CRISANTA KNIGHT

To Death & Back

Book Five in The Crisanta Knight Series

GEANNA CULBERTSON

BQB

Virginia

Crisanta Knight: To Death & Back
© 2019 Geanna Culbertson. All rights reserved.

Book Five in The Crisanta Knight Series

This is a work of fiction. All of the characters, names, incidents, organizations, and dialogue in this novel are either the products of the author's imagination or are used fictitiously.

Published in the United States by BQB Publishing
(an imprint of Boutique of Quality Books Publishing Company, Inc.)
www.bqbpublishing.com

978-1-945448-26-3 (p)
978-1-945448-27-0 (e)

Library of Congress Control Number: 2019930113

Book design by Robin Krauss, www.bookformatters.com
Cover concept by Geanna Culbertson
Cover design by Ellis Dixon, www.ellisdixon.com

First editor: Pearlie Tan
Second editor: Olivia Swenson

Books in The Crisanta Knight Series

Crisanta Knight: Protagonist Bound
Book One

Crisanta Knight: The Severance Game
Book Two

Crisanta Knight: Inherent Fate
Book Three

Crisanta Knight: The Liar, The Witch, & The Wormhole
Book Four

Crisanta Knight: To Death & Back
Book Five

Crisanta Knight: The Lost King
Book Six (2019)

Dedication

This book, like everything I shall ever accomplish, is dedicated to my mom and dad. You are my heroes, my coaches, and my best friends. I am thankful for you every day for more reasons than there are words in this book.

Special Thanks

Terri Leidich & BQB Publishing

For everything you've done, everything we'll achieve together, and for always being in my corner, *thank you*. A hundred times over, and sincerely from my heart, thank you.

Pearlie Tan

Whenever I talk about the publishing process, I always mention you and how much I value your work and trust your skill. You are a core part of Team Crisanta Knight and I appreciate you.

Olivia Swenson

I have valued your opinion since the beginning and with every book we work on together, I am increasingly grateful to have you on my team. You have made a big difference to me!

Alexa Carter

Thank you for being consistently, incomparably one of the dearest friends I could ask for and consistently, incomparably one of the best people I know.

Ellis Dixon

I am so glad to have you on my team! Thank you for helping me bring my vision for each Crisanta Knight cover to life. I love every cover more than the last and I know that wouldn't be the case if not for your skill and patience with the details.

I also want to thank The Fine Family, Bree Wernicke, Midnight Hour Studios, Girls on the Run, Read to a Child, Aimee Bender, all the other wonderful people who have supported this series so actively since the beginning, and my many fans who I hope to continue to amaze, enthrall, and surprise in the future!

Bonus Dedication

Since this is going to be an eight-book series, each book will include a bonus dedication to individuals who have significantly impacted my life or this series in some way. This one is for my brother Gallien Culbertson.

Brother, you and I spend a nice chunk of time sassing each other, but on a very sincere note, I honestly don't know what I would do without you. You are a wonderful older brother, but you are also a great friend. In fact, I consider it a privilege and a blessing to be able to say that I consider you one of my best friends. And that's just amazing. I mean, how many people get to say that about their siblings? Thank you for being my business consultant, life coach, pal, sports educator, TV and film debater, and the Robin to my Batman. (Just kidding; we're both Batman.) This might be the first book that is specifically dedicated to you, but you are a big part of every single one. Just like you are a big part of me, and everything I shall ever accomplish.

Prologue

You know how princesses are supposed to wear pretty dresses, be saved by heroes, and live happily ever after?

Well, if that's what you're into, you picked the wrong book.

As the daughter of Cinderella, I'm all for pretty dresses, but I prefer to pair them with combat boots. While a few of my hero friends have saved me on occasion, I've rescued them just as many times. And as far as living happily ever after goes, at this rate I'll be lucky just to be alive a few days from now.

My name is Crisanta Knight. I'm a protagonist and I hail from a world called Book—a magical realm that separates its citizens into main characters and common ensemble characters. One of the things our realm is known for is the Author—a mysterious prophet who writes the stories, known as "protagonist books," that detail protagonists' fates.

Each protagonist book starts with a prologue prophecy, a vague rhyme that predicts the general gist of a main character's story. Unfortunately, mine was a doozy. I was prophesied to decide the fate of the wicked antagonists plotting to overthrow our realm and eliminate all its main characters. At the end of this story, I would either be responsible for stopping them or helping them see their evil plan through.

Since learning of my prophecy, the antagonists had tried to strike me down at every possible turn. Protagonists in Book attend special private schools where they train for their fairytale destinies. As a princess and a protagonist, I'd always been trained to do good and be good, so the antagonists assumed that if I made it to the end of my storyline, I would enact the interpretation of my prophecy that implied I would stop them. As a result, they wanted to stop me first, and the only way to keep a prophecy from coming true is by killing its subject.

Regrettably for them, I was pretty hard to kill. And I had a team of fierce friends that made sure of that.

SJ (the daughter of Snow White), Blue (the younger sister of Little Red Riding Hood), Jason (the younger brother of the famous Jack who climbed the beanstalk), and Daniel (a hero with no previous ties to fairytales past) were always there for me when things got seedy.

I also had a Fairy Godmother–issue wand which could morph into any weapon I willed it into. I possessed the combat ability to utilize this tool dynamically, especially in the form of a spear. And above all else, I had magic.

My mother's Fairy Godmother had given me a spark of her magic when I was a little girl so I could operate the wand. This spark had developed into a singular, magnificent ability: life. As in, I had the ability to bring things to life and control them.

It was pretty awesome as far as powers went. Since realizing I possessed this ability a few months ago, I had spent a lot of time training to control and master it under the tutelage of the very Author who I once resented for supposedly controlling our fates.

Last semester my friends and I had discovered that the Author was actually a former Fairy Godmother named Liza Lenore who lived under the thumb of our realm's higher-ups. She didn't control our fates; she merely had visions of the future that reflected our choices. The higher-ups used her visions to keep order in our realm, convince the citizens of Book that their fates weren't their own, and separate people into protagonists and commons. Accordingly, Liza was imprisoned and isolated from the rest of the realm and was under an enchantment that made her live forever so she could be used in this way indefinitely.

Although Liza was a tool of propaganda for the higher-ups, she had become a valuable ally and teacher to me. The reason? She and I shared a similar problem known as Pure Magic Disease.

Magic normally works like a jacket. It's supposed to be easy to put on and use when needed, and simple to remove and ignore when not needed. However, every once in a while, magic irrevocably bonds to its host, resulting in Pure Magic Disease—an affliction that bestows great power with one ability, allows its host to see the future, and eventually corrupts them.

Liza was the only person I knew who had overcome the corrupting effects of Pure Magic, which made her the only person capable of teaching me the control to do the same. This involved tremendous focus and blocking out emotions—particularly negative ones—when I summoned my abilities. For while emotion made magic stronger, it also made it more unstable.

I had ardently tried to keep my emotions in check as my magic usage increased and developed, but that had become *a lot* more difficult lately thanks to Alex.

Alex is my older brother, and until a few days ago he was the beloved prince of our kingdom, Midveil. That all changed when he aligned himself with the antagonists and helped the common characters who had been rebelling in Book launch an attack on our home.

His betrayal had devastated me. He was no longer the hero, friend, and brother I once held dear. He was a monster working with Arian (the antagonist who'd been leading the charge against me since my prophecy appeared) and Mauvrey (the daughter of Sleeping Beauty, a former classmate at Lady Agnue's School for Princesses & Other Female Protagonists, and my long-time nemesis).

I wished I never had to see Alex again, but our stories were entangled. Alex and company, like me and mine, were now after Excalibur—King Arthur's legendary blade, which had been lost since his supposed death.

According to legend, Excalibur resided on Camelot's infamous Isle of Avalon under the care of the Lady of the Lake, waiting for someone worthy to claim it. The next person who would be able to do this was foretold by Merlin, Camelot's legendary wizard, in the Great Lights Prophecy. Enter my brother and me.

The Great Lights Prophecy indicated that a "Knight" of royal blood who was heir to the lion's throne was meant to claim Excalibur. Alex fit that description, as did I. We were royal, Knight was our last name, and Midveil's symbol was a lion. However, there was a deciding factor that could narrow down which of us had the chops to fulfill the prophecy: the Boar's Mouth, a mystical statue in Camelot. According to the prophecy, the Knight meant to claim Excalibur needed to get blessed by the Boar's Mouth in order to have any hope of completing the quest. The thing was, the statue only responded to people who had pledged a vow of loyalty known as The Pentecostal Oath to the king of Camelot.

Which brings us to the present.

Finding Excalibur was the key to accessing the memories of a lost Fairy Godmother named Paige Tomkins, who knew the location of Book's missing genies.

Our search for Paige Tomkins had brought my friends and I to Neverland. There, we discovered that the rightful king of Camelot, King Arthur, was not dead like everyone long believed. After being mortally wounded by his half brother Mordred, he had accidentally ended up in Neverland where biological time stood still, thus keeping him alive and also keeping him from aging.

We'd allied with Arthur and his Neverland friends—Peter Pan and the Lost Boys and Girls—and I had sworn The Pentecostal Oath to the king so I could receive the blessing from the Boar's Mouth in Camelot. Alex, meanwhile, had sworn The Oath to the person who had taken Camelot's throne in Arthur's place—only to learn he couldn't receive the blessing because the Boar's Mouth sensed Arthur, the true king of Camelot, still lived.

Now my brother, Mauvrey, Arian, and a buttload of their antagonist henchman intended to track down Arthur and force him to complete the pledge of The Pentecostal Oath with my brother. If the antagonists succeeded with this endeavor, Alex and I would both be eligible to get blessed by the Boar's Mouth.

This made my status to Arian and the antagonists more complicated.

While Alex and I had become opposites in a lot of ways, we were equals in terms of our chances at being the Knight of the prophecy. And since there was no guarantee that pledging The Oath would make the Boar's Mouth bless us, Arian and company weren't presently interested in killing me. They wanted to save me until Alex fulfilled *all* the requirements of the prophecy (the pledge *and* the blessing). In the meantime, I was their spare Knight in case he didn't cut it. Which meant Arthur was not the only one who needed to evade their capture. One wrong move and he and I would both become pawns in the antagonists' vicious game.

It was a dangerous, precarious situation to say the least. However, while I was wary about the immediate future, I was honestly not as intimidated as I once might've been. The antagonists were a fearsome group—cruel, cunning, and ruthless. That worked to their advantage. Nevertheless, they had a bad habit of underestimating me and that was their greatest disadvantage. We'd spent a lot of time together, my enemies and I, and if there was one truth that I carried away from our experiences, it was this:

The only thing better than being feared is being underestimated; because then nobody will see you coming.

I was coming for Excalibur.

If my enemies were smart, they would get out of my way.

The Spare Knight

ou know what's annoying? When your enemies don't attack at a reasonable hour.

It wasn't even dawn and our camp was under siege. Daniel woke me as the fairies and Lost Boys and Girls jumped into action. I snagged my black backpack before we made a break for the outside.

We'd been in the kids' belowground sleeping quarters. The only way to the main camp was through elevators in hollowed out tree trunks. We leapt across the bunker's trampoline floor, hopped into an elevator, and shot up. The seconds seemed like syrup-laden eons. I drew my wand in its sparkly hairpin form from my bra strap and transformed it back to its sleek, silvery state with the command word *Lapellius*.

At ground level, Daniel and I took half a step out of the elevator before I grabbed him by the jacket and yanked him sideways.

Shield.

My wand transformed just as a flaming cannonball took out the table where we'd eaten dinner. Big, angry sparks and lose embers sprayed from the explosion.

Surrounded by the cover of trees, the Lost Boys and Girls' hideout was a perfect woodsy camp with lots of open space to run and play. There was a fire pit surrounded by cushions, various obstacle courses, and treehouses overhead that were interconnected with zigzagging rope bridges and framed with strings of lime green lanterns. Now all that perfection was lost in chaos.

The forest was a flurry of fighting and fire. Antagonists were everywhere, laying siege to everything. I had the misfortune of knowing the foes leading the charge. Arian, Alex, and Mauvrey, along with no fewer than thirty henchmen, were engaged in various forms of attack across the forest area. Several henchmen mixed in throughout the space operated portable flaming cannonball launchers.

I was impressed that our enemies had narrowed in on Arthur's location and found the hideout so quickly, though I wasn't surprised. Our enemies sucked, but they were tenacious and shrewd. I didn't know where Arthur was in this pandemonium, but I worried it wouldn't be long before they located him—and me too. While they'd come here looking for the king, I was very aware they would happily catch and secure me as their spare Knight, so I had to avoid being seen if I could.

Many of our Neverland allies, including Dorothy Gale, had beaten us to the action and were already in full defense mode. The tall twenty-three-year-old protagonist from *The Wizard of Oz* was working with Tinkerbell and a fleet of fairies to fend off attackers. The fairies swarmed the enemy and blinded them with flashes of colorful light before Dorothy swooped in with a combination of brutal punches and kicks.

Some time ago, Dorothy and the rightful ruler of Oz (Princess Ozma) had been on a mission to Camelot. During their quest, the pair had gotten separated and a horrible monster called the Questor Beast had poisoned Dorothy with one of its venomous fangs. She should have died, but accidentally found her way to Neverland. Now, like Arthur, she would die if she left.

Dorothy and the fairies were doing a good job of kicking butt. The Lost Boys and Girls were also fighting hard and strong. The camp had more than enough weapons to fill an armory and, given that they spent their free time battling Captain Hook and his pirates, the kids had plenty of combat experience. However, these were ruthless, mostly adult antagonists we were dealing with. So as the fight scene unfolded with increased fire, arrows, and aggression, I wondered how long we could keep back the threat.

"Do you know where the others are?" I asked Daniel.

Suddenly muffled shouts came from overhead. Two of Arian's henchmen dropped out of the trees and landed face down on the ground beside me. Swiftly after, a third figure swung from a branch eight feet above us and landed in a perfect crouched position. Startling blue eyes looked up at me through a frazzle of dark blonde hair.

"Well, there's Blue," Daniel said as our friend rushed over to us, stepping on top of the incapacitated soldiers she'd knocked from the trees.

A flash of silvery light nearby encased three tree trunks in ice, three soldiers along with them.

"And there's SJ," I commented as our friend raced into the clearing. She was firing portable potions (crystalized, marble-sized potions of her own invention) using her slingshot. She aimed another potion at a couple of attackers encroaching on some smaller Lost Boys. Green slime coated our enemies. Distracted, SJ didn't notice the soldier behind her with his sword raised.

"SJ!"

She turned in time to see Peter Pan nail her would-be attacker in the head with a flying kick. Peter scooped SJ into the air, flying her over to us.

Let me tell you, if you've never seen Peter Pan take out an attacker while wearing pajamas, you haven't lived. It was awesome.

I loved that kid. The twelve-year-old boy was strong, fast, and quippy. His sassy personality actually matched up pretty well with what I'd always imagined based on the stories I'd read about him. I would just add that he was a lot cleverer than the stories indicated and could be a lot more serious if the situation called for it. He also had a heck of a knack for sword fighting, which he'd acquired from regular training with Arthur.

Peter deposited SJ beside me and I instantly felt better. She and Blue were my best friends and roommates at Lady Agnue's School for Princesses & Other Female Protagonists. Even with a million things to focus on, ensuring their safety was always one of my top priorities.

"What the frack, you guys!" Peter said, gesturing at the enemy soldiers. "We've never had an attack on our home base. Do you know these clowns?"

Another flaming cannonball obliterated a tree to our left. Peter managed to fly out of the way and Daniel and Blue braced themselves in time, but SJ and I were tossed to the ground from the force of the explosion. My backpack, much like her leather one, did little to break the fall.

Ow.

"Unfortunately, we do," Blue replied, offering me a hand up. "They're antagonists from Book and they're here for Arthur, and probably Crisa too."

A dozen men suddenly charged us. Peter drew his sword, leapt into the air, and flipped over the first three. He landed between the fourth and fifth antagonists in the onslaught. He kicked one, parried the other, and then flipped backward to ram the pommel of his sword into the chin of a sixth.

SJ fired a lightning potion that released a bolt as fierce as her gray eyes. Blue launched into a knife fight with a man wielding a dagger. Meanwhile, Daniel fought alongside Peter with his sword; as the airborne boy hit 'em high, Daniel hit 'em low with his own brand of swift aggression.

I had to say, I was always impressed watching Daniel fight. We'd faced a lot of enemies together, but few had ever rivaled his skill. In fact, I could only think of two swordfighters that might be his equal. And both were fifty feet away—and on the opposite team.

Arian and my brother Alex were making their way through the campsite. The fairies and kids tried to waylay them, but Alex and Arian were too good, smacking fairies aside before they could be blinded and deflecting kid attacks with ease. When the last of our nearby enemies dropped, and before Alex and Arian could spot us, I motioned for my friends to hide behind a jungle gym that had been turned on its side and was partially in flames. As we ducked down, however, in my peripheral vision I saw more attackers closing in. I transformed my shield into a spear. The silvery disc that I was holding instantly compressed and then elongated.

Incoming.

I rammed the blunt end into one soldier's chest, stabbed the blade end into the leg of a second, and then slammed the staff down on the shoulders of a third.

Blue rushed past me and punched one of two additional soldiers in the face. She then stabbed the first guy in the arm with her trusty hunting knife and hocked his leg out from under him while Peter shot like a comet into the chest of the second soldier and plowed him into a tree.

A few embers from nearby eruptions had caught onto Blue's faithful cloak, which was as blue as her eyes and namesake. She took a moment to pat it down. Peter's navy pajama bottoms and dark gray long-sleeves were also singed from the cannon fire and a couple of leaves were stuck in his tousled blond hair.

"Is this because of that Pentecostal Oath thing we were talking about last night?" Peter asked, all of us now taking temporary cover behind the jungle gym.

I nodded. "The Boar's Mouth must not have recognized the current leader of Camelot as the rightful king. Now our enemies have come for Arthur. I thought we'd have more time before they found him, but they're too good."

"And why would they want *you*?" Peter asked me.

"Because—"

"Hold that thought," Peter said, looking to the left. Twenty feet away a pair of soldiers had backed a few Lost Girls into a corner.

SJ grabbed a portable potion from the sack attached to her belt and fired with perfect accuracy. The orb squarely hit one antagonist and the lightning strike it produced blasted away the bad guy next to him. For good measure, Blue launched several throwing knives from her belt in their direction. Her belt was charmed to replace the knives as she threw them—a super handy enchantment that basically made her a walking artillery.

In that instant I looked up to see an archer in the trees taking aim at Peter.

Boomerang.

My spear transformed and I hurled the weapon. It smacked the archer in the head with blunt force and knocked him off his perch. The boomerang ricocheted back to my hand as Daniel ducked to evade a javelin that had been flung at him from a distance.

"They want me because I'm their spare Knight," I said to Peter, talking fast as we crouched for cover behind the jungle gym. "Remember how we told you about the 'Knight' of the Great Lights Prophecy? The antagonists want that to be Alex, but they're not sure the prophecy is about him, so they intend to capture me as a back-up until the Boar's Mouth gives Alex its blessing."

"Then we need to get you and Arthur out of here," Peter said, dodging an arrow.

"Not while the camp is in danger," I protested.

"I appreciate that, but I know the bigger stuff that's at stake," Peter argued. "If the bad guys claim Excalibur, this story is going to have a terrible ending. And anyway, the longer you're here, the longer the other kids and fairies are in trouble. The danger will leave once you're gone."

"Fine, we'll leave," Blue said. "But first we need to find Arthur *and* Jason. I haven't seen him since the fighting broke out."

She was right. Where was Jason?

Oh, crud.

I transformed my weapon into an archer's bow, picked up a fallen arrow, then stood and fired at a charging soldier. It hit him in the ankle, and he toppled over.

"Knight!"

Double crud.

There were only two people who addressed me that way. One was Daniel. The other was Arian. With an intuitive tingle up my spine, I whirled around.

From across the camp, Arian had spotted me. I was filled with fire at the sight of him—his familiar black hair and cruel eyes. The young villain in his twenties had two sides when he dealt with me—a cocky, condescending side where he treated me like a dumb princess, and a cold, merciless side where he treated me like a mortal enemy. I knew from the way he looked at me in that moment that today I was getting the latter.

Thankfully, a squadron of fairies attacked him a split-second later. We needed to disappear while he was distracted.

"Let's divvy up and look for Jason and Arthur," I ordered brusquely. "Once we've found them, we can meet at the edge of those cliffs where the Lost Boys and Girls taught us to fly yesterday. That's how we're going to get out of here."

"Crisa, you and Jason can't fly," Blue said, flinging another knife at an attacker. "Your minds couldn't host enough joyful thoughts or whatever to remain airborne."

"Then I'll secure another means of transportation," I stated. "Like this."

I transformed my bow back to a wand, dropped to one knee, and placed my free hand on a stone the size of a carriage wheel.

Come to life. Beat up the soldiers. Show no mercy.

Golden light burst from my hand and encased the rock. A moment later, the rock lifted off the ground and flew toward the nearest group of soldiers. It began to pummel them like a chef tenderizing a tenderloin.

I spun back to my friends. "Peter and Daniel, go find Arthur. Blue and I will find Jason. SJ, help the Lost Boys and Girls until we've got everyone. *Stay away* from Arian and Alex." I glanced around. There was no sign of my brother. "Wherever he is."

The others nodded in agreement and we broke apart. Arian was still too distracted to pursue me, and I counted that as a blessing. Blue and I made for the perimeter of trees and plunged into the forest in search of our friend. Worried thoughts assailed my mind as we searched for him.

Thanks to my Pure Magic Disease, I'd had a vision of the future that Jason was going to die sacrificing himself for Blue. My vision had shown it occurring next to a river during the day, so I knew that this fate was not going to play out here. But the only way to break a prophecy was if the subject died prematurely, so Jason's safety tonight was not ensured. There were so many enemies brooding in these woods, anything was possible. The image of my close friend getting stabbed with a spear as he stepped in front of Blue was hard to push away.

"Crisa."

Blue's voice drew me back to the present, and I came to a stop beside her. She pointed ahead at a clearing, where I spotted my old classmate and foe Mauvrey. She fought against three Lost Boys. A couple of them were in their teens, and each of them had a weapon—a sword, a sturdy hammer, and a large club. They were no match for her.

Mauvrey was wielding a pair of weapons that looked like bronze fingerless gloves. I knew from personal experience that they packed a punch. With her use of those unorthodox accessories, the fight wouldn't last ten seconds. Blue and I didn't have time to intervene, but we sprinted toward the clearing anyway, watching the fight unfold before us.

Mauvrey shot out her right hand. A pair of thin, shimmering wires emerged from her glove. They wrapped around the wrist of one Lost Boy like dual whips. She closed her fingers over her palm twice then yanked her arm back. The wires reeled in like a super-speed fishing line and Mauvrey nailed the boy in the face with a brutal punch from her other hand.

The whips released the boy and snapped back to starting position. He swung his fist, but Mauvrey ducked and bobbed around his side. She elbowed him in the spine and kicked out his knee. The kid went down and she whirled around to meet the other two boys charging at her.

The princess extended both hands and each of her metallic gloves fired a set of whips. They ensnared the boys' waists and Mauvrey pulled her arms apart, flinging the boys in opposite directions. They smashed into trees. Mauvrey unclenched her fists and crossed her pointer and middle fingers. In response, a charge of cackling energy surged down each set of whips and electrocuted the boys.

They shouted before the charge knocked them out. Again, Mauvrey closed her fingers around her palms twice and the wires reeled in with a rapid snap. Blue and I dashed into the clearing just as the first boy who'd attacked Mauvrey tried to get up, and she spun around and punched him in the head.

"Ladies," Mauvrey said with a wicked smile, turning to face us as the boy collapsed to the ground. She wore a purple leather jacket that matched her spiky-heeled ankle boots. With certainty in her eyes and confidence in her gait, she took a few steps toward us.

"Blue, go find Jason," I said.

"You sure?" Blue asked, glancing with concern at Mauvrey then back at me.

"Yes."

Blue nodded and took off. My fingers tightened around my wand.

"I was hoping we would find you here," Mauvrey said. "You have a talent for showing up when conflict breaks out. How fortunate that we will be able to secure you and Arthur in one siege."

"Like you even have a shot," I replied. "You and your people have been coming at me for months—unsuccessfully."

Mauvrey glanced up at the orange hue of the sky and the smoke drifting from the main battle. "Then maybe we just need to turn up the heat. Who knows, perhaps if we kill enough people and unleash enough destruction, you will come willingly."

I gulped and took in the fiery haze for myself. The antagonists may have been here for Arthur, but they'd gladly tear this place apart for me now that they knew I was within grasp.

Mauvrey made a *tsk tsk* sound and shook her head like she was disappointed.

"You know, Crisa, I pity your life choices. You could have avoided all the impending danger and death if you had stayed put in that coffin I sealed you in back in Midveil. By the way, I have been wondering, how *did* you beat the Poppy Potion I placed you under? That sleeping spell should have knocked you out for a full day."

"Poppy Potions don't work on me, Mauvrey," I replied bitterly, remembering her attacking me in my own home.

"Probably a side effect of your magic," Mauvrey mused, then shrugged as we started to circle each other. "Life, right? You must be getting powerful enough for the ability to expand in other ways."

I frowned. I genuinely hadn't thought about it. I knew I was getting more powerful, but I hadn't linked that to my weird Poppy immunity. It made sense though. My ability was generating life, and Poppies put people to sleep by means of draining life energy. My body must've been accessing my magic without my command when I came into contact with the toxic flowers. I guess I hadn't fully considered this possibility until now because I'd never tried to use my powers of life on myself. I didn't know that I could.

"Must be tempting to hold such power," Mauvrey continued. I eyed her bronze gloves, and the other weapons attached to her belt—a dagger within a sheath and a miniature crossbow with two arrows.

"Are you going to try and use that power on me?" she asked.

"I don't need magic to beat you, Mauvrey."

Mauvrey's cruel grin returned. "I was hoping you would say that."

She shot out her right hand.

Shield.

The whips from her glove bounced off my weapon as I raced at her. She closed her fingers twice, making the wires snap back. When I was four feet away, she extended her other hand. The whips came out. I ducked and rolled—*Wand*—landing to my feet on her other side.

Shield.

Again, I blocked a pair of wires headed for my chest, but I was unable to avoid the second set aimed at my legs. The whips snatched my ankle and Mauvrey yanked forcefully, pulling me off my feet.

My shoulders slammed into the dirt. I looked up and flung my shield at Mauvrey discus-style. It knocked her in the chest. She staggered back and her whips released their hold on me. I leapt up and grabbed the shield.

Spear.

I lunged, but Mauvrey sidestepped, spun, and evaded my strike. As she turned, she clapped her hands together. When she came out of the turn, her gloves were surging with electricity and she grabbed my spear with both hands. The staff acted like a lightning rod and the energy blasted me back. I let go of the weapon and was knocked against a tree. Mauvrey fired her mini dual-arrowed crossbow. It released two arrows attached together by a small wire. The wire caught my left wrist and pinned me down as the arrows plunged deep into the tree trunk.

I was still recovering from the electric shock and couldn't react quick enough. Mauvrey fired a second shot, which captured my other wrist before I could move. Then the princess was in front of me with a dagger in hand.

I glared at her. "Go ahead. I dare you."

Mauvrey smirked. "Not afraid of dying, Crisa?"

"Not afraid of you, Mauvrey. Besides, today is not the day for me to die. I know you need me as a fallback for the Great Lights Prophecy."

Mauvrey crossed her arms, grudgingly impressed that I was aware of their play. "You are just lucky the Boar's Mouth did not respond when Alex tested it. If The Oath he pledged to the current king of Camelot, King Rampart, had been accepted, you would be finished right now. Once your brother pledges The Oath to Arthur and gets the statue's blessing all bets will be off and I will kill you in the most painful way possible."

"You have no chance, Mauvrey. You'll never capture Arthur," I replied, struggling against my restraints. "You may have the numbers, but Arthur once ruled an empire. You really think you can beat him?"

"We can together," a familiar voice answered. "And we're not leaving until we do."

I turned my head to see my brother walk into the clearing to join Mauvrey. The pair of them stood not three feet from where I was pinned. Alex was four years older than me, built like a hero, and taller than Mauvrey by a good five inches. I didn't like how well they paired together—the blond hair, the blue eyes, the confidence.

It was weird. When I looked at Mauvrey, I felt spite and craved vengeance. When I looked at Arian, I felt hatred and intimidation. But when I looked at Alex, it was a mix of all four sentiments with the very distinct addition of sadness.

He'd betrayed my family, our kingdom, and everything that being a protagonist stood for. I wasn't sure if I could ever completely erase the love I once held for him, but at this point it was so frozen over that its frost would have inspired the snow queen to put on a jacket.

Alex studied me. His face was hard, his expression steely, but his eyes held a tinge of remorse. Mauvrey may not have seen it, but I did. He and I were too close; I could read him like a book. He may have fully committed to the antagonist role, but old habits died hard.

"You didn't hurt her, did you?" he asked Mauvrey, confirming my suspicions that a small part of him still wanted to protect me. This sentiment made me even more irate; after selling out our family to the antagonists and commons rebellion, and half destroying our castle, he had no right to pretend I still meant anything to him.

"Of course not," Mauvrey responded. "But she knows about the Boar's Mouth and the Great Lights Prophecy."

"I would expect as much," he responded. He pivoted back toward me. "Since we still don't know which of us is going to qualify as the Knight of the prophecy, you're going to have to come with us as a prisoner. I'm sorry about this."

I narrowed my eyes. "Well, I'm not sorry about this."

My pinned hands burst with light as I summoned my magic, retaining my focus and reining in my emotions like Liza had instructed. Such control was difficult around Alex and Mauvrey. My feelings toward them were vindictive and strong, and using my powers under such emotional influence tempted the dark, corruptible nature of my Pure Magic Disease. But I could control my rage much better now. Defeating Alex and Mauvrey may have been personal, but it was also business. And that was what I focused on.

As my hands ignited with their golden flare, I concentrated on the trees closest to Mauvrey and Alex. I wanted them to come to life and swat my enemies away like irritating insects. But almost immediately after the magical aura sparked around my fingers, a horrifying pain shot up my arms.

I winced. It was like someone had jabbed butter knives in my biceps and forks in my fists. My magic glow faded. When it did, so did the pain.

Mauvrey smirked. "You are familiar with Stiltdegarths, are you not?" she asked. "Marvelous creatures. The Fairy Godmothers use their magic-reversing properties to remove powers from people. However, the *blood* of a Stiltdegarth works as a great agent for cancelling out magic. It is one of only three substances known to have that effect. Avalonian glass is quite rare. And Jacobee stone is hard to cut, so it is best for bigger projects like constructing prisons. Given your abilities, Arian cleverly had all our weapons forged in Stiltdegarth blood, including the wiring of my dual crossbow."

I strained against the arrows and wire pinning me down.

"It does not matter how powerful you are," Mauvrey continued, moving closer to me. "You will never be able to summon enough strength to use your magic when restrained by something forged in Stiltdegarth blood. The pain will be too great and your instinct will stop you every time."

Out of the corner of my eye I saw movement in the bushes surrounding the clearing and a flash of a powder blue cape.

"I've said it before and I'll said it again, Mauvrey," I responded confidently. "I don't need magic to beat you."

"You are trapped, Crisa," Mauvrey said, rolling her eyes. "What, you have another wand up your sleeve?"

"No, I have something better. *Friends*."

Mauvrey and Alex whipped their heads around to see Blue, Jason, and SJ emerge from the forest. The instant they did, I used my restraints to leverage my weight and launch both feet into the air, roughly kicking Mauvrey in the chest. She stumbled backward.

SJ fired a silver portable potion. The orb exploded at Mauvrey's feet, encasing her in a block of ice.

Alex managed to jump out of the way, but Blue and Jason did not skip a beat. Blue threw a knife, which Alex ducked. My brother drew his sword in time to block a blow by Jason's axe. SJ fired a lightning potion. Alex dove under Jason's swing and avoided the bolt. She fired again and he rolled out of the way, somehow managing to block, parry, and kick Jason. Our heroic, long-time friend from Lord Channing's School for Princes & Other Young Heroes continued to spar with my brother as SJ launched potions at him.

"Need some help?" Blue asked, appearing by my side.

"Yes, please. My magic doesn't work on these things." I nodded at the restraints holding me down.

"Lucky for me, my kind of magic is much more powerful."

"What kind of magic is that?"

Blue raised her trusty hunting knife. "The magic of brute force."

My friend wedged the sharp blade of her knife between my wrist and the wire. She braced one boot against the tree and yanked. The knife sliced through the restraint.

Blue freed my other wrist as another lightning bolt erupted. Alex didn't move out of the way in time for this one and he dropped to the ground. Jason rushed in. He twisted Alex's arm behind his back and slammed one knee into my brother's spine to hold him down.

I stood in front of Alex. My brother met my gaze with an expression filled with nothing short of will and fire. I was familiar with that look. Good and evil aside, defiance was one thing we'd always had in common.

Blue retrieved my spear and handed it to me. I returned it to wand form.

"Crisa, what do you want us to do with him?" Jason asked.

I felt coldness in my heart—the iciness that came when faced with someone you used to love, but who'd hurt you too much to ever be forgiven.

Alex was working with the antagonists. Alex had betrayed my parents. Alex had attacked our home. Alex was dating Mauvrey. *Alex was my enemy.*

"Let him go," I said, the words escaping my lips before I thought better of them.

In spite of what he was and what he'd done, one thing surpassed everything else: Alex was my brother.

Jason thrust Alex against the dirt and stepped back, joining Blue and me.

"Seriously? You're just going to set him free?" Blue asked.

"Not quite." I gestured at the fourth member of our group. "SJ . . ."

My friend drew back her slingshot. Before Alex could get to his feet, a silver portable potion exploded in front of him and encased him in his own block of ice.

"Well, that's appropriate," Blue said as she gazed at the two chunks of frost. "An ice king for our school's former ice queen."

It was funny. But I didn't laugh. I didn't feel like laughing.

"Come on," SJ said. "We must go. There are still many soldiers, and let us not forget Arian."

Like I could ever forget Arian.

With one last glance at my brother—preserved like a handsome fossil for the time being—I turned and followed my friends through the woods. As we ran, Blue tilted her head in my direction.

"We probably should've killed them. It would've been smarter," she said.

The words caught me so off guard that I tripped over a tree root. I picked up my pace to make up for the falter and studied my friend. Her eyes were full of pensive darkness.

"That's my brother, Blue."

"That's our *enemy*, Crisa," she said. "And villains like them don't stay down. As long as they're out there they'll keep trying to kill us." She gestured at herself, SJ, and Jason. "When you're no longer useful, your brother will probably try to kill you too."

My stomach knotted as my friend's words sunk in.

A small part of me wondered if she was right. Arian, Mauvrey, Alex, and the countless other villains we'd encountered were relentless. It didn't matter how often we beat them or escaped their clutches; they kept regrouping and attacking with greater force. It was what bad guys did. So was Blue's assertion correct? Was it unwise to leave our enemies alive if they were just going to keep coming after us? Had I been wrong to let my relationship with Alex get in the way of my rational judgment?

I shook my head at such dark thoughts. I didn't know if Blue was right. But I also didn't know if I had what it took to kill someone, let alone my own brother.

CHAPTER 2

Picking Battles

e were the first to arrive at the cliff where we'd arranged to meet the others. It overlooked a massive span of Neverland's forest, the ocean a thick line of gray in the distance. Dawn was breaking, but my resolve was getting stronger.

As my three friends and I anxiously waited for the rest of our group, I pulled up the display on my Hole Tracker—the magic watch given to me by a White Rabbit named Harry. It was designed to display and lead the way to oncoming wormholes. Wormholes were dimensional tears that created portals from one enchanted realm to the next. The Hole Tracker projected a glowing, holographic map of Neverland. I spotted the desired wormhole, marked by a small, silver swirl of light. This was the way out of Neverland we'd been planning on taking today. It would open in two and a half hours.

Here's to an early start to the day.

Daniel emerged from the trees with Arthur and Peter right behind him. It was surprising to me how much the latter two looked alike. Arthur was in his mid thirties, extremely ripped, and had a much sharper jawline. But he had the same blond hair, thick brows, and blue eyes as Peter, and similar facial expressions too.

"Where are the fairies?" SJ asked when they reached us. "We need their fairy dust to fly."

"They're still defending the kids and the camp," Peter said. "You'll need another way to get out of here."

"I've got one," I said. I knelt, placed my hand on the ground, and concentrated. In response, the edge of the cliff we were standing on broke free and floated upward. Most of my friends wobbled a tad, but everyone recovered their balance swiftly.

"Are we making a run straight at the wormhole?" Jason asked.

"I don't think this means of transportation will get us very far," I responded. "We just need to get away from here. We'll worry about reaching the wormhole once we're clear of the camp."

"Hopefully once those guys realize you're gone, they'll stop attacking," Peter said, flying away from the levitating rock.

"Wait, kid, you're not coming with us?" Arthur asked.

"The Lost Boys and Girls and fairies are my friends. I have to defend them."

Guilt and worry overpowered me. Those kids and fairies, as well as Dorothy and Peter, were my friends too. "We'll stay then. Help you finish what we started," I said. My magic glowed brighter as I began to lower us down.

"No. You can't save everyone, Crisa," Peter said. "That's not your responsibility. You have a bigger mission. You need to pick your battles."

"He's right," Blue said. "We need to beat Alex and Arian to Excalibur. The wormhole to Camelot opens in a couple of hours and we can't miss it."

Every part of my instinct told me to stay and fight. It was completely opposite my nature to leave anyone behind. At the same time, our plan to leave was the best way to get the antagonists to abandon their assault on the camp.

"Fine," I said begrudgingly.

I started to move our chunk of terrain again, but Arthur suddenly jumped off. He landed on the cliff and rolled to his feet. He may have been a full-grown adult, but the former king of Camelot had all the athleticism of a young hero in his prime.

"What are you doing?" Jason asked.

"What the kid said." Arthur pulled a sword from a sheath on his back and gestured to Peter, his dusty blond hair catching the light of the sun appearing on the horizon. "Picking my battles.

This place has been my home for seven years. I am not abandoning Peter or any of those children either. I'll be fine. You five go."

"How can you tell us to leave when you're going to stay? The antagonists are looking for *you*," I argued. "If they capture you, they're going to force you to complete the pledge of The Pentecostal Oath with Alex, which will put him one step closer to being able to claim Excalibur. You staying here completely defeats the purpose of us—"

"Crisa," Arthur interrupted. "No more arguing. I can stop these antagonists—with or without Excalibur. You have no idea what I'm capable of. And right now, you need to get a lead on them. If they see me, they won't leave, and that will buy you a head start to Camelot."

"But—"

"Crisa, do as I say. *Go*."

I didn't usually follow orders. One, I didn't like them. And two . . . well, actually it was just the one reason. But Arthur projected more authority than anyone I'd ever known. Between that and the trust and respect I had for him, I nodded.

Arthur pointed his sword toward the swell of forest below. "Get to Camelot's citadel. In the castle, you'll find the Boar's Mouth statue. The rest is up to you."

I was about to direct our piece of cliff to take us away, but then I split my magic focus like I'd been practicing and directed additional power into a few nearby trees. My forehead crinkled from the strain. Telepathic magic took a lot of my strength, but I was able to do it.

Four trees glowed and sprung to life. Using their roots like feet, they took off into the forest to defend the camp.

Arthur gave me a look.

"What? I'm not allowed to pick more than one battle?" I said.

The king smiled and shook his head in a way that reminded me of how my mother reacted when I was being stubborn. "You can't help it, can you?"

"Nope." I turned to SJ. "Quick. Give them a Mark Two."

My friend swung the backpack off her shoulders and dug out one of our spare Mark Two magic compact mirrors. These nifty communication devices ran on the same kind of magic that *Beauty & The Beast*'s famous magic mirror did. They allowed you to contact anyone by speaking their name into the small looking glass within each compact.

We'd found a stall pre-selling them when we were in the Emerald City so each of my friends had bought one, and we'd purchased a couple of extras just in case. We had already gifted a Mark Two to Dorothy. This was a good use of the other.

"Just say one of our names and it will connect you to us," SJ said, tossing Peter the Mark Two. "If it buzzes, answer." Peter nodded.

I took a final look at our two new friends. "I'll bring Excalibur back to you," I said to Arthur. "I promise."

With that, I knelt down to touch the stone and released a fresh charge of magic with my commands. Like a falling star we sped from the cliff's edge. The promise I'd made to Arthur glowed inside of me with as much ardency as my magic aura around the slice of terrain we rode away like a magic carpet.

I didn't know for certain that I was the Knight of the prophecy, but I believed it in the same way as when you're little and you believe everything in life will be okay. It was a feeling rooted in optimism and heart.

I had to keep this promise to Arthur. Although I felt like his role in this immediate story was done and it might be some time before we all saw each other again, I knew his character's impact on our journey would resonate in the hard days to come. We were about to enter the world he left behind. We were headed for Camelot.

I realized our magical ride was speeding up. I was losing control as my emotions flared. My friends and I crouched to keep from being thrown off. When we neared the tops of trees at the bottom of the canyon, I focused as best I could and ordered the slice of terrain to slow down. We needed to land; the strain of controlling this big chunk of earth was pulling at me and I didn't think I could keep going. Using telepathic magic on those trees had drained me a bit, and I still felt somewhat woozy from getting shocked by Mauvrey's electric gloves.

I spotted an opening in the trees. It barely seemed wide enough for us to land, but it did the job. Following a bit of turbulence, we hit the ground roughly. I let out a breath I didn't know I'd been holding.

My hands stopped glowing and I wavered, feeling a little faint. It'd been a couple of days since I'd used my magic. Although my Pure Magic was powerful, I could only expel so much at once. If I pushed myself too hard, one of two things would happen: I'd run out of power and wouldn't be able to use it for twenty-four hours (Magic Exhaustion) or I'd use more than I could handle and would die (Magic Burn Out).

Ah, Pure Magic. Your caveats know no bounds.

We dismounted our rocky ride and took a moment to compose ourselves in the silent enclosure of dawn-drenched trees. My friends were also adjusting to solid ground, so they didn't notice how wobbly I was. Well, except for Daniel.

"You tapped out?" Daniel asked.

I glanced at him, startled. Then my eyes darted to my hands. They were trembling. I held up my right hand and focused. Golden light sparked off my fingertips.

"No," I answered. "Just tired."

I extinguished the glow. The magic needed time to rest. I huffed. It was sad how something that made me so incredibly powerful also made me so ridiculously vulnerable. Pure Magic came with so many rules, and Liza kept adding to the list:

- Don't power magic with emotion; the results might be stronger, but you could lose control.

- Don't use too much magic too often; you could exhaust yourself beyond repair.

- Don't reverse your abilities and take life away from things; it's a bad road to go down.

That last rule was the newest one. Originally Liza had stated that I *couldn't* reverse my abilities and take life. Out of curiosity I'd tried on an enchanted piece of wood and been successful. When I told Liza, she divulged that the reason she hadn't wanted me to do this wasn't because I *couldn't* do it, but because it increased my risk for turning dark.

When carriers of Pure Magic Disease used their powers to inflict mortal harm, the dark and corrosive nature of Pure Magic took a greater hold on them. The more power utilized this way, the stronger that hold became. It was crossing a line—a Malice Line, as it was called. And whenever you crossed it, the control you had over your Pure Magic was weakened, giving your Pure Magic a chance to control you instead.

Although I hadn't meant to inflict harm when I'd deactivated that piece of wood, I had crossed the Malice Line. I had the power to give life, after all. And by definition, reversing that power meant that I would be taking life away. Which, to quote Liza, was "one of the darkest actions a person can take, and a form of power that no one should have."

Taking life from that piece of wood alone wasn't going to make me wicked. But if I continued to cross the Malice Line, my already-low odds of avoiding the awful fate of Pure Magic Disease would decrease even more.

In a way, I was glad to know this. I hadn't put much thought into the philosophical and moral perspective when I'd taken life from that piece of wood, but I needed to be aware of the implications of using my powers just like I needed to be aware of everything I could do. I mean, I hadn't known that I could take life until a few days ago. That was important information. What if I could extend my abilities to other situations too, but in good ways like . . .

My eyes fell upon Jason.

That's when a brilliant, amazing idea sparked inside me.

Mauvrey's words about my life energy allowing me to overcome Poppies swirled in my head. *Where exactly did my powers end? Could I use my magic on myself? Could I use it on other people? Like Jason?*

My idea solidified like a sword forged in magma and left to cool. The notion was the perfect combination of beautiful and absurdly farfetched. I'd had a vision that my friend was going to die, but if I could become more powerful—powerful enough to extend my abilities to not only give life to inanimate things, but also restore life to people—then maybe I could save him!

"Knight," Daniel asked, completely unaware of my revelation. "What's our status? When is the next wormhole?"

"I, uh, I checked at the cliff," I said. "The next wormhole opens at 8:30 a.m., about two and a half hours from now."

"Let's get moving then," Jason said, jumping off the rock and onto solid ground.

I stared at him, still focused on my idea. I wanted to tell him but thought better of it. For one, we weren't alone and the rest of our friends didn't know about his imminent death. And two, until I could be certain that I could restore life, I shouldn't say anything that might get his hopes up. It would be wrong and it would be cruel.

"SJ, can you get out the Neverland map?" Jason asked.

SJ reached into her potions sack. The small thing didn't just hold her portable ammo. There was an enchantment on the bag that worked like a small wormhole, allowing her to retrieve anything if she knew its exact location and could fit it through the bag's opening. For example, hidden in our room back at school she had prepared an innumerable number of portable potions, which she was drawing from as we went along. Also hidden in our room were the maps of the Wonderlands we'd constructed before leaving Book.

Our realm may have been a Wonderland (one of fourteen magical realms in existence), but it didn't exactly sell maps of the other thirteen realms at the mall. So, since my Hole Tracker only displayed vague, general maps, my friends and I had done crazy intense research prior to leaving Book to create our own maps of the Wonderlands that we knew about.

SJ reached inside her potions sack and pulled out a rolled-up parchment. She handed it to Jason, who studied the map closely.

"Based on the size of Neverland," he said, "it should take us an hour and a half to get to the wormhole. But with the amount of trouble we get into, an extra hour of cushioning won't last long."

He was right. I checked the time on my Hole Tracker. It was just past six o'clock and every minute counted. My eyes lingered for a second on the other two accessories I wore beside my Hole Tracker: SJ's potion-laced SRB (Soap on a Rope-like-Bracelet, which we all wore to keep ourselves magically clean) and a special gold wristband that Alex and I used to share. I didn't know why I still wore it. Maybe because it reminded me of the goodness he used to have.

I shook my head as I followed Jason's lead back into the woods.

CHAPTER 3

Fish-Gut Slut

oly bananas, I can't believe that just happened."
Blue put her hands on her hips and looked around
in disbelief.

"I know," I said. "How did we make it here
without anything bad happening?"

We'd reached the spot where the wormhole was going to open
with fifty minutes to spare. The proximity sensor on my Hole
Tracker confirmed it. Amazingly, we'd arrived without running
into any villains, monsters, or woodland obstacles on the way.
That was certainly a first.

"It does not matter how it happened," SJ responded, putting
the Neverland map back into her magic potions sack and settling
down beneath a tree. "I am simply grateful. We could use a break
from evil."

"Truer words have never been spoken," Blue said as she
plopped down beside SJ. Blue lay back on the grass, folded her
hands behind her head, and closed her eyes.

I heard something in the distance and my ears trained on the
sound.

"Well, since we have some time I'm going to see if there's a
river nearby. I think I hear running water."

"Crisa, if you are thirsty, I could pull a canteen out of my
potions sack. I have several filled in our room back at Lady
Agnue's that are easily accessible."

"Thanks, but it's not really about the water," I admitted. "We've
got a little time to kill before moving forward toward inevitable
conflict, and you know how exploring relaxes me."

SJ furrowed her brow in concern. "You do realize that while you sauntering off alone might relax you, it stresses everybody else out."

I blinked, surprised, and pivoted toward Daniel.

"She's not wrong," he said. "People are always trying to kill or capture you."

"All right, that's fair," I said, shrugging. "Anyone want to come with me?"

"I will," Daniel offered.

"Me too," Jason added. He turned back to the girls. "Blue, there's still danger out there so don't—"

A potent snore emitted from my friend. Jason shot SJ a look.

"Do not worry," she said. "I will keep an eye out. Just mind the time."

I handed SJ my backpack for her to hold onto before the boys and I made our way toward the sound of rushing water. Bright morning sunlight spilled through the branches. I inhaled the crisp air and broke into a yawn.

"Maybe you should have followed Blue's lead," Daniel commented. "We have a long journey ahead. If you're tired, you might benefit from some sleep."

"With my dreams, sleep can be just as exhausting as being awake," I responded. "I'll be fine."

Daniel gave me a knowing look and dropped the subject. Like the rest of my friends, he knew better than to pry too deep where my dreams were concerned.

Seeing the future was both a gift and a curse of Pure Magic Disease. Sure, the power could come in handy. It gave me a heads up of what was to come. But it also showed me terrible things in my sleep that I would've preferred to stay innocent of. Like Jason's death.

Daniel pushed a large branch out of the way and we found the source of the water.

Oh, wow.

It wasn't a river. It was a cove. The crystal blue ocean was spilling into the small enclosure from the right. A wall of pale lavender rock rimmed the cove on the left. I'd seen this cove in a dream. Mermaids—five about our age, two a bit older—were presently perched on rocks poking out of the water. Two mermaids brushed their red locks with oddly shaped seashells. Three brunettes giggled near a flock of seagulls that stood beside them with the alertness of bodyguards. A mermaid with long black hair and a dark teal tail was floating lazily in the water and paddling backward strokes. And a blonde mermaid lay on one of the rocks, sunbathing. Her top was purple just like her tail.

I tilted my head.

No way.

"Lonna?" I called.

Lonna Langard, the mermaid princess of Book's undersea kingdom of Mer, sat up and looked at me with her familiar, bright purple eyes that nearly popped out of her skull when she recognized me.

"Carly!" she said.

All the mermaids whipped their heads in our direction. Lonna dove off her rock and swam toward us. The rest of her tailed friends followed.

"She can never remember your name, can she?" Daniel said as they approached.

I shrugged. "I guess I'm not very memorable."

"Must be your subtlety."

I looked up at him and we exchanged a smirk. Lonna burst out of the water alongside the other mermaids. She propped her elbows on the rocks at our feet and gazed up at us.

"I can't believe it's you, Carly," she said. "What's it been, a few months?"

"I guess that depends on what Wonderland time zone you've been spending your time in," I replied. "And it's Crisa. You remember Jason and Daniel?" I gestured at my friends.

"Ooh," one of the redheads cooed. "They're cute."

"Very cute," agreed the black-haired mermaid. "Lonna, since when do you know so many cute guys in Neverland?"

"We're from Book, actually," Jason said.

"I'll bet they're heroes," a brunette with a golden tail and off-the-shoulder top said. She batted her long eyelashes at my friends. "Either of you boys want to go for a swim?"

"Lay off, Stella," Lonna said. "Jason's with someone."

"I am?" Jason replied.

"Duh," Lonna said, tilting her chin. "What about Blue?"

"We're just friends."

"If I had a sea dollar for every time a boy said that . . ." Stella sighed. She pivoted toward Daniel. "How about you, handsome? You attached?"

"He's spoken for," I responded.

"Ooh, jealous much?"

"What? No, not by me," I said, taking a surprised step back. "He has a girlfriend. Her name is Kai."

"Whatever," Stella responded, flipping her thick wet hair. "Do either of you want to see the reverse waterfall on the other side of the cliff? It's just a short swim through an underwater cave. And it's way more interesting than this conversation."

"Well . . ."

"Oh come on, Crisa," Lonna interceded. "It's actually really cool. You'll love it."

Stella glared at Lonna. "I was talking to the boys."

"Story of your life." Lonna rolled her eyes then turned back to us. "Well, what do you say?"

Jason glanced at me. I checked my Hole Tracker and nodded. "Sure, we've got time."

Daniel, Jason, and I lowered ourselves off the rocky ledge and splashed into the glistening water. It was colder than I'd expected.

That'll wake you up.

I plunged beneath the surface to fully embrace the cold, opening my eyes to look around at the surreal blue seascape. Surprisingly, the salt water did not sting my eyes. Maybe it was magic water?

Jason, Daniel, and several of the mermaids were already making their way to the other side of the cove. I popped back up to get a swig of air before joining them. As I resurfaced, I heard Lonna curtly talking to Stella.

"Stella, that girl is my friend. You try and drown her and I swear I'll kill you myself."

"Ugh, you're no fun," Stella huffed. When she noticed me eavesdropping, she gave me a wicked grin and a wink before diving beneath the surface. Her golden tail slapped water in my direction.

"Don't mind her," Lonna said, paddling over. "She's a bit of a fish-gut slut."

"Pardon?"

"She goes through boys and leaves nothing behind but disheveled remains."

My eyes widened. "You don't mean she's going to *eat* them, do you?"

"What? Ew, no!" Lonna said. "Geez, Crisa. You shouldn't take things so literally."

"Sorry, I don't know a lot about mermaids," I replied. "I almost killed you with a bracelet once, remember?"

"I do." Lonna smiled. "The day we met. A lot has happened since then. Come on, I'll tell you all about it. But first, follow me. Stella may be a piece of work, but she isn't wrong. The reverse waterfall is awesome."

After swimming through an underwater tunnel lined with the most wonderful assortment of undersea plants, Lonna and I emerged in a secret pocket of Neverland beauty. What I saw was, in fact, awesome.

The reverse waterfall was exactly what it sounded like—a waterfall with waters that defied gravity by flowing upward instead of downward. It was incredible. And the bubbles in the stream sparkled as if made of magic dust.

While Jason and Daniel listened to Stella and the other mermaids explain the legend of the waterfall's origins, I sat off to the side with Lonna. I wanted to find out what she had been up to and how she had ended up in Neverland. Lonna insisted on my recap first though. She was super surprised to see us here. As I told her our reasons for ending up on the island, I felt somewhat surprised too. If I hadn't lived through the experiences, I would've had trouble believing them.

Our search of the Wonderlands had begun because of Paige Tomkins, the lost Fairy Godmother. She'd run away ten years ago because she was the sole guardian of the whereabouts of Book's trapped genies. We found her in Oz where, in order to best protect her secret, she'd gotten herself turned into a brainless scarecrow—a type of pathetic monster that had most of its brainpower and memories removed. The brainless scarecrows were victims of Glinda the Wicked Witch of the North, formerly Glinda the Good Witch. She and her sisters were carriers of Pure Magic and had all eventually succumbed to the evil, corruptible nature of the disease.

Paige had willingly let Glinda turn her into a brainless scarecrow to protect the location of Book's genies. That information was now trapped within her removed memories, which were contained in a nearly impenetrable stone in Glinda's lair. The stone was immune to pretty much everything—magic and brute force included. The only thing that could cut through it was Excalibur, the most powerful blade in existence. Hence the reason my friends and I had gone after the sword in the first place. We hadn't learned about the Great Lights Prophecy until later on.

Our team had a lot working against us on this quest, especially given that the antagonists wanted Excalibur and Paige's memories as badly as we did. However, our greatest obstacle was time. We had to successfully claim the sword and get to Glinda's memory stone within the next three days, because three days from now at 7:30 p.m. the Vicennalia Aurora would occur.

The Vicennalia Aurora was this great magic fluctuation event that took place across all Wonderlands simultaneously, despite the time differences. For us in Book, it happened every twenty-five years. Other lands like Oz, Neverland, and Camelot experienced it every five and a half years. When the Aurora occurred, beautiful lights streaked the sky and magic became very unstable.

"Great Lights" was the nickname people from Camelot gave to the Vicennalia Aurora. And the Great Lights Prophecy about Excalibur indicated that the sword would be retrieved on the day of the event. If we didn't get the sword in time for this one, we'd have to wait another five and a half years.

Past that, the Aurora was also our only chance to get into Glinda's lair and avoid being trapped forever. The witch's domain in Oz's North Mountains was protected under an In and Out Spell, which was a type of magical force field. Such spells came in different forms—for example, the antagonist kingdom of Alderon had a very strong half version that allowed people to be thrown in, but kept them from getting out. Glinda's version worked the same way, except on the day of the Vicennalia Aurora.

As mentioned, when the Vicennalia Aurora occurred magic was famously unstable. During our time in Oz we learned that this time around, ordinary magic specifically was going to become weaker. Meaning that In and Out Spells were going to become penetrable.

My friends and I were immune to certain types of In and Out Spells, but not this one. Thus, we had to go after the memory stone during the Aurora because it might be our only shot of escaping the In and Out Spell once we got what we came for.

"So now we're just waiting for the next wormhole to open so we can get out of here," I said to Lonna, finishing my story. "We'll try to claim Excalibur and then free Paige's mind from the memory stone. We can't let the antagonists have either, or the word *doom* will seem docile compared to what will happen next."

"Snap," Lonna replied. "That's a lot. And it sounds like you've had a rough few days leading up to this. You've dealt with a lot of monsters and bad guys already."

"Bad guys and monsters I can handle," I replied. "What worries me is the timing. I don't know how we're supposed to claim Excalibur and get back to Oz in three days. It seems impossible."

"Quests always seem impossible, Crisa. That's what makes them fun. Put your faith in the universe. If you're meant to succeed, you will."

I sighed. "The universe likes trying to kill me and my friends. I'm not putting my faith in it, I'm putting my faith in them." I tilted my chin in the direction of Jason and Daniel. "If we see this thing through, it will be because of those two, SJ, and Blue. I may be the one that the antagonists and magic hunters always want a piece of, but my friends make me strong enough to take them on. But enough about me. What have you been up to? And how did you end up in Neverland?"

"In a way, it was because of you," Lonna answered. "After you and your friends asked for my help finding that wormhole under the sea, I was inspired to kick my mischief-making up a notch. One day I got tired of everything—the routine, the expectations, the mermen—and I took a leap, or rather a swim, of faith. I came across a swirling red wormhole in the middle of the ocean and went through the portal it created. And from there, well, a lot of chiz happened."

Lonna told me how the portal had taken her to the frosty waters of the Wonderland called the North Pole. It was an icy, snow-covered realm, and Lonna would have frozen if a kindly polar bear wearing a striped scarf hadn't shown her the way to another wormhole.

The polar bear (named Leonard) had explained to her how the different colors of wormholes worked. Red or orange wormholes were Pop-Up Portals, which took you to the next realm in the sequence of fourteen Wonderlands. Red wormholes meant a counterclockwise jump in that sequence; orange, clockwise. Silver wormholes, meanwhile, were Portalscape Portals that led directly to the great intersection of all these magical realms—the Portalscape, a Wonderland in its own right.

Leonard bestowed Lonna with her very own Hole Tracker— evidently the North Pole had a huge elf population, many of whom were skilled at building magical knickknacks—and Lonna continued her travels from there. Armed with her Hole Tracker and the new information, she became a nomad of the Wonderlands, traveling from one realm to the next at her leisure.

"I've visited ten so far," Lonna explained as she and I compared Hole Trackers. "After the North Pole, I went to Atlantis, the Super Dome, Xanadu, the Portalscape, Limbo—which was weird—Oz, Cloud Nine, Camelot, and now Neverland."

"Dang," I replied. "And I thought I'd seen a lot. Are you going to keep going to the other Wonderlands?"

"Yeah, but I'm not sure when. I've been in Neverland a while. Other than Atlantis and Book, it's the only other realm I've come across with a mermaid population. I might not like Stella, but I owe her, so I'm sticking around. She and her sisters saved me from one of Captain Hook's fishing nets when I got here." Lonna huffed in disgust. "That guy sucks."

I nodded, remembering how I'd walked the plank on Captain Hook's ship. "Yeah, he does. You'll be happy to know that Blue punched him in the face and we burned down his ship."

"That was you?"

"Who else?"

Lonna smiled. "I only wish your destruction lasted longer. My mermaid crew and I were out at sea earlier and the ship is already halfway rebuilt."

"That was fast." I frowned for a moment, then changed the subject. "What's been your favorite Wonderland so far?"

"Probably either the Super Dome or Cloud Nine," Lonna replied. "The worst was Oz. A bunch of flying monkeys tried to snatch me out of the water like I was their lunch."

I shuddered at the thought of Glinda's flying monkeys. They'd attacked us during our time in Oz too.

I checked the time and called out to my friends that we had to go. The mermaids pouted when the boys said they had to leave. The lot of us began our return swim through the underwater tunnel. I loved being able to keep my eyes open during the swim. It was absolutely breathtaking.

And yes, that play on words was intentional.

My hand grazed the squishy, bright red algae at the bottom of the tunnel. Unusual fish with glimmering scales swam by lazily. My heart skipped a beat when what I thought were pink and lime-green flowers suddenly morphed into lime green baby octopuses with pink underbellies.

As we neared the exit of the tunnel, I looked up and saw Daniel. He seemed equally fascinated by the surroundings. When he saw me, he smiled. I smiled too. We came out of the tunnel and rays of light glimmered between our bodies as we rose. The two of us broke the surface at the same time and floated facing each other. Then Stella splashed me with a faceful of water and the moment was over.

Jason, Daniel, and I made for the rocky ledge and climbed out. The instant we exited the water, our SRBs sent a flurry of silver sparks around our bodies that dried us off in less than three seconds. Dang, I loved those things. SJ had invented SRBs to solve an under-discussed problem in all great adventure stories: how *do* the main characters stay clean and looking good along the way? This innovation—like her portable potions—was a perfect reflection of her brilliance and practicality.

Once again, I checked my Hole Tracker. We had five minutes until the wormhole opened.

"Thanks for showing us the waterfall, Lonna," I said. "I hope we cross paths again."

"Maybe we will," she replied. "I'll probably be moving on soon, going wherever the tide and mischief takes me." She nodded to Daniel and Jason. "Always a pleasure, boys."

"Good to see you, Lonna," Daniel said. He smiled at the other mermaids. "Ladies."

They giggled giddily and whispered to each other as they waved goodbye. I rolled my eyes. The three of us began our return march through the forest.

"Lonna's nice, but those other girls were weird," Jason commented.

"All girls are weird," I replied. "It just varies to what degree, and how proud we are to embrace it." I tilted my chin at Daniel. "You seemed to enjoy yourself."

"The waterfall was cool."

"And Kai wouldn't have felt threatened that a gaggle of sparkly, aquatic girls were the ones that showed it to you?"

"She's not the jealous type. Why would she be? You've met her. She's awesome."

It was a fair point. Daniel's girlfriend in Century City was beautiful, smart, kind, and an extremely skilled swordfighter. I guess if you were that awesome, you wouldn't worry about anybody else catching your boyfriend's attention. Nobody could threaten you. Well, except for me. Not in the traditional sense, but in terms of prophecy.

Daniel's prophecy said that I was going to be a key ally to him and Kai; however, it also indicated that I had the potential to destroy her. We didn't know any of the specifics in regards to how this was going to happen, but the possibility was an ongoing burden Daniel and I had to deal with.

For a time this had been a point of awkwardness between us. Luckily, we'd eventually made peace with it. Daniel didn't blame me for his prophecy, and he took full responsibility for trying to influence the outcome so Kai could be saved and the two of them could end up together. I had also volunteered to help protect her. I was just as adamant about controlling our fates as he was. And I saw no reason why—as I tried to shape a future where my magic helped stop the antagonists—I couldn't take steps to ensure Kai's safety as well.

Daniel may not have held me responsible for his prophecy, or for Kai's wellbeing, but I held myself responsible for his. He was my friend. And he'd been there for me too many times for me not to return the favor.

The boys and I entered the clearing where we'd left our friends. SJ was pacing while Blue sat in the branch of a tree.

"There you are. I was starting to get worried," SJ said when she spotted us. She tossed me my backpack and I swung it over my shoulders.

"You're always worried," I replied.

"You always give me a reason to be."

I shrugged, conceding that it was a fair accusation. No sooner did I do this than the air in front of us began to change, rippling and wavering us until a tear in reality created a silvery wormhole. The Portalscape Portal floated above the ground. It was the size of a throw rug—only big enough for one person to fit through at a time.

I consulted my Hole Tracker again. "This wormhole is meant to stay open for ten minutes." I moved a finger over the face of the watch with a light, circular motion. The action forwarded through time on the map. "The next portal in Neverland opens in eight hours."

"That's fast," Jason commented. "We had to wait a day and half between this wormhole and the last one."

"Looks like the holes are getting closer together," I replied, continuing my circular motion. "The next one may open in eight hours, but the one after that comes after seven. And look at tomorrow . . . six hours, four hours . . ."

"It must be the Vicennalia Aurora," SJ said. "The event causes magic fluctuation and instability across *all* the Wonderlands, so the barriers between the worlds are breaking down the closer we get to it."

"Then I guess we better take this head start on Arian while we have the chance," Daniel said.

Blue came up behind Jason and me and put her arms around our shoulders. "All right then. Who wants to jump through the inter-dimensional portal first?"

Before we could decide, a White Rabbit bounded out of the wormhole from the other side. Unlike my friend Harry the White Rabbit, this rabbit struck me as a no-nonsense type.

"Conflabbit, thirty-eight seconds late," the White Rabbit huffed, checking her Hole Tracker, which had a purple band that matched her velvet blazer. When she finally noticed us, her ears stood as stiff as the ruffled collar poking out of her jacket.

"What are you children up to?" she asked suspiciously. "Stay away from this wormhole. It's dangerous."

"It's not dangerous," I commented. "It leads to the Portalscape."

The White Rabbit raised her eyebrows. "Travelers, are you? Let me see your SVs."

"Our what?" Blue asked.

The White Rabbit totally freaked out. Her ears vibrated with the speed of mosquito wings and her eyes turned the color of fresh blood. Then—*blam*—she mutated. Her body expanded, but her head grew much larger, turning White Rabbit into a scary, gigantic bobble-head. Her ears were now sharp and stiff like swords, her face was Rottweiler-esque, her paws sprouted claws, and her body became thick and muscular.

"No visas, no access!" she snarled.

The intensity of the creature's roar caused an updraft that blew my hair back. I raised an arm to shield myself from some of the spittle that came with it.

"She means storyteller visas," Daniel said urgently.

"Whoa, whoa, whoa," Jason said, raising his hands to show the monster he meant no harm. "Sorry, we didn't get the SV abbreviation, but we do have visas." He approached the White Rabbit slowly, holding up the back of his hand.

The White Rabbit narrowed her red eyes but reached inside her jacket and removed a black wand from a massive zip-up wallet. She passed the wand over Jason's body. It glowed as she scanned him. After a beat, a formerly invisible stamp on Jason's hand revealed itself. It was in the shape of a crescent and sparkled a myriad of different colors in a matter of seconds.

"All access; no expiration," the lady White Rabbit said. In the blink of an eye, she returned to her normal size. Jason stepped away and the stamp on his hand faded.

Harry the White Rabbit had given us storyteller visas so we could travel the Wonderlands without interference. White Rabbits usually guarded the wormholes that led to the Portalscape because that realm gave you access to all the others. He had warned us that we wouldn't want to get caught by a White Rabbit without the proper access pass. Now I knew why.

"It is very rare that all access, no expiration visas are issued," the lady White Rabbit said, now in a perfectly amicable mood. "Let me scan the rest of you."

We all took turns being scanned. Each of our hands revealed the same stamp as Jason's. When the lady White Rabbit was through, she nodded to us. "You are all approved. Now hurry on your way before I change my mind."

"All right, all right." I stepped in front of the wormhole and took one last glance at the Neverland forest. We'd be back. I could feel it.

Just maybe not in this story arc.

"See you on the other side," I said to my friends. With that, I leapt from this realm into the clutches of a new one.

CHAPTER 4

Giants of Geene

 was not a fan of Portalscape Portals.

Going through a Pop-Up Portal to the next realm in the Wonderland sequence was like stepping through a door. The transition lasted a second, and other than not knowing what kind of environment you would end up in, the journey posed no physical danger.

Portalscape Portals were far more perilous. The instant you stepped through, you fell into an underground abyss that smelled like topsoil. It was a wonder that none of us dislocated a shoulder or sustained a concussion on the way down.

My hands and feet scraped against dirt and roots as I tumbled through the void. After about thirty seconds the tunnel opened up and spat me out into a massive room—the Portalscape. Regrettably, it expelled me at the top of that room, twenty feet above the ground.

At least there was something to land on. Directly below the ejection point was a comically large bed. My friends and I had learned from our previous trips to the Portalscape that the mattress was incredibly springy. So if someone landed beside you while you were still on it, the resulting bounce would send you flying. The second I touched down I leapt from the bed before my friends' incoming bodies could throw me off. Unfortunately, Blue didn't have time to do the same before SJ landed, so the both of them were flung to the floor when they bounced off the bed. Blue hit the ground hardest.

"Ow." She rubbed the side of her arm as she got up.

I took in the mystifying Portalscape. The entire realm consisted of a circular room forty feet in diameter and was filled with a mist that hung around our knees. A similar wraithlike fog drifted around the curved earth ceiling with the hole that spat us out at its very center. Vines dangled around the opening like creepy plant arms.

The main points of interest in the Portalscape, though, lined the walls. Each of the fourteen magnificent doors along the rounded walls of the Portalscape led to a different Wonderland. The doors were as unique as the mystical worlds that lay beyond their frames. Now that I was becoming familiar with the different Wonderlands, I could more easily peg which door led to what realm. The dark brown wooden door with vines sprouting orange tiger lilies, for example, went to Neverland. The bright yellow door led to Oz. The ice door decorated with holly and garlands led to the North Pole.

My eyes lingered on a forest green door opposite me. It was elegant and enchanting with a gold floral design etched into it.

It was the door back to Book.

Blue moved over and stood next to me, still rubbing her arm.

"You okay?" I asked.

"Fine. I probably deserved it after screwing up back there. My big mouth almost got us killed by a giant bunny."

"Bunnies are different than rabbits, Blue," SJ commented, dusting herself off.

Blue's mouth was halfway open with a retort before SJ cut her off. "And anyway, it does not matter that you made a mistake. It happens. Your combat skill and vast knowledge of all things fairytale have saved us on too many occasions for this incident to tarnish your record."

The indignant expression on Blue's face disappeared. "Thanks, SJ."

I allowed a small smile to curve my lips.

SJ, Blue, and I had been a dynamic trio for years, but because my friends were so different they often squabbled over trivial things. SJ was the perfect traditional princess—kind, graceful, polite—just like you would imagine the daughter of Snow White to be. Conversely, Blue was the scrappy, bold, and outspoken younger sister of the famed Little Red Riding Hood. While SJ preferred singing with birds and mixing potions, Blue fancied rough combat and weapons. SJ steered toward a logical, rational approach. Blue was driven by instinct and impulse.

Yet, despite their core dissimilarities, the two were true friends who cared deeply for one another. In moments like this it was easy to see the fondness and respect they had for each other.

"Now then," SJ continued. "Shall we?"

She was pointing to the gray stone door that led to Camelot. Silver and gold glitter stretched from the edges the way frost climbed windowpanes. In the center of the door was a familiar symbol—a cross with a ten-pointed star in the upper right quadrant. I had spotted the same symbol in the form of a birthmark on Arthur's left forearm yesterday. I would've never known it was there if it hadn't been for his sleeve getting accidentally pushed up when he was helping me out of a trapping pit. I wondered what the symbol meant.

Daniel stepped forward and opened the door. We saw the shadowy depths of a cave on the other side. Not promising.

He gestured to us. "Ladies first."

"You heard him, SJ," Blue said. "That's all you."

SJ rolled her eyes. "Fine." She walked up to the door, took a deep breath, then stepped through. I went swiftly after her. A breezy energy passed over me as I crossed into the new realm. Once in the cave, I looked back as the rest of our friends followed. From this side, the door we'd come through had the appearance of another silver wormhole.

The cave we found ourselves in was small with a low ceiling, but not dark. Streaks of light poured in from around the corner ahead of us—the way out. A large rock sat in the center of the cave where another White Rabbit sat, half asleep. His whiskers drooped and his fur had touches of gray. He wore the top half of a three-piece suit—a collared shirt, vest, and jacket—and held a cane in one hand. He looked feeble, but I regarded him with proper respect. I had no doubt he would turn into a monster if we crossed him. That cane would probably become a massive battering ram he could smash us with.

"Storyteller visas," he said in a rusty voice with a partial yawn, slowly getting up from his seat.

We all presented our hands and repeated the scanning process. When the White Rabbit was satisfied, he waved us along. My friends and I followed the sunlight around the corner and out of the cave. We stepped into the outside world and took in our first real sight of Camelot.

The forest before us was breathtaking, and not eerie like so many others we'd been through. The blossoms of a massive magnolia tree next to the cave filled the air with sweetness. Dandelions and mushroom circles sprang up from the grass. A rush of red-chested hummingbirds flew by, their updraft causing my dress to flutter.

Blue tilted her chin at me. "Right. Now we have to find our way to Camelot's citadel so you can get that Boar's Mouth blessing."

"So, we should head left then," Daniel said.

Blue gave him a skeptical look. "How do you know that?"

Daniel pointed at a tree. Hanging from one of the lower branches was an arrow-shaped sign with the word "Citadel" pointing to our left.

"Oh," she said.

Enchanted creatures we came across while trekking through the forest: six. Conversations we had that focused on topics unrelated to the Vicennalia Aurora: three. Minutes that went by without me worrying about one of our enemies: zero.

I think we were all still a bit wiped from this morning and didn't feel much like casual chatter. We also weren't in the mood to strategize yet. We briefly discussed a few thoughts regarding what awaited us at the citadel, and I mentioned that Mauvrey had given a name to the ruler currently on the throne—Rampart— but past that our focus remained on the hike itself.

There were additional sporadic direction signs mounted throughout the forest, but to get to the citadel we relied mainly on our map of the realm that SJ pulled from her potions sack.

Jason, as our primary navigator for the time being, studied it intently before leading the way. We walked for an hour and a half before we ran into an issue.

"That's weird," Jason commented as we paused by a signpost. One sign pointed right and was labeled "Canyon of Geene" while all others pointed left, one of which was labeled "Citadel."

"I don't know why the sign wants us to go left," he said. "The map shows this canyon as the fastest direct path to the citadel. If we go around it, it could take seven or eight hours. If we go through it, we can get to the citadel in, like, half that time."

"So let's take the shortcut," Daniel responded.

"I don't know, man," Jason said. "I know being the voice of reason is more SJ's thing, but don't you think there might be a reason that the sign is pointing that way?"

"The voice of reason agrees," SJ said. "There is probably something dangerous in that canyon. The terrain itself might be treacherous as well."

"What's a few monsters and a difficult hike?" Blue said. "We can handle a little danger."

"Let's take a vote," Daniel said. "All those in favor of a shortcut?"

He and Blue raised their hands.

"All those opposed?"

SJ and Jason raised their hands.

The four of them turned to me. "Crisa?"

I weighed the choices. "The next wormhole in Neverland was supposed to open eight hours after ours. That was an hour and a half ago. I don't think we can afford to take the long way. We need to get to the citadel as quickly as possible."

"The canyon it is then," Blue said.

And with that, we forged ahead into uncertain terrain.

The forest path soon turned rocky, and steep hills rose around us until we were completely engulfed by a canyon of black rock. Its mouth grew higher around us as we proceeded through. Boulders ten to thirty feet high were scattered everywhere, including on top of each other, forcing us to scoot through tight spaces between them or climb around.

The climbing wasn't that hard, but I also had to contend with a different issue. From the moment we'd entered the wasteland of black stone I'd begun to feel dizzy. It didn't affect my balance so much as it did my concentration, allowing the condition to go unnoticed by my friends. As we entered the second hour of our hike, I considered bringing it up. The further we delved into the canyon, the more warbled my head became.

I paused to catch my breath at the peak of an immense rock that we'd had to scale to get around. As I tightened the straps on my backpack, I gazed at the landscape ahead.

The end of the canyon was thankfully in sight, maybe a five-minute walk away. Hopefully once we weren't in the claustrophobic hold of this canyon I'd feel better. I could see green hills in the distance. Unfortunately, I could also see something else. My eyes narrowed on enormous footprints in the ground the size of beanbag chairs. The closest set abruptly stopped at a massive stone a few yards from the boulder I was perched on. Another set vanished at a stone about halfway to the exit.

Hm. That's troubling.

I hopped down from the immense rock a little too speedily and my head spun. It felt like there was static in my brain blocking my focus. Trying to shake off the sensation, I called after my friends.

"Hey guys, what do you make of this?" I jogged over to the nearest prints. "Look. There are footprints here, and they just stop next to this stone."

My friends glanced around, equally puzzled, until Blue spotted something. "Hey, is that a button?" She pointed at a short, flat rock next to her.

Further inspection revealed the rock's color to be slightly lighter than the others around it. Creases in the dirt around it formed an unusual outline. And it was smooth like it was frequently touched.

Blue lifted her foot.

"Blue, I wouldn't—"

Before Daniel could finish his warning, my friend stomped on the button with the full force of her boot. The moment she did, the huge rock next to us began to shake. Then it slid to the left, revealing an underground passageway.

The steps were enormous and stretched into darkness. I could only see twenty feet or so into the passage, despite small balls of glowing light strung on the walls. A cold draft accompanied by the smell of corned beef drifted upward as we stared into the depths.

"Blue," I said steadily, a bad feeling filling my stomach. "Close the passage."

She nodded and went back to the rock. There was no reverse switch, so she did what seemed most natural and stomped on it again. Her instinct was correct. The button rose up to its starting position and the massive stone slid into place, closing off the staircase.

I looked around the canyon warily.

"All these rocks . . . How many of them are just hidden passageways?" SJ asked nervously.

"And what exactly lives down there?" Jason added.

The latter of these two questions was soon answered. Suddenly, the other stone I'd seen footsteps leading up to began to move.

"Everybody hide," Daniel snapped.

We sought cover behind two stones—SJ, Daniel, and I hid behind the one concealing the passage we'd previously opened while Blue and Jason darted behind a rock ten feet over.

I poked my head out to see a creature emerging from another underground lair, but I only got a glimpse of a large, bald head before the rock we were hiding behind started sliding aside. My friends and I had to scramble into the open to avoid getting crushed. We didn't have any time to find new cover, and so had front row seats as an intimidating head rose from the passage. It was pale green like an aged flower, bald and smooth except for jagged ears on either side, and huge. Following the head came an equally intimidating body.

I'd never seen a giant in person, though I'd read there were many kinds and they came in various large sizes. Most of Book's were the size of trees and were locked in Alderon because they were dangerous, cannibalistic monsters. Thankfully, the type of

giants that grew to the height of skyscrapers only lived in the
Wonderland called the Giants' Keep, where Jason's brother Jack
was famous for getting into trouble.

The giant we faced now was not the size of a building, but
at fifteen feet tall he was still formidable. Despite his protruding
belly, the monster bulged with muscles. He clutched a large club
made of the canyon's black stone in his meaty left hand and hauled
it behind him like a little girl dragging a rag doll.

Further ahead, the giant who I'd only glimpsed coming out of
the other passage was now in full view. His club was curtly pointed
in our direction. "Morris. Behind you."

The giant named Morris turned. My friends and I stepped
back but could only go so far before our backs pressed against
rock.

Aw, crud.

"Well, well, well," Morris said. His eyes were dull gray, but
their spark was as sharp as his uneven teeth. The brown, patchy
beard on his chin matched the color of the skort he wore below
his bare chest. This unfortunate skort was adorned with a belt
that looked like it was made of human pelvic bones.

I inadvertently squeezed Daniel's arm.

"Don't you kids know it's dangerous to go wandering about
the Canyon of Geene?" Morris said. "You could get hurt." And
just like that, he raised his club and slammed it down. We barely
dove out of the way in time.

The club hit the ground so hard it created a pothole. Daniel
had rolled to the left while SJ and I went right. The giant followed
SJ and me and raised his club again. Just as he was about to bring
it down, Blue darted in from behind him and thrust her hunting
knife into his calf.

Purple blood oozed from the gash and Morris howled in pain,
giving SJ a chance to fire a portable potion. She pulled out a
red orb and shot it at the giant's chest. The potion released an
explosion that blasted him back a dozen feet. He didn't fall over,
but he slammed into a boulder, which cracked in half.

My friends and I made a break for it. Regrettably, three more
giants had risen from underground passageways in the distance

and another had popped out of a passage thirty feet over. SJ drew a couple more potions. She launched an explosion potion at the nearest giant and an ice potion right after.

The explosion potion caused him to stagger, but the ice potion didn't do anything to waylay his approach. Although its effects encased his leg, all the giant had to do was flex his muscles and the ice shattered. In retaliation, he picked up a black stone and flung it at us.

It crashed into the rocks behind us and smashed into a dozen bits. I lunged for cover and narrowly avoided getting bludgeoned by the pieces. I looked around and saw my friends were okay. Most of them had moved out of the way. Jason had utilized the enchantment on his axe, which projected a small force field when he willed it to with the word "Protect." Its glistening energy vanished as he deactivated the enchantment, and he offered SJ a hand up from where she'd dived to avoid being hit.

She took it with gusto, sprung up, and fired six explosion potions in a row at the nearest giant who'd thrown the rock. They pummeled him with fire and knocked him over. He didn't get back up, so I guess they knocked him out too.

"The exit to the canyon isn't far!" Jason shouted. "We just need to mow past these guys and make a run for it!"

Another enormous rock shattered in front of us, thrown by one of the farther away giants. The impact caused my brain to rattle in my skull. A glance behind me showed that Morris was getting up. It wouldn't be long before we had to worry about attackers on both sides.

We all dashed behind a rock for quick, shared cover.

"A head-on assault is suicide," Blue said. "We'll get crushed before we get close."

"I'll use my magic," I said. "They're not the only ones who can use these rocks to their advantage. I'll launch a few and knock them out of the way to clear a path. SJ, can you distract them? Keep any rocks from pelting me while I do this?"

"It would be my pleasure."

SJ scaled the nearest rock like an alley cat and began releasing one potion after the next. A trio of goop, lightning, and explosive fire assaulted the three giants ahead. She spun around and shot a lightning potion at Morris. Then she turned and launched four more potions at the giants in front.

I pressed my hands onto the nearest rock with the intention of summoning my powers to defend us until we were clear of the canyon. Despite having controlled the cliff chunk earlier, I knew I had enough power left to do this. The other day I'd manipulated an entire yellow brick road. This morning I'd controlled four trees at once. Heck, last semester I'd raised an army of bronze animals.

Given that, you can imagine my surprise when my magic didn't work.

The glow erupted from my hands, but when I focused on the rock, the static I'd been feeling in my head since entering the canyon grew stronger. The more I concentrated, the more that feeling escalated, making me dizzier until—

"Awgh!"

My magic aura suddenly exploded like an angry power surge. The golden burst blasted me back. I plowed into Daniel, who caught me by the arms. Every vein inside my body was tingling. I felt like I'd gotten punched with a cattle prod.

"What was that?" Daniel asked.

I gasped for breath and shook my head. "I don't know."

"Problem?" SJ called from atop her rock, still flinging potions in both directions.

"No!" I called back. I righted myself and tried again. I moved toward the rock and vehemently pressed my hands against it. Magic erupted from my palms as I channeled the full force of my power.

Okay, focus. You can do this.

Alas, the harder I tried, the more I felt like my head was going to explode. After a few seconds an even bigger burst than before blasted me off my feet. This time Daniel didn't catch me and I slammed against hard stone.

Ow.

I stood up slowly, shaking my head trying to clear it.

"Crisa, what's going on?" Jason asked, casting worried looks at me and then the approaching giants. "SJ can't keep this up forever. We need you."

"It doesn't work," I stammered. "My magic, it doesn't work."

"Then we need a new plan," Daniel said.

"I have one," Blue said. "Bob and weave." She looked up. "SJ! Come on, we gotta go. Crisa's magic isn't an option. Fire as you run."

SJ discharged another four potions before sliding down the rock. We darted through the canyon evading the stones that the giants chucked at us. Despite our desire to stay together, we had to separate as we bobbed and weaved around rocks and evaded the giants' heaved projectiles. Jason tended to be in the lead of our pack and SJ was at the rear due to the number of times she had to stop and launch counterstrikes. Every ten yards or so she scaled a stone to shoot off some of her potions, buying us precious intervals to run without having rocks thrown at us.

When we were about twenty feet from the giants blocking our exit, SJ shouted, "I will hit high! You all hit low!" She pulled back on her slingshot and nailed all three giants in the face with slime potions. They started swinging their clubs blindly while they pulled at the goop stuck to their eyes.

Daniel, Blue, Jason, and I raced beneath the monsters and attacked. Having transformed my wand into a sword, I stabbed the first giant in the ankle while my friends assaulted their own monsters.

Wand.

I rolled to the side as a wildly swinging club nearly smashed into me. I stabbed my giant again and his howl filled my eardrums.

"Move!" SJ suddenly yelled.

I didn't question the command and ran out of the way. I spun back on my heel just in time to see SJ fire a succession of twelve ice potions. Her shots were so hard and fast I thought her slingshot might snap under the pressure.

The three giants were frozen solid; they wouldn't be able to flex their way out of that many layers of frost any time soon. The only monster that still posed a threat was Morris. He'd freed himself from SJ's last potion and was now running toward us in ungainly leaps, only pausing to heave stones in our direction, lobbing them over his frozen friends.

He was too far away for SJ to get a good shot at him. Time to run. So we ran, Daniel in the lead followed by Jason then Blue then me, and lastly SJ trying to catch up.

The way out of the canyon was fifty feet away—a relatively straight shot, but we had to zigzag around the large stones scattered throughout the terrain. These same obstacles had made the exit to the canyon hard to see from ground level. However, I could see traces of green hills in the distance that promised freedom.

Debris from hurled rocks shattered all around us.

Forty feet.

Rock dust blew around me. The dirt and onyx gravel beneath my feet shook violently.

Thirty feet.

The exit was so close I could taste it. I glanced back. SJ was ten steps behind me. I couldn't see Morris, which meant I couldn't tell what direction the next soaring projectile would come from.

I looked forward again. The black rock walls funneled here, and my friends went in a single file line as they sprinted toward the green hills. I shoved my wand into my boot and exited the canyon second to last. I clambered through the gap then spun around the instant I touched down on the other side. SJ was picking herself up from the canyon floor mere yards from the opening. She must've stumbled. That's when I saw it—the light from the canyon exit glinted off a huge stone that was flying through the air.

"SJ!"

Reflexively, SJ flung herself sideways. The projectile missed her and crashed into the gap instead. Shards of stone broke from the rock and the force of the wind that came with it blew dust and gravel against me. I leapt back, covering my eyes with my arm. When I lowered my arm a moment later I saw that the opening to the canyon was now sealed off, and SJ was on the wrong side.

I raced up to the stones and made one final attempt to rally my magic. It was no good. When I tried to enchant the rock I felt intense brain pain and another surge blasted me away. When my butt hit the grass I decided to try something else.

Shield.

I transformed my wand and tried to bring it to life with the idea of riding it like a saucer-shaped sled. But although my glow shimmered around the shield, nothing else happened.

Ugh! What the frack?

I didn't have time to worry about why I couldn't use my magic right now. SJ was in peril, which meant time for Plan C.

Wand.

I put my wand back in my boot and dug my feet into the dirt. With all my fortitude, I willed a small patch of earth to lift off the ground just like I'd manipulated that slice of cliff in Neverland.

As my magic poured out of me and the earth began to move, I was filled with relief. It worked! The section of ground immediately surrounding me levitated into the air. I willed it high enough to allow me a view of what was happening in the canyon. As I crested the rock, I first spotted Morris's big head. I urged my earth platform to go faster, and soon I crested the entirety of the blockage. When I did, I saw SJ at the foot of it, whole but unmoving. Morris was headed straight toward her.

Dive, dive, dive! I commanded, doing my best to keep the section of earth together. It was not as sturdy as the piece of Neverland cliffside—too many separate particles to keep united. More of it crumbled with every second.

I shot down over the stones that blocked the canyon exit. I didn't think; I only knew I needed to protect my friend. About five feet from the ground I released control over the dirt. As it fell apart, I jumped, landing just between SJ and the giant as he reached for her. As a result, instead of grabbing SJ like he'd intended, Morris grabbed me.

SJ stirred right as the monster lifted me up to his eye level. "Crisa!"

My heart pounded in my chest. My arms were free, but the giant's grip cut off the blood flow between my upper and lower body. My wand was in my boot and I couldn't reach it over his massive fingers.

Fear and desperation boiled inside of me as I struggled. Then I met the giant's gaze—ten inches from my face. He laughed and opened his mouth wide.

White noise rang in my ears and I lifted my hands.

I don't remember thinking a specific command. I don't remember calling on my magic. My subconscious went silent and autopilot took over. Everything that came next was pure instinct.

Magic burst from my palms as I pressed my hands against Morris's face. My glow had never been stronger. It immersed the giant in half a second. He cried out in pain like the energy was searing him.

My glow radiated more fervently. It was vibrant gold, but hints of gray flowed around the edges. Fear whirred around my mind, flooding it with heaving emotions like a tidal wave. The stronger my emotions became, the more my magic seared the giant until . . .

What in the—

Morris started to disintegrate. Like literally. His green skin began to turn black like ash and dissipate into the air around us.

The giant dropped me and shouted. The thud of my body hitting the ground knocked me out of my emotional stupor. My thoughts sharpened and I was in control again. And that's when I knew what I'd done.

No.

It was too late. The giant clutched his face and screamed once more before stumbling and falling flat on the canyon floor.

He didn't make any more noise after that. The disintegration effect stopped and the energy that'd been surrounding him evaporated. He was dead. I could feel it. He lay there still as the rocks around us.

I got up slowly as SJ came beside me. We walked closer to the giant and saw how sections of skin across his body were charred while other parts were missing. There was no blood or exposed flesh. The parts of his limbs and face that had disintegrated had just disappeared, like an artist had come along and erased pieces of him from existence. I stood next to his face and knelt beside him, staring blankly at his lifeless form.

"Crisa . . ."
I looked up at SJ.
"What have you done?"

CHAPTER 5

The Mercy Pit

n this side of the canyon the shattered rock pieces created a rough stairway that allowed SJ and me to climb out. Once at the top, we stood for a moment. Our friends rushed closer when they spotted us. "You okay?" Blue called.

"Fine!" I responded.

SJ gave me a look.

"We'll talk about it when we get down there," I told her.

I observed the forest starting anew about a hundred feet away. With deep concentration, I brought a tall tree to life and had it come over. It took some effort, but despite my last action I wasn't magically exhausted.

Height-wise the tree reached the halfway point of the canyon barrier. I commanded it to catch SJ and me then set us on the ground. Once the telepathic order was given, the two of us carefully sat and pushed off the brink. We slid down the side of the canyon until the tree's branches gingerly caught us in a perfect cradle. It was a smooth landing, and the branches lowered us with great care. Once we touched the ground the tree went inanimate again, having done its duty.

After Jason consulted the map and confirmed our direction, our united group of five began to move through the forest and I finally proceeded to tell SJ, and the others, what had happened on the other side of the canyon wall and *how* it happened.

"It's called crossing the Malice Line," I said. "It's what happens when someone with Pure Magic uses their powers to inflict mortal harm."

"Have you done it before?" Blue asked.

"Not intentionally," I responded. "Remember that wooden plank I brought to life last semester? Remember how I took away its enchantment because it was causing a nuisance flying about everywhere? It's the same concept. I can take life just like I can give it, but I cross the Malice Line every time I use my power for taking life because that aspect of my ability literally translates to killing something."

"So you're not supposed to use your magic that way?" Jason clarified.

I nodded. "Liza said it was dangerous, that crossing the Malice Line would reduce my control over my magic and heighten my *magic's* control over me, pushing me closer to the corruptive darkness of Pure Magic Disease. Hence why I wasn't planning on ever using my powers that way again. Liza already taught me how to temporarily bring things to life so that once my commands have played out they can return to normal, like that tree back there. So there's no need for me to actively take life."

"Except for now," Blue commented.

"Except for now," I agreed sadly.

"How did you know you would even be able to do it?" Jason asked, pushing a branch out of his way. "A bit of wood is one thing. But taking the life of a living creature—you've never done that before."

"Honestly, I didn't know I could do it. I didn't even know that I was doing it. It just sort of happened." I shook my head dejectedly. "My magic wasn't working on the stones—which I still don't understand—SJ was in trouble, and I was about to get eaten. I remember this swell of fear and desperation, and then hearing this white noise, and then he was disintegrating. The magic reacted out of instinct, not my intent."

"Crisa, that is not good," SJ said. "You lost control. You lost control and you killed him."

"Lay off, SJ," Daniel said. "If she hadn't, you'd both be dead. Besides, that thing wasn't so much a *he* as it was an *it*."

"Exactly," Blue agreed. "It was self-defense. And it's hardly the first time Crisa's killed someone."

I blinked at her. "What?"

"Oh, come on," Blue said, swatting a fly that was pestering her. "On all the adventures we've been on, you're telling me you haven't offed somebody?"

"Of course not," I replied.

"*Really?*" Blue stopped and crossed her arms. "What about in Alderon? When we were trapped in that antagonist castle and were fighting for our lives to get out?"

"I don't think I killed anybody," I replied. "I was just fighting to escape like you said. I slashed and punched and stabbed like you guys—and wounded a lot of people, sure—but I didn't act with the intention of killing anyone. There was no moment when I thought 'strike to kill.' That's not me."

"What about on the magic train?" Blue asked.

We'd stopped walking. Sunlight leaked through the branches in different-sized rays and I felt like everybody's eyes were on me.

"When those magic hunters attacked, you used the exploding necklaces to blast them off the train," Blue said. "We were crossing over an enormous gorge at the time."

"There was a lake below," I argued.

"Would you have done things differently if there wasn't?"

I hesitated. Thankfully Jason came to my defense.

"Look, I don't think any of those instances count, Blue," he said. "If you don't know for a fact that any of the people you've fought are dead—and if you struck out against them in self-defense and not with the intention of taking their lives—then the slate is morally clean."

"Agreed," Daniel said. "And as far as today goes, that monster deserved to die and Knight is still plenty in control of her magic. So she slipped up for a second. Big deal. Considering the alternative was death, I'm glad her magic stepped in. It's not like there's any greater harm done." He turned to me. "You don't feel evil, right?"

"Um, no."

"See?" He gestured at me as if the matter was completely resolved. "She's fine."

I didn't know if I was fine, per se, but I did know I didn't want to spend any more time talking about it. The dizziness and brain pain I'd been feeling had vanished once we'd left the canyon, but Blue's assertions had knocked me off balance. What I'd done to that giant took a lot out of me both physically and emotionally, causing my head and heart to hurt in a new way.

It was only this morning that I'd wondered if I had it in me to kill anyone. And here I was, not even half a day later, with metaphorical blood on my hands.

Perhaps my friends were right. Maybe it didn't count because Morris had been a monster, not a person. Maybe it didn't count because it had been self-defense and he would've killed SJ and me. Maybe it didn't count because I hadn't actively chosen to kill him. My instinct had overpowered my control and stepped in.

Or maybe those were all just excuses and I needed to face facts. Whatever factors had been at play, I had taken an action and now I had to live with it.

After a couple giant-less hours of journeying through the forest, we emerged onto a great, flat valley. It was crowned by a mountain range miles to our right, and a dark line in the distance opposite us was likely another forest.

What caught our attention was what lay at the center of the valley. Rising up like a boil on smooth skin was a cluster of mountains that housed the citadel of Camelot. It was massive. It was impressive. It was intimidating. Structures were flawlessly woven into the rock. They rose and hid with the different levels of the terrain—wrapping around the sides of the mountains and delving into its folds.

While the majority of the citadel was seamlessly imbedded into the natural architecture of the mountains, a tall concrete wall had been constructed around the whole mountainous cluster about sixty feet from ground level. There was only one way through: a single uphill road that led to a main gate.

Hearts full of anticipation, my friends and I crossed the valley and began the climb to reach it. The sun beat down on us. The wall grew more menacing with every step. Its size alone was overwhelming, but I could also see guards walking along the top and cannons spaced out. I had no doubt that any approaching hostile would have a very high chance of being obliterated.

A muscular guard awaited us at the entry. He had a hard chin, tan skin, and a no-nonsense expression that reminded me of my teachers at Lady Agnue's. He pointed a finger at me.

"Name? Where are you traveling from? What is your reason for being here?"

Crisanta Knight; another realm; to claim Excalibur.

"Yeah, hi." Jason stepped forward. "We're iron importers from the Red Lands. We're here to discuss a deal with one of the local bladesmiths."

"Which one?" asked the guard.

"Dalhan and Son," Jason said without skipping a beat.

The guard raised his eyebrows suspiciously. "The Red Lands, huh? I hear those Graysnapper monsters can make travel very dangerous this time of year, what with mating season and all."

"Graysnappers only mate in the fall, actually," Jason replied. "And since they only come out at night, we didn't encounter any trouble."

SJ and I exchanged a look.

The guard seemed satisfied. "Very good," he said. "You may proceed." He motioned to another guard in a tower above the gate. In response, the weighty iron barrier rose up. Jason nodded and gestured for us to follow.

"Hey, one more thing . . ." the guard said.

Jason paused.

"Are you a first-time visitor, or returning?"

"First time," our friend answered. "Why?"

"You kids look familiar," the guard responded. "Never mind. Forget I said anything."

Without further delay, the five of us hurried down the concrete tunnel that led through the wall and into the citadel. When we were safely out of earshot, Daniel gave Jason a pat on the back.

"Nice job, man. Quick thinking."

Jason shrugged. "I spent a lot of time learning about these Wonderlands when we were making our maps. I remembered reading that the Camelot citadel does a lot of business with outside importers, and there's a bladesmith on almost every block. Camelot folk love their weapons."

"Meanwhile, the Red Lands are known for their iron product," Blue chimed in. "Which is always in demand here."

"Exactly," Jason said. "That's why I figured it was our best bet. And the Graysnapper thing was just luck. I didn't know they were native to the Red Lands, but I learned about them in an Animals from Other Realms course last year. I guess the guard was posing a trick question because he wanted to make sure I was telling the truth about where we came from."

"Impressive," I commented.

"Not as impressive as that." Jason pointed up.

We stood on the threshold of the citadel. All around us were bustling shops filled with drably dressed peasants and the occasional group of black-armored knights. The shops were decorated with colorful banners and streamers in shades of green, pink, and purple, probably in tribute to the Vicennalia Aurora.

Camelot flags and banners also hung from every balcony and tower. They were navy with golden accents in the corners to match the golden cross-and-ten-pointed-star symbol at the center. That symbol was popping up everywhere. I had to figure out what it meant.

"I'd presume the castle is on the other side of the mountains because we didn't see it from the valley," Blue commented. "We should find out exactly where it is."

"This might help," SJ said. In her hand she held a brochure titled "History of the Citadel Castle."

"There are directions on the back that can take us right to it," she said.

"Where'd you get that?" Blue asked.

SJ gestured at a nearby cart with a banner that read "Citadel Souvenirs." There was an assortment of free maps and brochures at the front. SJ cracked a smile. "You know, the four of you are always ready to face any fearsome challenge that comes your way, but you never stop to consider the absurd chance that there could be an easy, logical alternative."

"Yeah, yeah," Blue huffed. "Open the brochure."

SJ unfolded the document and gave a small gasp of delighted

surprise. The map was designed like a pop-up children's book, and the image that had leapt out was a 3-D rendering of the castle.

"Combining the different levels, the citadel castle is roughly 135,380 square feet," SJ read. "It took seven years to build, and the structure has seen many renovations throughout its history, the most recent being the addition of the M.C. Escher intersection. The only direct entrance is across the Reflection Bridge. Tours are offered on the second Monday of every month."

"Does it say anything about the Boar's Mouth?" I asked.

SJ scanned the brochure. "No," she said after a moment. "This is mainly information about the structure itself. For example, during the original construction a woodworking factory and kiln were built onsite to produce 30,000 bricks a day."

"Well, that's helpful," Blue replied sarcastically. "I guess we could always wait for a tour and chuck a brick through the window to break in."

"Calm your sarcasm, Blue," I said. "The Boar's Mouth is in the castle, which means one way or another, we'll find a way in so I can get blessed and—" My nose caught a whiff of something delicious. I pivoted toward the source of the smell—a nearby restaurant. "Come on," I said to my friends. "Let's get some lunch and regroup."

Weaving around mounted horses and vendors hawking their wares, my friends and I sat down at one of the tables outside the restaurant. A cute red-chested hummingbird flew onto the edge of the table and tilted its head at me. I smiled at it, but the creature flittered away a second later when a slender waitress exited the restaurant with a slam of the door. She wore a mustard yellow dress and had curls coming out of her bonnet. She brought us coffee, insisted that we try the house special Monte Cristo sandwiches, and then stepped back inside once we'd agreed.

Near our table, a man was hawking newspapers. SJ paid for a copy with some money from her backpack. She shrugged at my questioning glance. "It does not hurt to know more about your surroundings when you are on foreign territory. We should learn as much about the citadel as we can. It may help us conceive a better plan."

She wasn't wrong. We crowded around the newspaper.

On the front page there was coverage of the citadel's Vicennalia Aurora festivities, or "Great Lights" festivities as they were called here. The citadel was loaded with events and celebrations this week—pubs with discounts on food and drink, performance venues with grand shows, even nightly fireworks. In addition, a different sector of the city hosted a special activity for the whole citadel each night. Yesterday there had been a jousting contest among some of the king's guards. Tonight, there was going to be a big battle in something called the Mercy Pit.

The castle was also participating in a "higher class" form of merriment this evening. The newspaper described that King Rampart was hosting a grand party. All nobility across Camelot were welcome, so long as they paid the grandiose admission fee.

"I wonder how this Rampart guy got the gig of being Arthur's successor." Blue said.

"That doesn't matter right now," Daniel replied. "This party is our best way in. We still have plenty of ONC money, don't we?"

"We do," SJ responded. "It was a good plan to convert most of the money we brought from Book into Oz Neverland Camelot currency at that ATM in Neverland. But this gala will use it up. After all, we do not just need to pay the entry fee for the party; we need a change of clothes in order to look like nobility."

"All right, fine. We'll buy some new clothes." I replied. "We've got that covered."

"Do we also have *this* covered?" Jason asked. He had continued to flip through the paper while we were talking and pushed page six in front of me—the Wanted Ads.

"Crisa, if King Rampart was willing to help the antagonists by giving your brother The Pentecostal Oath in the first place, then we can assume they're on the same side. He knows we're coming."

With SJ, Blue, and Daniel crowding around me, I looked at the page Jason had pushed forward. It featured pictures of all five of us alongside a call to action.

"Wanted by King Rampart of Camelot for questioning. Should be detained on sight. Volatile and extremely dangerous. Reward for capture," I read aloud.

"Wait, why is there a caption under my picture?" Blue asked, pointing. I followed her finger. Sure enough, in tiny print below her name it read: *If unable to detain, kill with extreme prejudice. Threat to QB mortality. See authorities for details.*

"That's bizarre," Jason commented. "What do you think it means?"

A glassy look passed over Blue's eyes like she was thinking about something, but she quickly responded, "I don't know."

She was lying. I'd known her long enough to tell. I would have pressed her if SJ hadn't grabbed the newspaper. Her eyes lit up when she took in her picture in the Wanted Ads. She beamed.

"I made the list! They actually consider me a threat!" she said with delight.

I was happy to see her reaction. All the royals in our realm were supposed to be main characters and thus have protagonist books, but the truth was Liza didn't foresee every royal as a main character. As a result, our realm's higher-ups forged protagonist books for royals that Liza didn't have visions about. SJ was one of those royals.

Since learning this she'd had a massive bout of insecurity and identity crisis. Thankfully, her confidence was coming back and now she was trying to define her character anew.

"They don't just consider you a threat," Blue said, putting her arm around our friend. She pointed at the words. *"You're volatile and extremely dangerous.* That's a compliment if I ever heard one."

"Yup, we're all super important," Daniel said, rolling his eyes. "But how are we going to get past castle security? I think that guard at the gate recognized our faces but was too lazy to follow through. The guards at the castle will be way more alert."

"Then we won't use the front door," I replied flatly. "Forget the entry fee. We're spending our money on disguises, bribes, and . . ." I spotted the waitress approaching with a platter of food. "Sandwiches."

The waitress set a deep-fried sandwich in front of each of us. Cheese melted out of the sides, powdered sugar dusted the tops, and small cups of strawberry jam were presented beside each plate.

Blue looked them over. "Now that's money well spent."

After we devoured our sandwiches we worked our way through the streets of the citadel looking for a shop that sold clothes appropriate for the gala at the castle.

We were glad that the citadel was so packed with people, *and* that everyone seemed to be in a hurry. We didn't have any disguises and any person here could've read the newspaper today. All five of us made an effort to keep our heads down, avoid eye contact with anyone, and meld with the busy mess of people. Each of us had enough practice with stealth to blend in with the crowd just fine, but I still considered luck to be a big part of us remaining unnoticed.

As we maneuvered across the citadel's different mountainous layers, certain peculiarities started to stand out. Civilians ducked into shops whenever the black-armored knights passed by. Despite crowded tables indoors, no one sat in the patio areas of restaurants. There was a fairly high number of homeless people and beggars, but they hid whenever knights (on foot or horseback) came by. Numerous "missing persons" fliers were hanging on posts and in alleyways. And small gangs of children in rags ran about, scoping out targets for pickpocketing.

This place may have looked like an orderly, bustling metropolis at first glance, but it had a lot of internal problems.

Currently we found ourselves walking through a busy marketplace abundant in apothecaries, herbalists, and mystical tchotchke vendors. I ducked with the rest of my friends behind a candle vendor's tent when we spotted a cluster of knights heading our way. While stalled there, I overheard an exchange next door. I peered between a slit in the adjacent tent. This vendor's booth displayed jewelry all made from the same black stone. A burly knight and the stall's elderly vendor were speaking by the front table. The knight wore a navy cape attached to the shoulders of his black armor. I'd noticed quite a few knights around with similar capes, but this was the first I'd seen with a golden brooch on the left shoulder. The brooch looked like the face of some kind of animal.

"I will give you two bronze pieces for this pendant," the knight said to the reluctant vendor. "My lady will be quite pleased with such a trinket."

Blue waved us forward, signaling that the coast was clear, but I motioned for them to wait a moment so I could continue to eavesdrop.

"But sir," the elderly vendor protested. "The price is six silver pieces. This stone comes from the Canyon of Geene. It is incredibly hard to collect and even harder to shape."

"Ah, a bartering man, I see," replied the knight. "Then how's this? I'll counter your offer. *One* bronze piece, and my men and I won't pay your home a visit during this week's nightly raids. You live on Briar Street, don't you? And I believe you have a daughter who works in the castle stables?"

The elderly man froze for a second. Then he replied with more speed and worry in his tone. "On second thought, it's on the house, Sir Gaheris. Take it. Please. A gift to you in celebration of the Great Lights."

Sir Gaheris smiled. "Good man. Enjoy the rest of your week." He stashed the pendant in his pocket and mounted his white stallion. After he'd ridden away, I moved around the side of the stall to talk to the elderly vendor. It probably wasn't the best move, given that we were trying to keep a low profile, but my feet were already in motion and my friends were following me before I thought better of it.

"Good afternoon, miss," the vendor said, still a bit shaken. "Can I interest you in any of my pieces? They're quite rare and have a variety of special properties."

"That man who was just here," I said. "Why did you let him rob you? What did he mean by nightly raids?"

The elderly man gulped audibly. "You are not from the citadel. If you were, you'd know that under order of King Rampart, the citadel knights scour a different district every night in search of disloyalists."

"Disloyalists?" Blue repeated.

"Aye." The man nodded. "Anyone who might be affiliated with rebellions to overthrow the king, anyone who has not conformed to our leader's many ordinances or taxes, or anyone who just rubbed a higher-up the wrong way. We are all subject to the nightly raids. And those who are taken in the night are sent to the Mercy Pit or never seen again."

"What's the Mercy Pit?" Jason asked.

"It is an arena just outside the castle where accused citizens perform trial by combat—battling against one of Rampart's knights, or even King Rampart himself—to gain their freedom. Most of those poor people never stand a chance. Rampart's knights are formidable. And the king is a warrior with more kills under his belt than the Questor Beast." He shuddered.

"That is terrible," SJ replied.

"Aye," the elderly man said again. "But such has been the way of this land since the passing of—" he looked around to make sure no one else was listening, then lowered his voice to a whisper— "the great King Arthur. In the seven years that the king's been gone, we've had one cruel ruler after the next. Their reigns may not last long, but they succeed in tearing down King Arthur's legacy a bit at a time. King Rampart, however, has been the most hated, the opposite of King Arthur in every sense. He truly knows no pity."

I wanted to tell the jeweler not to lose hope, that Arthur was alive and we were on a mission to make sure Excalibur would be placed back in his hands. But since I was unable to do this, I settled for something else.

"Here." I dug a handful of ONC currency pieces out of my backpack and placed them on the table. "This ought to cover whatever that knight took."

The elderly vendor's mint green eyes nearly popped out of his head. "Miss, that is far too much money."

"Consider it an investment," I said. I looked around at the jewelry. "You can expand your business. You have some lovely product. You said these stones have special properties?"

"Yes, yes," the man nodded fervently. "This is Jacobee stone.

It is only found in certain regions, like the Canyon of Geene, and it is very difficult to shape, as only brute force can break it."

Jacobee stone . . .

A light went on in my brain. Mauvrey had mentioned Jacobee stone when she told me about the Stiltdegarth blood in her duel crossbow. And if this stone was the same stone found in the Canyon of Geene where we had encountered the giants . . .

I picked up a large black pendant in a gold setting. The instant my fingers closed around the stone, the dizziness and brain static I'd experienced in the canyon returned.

"Jacobee stone is one of only three substances known to suppress and repel magic," explained the vendor. "Wearing it is a sure way to deter unwanted spirits and supernatural forces. I also sell it in large, decorative rock form to put in the entryways of homes. The stones work as wonderful talismans to ward off any magical energy that might be nearby."

"Well, that explains a lot," I said, hurriedly putting the stone back on the table. The moment it left my hand, the faintness dissipated and I was myself again.

"Would you like one?" the elderly man asked. "It's on the house. A small tribute to your generosity."

"Um, no thanks," I said. "We will take directions, though. We're looking for some new clothes. The five of us are going to crash the party at the castle tonight, cause a little . . . *inconveniencing* for King Rampart."

The man's cracked lips turned upward in a small smile. "I can assist you with both." He pointed to the right of the marketplace and leaned in closer. "The apparel district is two blocks over. Take a left on Dalliant Street. And if I cannot repay your generosity with any of my wares, I will repay it with a favor to aid your mission. My daughter Ormé works in the castle stables. She can help you get inside. Just tell her that Jedidiah sent you, and show her this."

He gestured for my hand. From within the folds of his robe, he removed a small white card, which he placed in my palm. The card had a golden symbol on it—the letter G contained within the mouth of a dragon. He motioned for me to put it away, and I stuck it in my boot.

"Thank you," Jason said before I could ask about the symbol.

"No. Thank you," Jedidiah said. "But word to the wise, children. Do not let anyone else see that card." He glanced left and his eyes widened. I followed his line of sight and spotted a couple of knights on horseback getting close.

"Go now. Remember what I told you," Jedidiah said, shooing us away.

My friends and I moved back into the tide of people in the marketplace. I stole a glimpse over my shoulder at Jedidiah, considering returning to quickly ask him about the symbol on the card, but the flow pushed me along and I resigned to turning my attention forward again. We navigated up the block on our way to Dalliant Street as Jedidiah had instructed. I kept an eye out for knights as we continued up the road, but my mind buzzed with the latest information.

I had learned so many new things about my magic today. There were some bad revelations, obviously: I couldn't touch Jacobee stone without my magic going berserk and my brain fizzling up. But there was a pony hidden in the pile of manure too, and that was the idea that maybe, just maybe, my magic might let me save Jason.

I honestly didn't know if that was a stretch, if my magic could be developed in this way. And I didn't know how to test it in advance either. So while the notion lifted my spirits, for now I stayed committed to not telling Jason what I was thinking. I mean, what if this was all a false hope?

Daniel walked beside me at the back of the group.

"I guess we know why your magic didn't work in the canyon," Daniel said. "The stone was repelling your powers."

"Um, yeah." My brain switched gears. "Not the most convenient timing, but it's good to know that I'm not broken. Oh, and it finally put a cap on a question from last semester that I was never able to answer."

"What's that?"

"You remember when we were being held in the antagonist castle in Alderon? My wand couldn't cut through the stone walls of the prison. In the right weapon form, my wand's enchantment lets it cut through just about anything, but it didn't even make a scratch. And that magic pea we eventually used to escape got obliterated on impact with the walls. Knowing I had magic, the antagonists must've stuck us in a cell made of Jacobee stone."

"Makes sense," Daniel replied. Then he smirked at the satisfied look on my face. "That was really bothering you, wasn't it?"

"Hey, this story already has enough holes with wormholes appearing left and right. We don't need any plot holes too."

"Can't argue with that," Daniel said. "And it's good to know what your weaknesses are. Just be sure to tell your boyfriend when we get back to school that he shouldn't give you anything with Jacobee stone the next time he sends jewelry your way. Wouldn't want to give you a gift that incapacitates you."

I furrowed my eyebrows in confusion. "My boyfriend?"

"Chance Darling."

I laughed in disbelief and shook my head. "Chance is *not* my boyfriend. He's not even my friend. You know I can't stand him."

"You might feel differently about that soon," Daniel said. "Word gets around. Chance has been trying to change his ways to become someone worth your attention. I didn't believe he could do it at first. I hate the guy. He's a stuck-up, self-entitled prick. But you should see what he had in the works before we left school to meet up with you in Midveil. While you were gone, he seriously put his money where his mouth is. I think you're going to see him in a new light when we get back."

I crinkled my nose at the prospect.

The notoriously handsome and charming Prince Chance Darling—grandson of King Midas—had been courting my affections for some time. Until recently his attempts had been futile because I'd disliked the vain, egotistical boy since day one. However, at the start of the semester, Chance professed that his interest in me actually ran a lot deeper than both he and I initially believed. He claimed to have real feelings for me and that he could change into someone I might come to regard in the same way.

I seriously doubted this was possible, but he vowed he would think of some way to prove how much he cared for me.

I only needed to keep an open mind until then. If the prince's recent actions could inspire even Daniel to alter his estimations, I wondered just what miraculous gesture Chance had been conspiring in my absence.

And yet . . .

"I don't think there is anything Chance could ever do to change our relationship so dramatically," I thought aloud. "He and I have too much negative history. He irritates me and I find him insufferable. How could we possibly work?"

"I don't know," Daniel replied. "But you used to feel the same way about me and look at us now—having conversations about personal topics without either of us throwing insults or punches."

"Well, the day is young." I grinned.

He smiled and was about to say something else when his expression abruptly changed. "Do you hear that?" He paused to listen and I did the same, despite the mutters of annoyance of the people who had to push around us.

"Guys, come on," Jason called from ahead, pointing at a sign for Dalliant Street. "The apparel district is this way."

I gestured for him and the others to hold on, trying to pick up the noise Daniel had heard. "It sounds like . . ." I narrowed my eyes. "Applause."

It was coming from a street on the left. Daniel started to head toward the sound and I followed. The others had no choice but to come after us.

The sound of applause grew louder and the crowds grew denser as we made our way through the streets. I almost got run over by two horses pulling a carriage and nearly rammed into a woman walking three bulldogs, who aggressively barked at me.

Soon we reached a square that was packed to the seams. People were lining up at the entrance of a building on the far side, each holding a pale yellow flier. Knights guarded the outside of the building and I spotted others stationed in nearby cross streets and balconies.

Based on the noise, something big was happening just beyond this street, but we couldn't see anything. Because the citadel was built into the rises and falls of the mountain, the layout of the whole place was disorienting. The changing elevations skewed your understanding of how high on the mountains you were, and on what side.

A burst of applause came from a small alleyway off to the left. Maybe that route somehow had access to what was happening? Daniel had the same idea, and he led the way into the narrow street.

As soon as I entered the lane, I struggled to breathe. The musk of livestock and sewage was overpowering. Clotheslines hung from apartments high up. Daniel headed toward the end of the alley where light was flooding through a chain-link fence. He halted when he reached it, a look of shock on his face. Another roar—clearer and louder this time—burst out as the rest of us joined him and witnessed the dreadful and spectacular sight below.

Wind gusted around me as my fingers clenched the metal fence holding us back. A grand arena had been built into the enormous bowl-shaped canyon beneath us. Roughly circular and with no formal seating areas, the canyon was full of civilians sitting on rocks surrounding the perimeter.

About twenty feet from the base of the canyon the seating stopped. Concrete walls covered the natural rock and lined the circumference of the arena's smoothed-out dirt and sand floor. Several entryways in the concrete led onto the arena, and all were barred with iron gates.

Almost at my eye level, though fairly far away, several huge holographic screens floating in the center of the canyon projected the events unfolding on the arena floor.

Projection orbs.

Sure enough, I spotted several specks of light zipping about within the lower section of the arena. The canyon was utilizing the same type of magic tech that we used back home to relay real-time footage of our realm's favorite sport, Twenty-Three Skidd. Since Twenty-Three Skidd was played in the air on Pegasus horses, projection orbs allowed people in the stands to see what was happening. The same applied here, only in reverse. The audience was elevated in the canyon's seats, and the enchanted spheres helped them see the main event far below.

That event was a fight. The projection orbs transferred images of two men battling in the arena onto the holographic screens. One was a knight in black armor; the other was a skinny, poorly dressed man. Both wielded swords, but the commoner was clearly inexperienced.

I knew the dynamics of a fight too well and recognized what was coming. Right as the common man sidestepped and parried, the knight reversed the trajectory of his blade. I looked away as the audience roared. Carefully my eyes drifted back to the arena as the common man's body was taken away through the nearest tunnel.

"You kids won't get credit for watching if you don't get your papers stamped at the entrance."

I looked up to see a narrow-eyed woman sticking her head out a window above us. Maroon pantaloons hung from the clothesline next to her, fluttering in her freckled face until she yanked them off their hooks.

Blue stepped back slightly. "What do you mean?"

"Oh, you don't know? You must be from out of town," the woman replied. "I suppose you don't need to worry then. It's mandatory that all citizens of the citadel attend at least two Mercy Pit fights per week; four if you own a business. You receive a stamp on your tax document every time you attend, but visitors have no use for that. Lucky for you."

I was about to respond when the cheers suddenly escalated. I pivoted back to look at the arena, as did my friends.

"Ladies and gentleman," an announcer called, standing at the center of the combat zone. His face filled every one of the giant screens, and the projection orbs served to magnify his voice as well. "And now for a special treat. All rise and welcome . . . your king, Rampart Pendragon!"

The applause nearly drove me deaf. Every person in the canyon rose to his or her feet and turned to face a private viewing box that resided just over the concrete wall on the right. It was open on all sides and framed with gold and navy silks and Camelot flags. A railing at the front kept its spectators safe from the fall below. Just under that railing hung a massive Camelot flag that must've been at least twelve feet long. A man emerged from the tunnel beneath the flag. His face lit up the holographic screens. He had dark hair, was fairly tall, and based on his gait and the way he spun his sword, carried a little too much confidence.

"How is Rampart a Pendragon?" I said. "I thought Arthur never had any children and that he was an only child."

"He was," Blue responded. She was our resident expert on fairytale lore. "Mordred was technically his half-brother. But he was killed shortly after he 'killed' Arthur."

"So how is this guy related to him?"

The announcer's words overpowered our conversation as his voice, like his image, was amplified across the arena through the projection orbs. "And as for the challenger," he continued. "Here we have a traitor guilty of conspiring with some of the crown's most hated disloyalists."

A man with massive biceps, a bald head, and no shirt was forced out of a tunnel across the arena. He wore shackles on his wrists and was escorted by four burly guards. Upon reaching the center of the arena, the guards removed the shackles and then withdrew.

Three women dressed entirely in black came out of the tunnel beneath the private viewing box. Their long-sleeved dresses were fitted, as were the scarves they had wrapped around their heads to conceal everything but their eyes. Each pushed a cart loaded with weapons into the middle of the arena.

The bald man rubbed his wrists, shot Rampart a glare, then selected a spiked club from a cart. He looked around the canyon and took a few steps back, taking it in.

His build was much bigger than Rampart's. He would've given even Big Girtha—my burly, gigantic friend back at Lady Agnue's—a run for her money. Yet Rampart seemed unfazed. He waved to the audience and they cheered in response.

The projection orbs rotated their shots between Rampart and the bald man. My eyes followed the tiny figures of the announcer and the women in black. All of them made their way to the area beneath the private viewing box. However, while the women exited through the same tunnel they'd come out of, the announcer stopped just under the box.

One of the projection orbs cut to displaying him on a bigger screen and a sudden hush filled the entire stadium. A much older woman in regal attire appeared at the edge of the private viewing box. She had curly, white-ish blond hair and wore countless jewels that glittered in the afternoon sun. Next to her stood a golden gong on an intricate stand.

The regal old woman held out her right hand. A silvery glow came out of her palm and enveloped the announcer, who gracefully levitated off the ground to join her and the other courtiers in the box.

This woman—whoever she was—had magic.

The announcer raised his hands and the crowd hushed. Then he grabbed a mallet brought to him by an attendant and swung it against the gong.

"Fight!" he roared.

The applause started anew and the challenger charged at Rampart.

This fight was way more intense than the previous one. The man taking on the king clearly knew what he was doing. He was formidable and fast. On more than one occasion I thought his spiked club would take off Rampart's head. Alas, the king was also formidable and fast. The pair fought for three minutes—a nail-biting combat if I'd ever seen one.

One misstep of the bald man gave Rampart his opening. The king ducked underneath his opponent's swinging club and leapt forward, driving his sword up. Again I looked away, not wanting to see a sword impale someone's chest if I didn't have to.

The audience applauded the end of the fight. I opened my eyes to see Rampart bowing gallantly.

"Hypocrites," the woman above us said.

We glanced up.

"If you say anything about this place when you leave, tell the rest of Camelot that the citadel is full of hypocrites," the woman said. "Most of the people in that arena support the Gwenivere Brigade and hate Rampart. They would love nothing more than to see him killed after all the suffering he's caused. But out of fear, they applaud him."

"What's the Gwenivere Brigade?" Jason asked.

"The group that the crown considers the most dangerous kind of disloyalists. It's a rebel faction in Camelot started by King Arthur's wife after he was killed."

The woman shook her head with disappointment as if mourning a memory. "If you kids want a real show, come back this evening. Apparently, as part of King Rampart's big party, tonight's activity is a special fight. They say it's going to be something else. And given our ruler, that means *a lot* of pain and *a lot* of suffering."

With that the woman returned inside her apartment, slamming the shutters of her window. I took one more glimpse at the arena. Rampart was being levitated up to the private viewing box in the same fashion as the announcer. When he landed and the silvery glow around him evaporated, the old woman put a hand on his shoulder affectionately.

"Who do you think that woman is?" Daniel asked.

"I don't know," I replied. "But we have better things to do than wait around to find out. Let's get out of here. I'm tired of watching unfair fights."

CHAPTER 6

Dancing with the Enemy

I hate shopping," Blue remarked.

She was in the changing room next to mine so I couldn't see her face, but I could guess there was a scowl on it.

"It's hard to argue with the results though," I replied, stepping out of my own changing room. I stood in front of the full-length, three-paneled mirror and admired my gorgeous gown.

In search of the right royal clothes, we'd perused a few designer shops in the apparel district before finally settling on this one. Jason was in another part of the store trying on suits while Daniel was running an errand for SJ.

To say I loved my dress would've been an understatement. I adored combat boots and leggings (they were my usual jam), but that didn't mean I couldn't enjoy wearing gowns if they fit me properly and didn't limit my abilities. "Pretty" can apply to a lot of looks, both casual and formal. And this outfit made me feel just so.

My periwinkle blue dress had a sheen that caught the light just enough to catch someone's attention. The main bodice was like a fitted dress that only came to mid-thigh, so I could still move my legs. Additional thick material flared out from the waist at the sides and fell to my ankles, leaving my legs exposed in the front and covered in the back.

"And I thought I had seen everything," SJ said as she came out of her changing room.

She wore a fitted, floor-length dark purple gown with a slit up the right side that went well above the knee. The dress had one sleeve on the left arm, which featured a small cutout on the shoulder. The metallic belt at her waist matched her strappy shoes and the headband she'd placed over her braided, raven-black hair.

"Are you wearing high heels?" she asked in astonishment.

I looked down at my feet, which I had pushed into a pair of simple black pumps. With the front of the dress fully exposing my legs, I needed to look the part if I wanted to blend in with the royal crowd.

"Sometimes a girl's gotta make sacrifices," I replied. It was the truth and I could handle it. I'd been to enough balls in my life that I could maneuver just fine in heels, even if I was not a fan of them.

"Speaking of sacrifices . . ." Our heads turned to Blue peeking out of her changing room. "Don't laugh, okay?"

Blue stepped out in a crinkled chiffon dress that featured a plunging neckline and a high front slit. The dress was color blocked with long, vertical stripes from top to bottom in three shades: mint, cream, and light pink. The stripes of graceful fabric flowed behind her as she walked, and she completed the look with a waist-accentuating eyelet belt and strappy silver sandals.

"What are you talking about?" I said. "You look awesome."

"But there is hardly any place to put my weapons," Blue protested. "The only one I could fit is here." She lifted the right side of her dress to reveal a holster with her hunting knife strapped to the upper part of her thigh. "You're so lucky your wand changes forms."

I couldn't argue with that. I felt beyond grateful that my trusty weapon could be disguised as the hairpin currently attached to my bra strap.

"Even SJ is packing more than I am," Blue continued. "Or at least she will be once Daniel gets back with—"

"You all decent?" Daniel called from outside the changing area.

"Speak of the hero," I said.

"You can come in, Daniel. We are ready," SJ replied.

Daniel pushed aside the magenta curtain separating the women's dressing area from the rest of the store. He was holding a shiny metal necklace.

"Wow. You guys look great," he said, genuinely impressed.

"Thanks," Blue replied, playfully draping her arms around SJ and me. "Hope you're not having second thoughts about being the getaway driver. You'll be sitting in a carriage with the company of two smelly horses when you could be at a party with three stunning protagonists."

"Shut up, Blue," I said, laughing. "And anyway, Daniel volunteered."

We knew we needed to have a quick means of escape once we'd gotten what we came for. I didn't know how long it would take to find this Boar's Mouth, or figure out how to get blessed by it, but we could not afford to waste a single minute.

I honestly didn't know if Arian and his allies could capture Arthur and force the king to complete the pledge of The Pentecostal Oath with Alex. But I did believe that my enemies would send forces to stop us in our search for Excalibur. Based on when and where the next wormhole in Neverland had been scheduled to open, and the amount of time it took to get to the citadel, I figured the soonest Arian's goons could get here would be in two hours.

Unless they get eaten by giants, which is preferable, but unlikely.

Our plan was in motion. We had rented a carriage and a couple of horses. Daniel was going to act as our valet and drive us to the castle. When our ride merged into the traffic of arriving nobles, the four of us would head for the stables. Hopefully, once there we would find Jedidiah's daughter and she'd get us inside the castle. Maybe she even knew where the Boar's Mouth was. With any luck, my team and I would find it, get the job done quickly, and then meet Daniel back in the stables where he would be waiting for us to make a clean break.

"I realize this may be a bit unnecessary, but better safe than sorry given our history," SJ said as Daniel handed her the metal necklace.

On our way to the clothing shops, SJ had spotted a sign for

an ironworker who claimed he could forge any kind of jewelry design in thirty minutes or less. An idea had popped into her head and SJ had gone inside and drawn the man a sketch of what she wanted. True to his word, he had been able to create the necklace in under half an hour. Ten empty settings for round jewels sat in the thin iron collar design. However, SJ was not planning on sporting precious stones tonight.

My friend looked over her new accessory, very pleased, and began pulling portable potions out of her potions sack, which she snapped into each of the empty settings. A simple rubber hairband around her wrist would serve as her slingshot. She had practice firing with such a simple tool before, and as her sack and actual slingshot would clearly be out of place with her dress, they'd have to wait in the carriage with the rest of our stuff.

"Have I told you lately how brilliant you are?" I asked, marveling at the necklace.

"Not today," SJ replied with a smirk. "But it usually goes without saying."

I smiled. I liked it when SJ let her smarts and sassiness shine through. She was too modest about how amazing she was sometimes. The best friend I knew was finally coming back with confidence. Maybe even stronger than before.

"All right," I said, grabbing my backpack from the changing room. "Let's go see if Jason's ready so we can get going."

I shoved my clothes, Blue's clothes, and her utility belt of throwing knives into my backpack. SJ stashed her clothes, slingshot, and potions sack inside hers.

We carried our boots as we exited the dressing room. Blue stumbled as we entered the main store. She claimed she'd tripped on her flowy dress, but I suspected the falter had more to do with Jason. He was waiting for us. And he looked hot.

My friendship with the boy was as platonic as a relationship could be. He was practically like a brother, or a really close cousin. But the teenage girl part of me recognized that he looked as handsome as any hero ever could. Knowing how Blue felt about him, I understood why she had been knocked off balance.

"You all look awesome," he said as Blue composed herself.

"That seems to be the consensus," I replied with a playful grin.

We paid for our outfits and made our way outside. The carriage we'd acquired was rather plain. There was a rickety door on the right side, but the rear of the carriage was covered only by a thick tarp. A small ramp lay inside, folded against the floor, probably meant for loading heavy cargo. As my friends climbed into the carriage I headed for the front to sit next to Daniel, but he held up his hand.

"Not that I don't welcome the company, Knight, but if you're the princess and I'm the chauffeur, then I think you should ride in back. We're trying to blend in with the other royals."

"Oh, right."

I filed into the carriage behind Blue. There were built-in bench seats on both sides, which could be lifted to store cargo underneath. Blue put my backpack in the left compartment and I shut the carriage door. Then we were in motion, merging into the traffic.

As we moved forward, I propped my head on my hand and stared out the window. The roads were bustling and getting busier the closer we got to the castle. Daniel was using the street directions on the back of the brochure SJ found earlier to get us there.

I watched the people and places go by. The atmosphere was growing pink and hazy as the sun began to retire for the day.

After this there are only three more sunsets until the Vicennalia Aurora.

As shadows set in and the colors in the sky shifted, I thought about everything that had shifted since the commons rebellion attacks on my home and other kingdoms a few days ago.

Commons had tried to rebel against our realm's class system before, but this time they were gaining traction because the antagonists were helping them. I believed the antagonists were doing this to weaken the protagonists while the villains focused on their real plan for the realm.

I hoped Book's higher-ups could see that. Recently my friends and I had revealed to them the truth about the antagonists' plans to overthrow our realm and kill all its protagonists. However, a serious part of me suspected that the higher-ups hadn't disseminated that information to the rest of the populace yet. Our realm's ambassadors and Fairy Godmothers liked keeping the greater citizenry on a need-to-know-basis. And with the commons rebellion—a very real danger that everyone already knew about—needing to be handled, I doubted they wanted to throw more panic into the mix. I guess we would find out when we got back.

I checked my Hole Tracker for the time. It was quarter past six. Most of the shops had closed early for Vicennalia Aurora festivities. Conversely, the pubs were filling up fast. I watched a family of five—two parents, two boys, and a young girl—merrily stride into a tavern, chatting animatedly.

A twisting sensation filled my stomach and I realized I was jealous. I would never have such a moment again. Thanks to Alex, my family was broken. Resting my head against the window, I thought about how much my old life dissipated with each new chapter we turned.

I didn't know why the universe had decided to saddle me with so much responsibility; but I wasn't complaining. I accepted my role in this story and was going to do everything I could to influence the conclusion. The only thing that readily plagued me now was the understanding that on my way to achieving this ending, a lot of things would be lost along the way.

I knew all good things in life came with a cost. If you wanted to lose weight and get in shape, you ate healthy and exercised. If you wanted to get better grades in school, you studied more and partied less. If you wanted to achieve a goal of any kind, you had to do the work. But I hadn't realized that the cost of forging my new world would be sacrificing my old one.

If I could go back, in all honesty there was nothing I would do differently. Every ounce of pain, every obstacle, every choice had led me here. And here was where I needed to be. Still, that didn't mean the past was any easier to let go of. I missed Alex. I missed living in a world where people weren't always trying to hurt me.

As if reading my thoughts, Blue put her hand on my shoulder.

I glanced away from the window and she smiled at me softly. I returned her smile and sat back.

At least I knew a few people who would never try to hurt me. Blue, Jason, Daniel, and SJ were four pieces of my old life that I cherished more than anything. Their support gave me strength, their friendship gave me power, and having them by my side gave me hope.

At the end of the day, they were my greatest source of magic.

A charming clan of hummingbirds suddenly rushed past my window and zipped into the sky. Then, with a final turn in the road, the city streets and common buildings were left behind as our carriage followed others onto a long bridge that led to the castle. I could only partially make out the structure at this angle, but I could admire the intricate decoration of the bridge. Its base was stone, but the sides were encrusted with whimsically cut shards of mirrors, sea glass, and precious stones. Lanterns lit up both sides like a runway.

As this was the only way to reach the castle, the bridge was jammed with traffic, and we moved forward at a turtle's pace. The bridge passed over a moat thirty feet below. The waters reflected the pinks and oranges of the sky, sloshing against a gravely shore that shot up into a steep embankment of jagged mountain stone on either side.

Finally we made it to the end of the bridge and passed through an open gate. Most of the carriages veered right toward the main entrance, dropping off royal passengers before moving on to the stables. However, several of the plainer vehicles (like ours) went straight to the stables to drop off deliveries for the party. As our carriage moved to the left, I got my first good look at the castle. I gestured for SJ, Jason, and Blue to come to my window and have a gander.

There it was—larger than life—built into the rock to loom over this side of the mountain. The compound was made of giant bricks of gray stone. The last of the sun's rays were disappearing behind the tallest of the turrets that rose proudly from the front façade. Lit torches lined the outer curtain wall, which had cannons poking out at intervals just like the outer wall of the citadel. Far away on top of the curtain wall and by the castle's main entrance innumerable guards patrolled the area.

Our carriage continued left and the castle's grand intimidation went by in slow motion for extra dramatic effect. Soon we entered the stables and Daniel pulled on the reins. Ice sculptures were being unloaded from the carriage in front of us.

"Name?" I heard a woman with a deep voice ask Daniel.

"Yeah, I have a delivery for Ormé."

"I'm Ormé," the woman replied.

I leaned forward to see her through the window. She was a few inches over five feet tall. Her skin was dark, but her hair was light—a mixture of blonde and brown that blended together.

Daniel subtly reached into his jacket pocket and stretched out his hand. Concealed in a handshake, he transferred the card Jedidiah had given us into her palm. Ormé glanced at it before storing it shrewdly in her pocket.

"What can I help you with?" she asked.

"I have a delivery in the back that requires special care. Do you mind climbing inside to take a look?"

Ormé nodded. She walked around to the back of the carriage and pulled aside the tarp just enough to slip inside. She raised her eyebrows when she saw the four of us in our fancy outfits.

"Long story," I said, holding up my hand before she could ask anything.

"That's an understatement," Blue huffed. "We have enough backstory to make up a book series."

"The short version is that we helped your dad today and he said you might assist us in return," I explained. "We need to get inside the castle, and we need to know how to find the Boar's Mouth statue. If you could tell us anything you know about it, that would help too."

"Of course," Ormé replied. "I just met with my father at dinner. He told me everything and I am happy to be of service. I'll get you inside in a moment. As for the Boar's Mouth, it is housed in a temple within the heart of the castle beneath the Knights'

Room. Before one of the Knights of the Round Table goes on a quest, it is tradition that he goes into the temple and states his intentions while placing his hand within the Boar's Mouth. The statue is enchanted. If the knight's quest is worthy and his heart is strong enough to complete it, then he will receive a blessing from the statue. If not, the statue will bite off his hand."

"Oh, is that all?" I scoffed.

"There's more," Ormé replied. "The temple is protected by a door made of Jacobee stone. And there are plenty of traps in place should anyone try to blast past it or pick the lock. The only way to gain access is with a gold key with a twisted handle. There are only two such keys. The king has one, and the second is rotated amongst his five most trusted knights. You'll recognize them by the golden brooches on their shoulders; each is in the shape of a boar's head. Alas, there is no way to tell which knight is in possession of the temple key at any given time."

"And the news just keeps getting better." Blue sighed and cracked her neck. "All right, let's get this over with."

Ormé hopped out of the carriage and pointed Daniel toward a loading bay. I heard Ormé talking with some people as we passed. A few seconds later, her head poked through the tarp of our carriage.

"Come quickly. There's a secret passage behind the purple tapestry that leads to the castle gardens. I just sent the workers back to the kitchen with the ice sculpture deliveries. They've all gone so you must move now. You have about thirty seconds before they return."

She didn't have to tell us twice.

"Thank you," I told Ormé as we scurried out.

"No. Thank *you*," Ormé replied. "Even peasants have heard the Great Lights Prophecy. It is common knowledge across Camelot. I saw your name and picture in the paper this morning, and I have heard whispers throughout the castle. You could be the Knight of the prophecy we've been waiting for. So good luck, Crisanta *Knight*."

My mouth dropped in surprise, but Ormé ducked around the

side of the carriage before I could get any words out. With no time to say goodbye to Daniel, I dashed after my friends through the loading door.

It was obviously harder to run in heels than in boots, but like I said, I could handle it. I supposed I owed a thank you to our ballroom dancing professor at school for making us change into heels for every class. Those mandatory lessons had given me the strength and practice to stay on my feet.

We hurried down a stone corridor with tapestries lining the walls. When we came to a purple one embroidered in gold, Blue pulled it aside and sure enough, there was a door. We heard footsteps coming. Blue gave the door a solid shove and it popped open. We disappeared inside seconds before the workers returned.

The four of us were now in a stone tunnel. Only old, dim lanterns every twenty feet provided illumination, so we proceeded carefully.

"I know we talked about it earlier," SJ commented as we walked. "And I know that this party is our best means for penetrating the castle. But I just want to say it again—are we certain waltzing into a room full of nobles and knights who could recognize us from those Wanted Ads is a foolproof plan?"

"A, there's no such thing as a foolproof plan," Blue responded. "B, like you said, we all agreed it's our best and only means for getting in there. And C, relax. When you're wanted by the man, the last thing people expect you to do is attend a party at his home. We're being so bold we'll be invisible. It's literally the definition of hiding in plain sight."

I agreed on all accounts but didn't say so because we had arrived at a dead end—or so it seemed. I was familiar enough with secret passages around my own castle and knew there had to be a way out.

I felt around the stone wall until I found an indentation. I gave it a good push and heard something click. The wall rotated out and we emerged in the castle gardens exactly like Ormé had said we would. We checked to make sure the coast was clear then we slipped out. Jason shut the tunnel door behind us.

My friends and I dusted ourselves off then began to walk through the gardens. Rose bushes lining the pathways filled the air with sweetness. The sky was fading from pink to reddish gray. I easily spotted the windows of the ballroom. Light spilled through a wall composed entirely of stained-glass windows.

"Okay, everyone. Look natural," SJ said once we'd arrived at the end of the path.

"We're a bunch of kids hopping from realm to realm on a quest to get a sword, save a Fairy Godmother's memories, and stop a lot of villains," I replied. "I don't think I know what natural is anymore."

"Fine, then look like a princess. You still know how to do that, right?"

"Did I ever know how to do that?"

Blue and Jason grinned in amusement. SJ rolled her eyes and proceeded inside the ballroom through an open iron doorway with an elaborate opaque design. We followed. My heels clicked against the cherry wood floor and I took in the sight of the party.

"Dude, this place is packed," Blue commented.

"That's good for us," Jason said. "It means there's less of a chance of being spotted."

I nodded in agreement. There must've been close to two hundred noble guests in the ballroom, all of whom were dressed in gorgeous attire. I noticed a trend amongst the women in particular. Their outfits, like ours, were designed with high slits, cutouts, and metallic accessories. By luck we had picked a very in-fashion boutique to get our dresses from.

Iron chandeliers dangled from the ceiling of the ballroom. An enormous one with thorns like a deadly rose bush hung over the center of the dance floor. Guests in three interconnected dance circles were in the midst of a fast-paced number. The couples twisted and turned and dipped and spun. It was so mesmerizing that I couldn't stop watching. Each pair kept perfect beat with the orchestra. The musicians that comprised it emitted such energy, you'd think their instruments were made of magic.

At the front of the ballroom was an elevated platform with three thrones. It was a little hard to see over the crowd, so I only caught a glimpse. In the center throne sat Rampart. To his left was a poised but sad-looking redheaded woman with a crown, who I imagined was his wife. And to his right sat the blonde, older woman with the levitation powers.

"There's that knight from the marketplace," Jason said. He pointed out Sir Gaheris, the jerk who'd robbed Jedidiah. He was on the right side of the ballroom where the stained-glass windows faced the garden. In front of the windows, a lavish buffet was spread out over nine silk-draped tables.

Sir Gaheris was talking with several courtiers and a petite woman in a crown. I narrowed in on the same golden brooch on his shoulder that I now knew marked him as one of the five knights that Ormé had mentioned. When he pushed back his navy cape and turned to serve himself from the buffet, I noticed a key ring poking out of his back pocket. Unfortunately, I couldn't tell if the gold, twisted key we sought was on it.

Okay, that's one.

We slowly scanned the ballroom, eventually locating the other four knights with golden brooches. Three were dancing; a fourth was chatting with people by the orchestra. Their capes got in the way of a direct visual, but my friends and I confirmed that they all had key rings. We'd need to examine each one closer to find what we were looking for.

"Okay, chief," Blue said. "What's the plan?"

I nodded at the dance circles. "That's our plan. Do you see the pattern?"

My friends stared at the couples. After a minute, Blue spoke. "Tango left, tango right, thrust, dip, salsa, salsa, turn around back, turn around forward, tango left, tango right, thrust, spin in, thrust, turn in, turn out, pull in for another dip, thrust, lift, fancy arm movement, assisted spring, toss, toss, tango right, repeat."

"Very good," I said.

"Blue, I am impressed," SJ said, flabbergasted. "I never knew you had such an eye for picking up dance moves."

"It's no different than picking up fighting moves," Blue replied with a shrug. "Ballroom dancing and combat are basically the same thing. It's all about timing, agility, and precision. In ballroom dance, though, the guy is leading so he is always on offense and the girl is always on defense. He makes a move; she parries or counters."

"I think you just found your senior thesis project for next year," I said. I turned to the others. "Jason, SJ, do you follow?"

The current song began to fade into the next, but the same dance continued without missing a beat. Jason and SJ took another moment to memorize the movements.

"Yeah, I think I got it," Jason replied. SJ nodded in agreement. All of us had years of ballroom dance training. We could do this.

"Good," I said. "Everybody huddle in. I've got a plan."

For the first time in my life, I approached a buffet with no intention of eating.

"How's it going?" I said, abruptly stepping in front of the woman that Sir Gaheris had been talking to.

"Um, pardon me, but we were having a conversation," protested the petite but pudgy woman wearing a crown.

"And now *we're* having a conversation," I said gesturing to Sir Gaheris and me. He looked me up and down and smiled.

"Miss," one of the courtiers insisted. "Have you no decorum? This woman you just spurned is a princess."

"Aren't we all," I responded with a confident smile. I turned back to Gaheris. "Princess Marie Sinclaire." I stretched out my hand to shake his. "And yes, I am this assertive in real life. Wanna dance?"

"I would be honored," he said, setting down his plate of food and taking my hand.

And SJ says my flirting style is too aggressive. So what if I've never had a boyfriend or been on a date? I'm a girl with confidence and a pretty dress. With those two factors alone, I could conquer worlds.

I walked slowly to the center of the room, pacing it out so that we would enter the desired dance circle in just the right place. Before I'd gone over to Gaheris, my friends and I had done the math to ascertain where we all needed to be in relation to one another.

Accordingly, Blue and SJ had already taken their partners and were in the dance circle. Blue had paired with the other knight with a golden brooch who hadn't been dancing. SJ had taken a miscellaneous partner as an excuse to join the dance circle. With all five brooched knights now in play, we'd be able to reach each of them in the course of the dance. Once we did, it was only a matter of time before we collected what we came for.

Just one of the benefits of having a friend like Blue who has mad pickpocketing skills and taught me (and SJ against her will) how to master the ability too.

Gaheris and I entered the dance circle—one couple between us and another knight with a golden brooch who was enjoying the dance with his own partner. The three interconnected dance circles provided good cover and I felt certain that Rampart wouldn't see us. It was beautiful, distracting chaos. Choreographed chaos, yes—but chaos nonetheless.

Gaheris pivoted me in front of him.

All right, let's see how well I was paying attention.

In the heat of the dance circle the music felt louder, or maybe that was just my heart pounding. The exhilaration was powerful and visceral. Every beat was like another high—enticing, entrancing, invigorating.

I held Gaheris's gaze. He smiled at me and I kept his attention through every twist, turn, and thrust.

That's right, buddy. Eyes on me.

My moment was coming. He turned my hand and I spun behind him. In that split second, my free hand pulled the key ring from his back pocket. He turned me forward. I kept my eyes locked with his so he wouldn't notice what was concealed within my fist.

Careful not to let him detect the key ring, my hand returned to his shoulder and we moved left then right. With that, he spun me out. As I spiraled away, I was able to check the contents of the key ring.

No gold key.

I whirled back into him, wrapping my left fist under my right arm as I came against his chest. As I spun out a couple more times,

I kept my hand concealed and his attention focused elsewhere. It wasn't hard. *Remember: never underestimate a confident girl in a pretty dress.*

When he pulled me in for a dip I slipped the key ring back into his pocket. Then he spun me out. I saw Jason patrolling the perimeter of the dance circles waiting for one of us to signal him. He made eye contact with me and I shook my head. No luck here.

Gaheris pulled me in for a lift. All the ladies in the dance were raised high above their partners. Blue, SJ, and I exchanged a glance from across our dance circle. Blue—who'd been dancing with one of the other brooched knights—shot me a look that said she hadn't had any luck. I mirrored her expression.

Gaheris lowered me to the ground. When I landed, we went into this fancy arm movement timed perfectly with the music. My hands pressed over his and he thrust me to his left while I leapt in the air. I was thrown into the arms of the next man in the dance circle. Then this man launched me to the side, tossing me to my new partner.

Now I was dancing with the next brooched knight. The music did not hesitate and neither did we. The pattern repeated. I was disappointed to learn this partner did not have the correct key either. However, this time when I was lifted off the ground, SJ gave me and Blue a clear nod. The brooched knight she was dancing with had the key. She'd found it.

Having received the signal from SJ, Jason selected his own dance partner—a pretty blonde in a pink dress. He pulled her into the dance circle right beside the brooched knight we were after.

I did the math; Blue and SJ were no doubt doing the same. Based on the number of couples in our dance circle, it should've been Blue who reached our target first. However, several more couples suddenly joined the circle, throwing off our count. Recalculating, I soon realized Blue would be one partner change off. The next one of us who would land in the arms of our target was me.

The music seemed to move faster as my turn approached. And then—

Press, toss, hello there . . .

I stepped into the music and the line of sight of the target knight. Jason was right beside me. My handsome friend was now dancing with a dark-haired beauty in a mint dress. Her long legs swayed around his with such seductive grace it made me glad that Blue was not near enough to notice.

I twisted around my dance partner, snatching the key ring out of his pocket. Coming back around, we fell into a left tango then right. I used every ounce of my stealth powers to keep the key ring hidden. When my partner proceeded to spin me out, I stretched out my free hand to pass it to Jason. Alas, this knight was ahead of the beat. He reeled me in before my hand could reach Jason's.

With a thud, I spiraled against the knight's chest. I didn't have time to regain my bearings. He thrust me out again and whirled me back toward him just as quickly. I only had one more thrust left before our opportunity expired, one more chance to reach Jason.

Harnessing all my feminine fire and focus, I kept my partner's attention on my face as my left hand hovered behind his neck with the key ring still clutched in my palm. He dipped me and then thrust me out a final time.

The timing was perfect. As I flung out my left arm, Jason took the key ring and pocketed it before his own partner spun back in. My brooched knight raised me up for the lift. I met eyes with Blue and SJ and winked. An instant later I was lowered and tossed into Jason's arms.

"Nice," he whispered just before launching me to my next partner.

To be courteous, and remain inconspicuous, I danced with my new partner for a few beats before expressing my wish to retire from the dance circle. SJ excused herself next, followed by Blue, and then eventually Jason.

After we'd ditched our dance partners, we met by the buffet. My eyes wandered to the prime rib on the center table, but I reminded my brain to stay focused.

"I've got the key," Jason said, patting his pocket. "And I also found our way out of here. I was talking with one of my dance partners, and the Knights' Room is down the hall past the music quarters and the library. Since guests have been going in and out of the ballroom, I think we can slip out unnoticed."

"Okay, what about Rampart?" I asked. But as I looked through the crowd, I realized the king wasn't on his throne anymore. His wife or whatever was still there. But he and that elderly, regal woman were gone.

"He got up and left a couple minutes ago with his grandmother."

"His grandmother?"

"Oh yeah," Jason said. "I found out that the old woman with the crazy levitation magic is his grandmother Morgause. She is very powerful and not very forgiving according to another one of the girls I was dancing with."

"How many girls exactly *did* you dance with?" Blue asked, her hands on her hips.

"Morgause," I thought aloud, changing the subject before Blue could grill Jason further. "She is one of King Arthur's relatives, right?"

"Yeah," Blue replied, reluctant to give up her previous topic, but too compelled by the fairytale history nerd inside her not to answer the question. "She is his aunt—the sister of Arthur's late mother Igraine. Morgause married this guy named King Lot and had a bunch of kids, but she also had an affair with Arthur's father, Uther Pendragon. That's how she sired Mordred."

"But Rampart is a Pendragon," I said. "And Arthur never had any brothers or sisters. If Morgause is Rampart's grandmother, then that means Rampart is—"

"Mordred's son," SJ interrupted. "The current king of Camelot is the son of the man who killed King Arthur."

"I'm beginning to understand why a lot of his citizens don't like him," I commented. "Hardly the people's choice award for best legacy. How did a guy like that even come into power?"

"I don't know," Jason replied. "But Blue can check the history books about that later. Right now, we should leave while we have the chance." He nodded at a set of open double doors on the other side of the room.

We made our way through the glittering crowd, around the dance circles, and past servants waiting on guests. I kept vigilant. Just because the king wasn't in the room didn't mean we were in the clear.

"If Rampart's not here, then he's somewhere in the castle. We'll have to watch our step," I said, following Jason out.

"SJ is rubbing off on you, Crisa. You worry too much," Blue said, maneuvering past a trio of excited courtiers. "Considering what we just did, I think we've taken 'watching our step' to an art form. That, and utilizing our feminine wilds."

Jason cocked his eyebrows. "Your what?"

"Feminine wilds," Blue repeated.

"I think you mean *wiles*."

"No, it's *wilds*," Blue insisted. "As in, animalistic instinct that can't be tamed."

"I don't think so," Jason responded. "SJ, can I get a ruling?"

SJ shook her head, exasperated. "We shall look it up in a dictionary later. For now, can we focus on the task at hand?"

"Ugh, fine," Blue huffed. "But I still say it's wilds."

I laughed.

And I thought I provided the comic relief in this story.

CHAPTER 7

Heart & Soul

feel small," Blue said in a low voice.

Stepping into the Knights' Room—the room that Ormé said was above the Boar's Mouth Temple—I had to agree. Gray marble floors supported massive obsidian pillars that led up to a ceiling of overlapping large mirrors. The mirrors reflected the great centerpiece at the heart of the room: an enormous round table. And by round table, I mean *the* Round Table.

The mahogany wonder must've been thirty feet in diameter. There were fifty tall-backed chairs surrounding it, each constructed from dark wood with a navy velvet seat and back cushion. While all the chairs were carved with fine designs, one seat at the other end of the table was significantly larger and more intricate. I drifted toward it, running my fingers along the backs of the chairs as I went.

When I reached the grand chair—the king's chair, no doubt—I looked around the room. Lit torches lined the walls and added to the strong, commanding atmosphere. I could feel power emanating around us as potently as if it were blended in with the oxygen.

Above the door we'd entered hung five large tapestries. The first held a familiar inscription. It was the Great Lights Prophecy— the prophecy that had set me and Alex on this violent opposing path:

"A game of four kings
Three of them lost
A struggle for the realm
Where one king pays the cost.

This fate will be forged
By one Knight alone
Born of royal blood
Heir to the lion's throne.

The Oath pledged to Camelot's king
Endowed with the quest
And blessed by the Boar's Mouth
With strength to pass the test.

The Lake shall be crossed
And the Sword will be found
To the rightful king returned
When Great Lights strike the ground."

I felt bitterness as I read it. I also felt resentful at the wizard Merlin who'd spoken the prophecy into existence and shackled me to its direction. People needed to stop having prophecies that involved me. I was trying to forge my own path and define my own fate. That was a lot harder to do when magical, powerful people kept spitting out destinies for me to fulfill.

I valued Liza as a mentor and an ally, but if I was being completely honest with myself, I think I would always feel a little bitterness toward her for starting all this trouble in my life with her prophecy. Since the woman had become so important to me, and I cared for her, I knew I could never tell her this. Nor could I smack her. But Merlin was a different story. If I ever met him I'd be severely tempted to give him a good thump on the back of the head. Unfortunately, according to Arthur, the wizard had been missing for years.

My gaze drifted to the other tapestries above the door and I paused on one in the middle. It was gold and black with a set of crossed swords at the center.

"Over here."

SJ's voice echoed across the chamber. She was standing near the back wall next to a gargantuan fireplace. Gold floret designs decorated the mantle. The fireplace itself was so clean that it looked like it had never been used. SJ stepped inside it and promptly disappeared from view.

"Just as I thought," her voice echoed. "There is a passageway through this fireplace."

"How do you know?" Blue asked.

"There is no ventilation system in here," SJ called. "There is only stone overhead, meaning this is a fake fireplace. And look . . ." She stuck her head out and pointed at the floor. "These dust patterns do not fall naturally. It is as though something has moved across this space repeatedly."

"That must be the entrance to the Boar's Mouth Temple," Jason said. "Any ideas on how to open it?"

"It's best not to overthink these things," Blue responded. "People are suckers for consistency, so let's go with classic fairytale logic. If fireplaces, bookshelves, and tapestries are the most common hiding places for secret passageways, what are the most common ways to open them?"

"I'd go with moving a book on a bookshelf, wall candelabras that double as levers, and . . ." I glanced around the room and spotted a life-size statue of a lion. "Buttons hidden inside statues."

Our group moved toward the statue. It was made of marble, but its eyes were glittering emeralds. The four of us studied it, searching for a clue. I peeked inside the lion's mouth and saw that the opening ran deep. Something shiny inside caught the light for a split second.

I stepped back. The lion's mouth was too narrow for me to fit my arm inside. I knew what I had to do.

"And history repeats itself," I said, drawing my wandpin.

Transforming it into a sword, I shoved the blade inside the lion's mouth until I felt it press against something. A button.

Like I had with the dragon statue back at the Capitol Building at the start of this adventure, I twisted my sword inside the lion's mouth and unlocked the secret passage. The sides of the fireplace slowly pushed outward. We heard the sound of various locks and tumblers moving within the wall. Then the stones directly in front of the fireplace pulled apart, revealing a stairwell.

"You were right," I said to Blue, returning my wand to pin form and tucking it within my dress. "People are suckers for consistency." I turned to Jason. "You still have that Mark Two on you?"

While Blue, SJ, and I had no place to keep our communicative magic mirrors, Jason's suit had pockets. He pulled out his compact and tossed it to me.

"SJ, can you keep watch while we go down?" I asked. "If anybody comes in, I think your potions might be our best bet for evading trouble."

"I agree. Should I call Daniel to tell him we will be out soon?"

"You read my mind." I handed her the Mark Two.

Leaving SJ behind, we descended the dark staircase. There weren't any torches to light the way. However, every step was encrusted with a flat, glassy substance that made the stairs glow vaguely like they'd been coated with the saliva of stars. When we reached the bottom, we faced a grand door made of Jacobee stone. A boar's face was carved into it and there was a lock beside the handle.

Jason removed the key ring from his pocket. There were four keys on it. He placed the gold one inside the lock and turned. With a mighty, ominous creak, the door hinged open. We stepped into a temple of shadows.

The only light came from the floor and ceiling, which were partially constructed from the same luminescent material as the stairs. Fewer sections of the floor and ceiling glowed the farther from the door you got, and as a result the far sides of the room were shrouded in darkness, concealing the true size of the temple.

Twisting pillars stretched up and connected in curved arches all around us. A row of parallel empty silver braziers led to the rear of the room where a massive statue in the shape of an open-mouthed boar's head was mounted.

The statue was three times bigger than the head of an actual boar. It was mostly composed of gold, but its eyes, tusks, and teeth were made of dark blue sapphires—sharpened so finely they would've mortally impaled any beast unlucky enough to fall upon them.

"Okay, it's all you from here," Blue said, gesturing from me to the boar.

I took a deep breath and approached the statue. Ormé had said that I needed to place my hand inside its mouth and state my quest. If it was a worthy mission and my heart was strong enough to complete it, then I would receive the blessing.

Gingerly I placed my hand inside the Boar's Mouth. My wrist lay upon the prickly points of sapphire teeth between the two tusks.

I gulped.

Prophecies were vague. My friends and I had learned from our own prologues not to expect the obvious when it came to their outcomes. Camelot's Great Lights Prophecy could be no different. I genuinely might not be the "Knight" with the potential to retrieve Excalibur. It could be Alex, or it could be someone else with no connection to either of us. Believing that I was the one and offering myself up to this boar was a gamble. If the statue didn't bless me, it would bite off my hand.

I shuddered. Then I exhaled slowly to chase away my nerves.

You can do this. If you don't believe that, neither will the boar.

I stared directly into the eyes of the glittering animal. Alex had been here recently. He hadn't gotten his hand bitten off; according to Mauvrey, pledging The Oath to the wrong king caused the statue to not respond at all. But this wouldn't be the case with me. This was going to end one way or the other. Might as well get it over with.

I wasn't sure how formal a proclamation I had to make, but I decided to wing it.

"I seek Excalibur," I said bluntly. "I want to retrieve it from Avalon and use it to free the mind of our friend Paige Tomkins from Glinda's memory stone, learn the secret of the genies' whereabouts before the antagonists do, and once this is done, return the sword to Camelot's rightful king just like the prophecy says. I will return it to Arthur."

It was quiet for a second, and then—

"Argh!"

I screamed as an unexpected force sucked my entire arm inside the Boar's Mouth. My shoulder was jammed against the tusks and I couldn't get free.

"Crisa!"

My friends rushed to my aid but stopped when the room began to rumble and a great wind blew them back.

A bone-chilling voice echoed all around us. "Your mission is worthy," it said. "But there will be a price to pay." The boar's voice boomed like a megaphone, resonating deep within my head and chest. The statue's eyes glowed ardently, pulsating with every word.

"Another will seek the sword. Another sword will seek you," the boar continued. "What you gain will be beyond compare. But the cost will shift your fate beyond repair. Do you accept these terms and assert that your heart is strong enough to pay the price?"

A chill passed over me. The boar spoke in riddles and it felt like I was signing a contract I hadn't read. I wondered if this was how the Little Mermaid felt when she went to the sea witch to exchange her voice for legs.

Girl definitely didn't read the fine print on that deal.

That part of the Little Mermaid's story always felt like a cautionary tale to me, like a warning against entering into legal arrangements without having all the facts. And yet here I was making a similar, unadvised exchange. I didn't know the specifics of what the boar was talking about, so agreeing to the terms was an act of faith.

But I suppose that's what all choices—and this quest—came down to in the end.

"I do," I said. "I accept these terms and all that comes with them."

A brilliant white light exuded from the statue's mouth. It was so bright I had to shield my eyes with my other hand. A tingly feeling spread through my body. It was peaceful and almost cleansing, like a spa treatment for the soul. At least until I noticed what was happening. A white substance like smoke was seeping out of my skin and pulling away from me. When it left, I felt exposed and raw.

The aura twisted next to me in a morphing cloud for a few seconds before transforming into a full-size ghostly representation of me. Ghost Crisa blinked and wailed. Then she shot across the room and dove into a section of normal marble floor. When she absorbed into it, the normal bit of flooring changed and took on the same eerie, mystical glow as the stairs that led here and other parts of the temple's floor and ceiling.

The light receded from the Boar's Mouth and my arm was released. I eased it out of the cavity and took a few steps back, joining my friends

"You have been blessed," the boar's voice boomed. "Retrieve the sword and bring back Camelot's lost king. Only when he sits on the throne will your mission be complete and this fragment of your soul be returned. Fail, and your physical body will wither within the year and the rest of your soul will be trapped here forever."

The boar's sparkling eyes extinguished and all went silent.

"So that's what's causing the floor to glow," Jason thought aloud in awe. "The souls of the people who came down here, got blessed, and never completed their missions."

"Seems kind of like overkill," Blue commented. "We already have a bunch of people that want to eliminate us and like a dozen magical obstacles to worry about. Was another bit of hindering hocus pocus really necessary to the story at this point?"

"Probably not," I replied. "But it doesn't matter. I'll likely die six other ways before some stupid missing piece of my soul takes me down."

"Fair enough," Blue shrugged. "Still, I wish someone would give us all the information about what we're getting into ahead of time. You know, 'Do this. Watch out for that.' I realize we were in a rush this morning, so Arthur didn't write down any instructions before we left, but it would've been nice if Ormé had warned us about this part of the deal."

"She may not have known," I said, rubbing my arm. "In any case, it's inconsequential now. What's done is done."

"I couldn't have said it better myself."

My heart froze and the three of us spun around. Two figures appeared from the shadowy depths of the temple: Rampart and Morgause. I had a feeling they'd witnessed the entire ordeal.

I took a good look at the king. Rampart was near twenty-five years old. He had thick, black curly hair that made a nice bed for the crown on his head. His eyes, like Morgause's, were dark brown and cruel. Unlike his pale grandmother, he had olive skin that suggested his mother had been of exotic descent.

"So Arthur really is alive," Rampart said. "When the Boar's Mouth would not wake to your brother's touch, I knew that could be the only explanation. My reign is still in its infancy and no knight had come to me seeking a quest before your brother, so I had not discovered the truth. Needless to say, I was disappointed."

Ten knights emerged from the shadows behind Rampart and Morgause. The king removed a Mark Two magic compact mirror from his pocket and passed it to Morgause. "Grandmother, tell Arian that we have her. And that if he gets here soon, he'll also have that show I promised."

Morgause brusquely raised her other hand.

There was no time to act. Silver light coated Morgause's palm and instantly consumed Jason and Blue, slamming my friends against the back wall so hard it knocked them out.

In the next instant the same silver light enveloped me. I was curtly pulled forward onto the floor at Morgause's feet. Several knights lunged in and cuffed my hands together. I tried to summon my magic to defend myself but was met with a surge of pain.

"Game over, Crisanta Knight," Rampart said. "Though for your friends, it's only just begun."

CHAPTER 8

The Gwenivere Brigade

Good news: After climbing out of the temple, I saw three guards frozen in blocks of ice near the entrance of the Knights' Room, but no SJ. Which meant that hopefully Rampart's men hadn't captured her.

Bad news: After being knocked out by Morgause's levitation slam, Rampart's guards had taken Jason and Blue away. I didn't know where they were, which made me uneasy. Another thing that made me uneasy was the fact that I was currently being escorted through the castle's dungeon by Rampart and several of his men.

I fidgeted under the weight and discomfort of the shackles.

"Don't bother trying to get out," Rampart said. "Those cuffs were forged in Stiltdegarth blood. You won't be able to use your magic."

Yeah, thanks. I figured that out already.

My escorts and I had taken a staircase behind the throne room to reach the dungeon. My heels clicked with every step we took deeper into the mountain. A draft caused goose bumps to rise on my skin.

Up 'til that point, I'd been preoccupied with thinking of an escape plan, running scenarios through my head as I sized up my captors. But as we turned a corner something red and shiny caught my attention. Through the lone barred window of a solid steel cell on my left, I noticed a glittering silver and ruby object zoom by. It seemed to hesitate for a moment by the window, allowing me a good look before it zoomed on.

Holy cow.

The right shoe of Dorothy's famous "there's no place like home" magic slippers was imprisoned in Camelot. I couldn't believe it. Dorothy's slippers could not only send their wearer home with three clicks of the heel; they could send messages too. When Dorothy and the ruler of Oz, Princess Ozma, were attacked in Neverland by the Questor Beast, they had sent one slipper to the Emerald City to let Julian (the Wizard of Oz and Ozma's older brother) know they were in trouble.

My friends and I had recently visited the Emerald City. While there, Julian had shown no sign of ever having heard from his sister. However, when I explored his home, I had found a secret room where this slipper had been locked away. I'd freed the slipper, and it had taken off through a window to find its mate, as it was designed to do after delivereing its message. Seeing the glittering shoe inside the cell now made me realize the truth.

"Ozma . . ." I said aloud. "She's here."

Rampart turned to smirk at me. "You're pretty smart."

"And you're pretty stupid," I replied. "Ozma is the rightful queen of Oz. She has powerful magic just like her brother and his wife. How long do you think you can hold her here before one of them comes looking for her?"

"Fairly long given that they do not want her back," Rampart replied. "I have specific instructions from the ruler of the Emerald City to keep her here indefinitely."

I felt darkness sink inside of me. Rampart had just confirmed my suspicions about Julian. When Ozma disappeared he had become the sole ruler of Oz. He'd left her to the wolves so he could continue to rule in her place.

"So long as they don't know that Ozma had her Simia Crown at the time of the abduction, they have no reason to care what I do with her," Rampart continued.

"What's a Simia Crown?" I asked.

"Hm." Rampart gave me a patronizing look. "Maybe not as smart as I thought. Tell me, Crisanta Knight, haven't you wondered how Arian and I came to be working together in the first place?"

I had wondered about that. While the antagonists wanted

Excalibur to access Paige's memories like we did, Alex and Mauvrey had already been in pursuit of the sword before they learned about the whole memory stone situation. Which meant they wanted Excalibur for another reason too. I just didn't know what that was.

"I don't suppose you'd like to tell me?" I asked, raising an eyebrow.

Rampart smiled. "Where would be the fun in that?"

His guards shoved me forward and we continued past a dozen more cells, several of which were uniquely customized. There was one made entirely of crystal, inside of which a number of pixies buzzed around angrily. Another was pure silver, holding back a black wolf with red eyes. Next came a cell that was modeled like a large fishtank. A mermaid who was floating inside screeched loudly when she saw us, like she was trying to break the glass with her voice.

Finally, the guards directed me to a cell constructed compeletely of black rock. The cell opposite was hidden by a green velvet curtain.

"Let me guess," I said. "Jacobee stone?"

"Precisely."

"I don't know whether to be intimidated or flattered, Rampart," I scoffed as one of the guards opened the door. "You built this cell just for me?"

"Aw, there's more of that cockiness Arian has told me so much about," Rampart said. "This cell wasn't built for you, Crisanta. If I ever find where that old fool Merlin is hiding, this will be his prison. But since Arian tells me you have Pure Magic like Merlin, this shall be your cell until I am ready to bring you out."

A couple of epic questions popped into my head:

Merlin has Pure Magic?

Bring me out for what?

However, the question that actually escaped my lips was: "What's behind the curtain?"

I gestured to the cell across from mine that was concealed behind the hefty drapes.

"Interesting choice of words . . ." Rampart said. He nodded

to one of his guards, who pulled on a golden rope to reveal the
hidden cell beyond.

It'd been thirty minutes since Rampart had left me in my cell.
Since then, I'd had nothing to do but play with my Hole Tracker,
formulate ideas for escape, and stare at Ozma.

The missing ruler of Oz was imprisoned in the cell across from
me in some sort of suspended animation. Her cell was made of
thick glass and filled with a translucent blue gel, which I assumed
was magic in some way. She floated in the middle of the gel
peacefully. I studied her with fascination and pity.

Ozma looked a lot like her brother. She had dark hair and a
regal jaw line. Her nose was like a pixie's and her eyebrows were
perfectly arched. I knew from Dorothy that she was only thirteen,
but she looked painfully young.

Her mint green jacket, white top, and black pants were
tattered—no doubt the result of her encounter with the Questor
Beast. While one of her feet was bare, the other featured Dorothy's
second slipper.

I wished I could get her out, although for the moment I was
as stuck as she was. I still had my wand, but it would be useless
against the Jacobee stone. Add to that, I couldn't even transform
the wandpin out of its clandestine state, let alone into another
weapon while I was cuffed. It only took a tiny bit of magic to
change the wand's form, but when I tried to summon even that,
I received a substantial shock. It seemed where Stiltdegarth
blood was concerned, *any* amount of magic was met with absolute resistance.

In another attempt I tried to pick the lock on the cuffs with
the wandpin. When that didn't work either, I huffed and sat back
on my stone bench and stared at Ozma again. Looking at her, I
was filled with all kinds of emotions. Sadness, because this young
princess had been captured by an evil jackwagon. Anger, because
her older brother had sold her out. And empathy, because exactly
the same thing had happened to me.

Yet Ozma's presence also filled me with another, much stronger emotion.

Hope.

When my friends and I met Julian in Oz, we'd also met his wife Eva, who used to be the Wicked Witch of the West. As mentioned, she and her three sisters (Glinda included) had all been carriers of Pure Magic Disease, which caused them to turn evil. But Eva had overcome her disease. The former Wicked Witch of the West hadn't beaten it by will or control like Liza; she'd been cured. During Dorothy and Ozma's first quest to Camelot, they'd recovered a magic liquid from the Isle of Avalon called the "Four Waters of Paradise." These enchanted waters were said to be the most powerful magic cleanser and purifier in all the dimensions.

Mixing the sample they collected with a bucket of regular water, they'd doused Eva during the Vicennalia Aurora—when carriers of magic are most vulnerable—and cured her of Pure Magic Disease. Eva still retained her magical ability of producing fire, but it was now normal magic. This meant that it was not nearly as strong, but it wouldn't corrupt her with power.

Before hearing this story, I'd thought that there was no cure for Pure Magic Disease. But now there was proof. Eva had been cured. Which meant if I found the Four Waters of Paradise on the Isle of Avalon while searching for Excalibur, I could be cured too. And that was so tempting a possibility it churned my stomach with optimism.

Suddenly, I heard footsteps coming down the corridor. Three guards arrived alongside Rampart.

"Time to go," Rampart said as a guard opened my cell.

"Not until you've told me what you've done with my friends," I replied.

"Jason Sharp and Blue Dieda," Rampart mused. "I was particularly interested in meeting the latter. Fate has predicted an interesting course for her life. Not that she will ever see it. You can, however, see them if you come with me."

Reluctantly, I followed him down the corridor. I glanced back

at Ozma before we turned a corner, adding her to the long list of
people I intended to save one day.

"So at what point did you spot us?" I asked Rampart curiously.
"Was it the second we entered the ballroom, or was it during the
dance?"

"You don't give yourself enough credit," Rampart said. "In
all truth, neither me nor my men actually recognized you at the
gala. Arian had warned us that you were on your way, and I knew
that the best time for you to make a run at the Boar's Mouth was
during the party. Soon after the festivities began, my men and I
concealed ourselves in the temple. Based on everything I'd heard
about you, I was sure you'd eventually find it. It was only a matter
of waiting to see if you received the boar's blessing."

"You wanted to know whether or not you could kill me."

"Precisely. I want Excalibur, so it was a win-win either way.
If you were blessed, then we had a back-up Knight to go after
the sword should your brother not prove adequate. If you failed,
then we could kill you and I would get to see the boar bite off your
hand. I've never witnessed that phenomenon. As I mentioned,
knights don't ask for formal quests anymore; they're such an old-
fashioned thing. It's a shame really . . ."

We turned and continued through a narrow tunnel. I felt us
going deeper beneath the mountain still. I hoped Camelot never
suffered from earthquakes. There was probably ten thousand
pounds of rock above our heads right now.

At the end of the tunnel we arrived at a circular door made
of metal. One of the guards pulled a crank on the wall, causing
the door to spiral open and reveal a moderate-sized capsule with
a low ceiling. Fashioned like an escape pod, it was maybe five
feet in diameter. The floor and couch inside were white. The top
half of the capsule was made of glass and offered a view of the
dark, narrow tunnel ahead, which was rimmed by a runway of
tiny lights.

Another crank opened the capsule. When it did, bright white
lights glowed on the capsule's floor. The metal table in the center
of the pod shone.

Rampart gestured for me to enter the capsule. I stepped inside and the guard behind me secured my shackles to a set of short chains attached to the table. I sat on the couch as Rampart and the second guard entered. They took their seats, Rampart placing himself across from me. One guard remained outside. He used the cranks to close the capsule and shut the circular metal door.

One of the guards sitting next to me pulled a handle that protruded from the ceiling of the pod to reveal a simple control panel. It had several buttons, including a red one beside a black knob with numbers from one to ten going around its circumference. The guard pressed the red button and the capsule jarred into motion. Then he twisted the black knob slowly to number six; the capsule increased in speed correspondingly.

"I suppose you must be wondering where I'm taking you," Rampart said.

"When you get captured as often as I do, you learn to roll with the punches," I replied with a shrug. "And anyway, it doesn't matter. I'm getting out of here pretty soon."

Rampart looked me over. "You're an interesting protagonist, Crisanta. I can see why Arian and the antagonists are so obsessed with catching you. It almost makes me hope that Alex won't be blessed by the Boar's Mouth. If you're the only one capable of retrieving Excalibur, then it means I won't have to kill you. At least not for the time being."

My brows furrowed at the mention of Alex's name, which caused Rampart to smile.

"Sore subject, isn't it?" He leaned back. "Your brother betraying you the way that he did? Well, it is a good lesson for you. There's no room for heart where thrones are concerned, Crisanta. It all comes down to one crown and how many people you're willing to step on to get it. So what if some folks die or are betrayed along the way? History will forget those people. The only ones who truly matter are those who win in the end. Take my grandmother, Morgause. She wanted to rule Camelot, but it was her sister Igraine who married King Uther Pendragon. So she hatched a different plan, one that required patience and many years of planning.

"She married King Lot of Orkney and had six of her own

children, but also seduced Uther and bore a son with him—my father Mordred. Over the years, she secretly worked with various rebel factions throughout Camelot to start a war. And when Uther died and Arthur took power, she heightened her efforts and trained my father to defeat Arthur, which he eventually did. Father took power for a short while, but the realm was in turmoil, and he was weak. My grandmother never had faith in him as a ruler. She just used him as a tool to get Arthur out of the way.

"She had a similar lack of faith in my older brother Melehan. So when war ravaged the land and my father was killed, she chose to smuggle me to safety alone. Melehan was eventually tracked down and killed, as were the series of kings that succeeded my father through wars, coups, assassinations, and what have you. Then when the dust settled, the armies my grandmother had assembled took the citadel and I—the last living noble with Pendragon blood—claimed the throne as the true king and heir of Camelot."

I rolled my eyes. "You're right, Rampart. Your grandmother's ruthlessness is exemplary. But excuse me if I take a different world view."

"You'll understand soon enough," Rampart said. "It's easy to stay on your high horse when you've never faced tough choices—when you've never had to decide who lives and who dies based on what you want and what would benefit your needs. If push came to shove, you would be no different than your brother."

"I am nothing like my brother!" I snapped. Surprised by the rage in my voice, I reined it in a little. "And for the record," I continued, "even if Alex doesn't get blessed by the Boar's Mouth and you have to keep me alive to retrieve Excalibur, I won't be retrieving it for you. I'll be doing it for Arthur. I'm not some pawn in your game."

Rampart shrugged, unfazed. "I have faith in you, Crisanta Knight. You're capable of a lot more than you might think. You'll play your part one way or the other. And as for Arthur, I am not concerned. Arian and Alex have already taken a wormhole from Neverland to Camelot. What do you think that means for your king?"

My eyes widened.

Oh no. If Arian and Alex were coming to Camelot, that meant they'd gotten to Arthur and forced him to complete the pledge of The Pentecostal Oath with my brother. They wouldn't have left Neverland if they hadn't. I couldn't believe it. I genuinely thought Arthur was unbeatable. And if my enemies already had what they wanted from him, did that mean . . .

A horrible feeling sank in my chest.

"Is he dead?" I asked.

"Not yet," Rampart replied. "Arian informed me of Arthur's condition. Your king can't leave Neverland or the poison of my father's blade will kill him. We have him imprisoned there for the time being. I want him kept alive long enough to see me reclaim Excalibur. Whether it is you or your brother who helps me, I will be the rightful king that fulfills the prophecy and Arthur will go to the grave knowing so."

Our conversation stopped when one of the guards pulled the handle in the ceiling again. He turned the black knob slowly. As it went from six to five, to four, and so on, a sound like metal grinding against metal emanated around us. I felt the capsule slow down. Shortly thereafter, our ride was ejected from the tunnel and emerged in a large, circular cavern. The reddish rock interior had enormous white lights built into the jagged ridges. The top of the cavern was far above us.

The capsule came to a complete stop at the end of its pathway, docking in a port next to several other capsules on their own tracks. A waiting guard pulled a crank on our port, opening our capsule. I was unchained from the table and pushed outside. There was a dirt tunnel across from where we docked. Applause was coming from the other end. I had a bad feeling about where it led.

I was taken to the left side of the cavern where a metallic ramp ran twenty feet up to an immense iron door. Rampart led us to it with guards in front of and behind me in case I got any ideas.

I glanced over my shoulder at the other side of the cavern. Past the last capsule dock, a set of glass doors provided access to a white room built into the rock. It was full of weapons. Six women in black outfits and headscarves were inside arranging an array of the arms into carts. I thought one of them shot me a look through the eye slit in her headscarf as she loaded knives onto her cart, but a guard stepped in front of my line of sight before I could be sure.

At the top of the ramp, Rampart thrust open the door with a massive push. My fears were confirmed. The applause and illumination hit me like a tidal wave as we stepped out onto the private viewing box of the Mercy Pit.

While the night sky was a smudge of purple and gray, giant spotlights—each the size of a carriage—were mounted on high posts across the canyon, illuminating the packed arena.

There were a dozen knights and a slew of courtiers and nobles gathered in the viewing box, many helping themselves from a buffet table. They bowed or curtsied as Rampart walked past and I was led forward to the front railing.

Three people awaited us at the head of the viewing box: the announcer I'd seen earlier, Rampart's wife, and Morgause. The two women sat in ornate thrones with an empty throne for Rampart nestled between them.

While Rampart took his seat, a guard approached me and locked the chain of my shackles to another chain on the railing. I eyed his sword and the dagger attached to his belt as he stashed his key ring within his right pocket and moved to stand with the guards at the back of the viewing box. Now shackled in place, I turned my attention to the pit below. The drop to the arena floor was nearly twenty feet.

The announcer came to stand beside me, as did Morgause. The latter smiled wickedly before summoning her magic and gently levitating the announcer to ground level. I watched him walk to the center of the Mercy Pit. The projection orbs followed him like obedient servants, lighting up the sky with his image. When he held up his hands the stadium fell silent.

"Our king promised you a special fight tonight, and by his good grace, he has delivered! Wanted in Camelot, enemy to this realm and many others, and guilty of conspiring against the king in the highest order—please give a round of applause for this evening's challengers!"

The barred gates of a tunnel on the other side of the arena were raised and Jason and Blue were pushed out into the Mercy Pit. The projection orbs zipped around them excitedly, broadcasting their bewildered faces on the enormous holographic screens. My hands tightly clutched the railing.

They were still in their fine attire from the party but their hands were shackled. Guards herded them toward the center of the arena. Three women in black appeared from the tunnel below the viewing box pushing weapons carts.

"These protagonists are some of the most formidable in the realm of Book!" the announcer continued. "So I'm sure we're in for a good fight! Now then," he turned to Jason and Blue. "Choose your weapons!"

The guards uncuffed my friends and went to stand beside the announcer. Blue and Jason looked at each other before moving toward the carts. When Blue bent over to grab a weapon. I thought she hesitated for a moment when she bumped into one of the women in black.

Jason selected an axe and Blue picked up a sturdy dagger. I leaned over the railing and watched the women push the carts back inside the tunnel, passing beneath the twelve-foot Camelot flag that flowed below the private viewing box.

"And representing the king," the announcer boomed, "please put your hands together for the senior members of his majesty's roundtable!"

The five knights that Blue, SJ, and I had danced with at the ball emerged from another tunnel. They carried gleaming weapons, but Blue and Jason didn't even flinch. A smile crept in at the corners of my mouth.

These knights have no chance.

I pivoted toward Rampart with a smirk on my face. "You're going to need more men."

The guards who'd escorted my friends into the arena returned to their tunnel while Morgause levitated the announcer back to the viewing box.

"Your confidence is admirable, but foolish, Crisanta," Rampart said condescendingly as he sat in his throne. "Here's what's going to happen. You're going to watch your friends get killed. My men are presently searching the castle for your other companions and will bring them here to face the same fate. And by evening's end, Arian will be here for you."

Morgause settled into her throne as the announcer headed for the golden gong. I leaned back against the railing as I met the collective gaze of the king and his royal family.

"Not a bad theory," I responded. "But here's what's *actually* going to happen. My friends are going to best your men and expectations. I'm going to escape. And we're going to leave you here looking like a fool in front of your people, having to explain to Arian how you let us get away."

Rampart scoffed. "Like I said, Arian mentioned you were cocky."

"Did he also mention that I was *good*?" I replied. "The guy's been hunting me for months, Rampart, and I embarrass him at every turn. What makes you so certain I won't do the same to you?"

The announcer grabbed his mallet and swung it against the gong. "Fight!" he boomed.

I directed my full attention to the arena. The five knights charged and I held my breath. I had full faith in my friends, but these were the king's best. I pulled at my cuffs. It wasn't easy watching my friends fight for their lives when I was stuck on the sidelines.

Jason and Blue kept close to each other, working as a team like they always did. It took thirty seconds for them to take out the first two knights with their dagger-axe combos.

Now there were only three opponents left. Blue used her free-flowing dress to her advantage, twirling her long skirt wildly and distracting the knights like a red cloth waved in front of a bull. Jason's defensive and offensive axe moves never ceased to amaze me. I pitied anyone who went up against him.

When my friends dropped the third and fourth knights, I

glanced smugly over my shoulder at Rampart. "Told you that you needed more men."

My friends had successfully knocked out all but one of the knights. And unlike the fights we'd witnessed earlier, Jason and Blue had been triumphant without murdering their opponents for the entertainment of the crowd; their attackers were either knocked out or severely injured. It was an epic display of skill paired with restraint and mercy.

The last knight left was Sir Gaheris—arguably the biggest and most adept of the lot. He was making them work for the win. My friends split up and attacked Gaheris from both sides, but he fought like a beast.

Jason jumped out of the way to evade the point of Gaheris's sword. Blue dashed around the knight's other side. He swung. She ducked to avoid his blade. From her crouched position she sliced her knife across his thigh, but he was unfazed by the wound and kicked her in the chest. Blue stumbled back and dropped her dagger. Gaheris kicked it out of her reach.

Jason took a swing at Gaheris with his axe. The knight expertly side-stepped and drove his sword straight into Jason's side.

I gasped and clutched the railing so hard I thought it might shatter. On the enormous holographic screens, I saw Jason stagger. A thin line of blood stained his shirt, growing wider and darker with every second. Gaheris struck out again and Jason managed to block the strike, but after the injury he hadn't had enough time to properly brace himself. Gaheris knocked his axe away and punched Jason in the face. My friend fell to the ground.

Gaheris lifted his blade and was about to bring it down for the kill shot when Blue stepped in.

Blue was small in comparison to Gaheris, but she was all muscle. She used every ounce of her strength to plow-drive into Gaheris's side, knocking him away from Jason and into the dirt.

Gaheris reacted quickly, wrapping his arm around Blue's neck and slamming her down. Blue scratched his face before reaching for her secret weapon, the hunting knife she'd hidden in the holster on her leg. She used her knife-wielding arm to block his sword-wielding one as it drove toward her. She stopped his weapon, but she didn't stop his other hand as it rushed in and gripped her neck.

"Blue!" I yelled.

Gaheris slammed her into the dirt once more, choking her with one hand, crushing her throat. He thought he'd won. He didn't see what was coming up behind him.

While Gaheris had been throttling Blue, Jason had staggered upright and now stood behind Gaheris. He grabbed the knight's head between both hands, twisted, and . . .

SNAP.

The orbs projected the sound across the Mercy Pit at full volume. I froze.

Gaheris collapsed to the ground, his neck broken. Morgause stood up behind me and screamed. I was surprised by how genuinely horrified she was.

Her cry was drowned out though by the sounds of the arena going wild. On the holographic screens, I watched Jason take a step back with a look of shock on his face. He'd killed Gaheris.

"You're right," Rampart said.

I turned to face him. He was holding Morgause's hand but looked at me with vengeance. "I *could* use more men."

He waved at the announcer, who smacked the gong twice.

"Round Two!" The announcer's voice boomed.

Fifteen more knights entered the arena from tunnels all around the combat floor and charged at Blue and Jason. My friends braced themselves for the attack. Jason clutched his injured side with one hand. Blue stood near him protectively.

The threat was thirty feet from them, twenty feet, and then . . .

One of the massive lights illuminating the canyon exploded, shot by an arrow. Screams emitted from the crowd as sparks flew. A second light experienced the same fate, followed by a third, fourth, and a fifth in perfect succession.

Panicked shouts filled the air as darkness fell over the Mercy Pit. The knights who were supposed to be battling my friends looked around trying to find out where the shots were coming from. Blue and Jason took advantage of their distraction and ran toward my side of the arena.

My eyes darted from one side of the arena to the other. So much was happening. For a second, I saw a gaggle of knights chasing a woman in brown robes in the higher part of the canyon. But when a sixth light was taken out, that part of the Mercy Pit dropped into shadow.

Knights and guards in our viewing box hurried for the door that led to the stairs. Before they could exit, the force of an eruption on the other side pushed them back. There was no smoke or fire, but the door rattled like something powerful had punched it. Green slime seeped beneath the doorframe.

SJ!

An arrow suddenly sailed above our heads. Two more arrows followed—each attached to a zipline. Seventy percent of the Mercy Pit's lights had been taken out by then, so the approach of the assailants was concealed by the darkness. The projection orbs flashed disorienting shots of screeching people in the stands and chaos in the canyon.

More arrows struck our box—and the people inside. The courtiers screamed as knight after knight was hit. Three women in brown robes and headscarves ziplined onto the viewing box. Each of them carried a quiver of arrows and a bow. They advanced on the remaining armed men. A gold emblem was sewn onto each girl's right shoulder—it was the letter G contained within the mouth of a dragon.

Conflict ensued around me. The guard who'd shackled me to the railing wasn't far and he was attacking one of the robed girls. I saw Rampart about to slice a different robed girl in half. The closest person to me was the announcer and I kicked him in the lower back. This sent him sailing into one knight, who then toppled into Rampart. They all fell like dominoes.

The girl I'd helped looked in my direction. Her brown eyes met mine and I knew we were on the same side.

"I need the key!" I said urgently, lifting my shackled hands and tilting my chin at the guard that had it.

The girl nodded and spun, hocking the nearest knight's leg out from under him. She slammed her bow into the face of another attacker before pivoting around, punching the guard I sought, and kicking him in my direction.

He fell against the railing. I dashed in and powerfully back-fisted him in the face with my left hand before reaching down and grabbing the key ring from his pocket with my right. He tried to come at me, but I kicked him in the kneecap. He folded. My fingers clasped around the key ring like brass knuckles and I drove in with a ruthless back-fist, right hook, back-fist combo, finishing with a good kick to the teeth. He slammed back—knocked out— and I had my opening.

I freed myself from the railing but still had my original cuffs and chain to worry about. More knights charged. I bobbed around the first knight's sword then ducked beneath the second knight's dagger. With a kneecap kick and a body slam, I took the first knight down. The second knight lunged in with his dagger again, but I raised the chain of my cuffs and used it to block then wrap the knight's weapon and wrist. With a tug, I yanked him to the railing and stomped my heel into his foot. He dropped his dagger and I pushed him over the railing.

Another explosion erupted somewhere beneath the viewing box, causing everyone to stagger.

"Get down to the arena!" one of the robed girls shouted at me. "Exit through the tunnel below the box!"

All right. But how am I supposed to get down there?

I couldn't climb down the smooth cement wall below the box. The archers were too busy to help me any more than they already were. And I still had my cuffs to worry about.

I spotted the dagger on the floor then looked over the railing at the flag.

Oh, this is a bad idea.

Before good sense could talk me out of it, I kicked off my heels, grabbed the dagger, and hopped over the railing. As I fell, I stabbed the dagger through the flag. By cutting through the thick material, I was able to slow my drop tremendously. Until I reached the end of it.

When the flag ran out I fell the last eight feet on my own. I braced myself as best I could, rolling on impact, but I hit the dirt hard.

Ow.

After the initial shock of the landing, I forced my will and adrenaline to compensate for the pain and pulled myself up.

I was scraped and sore and a little woozy, but I had to keep going. I looked around. The Mercy Pit was massive from this vantage point. Now eighty percent dark, it'd become a chamber of screaming, frightened civilians.

"Crisa!"

Blue and Jason called to me from the tunnel below the viewing box. The gate in front of it had been blown apart from the inside. That must've been the explosion I felt a minute ago. I was overjoyed and relieved to reunite with them.

"Good to see you in one piece," Jason said.

"Same," I said as the three of us high-tailed it down the tunnel.

"I see you left *both* your shoes behind before making a break for it," Blue commented with a grin.

"Ha ha. Yes, I get it," I replied dryly, grateful that Blue was in good enough shape to be cracking Cinderella jokes.

We came out the other side of the tunnel. I looked up and noticed that the door to the viewing box was encased in a wall of green goo and the ramp leading up to it had been obliterated. Also, the only person within the cavern that was not frozen in a block of ice was one of the women in black who'd pushed out the weapons cart. She pulled off her headscarf.

"SJ!" I exclaimed.

"Come on," she said, waving us toward the capsules.

SJ selected a different capsule than the one Rampart and I had arrived in. Blue heaved the crank on its dock. The capsule opened and we started to hop in, but then one of the knights from the arena came rushing in through the tunnel—the guy I'd thrown over the railing.

SJ pulled down the neck of her black dress to reveal her necklace of portable potions. She had three orbs left—one explosion, an ice, and a lightning. She drew the explosion potion and fired it at the ground a few feet in front of the knight.

The closer the range of her shot, the smaller the effect of her potions. From this distance, her shot caused a moderate eruption that blasted the knight back. Blue grabbed a rock the size of a cereal bowl and waved us into the capsule. When we were inside, she heaved the rock at the crank, hit it square-on, and the capsule sealed.

"How do you make these things go?" SJ asked, looking around the pod desperately.

"I've got it." I hastily yanked on the handle in the ceiling, revealing the red button and black dial. "Everybody hang on." I punched the red button. The capsule had barely started to move when I turned the black dial to its highest setting—number ten—with a swift twist. The capsule took off furiously down its track beneath the mountain and I was slammed into the seat between Jason and Blue.

"Who were those women in the brown robes?" I asked.

"The Gwenivere Brigade," SJ responded. "That resistance group trying to overthrow King Rampart and restore the throne to Arthur's wife, Gwenivere. Ormé is their leader. When the three of you got captured, I escaped from the Knights' Room and communicated with her and Daniel through the Mark Two. We came up with a plan."

"We left them behind in the arena," Jason said. "Those Gwenivere Brigade people, I mean. Should we be worried about them?"

"They have an escape plan of their own," SJ responded. "We will rendezvous with a few of them when we meet up with Daniel. Now then, let us get you free." She gestured for me to put my cuffs on the table.

"They're made of Stiltdegarth blood," I said. "They're blocking my magic and I don't think you can cut through them with a regular blade."

"Then we will use more than just a blade." SJ said. She turned to Blue. "Your hunting knife please."

I put my cuffs on the table in the middle of the capsule. SJ stretched out the chain between the cuffs and placed her last ice potion in one of the center links. "Brace yourself," she said. Then she smashed the portable potion with the heel of Blue's knife. Because of the proximity of the impact, the eruption was contained to the area around the table. When the poof of smoke cleared, the chain connecting my cuffs was frozen solid.

"Jason, your axe please," SJ said.

He handed her the weapon and she swung it down on the table, shattering the ice and the chain between my cuffs.

Success! The cuffs were still attached to my wrists, impairing my magic, but at least I had full range of movement now.

"Nice swing, SJ. Thanks." I stretched my arms and pivoted toward Jason. "How's your—" I saw his blood-soaked shirt. "Jason!"

"I'm fine," he said, swatting me away. "Just got grazed by Gaheris in that last fight."

I watched as small silver sparks flickered around Jason's side. SJ's SRB was trying to clean up his shirt, as it was designed to do, but since the wound was still open, the accessory's enchantment was not holding. When I'd first reunited with Jason and Blue in the Mercy Pit his shirt hadn't looked like this at all; at the time the SRB must've just finished restoring it to a clean state. Now the blood had overwhelmed it again and the enchantment was doing its best to counteract the new stain.

"That's more than a graze, Jason," Blue replied. "You're seriously hurt."

"And we seriously don't have the time for it," he said. "I'm fine. Let's just focus on getting out of here. Crisa, can you slow down the capsule?" He pointed at the fast-approaching end of the tunnel.

Oh, snap!

I hastily turned the dial down. I managed to get it from a ten to a five before we came to the end of the track, but our capsule still plowed through its dock at the end of the runway and demolished the area that held the crank to open it. The crash had cracked the glass of the capsule though, so I picked up Jason's axe and finished the job.

"Watch out," I told the others. I swung at the glass until it shattered completely. I offered the axe back to Jason, but he shook his head.

"Leave it," he said. "It's not mine. It's a random one from the weapon's cart. Mine's still in our carriage."

I ditched the weapon and hopped out of the capsule. SJ followed, then Blue. Jason leapt out next, but when he landed he crumpled to his knees, clutching his side. Blue hurried over and helped him up.

"I told you that was more than a graze!" she said. "If you weren't injured, I'd smack you."

"That's comforting," Jason grunted.

"You know what I mean," she huffed. "Now hold onto me, you valiant idiot. SJ, I take it you know where we're going?"

"Yes. I charted this route with the help of the Gwenivere Brigade. Follow me."

Our team pursued her up a staircase that deposited us into an open corridor. We dashed down it to an elevator, which we rode for ten seconds. When the doors opened we were in a hallway with three doors. SJ went for the third one, but it was locked.

"Darn it," she said. "Blue, can you—"

"Crisa, hold this." She passed Jason to me and I let him lean on my shoulder while Blue kicked the door in. She swiftly resumed her post as Jason's crutch and we continued on our way.

A minute later we found ourselves in a wine cellar. We darted through rows of barrels and bottles until we came upon another staircase, this one wooden. SJ grabbed a wine bottle from a rack before ascending. I didn't ask why.

She pushed open the hatch at the top of the stairs and we arose into another, much smaller wine cellar. This one seemed more for show; the bottles weren't dusty and they were displayed in open glass cases rather than on wooden racks.

There was a fireplace in the corner of the cellar. SJ hurled the wine bottle at it. When the bottle shattered and the wine splattered, the liquid seeped into carvings forged in the stone— forming the shape of a cross with a ten-pointed star in the top right quadrant. That same symbol we kept seeing everywhere in Camelot.

The fireplace pulled itself apart in four distinct sections, revealing a tunnel. We hastened inside. Just after we crossed the threshold, the fireplace sealed shut behind us. We raced on almost blindly in the dark. There was a small crack of light ahead that we maneuvered toward. It was bleeding from beneath a wall.

"Help me push," SJ said when we reached it.

I rammed my shoulder into the wall alongside my friend, which as it turned out was not made of stone. It was a stack of crates. After we pushed a section away, we slipped out of the tunnel into a storage room.

The room connected to stables where we discovered our carriage parked by the main doors. The horses had been changed out. The older, shabbier steeds we'd rented had been replaced with a pair of sleek black stallions.

Daniel was waiting beside the carriage with a woman in a brown robe. Unlike the others I'd seen, this woman's headscarf was golden. She pulled it down and I recognized the face underneath. It was Ormé, the leader of the Gwenivere Brigade.

When Daniel noticed Jason leaning on Blue, his eyes widened with panic. "What happened?"

"I got side-swiped in the Mercy Pit," Jason said, struggling. "It's nothing."

"Now I'm going to smack you twice when you get better," Blue grunted. "Guys, help me get him in the carriage."

We flung back the tarp at the rear of the vehicle.

"Get the doors!" Ormé shouted at two more robed girls who stood nearby. They pushed open the stable doors as we assisted Jason into the carriage. Daniel joined Ormé on the front seat and grabbed the reins. The other robed girls jumped in the back with us and an instant later we took off. I looked out the window. We were racing around the castle the way we'd come.

"Where are we going?" I asked one of the Gwenivere Brigade girls.

"There's only one way in and out of the castle," she said. "The bridge over the moat."

Sure enough, I saw the bridge we'd crossed earlier coming into view. The lanterns on both sides lit it up like a runway.

"We have a problem!" Blue shouted. She was looking out the window on the left. "Cannons."

Our carriage abruptly swerved and there was an explosion behind us. We were tossed around inside and the tarp at the rear of the carriage caught fire. Blue sliced her knife across the top of the burning material. It fell away, giving us a perfectly clear view of the castle as we sped onto the bridge. Through the opening we saw the next cannonball. It arced over us in a blazing streak against the dark sky.

"Hang onto something!" Ormé called back.

The cannonball obliterated a section of the bridge twenty-five feet ahead but Daniel did not slow down. He urged the horses to canter faster and we leapt straight over the gap.

One of the girls from the Gwenivere Brigade shrieked as she lost her grip and flew backward. I stretched out my hand and managed to grab her before she fell out of the carriage. A few supplies toppled from the vehicle and fell into the open—a couple of bags, some bundles of rope—but I refused to let this girl go with them.

We slammed down on the other side of the gap, safely reconnecting with the bridge. The impact jolted the ramp attached to the rear of our carriage, which began dragging behind us, its metal scraping against the stone. I yanked the Gwenivere Brigade girl back inside.

"Thanks," she said.

"No problem," I said. Noticing that her bow was about to fall out of the carriage, I reached for it. "Here, you dropped your— Argh!"

I lost my balance as the carriage swerved to avoid another cannonball. I tumbled down the ramp and fell onto the rough stone of the crumbling bridge. I only had a second to process the carriage continuing on without me before the ground gave way.

I fell thirty feet until I splashed deep into the cold, dark waters of the moat. I scrambled to the surface, gasping for air. Then I immediately dove back under and swam out of the way as another section of bridge came down. Giant hunks of rock crashed into the water behind me.

I kicked my way to the surface once more. Wiping the water from my eyes, I spotted our carriage. It had made it to the other side of the bridge and was pulling behind a turn in the road to take cover from the continuing cannon fire. I was glad my friends were out of range. I wasn't sure if they would come back for me or if they thought I would make it to them. Either play was dangerous. For now I simply had to act on my own.

Shouts from above made me look up. Countless guards had stormed out of the castle in pursuit of my friends, but they could not cross the massive hole in the bridge. Instead, a number of them were descending the jagged embankment—determined to cross the moat and come after us that way. An arrow whizzed by my head.

Aw, crud.

Some knights had raced onto the remaining bridge and had spotted me in the water. They began firing more arrows at me.

I held my breath and dove, trying to conceal myself from their line of sight. I swam as fast as I could toward the other side of the moat, zigging and zagging as arrows punctured the water. It was difficult due to the weight of the metal cuffs I still had on my wrists, but I was a strong swimmer. I hadn't always been, but I had dedicated many weeks to improving the skill recently when I was home in Midveil. Thanks to all the practice, now I could move underwater with great agility and hold my breath for long periods of time.

When I made it to the other side of the moat, I heaved myself onto the gravel and made a run for cover. The first surge of guards was ten feet from reaching the edge of the opposite embankment. They would soon be in the water. The SRB on my wrist caused a swarm of silver sparks to flurry around my body that dried me off. This effect was super unhelpful at the moment, as it made me an obvious target. I ducked behind the safety of a large rock and narrowly avoided being caught by a volley of arrows.

It was fairly dark, but lights from the remaining portions of bridge provided enough luminescence for me to see the people on the bridge and the surrounding area. Right then I caught a glimpse of someone high above.

SJ.

I recognized her silhouette even from this distance. The knights on the bridge hadn't spotted her yet.

Plan. Plan. I need a plan.

I had only seconds before two dozen men entered the water. If I tried to climb up the embankment I would be hit by one of the castle's archers. If I stayed where I was, it was only a matter of time before these guys swam across the water and reached me.

Wait. The water.

I looked at the moat, thinking about the shards of mirror and glass that decorated the sides of the bridge.

"SJ!" I called up, pointing at the bridge. "Hit it with lightning!"

She was smart; she knew what I was thinking. And she was speedy enough to act before the knights could intervene.

My friend drew the last portable potion from her necklace and fired at the bridge. She seemed to have her slingshot now, and her aim was perfect. With the distance of the shot being so great, the resulting bolt was huge.

When the portable potion impacted a mirror shard on the bridge, it released a lightning bolt that ricocheted off the mirror and arced into the moat. A massive electrical surge lit up the water. The moat crackled like a deadly eel and all the guards who'd been about to dive in held their positions, lest they be electrocuted to death.

Glancing up again, I saw Ormé and the two Gwenivere Brigade girls from the carriage arriving at SJ's side. Ormé handed SJ her magic sack while the other girls brought shields to protect SJ and Ormé with.

"We'll cover you!" Ormé shouted to me. "Climb!"

I did. While Ormé used her bow and arrows to take shots

at our enemies on the bridge, SJ fired explosion potions at the attackers and sent more lightning potions to electrify the water.

With a bit of effort, I scaled the ragged embankment. I was glad that I'd ditched my heels long ago, but I wished that I'd had my boots for better grip and protection. One wrong move and I'd seriously hurt my feet.

Once I arrived at the top, the five of us ran along the road until we reached our carriage. Only Jason was inside. Blue and Daniel were busy fighting off more knights who must've been patrolling the streets of the citadel and been informed of what was happening.

SJ blasted back half the battalion with an explosion potion then stuck the rest of the attackers in place with a couple of slime potions.

Ormé, Blue, one of the Gwenivere Brigade girls, and I bounded into the carriage. SJ—armed and dangerous—jumped on the front seat next to Daniel. The remaining Gwenivere Brigade girl swung onto the roof and took up an offensive position there.

Our horses galloped down the streets of the citadel. It was a wonder that our archer up top didn't go flying; girl must've had incredible balance and action training.

Pedestrians screamed and other carriages swerved as Daniel yelled for people to get out of the way. I occasionally saw knights mounted on horses, but the second any of them started to chase us, an arrow fired from our roof or a potion launched from the front seat would prevent them from getting too close.

Unfortunately, the onslaught would not stop coming and their numbers were increasing. The closer we got to our exit, the more knights came at us. I could see the outer wall of the citadel. Daniel was a dangerously intense driver with a propensity for speeding, but boy was he effective. We raced past the guards at the tunnel entrance and sped through. Looking out the side window, I saw that the iron gate on the other side was closed. To remedy the situation, Daniel slowed the horses with a sharp yank on the reins, allowing SJ to fire a series of explosion potions. The gate was obliterated and we shot to freedom through its smithereens.

Our carriage careened downhill, bouncing wildly on the uneven stone road that led from the mountains to the valley below.

"Turn left toward that forest!" Ormé shouted to Daniel. "I know where we can lose them!"

We'd originally come from the forest on the right side of the valley, so this was unknown territory. We had to trust our new ally.

Daniel pulled on the reins and jerked our carriage to the left. Speeding across the vast, open valley was both peaceful and terrifying. Peaceful because it was smooth terrain with nothing but wind and night air whizzing by us. Terrifying because of what was pursuing our vehicle. Six other carriages—those of the citadel knights no doubt—had emerged from the mountain pass not long after we hit the valley. They were after us now, as were several cannonballs fired from the citadel's outer wall in our wake. I was beyond grateful that Daniel was so skilled at getaway driving, and that I hadn't eaten anything from the buffet at the castle party. With all the abrupt movements of our carriage, I definitely would have tossed my cookies by now.

Finally, we reached the forest. The temperature dropped twenty degrees and thick mist consumed us the second we entered. Anything more than fifteen feet away was instantly lost to sight.

"Quick! Daniel, pull over!" Ormé ordered

Our carriage came to a halt. We had about a minute's lead on the knights of the citadel. We'd need to move fast to elude them.

"Everybody grab what you need," Ormé told us. "We're ditching the carriage."

I pushed up the seat of the bench compartment where we'd stored our stuff and pulled on my combat boots. Jason chose not to grab his regular clothes. He was having a hard enough time simply standing. He grabbed his axe sheath and my friends and I assisted him out of the carriage. SJ scurried around back and I tossed my friend her backpack before slinging my own over my shoulders.

"Let's move," Ormé commanded. She gave one of the horses a solid slap on the rear. He whinnied and the steeds cantered off with the carriage.

"The citadel knights don't know the Forest of Mists like we do," she said. "They'll never find us. Come on."

Ormé and the other two Gwenivere Brigade girls hurried into the mist. I didn't know where they were taking us, but our only alternatives were getting captured by citadel knights or getting lost in this freezing forest, so into the mist we walked.

CHAPTER 9

Morgan La Fay

e trekked through the forest for about five minutes before Jason collapsed.

"Everybody, stop," SJ ordered.

"We need to keep going," Ormé said. "We haven't put enough distance between us and the enemy."

"Jason cannot keep going like this," she argued. "This will only take a moment."

She reached inside her magic potions sack and removed a little bottle filled with pink liquid—the second of two improvised healing potions she'd whipped up before leaving school.

"Jason, sit," SJ said.

We helped Jason onto a log and SJ administered the liquid to the wound on his side. When she'd previously done this for Blue following an arrow injury, the concoction had sizzled, the blood had evaporated, and the wound had been closed with a splotch of glowing pink goo. Although Jason's wound sizzled when the potion made contact with his skin and the blood melted away, it did not turn to goo and close. Nor did it start to glow. It flashed a shade of peach then dissolved inside the deep injury. Jason's wound did not heal. A thin layer of skin formed over the injury, but the layer was nearly translucent and you could see blood coagulating beneath it. The wound was trying to reopen.

"It didn't work!" Blue exclaimed.

"Why isn't it healing him?" Daniel asked SJ.

"This potion can only heal flesh wounds," SJ responded gravely. "Jason's wound is too deep."

"So what do we do now?" Blue asked.

"I am not sure," SJ admitted. "I believe the potion should help with the pain and keep the wound from reopening for a while, but once it wears off . . ."

"SJ, come on," Blue snapped angrily. "Pull something else out of that bag of yours and *fix him*."

"Blue, I—"

"We have a healer," Ormé interrupted. "The place where we're going. Her name is Elaine. She can fix your friend; we just have to get him there."

"Should we do any more first aid first?" I asked. "We could bandage you up, Jason."

Jason glanced at his injury then put down his shirt and stood up. "Looks like SJ's potion is holding as a second skin. And she was right; it did make me feel better. Some of my strength is coming back. Let's not waste any time and keep moving while I can."

Our group moved through the trees with renewed urgency.

"Follow the fireflies" was the only guidance Ormé gave us as we delved deeper into the mist. "The more of them we see, the closer we'll be to our destination."

"Which is *where*, exactly?" I asked, hurrying after them.

"The home of a friend," Ormé replied vaguely.

Against my normal instincts I didn't bother her with further questions. We needed to move. And move we did. It was really lucky that SJ's potion had given Jason a burst of energy and temporarily sealed his wound. He still leaned on us for a bit of support now and then, but he wasn't struggling like he had been in the citadel.

After half an hour, Ormé reckoned we had put enough distance between us and the enemy. We stopped for a few minutes to let Jason rest. During the interval, Blue finally had a chance to take a proper look at my cuffs. She was seriously one of the greatest lock-pickers I'd ever seen. It only took her a few minutes to free me from my restraints. I released a huge sigh of relief when the shackles fell off. My wrists no longer felt strangled and neither did I. The Stiltdegarth blood used to forge those cuffs was no joke. I may not have fully appreciated it while they were on, but in weakening my magic they also weakened me. I felt so much better the moment they were gone, my strength returning in a powerful rush.

I only wished I could share that strength with Jason. He was trying to hide it, but I could tell that his pain was returning. We were running out of time.

For months I had been worrying about the future I'd envisioned where he would die by that river. I'd planned to stop this outcome—just this morning I'd had the idea that my magic might be the solution. But I didn't consider that another way of preventing the foreseen fate was if Jason never made it that far.

I'd long thought of my visions of the future as being fixed points. If I saw it, it would happen. The only way to manipulate those futures was to either influence what happened before or after. However, I now appreciated that there was another option. The only way to completely stop a prophecy of fate was if the subject died before reaching it. This was why Arian had been trying to kill me for months: to prevent my prophecy from coming true. Given that, I realized the same must be true for visions. They were not finite and could be avoided if their subjects were killed unexpectedly before the foreseen fate occurred.

Looking at my struggling friend, I had never hoped so badly that we would arrive at the future I'd envisioned. Jason couldn't die now. It was too soon and I wasn't ready. I had no idea if I had the power to pull off a magical resurrection. The anxiety churned my stomach like spicy curry.

We kept moving for another fifteen minutes before my friend's injury started to slow his pace again. Ormé reassured us that we were closing in on our destination and five minutes later, she stopped and held up her hand. "We're almost there, but you need to be careful. There's a big slope here."

I squinted through the mist to detect a drop in front of us. I definitely wouldn't have seen it if she hadn't pointed it out.

As we worked our way down the incline, I saw the vague silhouettes of thorn trees around us. The ground beneath my boots was squishy, like moss. Swarms of fireflies flickered through the air.

"You're going to start to feel a little groggy," Ormé said once we reached the bottom of the slope. "Try not to pass out."

I wasn't sure what she meant. A few minutes later, I still felt as alert as ever. But when I glanced at my friends I detected a shift. All of them—even Ormé and the Gwenivere Brigade girls—appeared to be moving sluggishly. Blue rubbed her eyes sleepily.

The fireflies were everywhere now. They had more light in each of their rear ends than my friends did in their eyes. What was happening to them? And why wasn't it happening to me?

We arrived at a curtain of weeping willows. "All right. We're here," Ormé said with a yawn. "Nobody take another step. This castle has the best protective border you'll ever see."

Ormé pulled aside a draping branch to reveal something that was both breathtaking and dangerous. About three hundred feet in front of us was a tall stone castle. Despite the heavy mist, we could make out the entrance thanks to the thousands of golden fireflies that floated in the vicinity.

That was the beautiful part. The dangerous part was the magnificent blanket of purple and red flowers that surrounded the castle on all sides.

Poppies.

That's why my friends had grown so lethargic. Poppies knocked you out instantly if you touched them, but they also produced a potent type of mist that made you sleepy. The greater the number of Poppies, the stronger the mist's effect.

"This castle belongs to Gwenivere Pendragon. She leads our rebel faction," Ormé explained. "After King Arthur died, she and the rest of her family settled here because it was the only place they knew they'd be protected from Morgause and Rampart. No one can cross a Poppy field. Even if you managed to shoot an arrow into one of the towers and tried to climb or zipline across, you'd never make it. Hovering over such an immense sea of Poppies still exposes you to their drowsy gas. In the end, their power will knock you unconscious before you even reach the halfway point. Believe me, we've tested it."

"So how do you get across?" Blue asked, stifling a yawn.

"Morgan La Fay," Ormé responded. "King Arthur's half-sister. She has a very specific kind of magic that can transport us across. She lives here with Gwenivere, but we'll need to get her attention by firing a sonic flare. There's a device in the castle's tallest tower that detects very specific sound waves. One of our Gwenivere Brigade sisters is always on duty monitoring it. Once she hears it, she'll find Morgan, who will use her magic to bring us over to the castle. Mindy, hand me a flare."

The Gwenivere Brigade girl that Ormé was gesturing to froze. She lowered her headscarf. Up 'til now, I'd only seen her light-colored eyes. Now I saw her dark skin and fuchsia lipstick, which had somehow managed to stay on during the fight. Her thin eyebrows were furrowed in worry. "Ormé, I'm sorry. I think the flares were in one of the bags that fell out of the carriage on the castle bridge."

"Well, that's just terrific, Mindy," the other Gwenivere Brigade girl said, annoyed. She lowered her headscarf and bushy orange hair spilled out. "Now we'll have to wait until morning to get inside. No one is going to see us through this mist at this hour. And unless you want to attract Magistrakes or Samaracks, we can't exactly yell for help."

"Does anybody in there have a Mark Two?" Daniel suggested.

"Yes, but we don't," Ormé replied, frustrated. "They're still a newer innovation around here and we only have so many. Our team's was in the same bag as the flares."

I narrowed my eyes at the entrance of the castle. "Is there a knocker on that door? I can't tell from here."

"Um, yes," Ormé replied. "But I don't think it's been used in millennia, not since the Poppies grew in."

"All right, so I'll just go knock on the door then."

The Gwenivere Brigade girls stared at me like I was insane. I simply shrugged.

"Poppies don't affect me. I can get across the field." I tightened the backpack around my shoulders before taking a deep breath and a few steps forward.

All right, here we go.

With a confident stride I walked into the Poppy field. The second my legs brushed against the flowers, the veins in my arms turned a sickly purple color, a consequence of direct skin contact with Poppies. But as I'd come to expect, my body began to produce its own soft golden glow that fought against the purple in return. Thanks to Mauvrey, I now understood this was my magic reacting like a reflex—refilling me with the very life energy that the Poppies were designed to take away.

Awesome.

The castle grew spookier the closer I got to it. A rapture of ivy clung to the stone walls, covered the windows, and snaked between the crumbling arches that decoratively framed the outside. Two ancient-looking wolf statues the size of buildings—hunched over like they were bowing—guarded the iron gate, which was old, rusted, and teetering half open in front of the castle.

My glow burned brighter the further I delved into the sea of flowers. I was lit up so intensely by the time I reached the castle that I wagered the fireflies thought I was some sort of god.

The Poppies grew right up to the castle's iron door. I gazed up at the silver knocker, which protruded from a monstrous gargoyle face at eye level.

Knock. Knock. Knock.

Soon I heard noises inside. I pressed my ear to the door.

"Who could possibly be knocking?" someone said.

"I just looked out the window and it's a girl in a fancy dress with boots. She's *glowing*," another voice replied.

"How did she make it across the Poppies?" asked the first voice.

"I don't know. Why don't we open the door and ask her?" replied the second voice.

"All right. You open the door and I'll wield the mace to kill her if it's a trap. Be careful not to let the Poppies touch you."

I took a step back. The door opened and I was face-to-face with two girls in brown robes and headscarves. One held the door open; the other wielded the mace as discussed.

"Whoa, whoa," I said, raising my hands to show I meant no harm. "Not an enemy. I'm here with Ormé. She didn't have a flare, so I had to knock on the door. They're over there." I pointed across the field.

Careful not to step too close to me or the flowers outside the door, the girl without the mace reached for a pair of binoculars hanging around her neck. She flipped a switch, which caused the rims of the lenses to glow green, then peered through.

"Yup, it's Ormé," she said.

"Right," I said, turning back to the girls. "Now can I come in? These Poppies are making me purple." I gestured to the pulsing veins in my arms.

The girls seemed more confused than reluctant. They stepped aside so I could enter. The moment I moved out of the flowers' touch, my veins returned to normal and my golden glow faded.

However, when the colors in my veins disappeared, I realized I had faint burn marks on my arms. The marks were dark gold and they throbbed with light pain.

Hm. That's new.

I didn't know what to make of the marks. They were hardly as noticeable as the other scrapes and cuts on my skin. I'd gotten a tad beaten up during our escape between my fall to the Mercy Pit and tumble out of the carriage onto the bridge. Still, I knew where those injuries came from. Not knowing what produced these new marks made me uneasy. I'd have to figure it out later though; there were more important things to do right now.

I cleared my throat and addressed the Gwenivere Brigade girls. "Ormé said that Morgan La Fay could help the others get across the Poppy field. Where is she?"

"She's right here."

I turned around and discovered a tall woman coming down the candelabra-lit hall. She was in her early forties and had black, wavy hair. The bodice of her silk dress was olive gray with bronze embroidery. Each shoulder had a cutout and her sleeves were so long they almost touched the floor. At her hips the ombre skirt flooded into a shade of wine, then mauve, then purple.

"Who are you?" the woman asked as she came closer. She walked so gracefully that it looked like she was floating. I felt the odd compulsion to curtsy.

"My name is Crisanta Knight," I replied. "My friends and I are seeking refuge from Rampart and the citadel knights. Ormé saved us when he sentenced us to the Mercy Pit."

The woman nodded. "Crisanta Knight. My name is Morgan La Fay. You have come to the right place. Any enemy of Rampart's is a friend of ours. Follow me. We will bring your friends over."

She turned and headed back up the hallway. The girls who'd let me in closed the main door and proceeded after her. I followed.

"I saw your glow from one of the windows," said Morgan, glancing at me. "It's been a long time since I've met someone with Pure Magic."

Her comment surprised me. "You can tell by my glow that I have Pure Magic?"

She nodded. "All types of magic have a specific glow. Normal magic is usually silver. Fairy Godmother magic comes in shades of red. Pure Magic glows gold until Pure Magic Disease corrupts the carrier. Then it becomes darker until it turns black."

I slowed my pace. When I took the life from Morris the giant, my glow had turned partially gray. The realization made my heart sink. It was only my second time crossing the Malice Line, and it had been by accident. Could my magic really already be turning bad?

"This is not common knowledge," Morgan continued. "Not many humans have magic, so the odds of knowing people with all the different types and making this connection are low."

Lucky for me. Otherwise people who weren't my friends might figure out I have Pure Magic, like Book's Fairy Godmother Supreme (a.k.a., Liza's sister) Lena Lenore. Lenore was arguably the most powerful person in Book and disliked me tremendously. If she could confirm I had Pure Magic, I would be sentenced to Alderon like all the other carriers of the disease who—as a safeguard—were put there before their magic could turn dark. Thus far, Lenore didn't have the evidence she needed to prove that I had Pure Magic. I definitely wasn't going to mention this magic glow color-code to her.

I continued to hurry after Morgan and the Gwenivere Brigade girls. They led me through the castle and up one of the towers. After what felt like too many steps, we stood on the edge of the castle's outer wall. A few more Gwenivere Brigade girls had joined us on the way up.

The landscape was mystifying from this height—the Poppies, the fireflies, the stone wolves.

"How are you going to get them over the Poppy field?" I asked, trying to make out the blurry silhouettes in the distance and wondering how Jason was. "Ormé said that even if you don't touch the Poppies, the mist is still strong enough to knock you out."

"That is true," Morgan replied. "Which is a lucky thing since my aunt Morgause has great levitation powers. She would have used her magic to assail our castle long ago had it not been for the Poppies' mist. My magic, however, will get your friends safely across."

Her aunt is Morgause . . . Of course. I wanted to mentally smack myself. Ormé had already told us Morgan was Arthur's half-sister, but I'd been so distracted I hadn't put two and two together.

Morgan took a quick deep breath and raised her hands. As she exhaled, a silvery glow emanated from her fingertips. I felt the wind pick up. *A lot.* My dress and hair flapped around me. The mist below began to blow too, churning uneasily.

Across the Poppy field I saw the mist swirl so tightly around my friends that a cocoon of wind formed around them. The whirling orb lifted my friends off the ground and steadily transported the group over the field as silver energy poured out of Morgan's hands.

I was super impressed. Morgan must've been exerting a ton of energy to be controlling the winds like that. It was amazing. She moved her hands in soft circles as the wind orb traveled closer. She shifted her stance as it came above the wall and then carefully lowered it until it touched down beside us. With that she spread her arms and extinguished her glow. The winds instantly dispersed wildly and I was almost blown off my feet.

Ormé stepped forward. "Thank you, Morgan. I will explain everything shortly. But first, this one needs to be taken to the healing room immediately." She gestured to Jason, who was looking alarmingly pale.

Morgan nodded. "Merriweather. Lavern," she said to a pair of Gwenivere Brigade girls. "Run and fetch Elaine. Fast as you can. Meet us in the healing room. The rest of you, help the boy."

Merriweather and Lavern dashed ahead. The other Gwenivere Brigade girls aided Jason inside. We all followed, descending through the stone stairwell of the tower.

"How did you and Morgause both end up with magic?" I asked Morgan.

"My grandfather was King Amlawdd Wiegg," she explained. "When he was young, he saved a pixie queen. As a reward she gifted all of his children with magic, including my mother Igraine and my aunt Morgause. When they had children, it was not passed on to all of their progeny, just some. While my older sister and I developed powers, my half brother—who you might know as King Arthur—was not born with magic. Morgause's son Mordred and his children Rampart and Melehan were not gifted with magic either. Neither were most of the children she had with her former husband, King Lot of Orkney. Of her six children with him, only her daughter Clarissant developed powers. Most of us have been unharmed by the gifts. But Clarissant's magical abilities developed into Pure Magic."

"What happened to her?" I asked, though I was pretty sure I already knew the answer.

"She was driven mad with power and eventually killed by magic hunters."

Yup, that's about right.

"We're not in any danger from magic hunters here," Morgan continued. "There is a large population of them living in the Passage Perelous, but the Poppies keep us safe from them just as they keep us safe from Rampart's forces. Before Gwenivere and I came here when Arthur died, this castle had been vacant for generations because no one could get across the field. Only my wind orb can deflect the Poppies' drowsy gas."

And me, apparently.

We arrived at a chamber with a golden door. It matched the color of the many silks that lined the hallway.

Morgan opened the door and we were met with the warm

glow of a hundred candles. In the center of the chamber was a raised bed covered in white linens. Just as we began to make our way inside, Merriweather and Lavern returned alongside a woman with braided strawberry blonde hair and kind brown eyes. She was around the same age as Morgan, though several inches shorter.

"This is my older sister Elaine," Morgan explained. "Our father was Gorlois of Tintagel, the Duke of Cornwall—our mother's first husband before he died and she married Uther Pendragon. Elaine has healing magic. She can help your friend."

The Gwenivere Brigade girls assisted Jason onto the bed. He immediately closed his eyes and his chest rose and fell with short, shallow breaths. His shirt was turning red with blood again. SJ's potion was wearing off. Blue held his hand and the rest of my friends and I crowded around him until Ormé shooed us away.

"Come on. Elaine needs space and silence. Everyone out."

"But—" Blue started.

"Don't worry," Elaine cut her off. "Everything will be fine. Your friend will be all right. You can trust me."

If Morgan hadn't told us that Elaine had healing magic, I would have thought her power was hypnosis. Her voice was so calming and reassuring, I genuinely believed everything she was saying. My friends and I made our way out of the room. Blue was reluctant to leave, but as she stepped through the doorway, Elaine reached out and touched her arm.

"I'll take good care of him."

Ormé shut the golden door behind us, leaving Elaine and Jason alone in the healing room.

"Elaine's magic is not as strong as mine," Morgan said. "Depending on the extent of the injury, it may take a few hours to heal your friend. Until then, I suggest we head for my study. There is much to discuss."

"I'll say," Daniel commented. "And given that you're Arthur's half-sister, I think I know where to start. Your brother's not dead, Morgan. He's alive."

Morgan stopped cold. She turned and stared at Daniel. After a moment, her eyes shone as she realized he was speaking the truth. Daniel had always had a confident earnestness in his eyes that let you know that when he said something—good or bad—he was being sincere.

"Ormé," Morgan said. "Go get Gwenivere. *Now*."

CHAPTER 10

The Queen & I

rthur's wife was absolutely stunning.

After attending a school for princesses for more than six years, you would think that I was used to regal, radiant girls. But Gwenivere Pendragon—formerly Queen Gwenivere of Camelot—was on another level.

She had chocolate-colored skin, much like Liza's. Despite being in her late thirties, not a wrinkle marred her face. Her eyes were a strange, entrancing shade of navy. High cheekbones made her look like the very definition of royalty. Her hair was a cascade of dark brown curls that fell to her lower back.

Again, I felt the compulsion to curtsy. This time, on seeing the example Ormé and the Gwenivere Brigade girls set, I heeded it.

My friends and I curtsied or bowed to Gwenivere as she entered Morgan's study. Gwenivere's dress was a lavender velvet, off-the-shoulder number with fitted sleeves covered in gold embroidery. The gold matched the headpiece nestled in her hair and the design at the bottom of her skirt. Her dress was trimmed with the same cross-and-star design I'd seen on the flags in Camelot's citadel, and on Arthur's arm.

After sitting on the various armchairs and sofas in Morgan's study, my friends and I dove into our very long story. We told Gwenivere, Morgan, Ormé, and the other present members of the Gwenivere Brigade about everything—what happened in the citadel, my magic, Paige, Alex, Arian, Ozma, and so on. We also explained about our current objective to recover Excalibur and how we'd found Arthur.

When we recounted that the king was alive, Gwenivere gasped. When we told her that he was trapped in Neverland, the muscles in her face tightened.

"Now we need to get to the Isle of Avalon before the Vicennalia Aurora," Daniel said, finishing our tale. "Excalibur is our only way of piercing the stone that holds Paige's memories."

"Paige used to be a Fairy Godmother," Blue reminded them. "Before turning into a brainless scarecrow, she was the only one who knew where our realm's genies were hidden. If the antagonists get that information first, it's game over."

Midway through our tale I had migrated to the window to stare out at the mist-covered Poppy fields. I could not sit still. Retelling our story was an in-your-face reminder of how much we had done and how much we still had left to do. There were so many elements working against us, particularly time, and so many unknown variables, including Alex and his run at claiming Excalibur.

"Crisa?"

I turned when Blue spoke my name. "Yeah?"

"What are you thinking about?"

"Just something I've been wondering for a while," I admitted. "Rampart reminded me of it when I was captured." I stepped away from the window and met the collective gaze of my friends. "Why were Alex and Mauvrey already going after Excalibur before Arian knew they needed it to free Paige's memories?"

"They must have been retrieving it for Rampart," SJ suggested.

"Yes, but *why*?" I urged. "Arian and the others are trying to overthrow our realm. They're hardly going to waste time and resources doing favors for villains in other realms unless they get something out of it. Mauvrey and Arian selected Alex for this task a long time ago. Rampart must have offered them something in return that has nothing to do with Paige or the genies."

"But what?" Ormé asked.

"I don't know, but it has to be important." I sighed and crossed my arms, wincing slightly from the pain of my injuries and the new, weird burn marks on my forearms. My friends had definitely noticed the marks but had been circumspect enough not to mention them until now.

"You need to go see Elaine," SJ finally commented upon seeing my grimace.

"She's still working on Jason," I replied.

"Then allow me to help you," Gwenivere said suddenly.

I was taken aback by her commanding voice. She hadn't said two words during our retelling—Morgan had been the one to direct the questions. I could understand why. Learning that your husband—long thought dead—was alive and trapped on a magical island was a lot to process.

"Girls . . ." Gwenivere looked to Ormé and the rest of the Brigade. "Take Daniel, Blue, and SJ to our guest rooms so they can rest. They must be exhausted. And prepare them something to eat. Crisanta, you and I are going to spend some quality time together."

Gwenivere's private workshop was located at the very top of one of the castle's towers. It was lovely. A green glass ceiling cast everything in viridescence. Countless shelves of herbs and plants—fresh, dried, and infused in oils—surrounded a workstation at the center.

Gesturing for me to sit on a cushioned windowsill, Gwenivere collected ingredients as I gazed out the window. I stretched my sore shoulders. One of the Gwenivere Brigade girls had offered to take my backpack to my guestroom while I went with the queen.

"I do not have magic like Morgan or Elaine," Gwenivere said as she worked. "But during Arthur's reign, Merlin taught me the power of potions. I learned to create all sorts of concoctions, from low-grade healing brews to poisons. He may have been the most powerful wizard in our realm, but only one of his abilities came from his magic—invisibility. The rest of his powers were based on his mastery of potions. He was arguably the greatest potionist in all the realms, with the exception of the Wizard of Oz and his son."

I rolled my eyes. "Yeah, we've met Julian."

"You don't like him?"

"I don't trust him," I replied. "I had my suspicions about Julian before, but Rampart verified my worst doubts when he was holding me prisoner in Camelot." I sighed. "Despite what I've come to learn about people—*and brothers*—I hoped that maybe Julian wasn't the scum I suspected. But finding Ozma and Dorothy's enchanted slipper in Rampart's dungeon totally confirmed it. Julian's been letting his sister rot in Camelot so he can rule Oz in her place."

"That is a serious accusation," Gwenivere commented as she searched a cabinet for ingredients. "But it wouldn't surprise me. Family members stabbing each other in the back in pursuit of a throne is hardly a new narrative. Mordred was Arthur's half-brother. Morgause is his aunt. It's a hard lesson to learn, but the people closest to you can betray you if you stand in the way of what they want."

"Rampart more or less said the same thing," I responded sadly. "I guess I was just hoping that people were better than that."

"I think they have the potential to be." Gwenivere began lightly pounding ingredients in a mortar dish at her workstation. "But that would require truly caring about someone else's well-being ahead of your own. That's a rare thing, Crisanta. You know, I love Arthur more than anything." She paused, her expression sorrowful. She'd been stoic since finding out about her husband, but I bet tons of emotion was boiling beneath the surface.

"So given the option," she continued, clearing her throat, "I would always put him first. Merlin was the same. He dedicated his entire life to serving Arthur and the realm to the best of his ability, no matter the personal cost. But loyalty like that is not commonplace. It is special."

Gwenivere took a copper blowtorch from a drawer and began smoking the ingredients in her mortar dish. "I think it's wonderful that you want to believe in people, but I advise you to be careful with such faith. Games of crowns and thrones are never-ending. And most people play dirty. Look at me. I consider myself kindhearted, and I believe in ruling with benevolence, fairness, and compassion. But I will stop at nothing to reclaim what was stolen from Arthur and our family.

"Since Rampart took the crown, I have been leading a rebellion from this castle. I established the Gwenivere Brigade to take the throne away from Rampart and restore it to me. We have countless followers throughout the land. We are organized and unyielding. And in the last few weeks, we have finally attained the numbers we need to attempt a full-scale assault on the citadel. When we enact our plan, do you really think I am going to concern myself with mercy? I might be related to a good number of people in Rampart's court, either by marriage or by blood, but I will not hesitate to bring down anyone who stands in my way. Enemies should be destroyed and villains should be killed. Any ruler who doesn't agree is foolish."

I was stunned. Her straight talk had the same chilling bluntness as Rampart's words to me as we journeyed to the Mercy Pit. And Blue had addressed the same topic this morning in reference to my brother. Were they right? Was it foolish to show mercy to villains? Was it foolish to choose faith in humanity over pragmatism?

Gwenivere extinguished her torch and picked up a flask filled with purple liquid. She poured it into the mortar. When the liquid made contact with the ingredients, a plume of smoke that smelled like nutmeg and cinnamon rose from the dish.

"Come." She gestured to me.

I went over to the workstation and eyed the fizzling black concoction. How could something that smelled like pumpkin pie look so terrifying?

Gwenivere placed a small washcloth in the dish. The washcloth took on the same black hue and steam started rising from it. Gwenivere wrung out the excess liquid and presented me with the washcloth.

"Wipe this across your injuries," she instructed.

I took the washcloth with the intention of starting with those weird burn marks I'd received after my trek through the Poppy field, but I discovered they were gone. My eyes widened in surprise. I was already confused about how the marks had appeared. Now I was more curious about why they'd vanished.

I began to wipe the washcloth over my skin wherever I saw scrapes and cuts. I cringed as the wounds began to sting then watched in amazement as every injury sewed itself closed until I was completely healed.

"Wow," I commented. "You're good."

I handed the washcloth back to Gwenivere. She raised her eyebrows. "You missed a spot." She signaled for me to turn and I felt her press the washcloth against my right shoulder blade. I must've had a large cut there, because the stinging was intense.

"All right, you're all finished," Gwenivere said as she put down the washcloth and wiped her hands on a clean towel. She offered another towel to me, but I'd already wiped my hands on my dress. I felt a tad embarrassed. I probably should've taken a more ladylike approach in the presence of a queen.

"Shall we return downstairs?" Gwenivere asked.

I nodded and followed her out of the workshop. We descended the spiral staircase of the tower in silence. The queen didn't speak again until we reached the main floor.

"After you and your friends reclaim Excalibur and use it to acquire those memories you are after, will you return the blade to Arthur?" she asked solemnly.

"That's our intention. You can bet the rightful king mentioned in the Great Lights Prophecy isn't Rampart. We would never let him have Excalibur."

"But right now, Rampart has Arthur," Gwenivere said bitterly.

"The antagonists who've been chasing us have him," I corrected. "Rampart wants to keep him alive in Neverland so Arthur can witness the moment that Rampart claims Excalibur. But I promise you that the only thing he'll witness is our victory. We will get Excalibur first, see our mission through, and then free Arthur. And once that's done—"

"My husband will still be trapped in Neverland," Gwenivere finished.

"We can take you to see him," I replied earnestly. "You can even have my Hole Tracker if you want, so you can visit him regularly."

She shook her head sorrowfully. "Make no mistake, I am eternally grateful that you and your friends have informed me that he still lives. The idea of seeing him again has made me happier than you can imagine. But the thought that he can never return here . . ."

The queen gazed at me with her mesmerizing eyes. They were both glassy from sadness and steely from determination. "I want to take back the throne because Rampart has done a great disservice to this land. Camelot needs a leader who can restore Arthur's vision for an honorable and prosperous realm. But passionate as I am about the endeavor, I am not the rightful ruler of this world. Arthur is. The idea of ruling in his place while he is sentenced to live out his days on an island of immortal pirates and children . . . it is very difficult to accept."

We turned and entered an enormous corridor lined with twenty-foot-tall suits of armor.

"Maybe there *is* a way he can return," I said slowly.

Gwenivere paused. "What do you mean?"

"Look, I'm not promising anything. But the Boar's Mouth said my quest wouldn't be complete until I brought back the lost king and he sat on the throne. Which means I have to trust there is a way that Arthur can return here without his mortal wound killing him."

This was the first time I had actually spoken this idea out loud, but I believed it was the truth. I didn't think the Boar's Mouth would give me a task that was impossible to achieve. The mystical statue thought I could bring Arthur back, so I had to have faith in the same thing.

"You're giving me hope, Crisanta," Gwenivere said steadily, eyeing me more like a threat than a friend. "That is a dangerous thing."

"So are explosives," I replied. "Both just need to be planted in the right place."

The queen sighed wistfully. "I wish we could consult with Merlin."

We passed under a stone arch and entered a hall decorated with intricate, handwoven tapestries. They were so fine they would've made my sewing teacher at Lady Agnue's reevaluate her life.

"Rampart said Merlin went missing a long time ago," I responded. "Do you know what happened to him?"

"I'm afraid not. A few months before Mordred killed—or *tried* to kill—Arthur, Merlin vanished. He was in love with a girl named Nyneve. She was his potions apprentice and many people think he ran off with her and left the realm. But I believe she did something to him. Arthur was like a son to Merlin; Merlin would never have left without saying something. And I never trusted Nyneve. She was half magic hunter on her mother's side. And with Merlin being a carrier of Pure Magic, goodness knows what she could have done to him when he let his guard down."

"So Rampart was telling the truth," I thought aloud as we arrived at a grand oak door. "Merlin's magic was *Pure* Magic."

"Indeed," Gwenivere replied. "An incredibly powerful gift and curse, as I'm sure you're well aware. A Fairy Godmother blessed him with a spark of power when he was young to thank him for saving her life from the Questor Beast. It fused to him and the rest is history. To this day, I still don't know how he managed to avoid being corrupted by the disease. But whatever the miracle that saved him, we were all grateful for it. Having him on our side was the key to Arthur achieving everything that he did."

I felt a flare of warmth in my heart like someone had just added kindling to the hope that earnestly burned there.

Merlin had evaded the curse of his Pure Magic Disease. It didn't turn him dark. With him and Liza that makes two. Which means maybe I really can do this.

I wasn't comparing myself to Merlin—the most famous wizard of all time—or Liza—our realm's all-knowing Author who'd had 150 years to learn to control her magic—but this improved my odds a little. And therefore it strengthened my resolve.

"Merlin's Pure Magic gave him psychic dreams that were often helpful in tumultuous times," Gwenivere continued. "With him gone, perhaps you can fill that void. Your Pure Magic must be very powerful for you to be immune to the Poppy fields. I have never seen anything like it. We will make good use of you."

A slight shiver of wariness went through my body. If there was one thing I didn't like, it was being controlled. With all the prophecies about me and my growing power, it was hard not to feel like people were always trying to use me. Arian, Rampart, Gwenivere—whether a friend or an enemy, they all had their own agendas. As our story progressed, I wondered if the players we met would continue to see me as a tool first and a person second.

"A lot of people seem to feel that way," I responded bluntly.

Gwenivere raised an eyebrow. "I intended no offense, dear. I only mean the timing of your arrival is ideal. Having you and your powerful protagonist friends here gives us an advantage. I must talk with Morgan and the senior members of the Gwenivere Brigade now." She touched the oak door in front of us. "I will speak with you tomorrow."

Hm. I guess I'm not invited to whatever meeting the queen is about to attend.

That insulted me a bit and reinforced the idea that my friends and I were just tools to be called upon when it was convenient for the people whose roof we happened to be under.

"Head down that hall and you'll find your way back to the study," the queen instructed. "One of the girls there can show you to your room, or to the kitchen if you'd like to have something to eat."

Now I was less insulted. After the day I'd had, I'd much rather have a snack than talk strategy.

"Thanks," I said. "I'll see you tomorrow."

"We shall have much to discuss by morning," Gwenivere replied. She turned the handle and pushed the door open just a crack so I could not see inside. She glanced over her shoulder. "Rest well, Crisanta Knight. Things are about to get very interesting."

The Hero's Standard

I walked down the hall to find Mindy in the study, who then showed me to the kitchen. Once there I chowed down on a cold mutton leg with a glass of milk, grateful for the food and that my escort had left me alone to enjoy it.

I'd gotten up early and it was getting late, but I still wasn't ready to go to sleep—the curse of an active mind mingled with my dread of nightmares. In addition, Mindy had told me that Jason was still in the healing room and would probably be there for another hour or so. I wasn't about to go to bed without knowing for sure that he was all right. So, to kill some time after I finished my snack, I explored the castle.

Eventually I found the library. Given my history of getting attacked in libraries—Century City, the Forbidden Forest, my castle in Midveil—I probably should've been less comfortable in such a place. But this room was the most peaceful setting I had come across in a while. The fireplace roared with cozy flames. The dark-green velvet couches looked plush and inviting. Warm walnut shelves held books with beautiful, shimmering bindings. The decorative artwork in the room depicted tranquil landscapes. I was content to stay here for a while.

After browsing through the shelves, I selected a book about Avalon with a lovely silver cover and one called *Beasts of the Land*, which was ruby red with a glittery spine. I nestled onto a couch to peruse them both, starting with the ruby one. When I flipped it open, however, I gasped and almost dropped it. An inscription inside the front cover read,

Dear Crisanta Knight,
    This book contains some of the lesser-known details about the beasts in our land. I recommend the section on the Questor Beast. Might help later on.
—Merlin

My eyes nearly bugged out of my head.
What the frack?
Merlin had Pure Magic, which meant he could see the future just like Liza and me. This note implied that—at some point—years ago before he disappeared, he'd foreseen me being in Gwenivere's castle and had planted this book for me to find.
But why did he care? Who was I to him?
I sped to the section on the Questor Beast. There were plenty of illustrations of different nightmarish animals in the book, but when I found the monster I was looking for I was certain that it was the most fearsome of them all.

My arm hairs stood on end as I read about the oddity known as the Questor Beast—a creature that dwelled in the Passage Perelous, which my friends and I would have to go through to reach the Isle of Avalon. When we were in Neverland, Dorothy described the monster as frightening and gruesome. But seeing the various renderings in this book paired with the description of the monster's abilities put a face to the wickedness and gave fear a context.

The creature was massive. It had the body and thick legs of a dragon but from the shoulders sprouted five snake-like necks. Each neck bore the head of a leopard. A golden, spotted coat covered the monster's skin. A long, thin tail protruded from its backside, ending in a rounded, spiked tip like a mace.

The Questor Beast had great strength and speed, and given enough time it could grow back its heads if they were chopped off. In addition, it could spit acid, produce fog to camouflage itself, and kill anything with its poisonous teeth and claws. A single bite or scratch was deadly.

As I read on, I learned that the Questor Beast was also all-but-impossible to destroy. Over the years, many former Knights of the Round Table had dedicated themselves to hunting it. Some had even succeeded. But there was a difference between killing the creature and destroying it. Unless it was properly slain, the monster would disappear and reform somewhere else in the Passage Perelous.

The only way to stop it permanently was by piercing the Questor Beast through the heart, which was located under the chin of its center head. But even this had a catch. According to the book, the Questor Beast would only be forever destroyed if it were "stabbed through the heart by someone with the death blood of their one true love on their hands."

Yikes. I hoped we would not encounter that thing on our way to Avalon. Unfortunately, Merlin's note left me with a queasy feeling that it was inevitable.

As I flipped through the book, each passage and picture relating to the Questor Beast was more awful than the last. When I turned to the page that described how the monster could lock onto the fear of its prey and track them like a possessed hound, I shut the volume. That was more than enough horror for one day.

I tossed the copy aside and picked up the other text I'd plucked from the shelf. Skimming through the table of contents, the chapter on the Lady of the Lake caught my eye and I turned to the corresponding section. As I read, I remembered some of the information that Arthur had shared with us back in Neverland.

The Isle of Avalon was home to all kinds of enchanted obstacles. The Lady of the Lake—the guardian of Avalon—was one of them. We had to show her respect and do *exactly* as she asked. If we deviated even a little from her instruction, we would die. If the spirits of her lake did not deem us worthy, we would die. And if we didn't pass any of the tests awaiting us on the isle, we would also die. Basically, there was a high probability that we would die.

What else is new?

I passed through the pages until I saw an entry about another familiar topic—the Excalibur Decision.

If we managed to reach Excalibur, whoever claimed the sword (me, hopefully) would need to sacrifice a decision. What that meant was there would come a time in my future when I would be faced with a life-defining choice and I would not choose wisely. That was the cost of claiming the great power of Excalibur—relinquishing some part of my fate to a negative consequence of my own design.

I had no way of knowing what this decision would be, nor when it would occur. I only knew that when I made the bad choice, the Lady of the Lake would appear before me to confirm that I had finally paid the price.

Staring at her rendering in the book—a pale-blue ghostly woman with raven eyes and dark flowing hair—I shivered at the thought.

I'd had to pay some hefty prices on this journey. Heck, just a few hours ago the Boar's Mouth had sucked out a piece of my soul. But the idea of surrendering a decision to poor judgment made me more uneasy still. If there was one thing I valued, it was the ability to make my own choices. Choices were what defined us and gave us power over our destiny. To have to sacrifice one was a hard cost.

Sigh. Sometimes being the lead protagonist on an adventure can really suck.

I read for a bit longer until my eyes started to droop. I knew I needed sleep, even if that meant having bad dreams. Looking at the clock on the wall, I confirmed it had been over an hour since I'd spoken with Mindy. I hoped Jason was all done being healed.

My friends and I had been invited to stay in the guest rooms on the fourth floor. Mine was to be the fifth door down the hall while Jason's was the first. Mindy said he would be taken there once Elaine finished with him. After I put away the library books, that's where I headed.

When I arrived at Jason's room I knocked on the door. When there was no response, I slowly pushed it open.

"Jason?" I whispered.

I peeked into the room and spotted him propped upright with pillows in a dark blue canopy bed. The bedframe was gold and reflected the glow of the blazing fireplace. His chest was wrapped in a thick bandage. The jacket he'd been wearing at the party hung on a coatrack beside his bed. When he saw me he held a finger to his lips and pointed across the room. Blue was fast asleep on a navy velvet couch, her face smushed into the armrest at an odd angle.

Jason waved me over to the bed, so I shut the door quietly and went to him.

"I didn't want to wake her," Jason whispered, gesturing to Blue. "After Elaine brought me here, I told Blue a dozen times that I was healed, but she refused to leave. She passed out ten minutes ago."

"*Are* you healed?" I asked quietly.

"Elaine did a great job. She said I need to rest, but I'll be on my feet by morning." He patted the bed. "You wanna sit? I'd offer you the couch but . . ." His eyes drifted to Blue again.

I climbed onto the bed next to him, scooching against the pillows. We stared companionably at the fire.

"How are *you* doing?" he asked after a minute.

I was so surprised by the question I let out a slight laugh. "I'm doing great. You?"

"Fantastic," he replied with a smile. Then after a beat his smile faded and a troubled look crossed his face. "Crisa . . ." he began. "Your magic is getting stronger. Isn't it?"

I pivoted my body to face him. "Yeah," I responded slowly. "It is. Why do you ask?"

"I don't know," he said slowly. "I've just been thinking. I've seen you do some amazing things lately. You literally drained the life energy from a giant this morning. It just makes me wonder . . . If I'm going to die like your vision foresaw, do you think there's a chance you can bring me back? Your power is *life* after all, right? There could be endless applications."

I let out a deep breath. "Honestly, I've been thinking the same thing. I just didn't want to say anything until I knew for sure. Eventually my powers might grow strong enough to restore life to a person. But we don't know when that vision of you dying will come to pass. There's a difference between it occurring next week or next year. Yes, I took the life from that giant this morning. But that was an accident. My magic just reacted, like it did when

I crossed the Poppy field. I still don't know how to consciously make it that strong and completely control it. And if I'm being reasonable, I don't know if I'll be able to figure it out in time."

Jason looked at me somberly. The expression stirred empathy inside me and also an additional layer of drive that I'd been too timid to acknowledge until now.

"But then . . . I've never been known to be particularly reasonable, have I?"

Jason's expression shifted. I knew I was playing with fire, but I didn't care. Jason was one of my best friends and despite my dark moments, I was a girl rooted in hope, not cynicism. Every part of me and my story was embedded in the idea that the things we wanted most in life might be the hardest to get, but they were worth fighting for. So no matter the odds or the toll, I would not stop fighting for the win, nor would I ever stop believing that the win was possible. I had to believe that. There was no life to live if I didn't.

I sat up straighter and looked Jason straight in the eyes.

"When we were in Neverland, I told you that I believed we could save you," I said. "My magic might be able to do that. So I don't care about the odds against us. I don't care how much time or power it takes. I'm going to make myself strong enough. I will learn to control my magic so that when you sacrifice yourself to protect Blue like I've foreseen, I will be there to resurrect you. Nothing in this world—or any other—can stop me."

Jason didn't say anything; he just stared at me.

"You believe me, don't you?" I asked.

"I do," he responded. "And I trust you, Crisa, I just . . . I worry about another deadline."

"What's that?"

"The Vicennalia Aurora. When Julian and Eva told us about the Four Waters of Paradise, I know we were all thinking the same thing. Those waters can be your salvation. If we recover them on Avalon when we're looking for Excalibur, you could use them to cure your Pure Magic Disease the same way she did during the event."

"Yeah," I admitted. "I was counting on it."

"Are you sure that's what you want?"

His question confused me. "Why wouldn't it be? Liza's prophecy says I'm either meant to be responsible for stopping the antagonists or granting them success. The outcome has to be linked to whether my magic turns me dark or not. If I were cured of Pure Magic Disease, I would never have to worry about that again."

"Yes, but curing you would mean that your magic would become normal; it would lose its purity, and as a result a lot of its power."

"I know," I said. "And I know that power has helped us a lot recently. But it still might be too much of a gamble to keep. Liza has been training me to control my magic, but the fact remains that she, and apparently Merlin, are the only known carriers of Pure Magic Disease who didn't turn dark. The idea that I can defy the odds too has been fueling me forward up 'til now, but if I'm offered an out, wouldn't it be more sensible for me to take it?"

"You've never been known to be particularly sensible either, Crisa," Jason replied. "What does your heart tell you?"

"My heart." I laughed bitterly. "My heart tells me that if I continue down this path, I might not have a heart to worry about anymore. It'll turn dark and be worse than useless—it'll be dangerous." I leaned back against the headboard. "You want to know something that I haven't admitted to anyone? I really like my magic. I like feeling powerful, and I'm grateful for all the things I've been able to do and all the people I've been able to help. But I'm scared. I don't want to turn dark. And after today with that giant, I'm worried that if I stay on this road I won't be able to stop."

"Crisa, I can't tell you what to do when it comes to deciding whether or not to keep your Pure Magic if we find the waters on Avalon," Jason said. "From a selfish point of view, I hope you decide not to take the cure when the Vicennalia Aurora hits. You probably won't have the strength to bring me back if my death comes after you're cured."

Hmm. I hadn't thought about that.

The Vicennalia Aurora was the only day when the Four Waters

of Paradise could work because the day's magic fluctuations made carriers of magic vulnerable. If Jason's death happened afterward and I'd already been cured, my promise to save him would fall flat. Normal magic wouldn't be able to revive him; I hadn't even proven that Pure Magic could.

"That aside," Jason continued. "I want what's best for *you*, and as it happens, I also think that means saving your Pure Magic. Your turning dark may play a key role in the antagonists' triumph, but I believe you using your magic for good is what will lead to their demise. You've been given an important gift. You can do incredible things. That giant of Geene is just one example."

"How can you call that incredible?" I responded. "Don't you think it was wrong of me to suck the life from another living creature? To kill that giant in cold blood?"

"No. I don't," Jason said plainly.

He paused. The firelight reflected in his bright blue eyes. "Crisa," he said. "How much do you know about Lord Channing's?"

His question came as a surprise.

"Um, I know all about Twenty-Three Skidd since I love the sport and made it onto one of your school's teams this semester," I said. "You've mentioned some of your classes over the years and I know students can leave school periodically for quests. But that's about all I've got. I really don't know that much about your day-to-day."

"That's probably for the best," Jason responded.

"How do you mean?"

"There's a lot about Lord Channing's that you don't know, Crisa," Jason said. "Aside from the fact that our school doesn't have an In and Out Spell protecting it like yours does, there's a reason why Lady Agnue's students are never invited to our campus except for the Twenty-Three Skidd finals matches in the spring. Just like all of your students have to take Damsel in Distress classes, we have requirements of our own—ones that may not reflect the personalities of every student, but that are mandatory for all heroes and princes nonetheless."

The serious tone of Jason's voice told me that he was about to divulge something important. I sat uncharacteristically still and listened quietly.

"At Lord Channing's, we're taught the importance of vanquishing enemies," Jason said. "That's why we're allowed to go on quests. In fact, it's mandatory we go on at least two before we graduate because there are two tests we need to pass during our junior and senior years. They're called Valiancy Tests. The first requires that we slay a monster. The second . . . well, we have to kill an antagonist."

"You mean to tell me that the students at your school can't graduate until they've *killed* somebody?"

"Not just somebody," Jason replied earnestly. "A bad guy. When you're a hero, you have to be able to stand up to a villain and have the courage and strength to end them. That's what's expected of us. I'm not saying it's right. I'm just saying that it's a part of our archetype. While princesses are expected to show justice in the form of mercy, we're expected to exhibit justice in the form of decisive, deadly action."

He took a deep breath. "Didn't you ever wonder why Daniel and I weren't punished for ditching school last semester? You, Blue, and SJ were given detention for an eternity. We got a slap on the wrist. Why do you think we didn't get reprimanded more severely?"

I stared at him.

"Crisa, we didn't get into trouble because the quests counted toward our class credit. Daniel and I each passed our first Valiancy Test last semester when we went looking for the Author. I know you're the one who stabbed it, but Daniel took credit for slaying that Magistrake when the two of you were alone in Alderon. And he let me take credit for slaying the log monster we encountered in the Forbidden Forest. But today, I officially passed my *second* Valiancy Test. All that minutia we got into today about past battles and self-defense aside, there is no mistaking what I did in the Mercy Pit. I struck with the intention to kill. Ending Gaheris was a choice and that makes it official. I'm a hero, by Lord Channing's standards anyway."

Jason's expression was hard to read. He didn't seem upset or remorseful, but he wasn't happy either. He spoke everything like it was simply fact.

I felt stunned, a little sad, and partially confused. I understood that being able to slay a monster or a bad guy was traditionally as much a part of being a hero as being a damsel was a part of being a princess. I just couldn't believe that it was a mandatory requirement. I had been beating myself up about what I'd accidentally done to that giant in the Canyon of Geene, but Jason, Daniel, Chance Darling—and every hero and prince I knew— was meant to go out into the world and intentionally eliminate antagonists.

"Has Daniel killed anyone?" I asked, surprised by how much I cared about the answer.

Jason shook his head. "I stand by what I said in the forest today. If you don't know for a fact that someone you've fought is dead, and if you never struck out against them with the intention to kill, then you're in the clear. Daniel is an amazing swordfighter—the best I've seen. It's because of that skill, and my own, that we've been able to avoid passing the second Valiancy Test until now. Every time we've been attacked by antagonists, we've fought to defeat them by wounding or knocking them out. Daniel hasn't officially crossed that line yet. Not like I did today."

I paused for a beat.

"That's a lot to process, Jason."

"The Valiancy Tests, or me killing someone?"

"Both, I guess. How do you feel after killing Gaheris? I mean, ever since killing the giant I've been racked with moral conflict."

"Honestly," Jason said, "I hope you don't think less of me for it, but I feel fine. Blue saved my life in the Mercy Pit. She was a third of Gaheris's size and she threw herself at him to protect me. The guy would have killed us both if we'd hesitated, so I killed him first. It's that simple, and I'm glad I did it. It's not like I was going to let the girl who just sacrificed her safety for mine get stabbed in an arena." He looked at the blank expression on my face. "You're disappointed, aren't you?"

"I'm not," I said, meaning it. "It's just a big concept to wrap my head around. I don't judge you for what happened today. You did what you had to do and I respect that. It was the right decision."

"You made the right decision today too," he said seriously. "You defending SJ by killing that giant is no different than me defending Blue by killing Gaheris. We care about them, so there was nothing more important than protecting them in that moment, no matter the cost. You may only have three days left to decide whether or not to cure your Pure Magic Disease, Crisa. But when the Vicennalia Aurora hits, if we've found the Four Waters of Paradise and you have to face that choice, I hope you take this into consideration and trust your instincts like you did in the Canyon of Geene."

There was a knock at the door and Daniel poked his head in. He noticed Blue, then Jason and me, and quietly walked over to join us, coming to stand next to me by the bed.

"Hey, man," he said to Jason. "You doing okay?"

"Fine," Jason responded. He tilted his chin toward me. "I just told Crisa about the Valiancy Tests."

Daniel's eyebrows shot up. "Dude, I don't think we're supposed to talk to anyone outside our school about those." He looked at me. "No offense."

"None taken," I replied. I decided to give Daniel and Jason some time to themselves. They were friends and roommates too; they deserved a minute to hang out on their own. I touched Jason on the arm and slid off the bed. "I think I'm going to turn in for the night. I'll see you guys in the morning." I gave Daniel a nod and glanced over at Blue. "If she starts snoring, just prop a pillow under her head. SJ and I do it all the time." I left and made my way down the hall to the fifth door, which Mindy said was for me.

My room was similar to Jason's. There was a roaring fireplace, candelabras, fancy paintings, and a large bed. Unlike Jason's bed, dressed in dark blue and constructed of gold, mine was light pink with a silver frame. My room also had an intricate, old-fashioned mural painted on the ceiling abundant in cherubs, lyres, and clouds.

My backpack was on the silver nightstand beside my bed,

delivered here by a Gwenivere Brigade girl earlier. I kicked off my boots. There was a nightgown folded on the comforter—probably a loaner from one of the GB girls as well. I changed into it and flopped on the bed, thinking about my conversation with Jason and comparing the hero's standard for justice against the princess's.

I couldn't name a single princess who had ever killed anyone. It was just not our way. But heroes could kill; in fact, they frequently did. They slayed villains. They stopped the bad guy and they were praised for it. Meanwhile, princesses were praised for showing mercy. Jason was right—that was our equivalent of triumphing over evil.

Did that make princesses stronger than heroes or weaker I wondered. And which was right—ending an antagonist before they could do harm to anyone else, or showing mercy and waiting for a more judicial form of trial and punishment?

The truth was, I didn't know. I had never really thought about it. Part of me, the princess side I supposed, believed that killing others, even if they deserved it, was wrong. I should be better than that. At the same time, I was a hero. Which made me consider that maybe killing someone who deserved it wasn't evil, as Jason had suggested. Maybe it was just and wise.

Blue had been correct in Neverland this morning. If I'd learned anything about bad guys it was that they didn't stay down for long. Villains would always be looking for a way to wreak more havoc. So appeasing a supposedly higher sense of morality by leaving them alive could be a foolish, selfish choice if it meant potentially exposing innocents to more of their wickedness.

I stared at the ceiling. The angels painted there made goodness look so easy, so simple. I was beginning to realize that real life was not like that. I didn't know why killing was okay for heroes but not for princesses. And I didn't know which I saw as greater justice or goodness. Both came with a set of caveats. Moreover, as an aspiring hero-princess, I wasn't sure which path best suited the type of character I wanted to be.

It looked like the hero way was a better option given the circumstances, but with my Pure Magic making me susceptible to darkness, I had to consider what that might do to me; what embracing the hero's standard over the princess's standard might turn me into.

And I really had to ask myself: *What was goodness?*

My backpack started buzzing. I dug inside and pulled out my Mark Two. I was getting a call. I hoped it was Dorothy, or Peter, or even Arthur himself calling to tell us that he had escaped Arian's men and was safe. But it was most likely Liza calling to check in on me. I hadn't spoken to my magic mentor since we were in Neverland. I wasn't looking forward to telling her about crossing the Malice Line in the Canyon of Geene.

I flipped open the compact.

"I thought it might be you," I said to Liza's reflection.

Our realm's mysterious Author met my eyes through the looking glass of the Mark Two. Her dark curly hair took up much of the mirror and, as always, her expression was a combination of stern, worried, kindly, and slightly judgmental.

"You seem tired," Liza said.

"It's been an exhausting twenty-four hours," I replied.

"How many people tried to kill you today?"

"I honestly lost count."

I proceeded to give Liza a recap of my story. I skipped over what had happened in the Canyon of Geene at first but felt guilty and circled back to recount the incident at the end.

"It just happened," I confessed. "One minute I was staring into the giant's open mouth and then everything turned into white noise and my magic sucked the life from him."

"Crisa! How could you?" Liza reprimanded.

"I'm sorry!" My emotions rose up. I couldn't help it. Although my talk with Jason had given me a new perspective on the morality of taking a life, and I'd tried to remain calm after the incident to reassure my friends, in that moment the reality that I had used my magic to kill someone washed over me and I felt awful about it. Unlike the morality of taking a life, the Malice Line had no gray area. Crossing it was bad for my Pure Magic, and Liza had repeatedly warned me about the dangers of doing so.

"Crisa, how am I supposed to help you beat this disease if you

flagrantly disregard the tools I give you to keep a handle on it?"
Liza exclaimed.

"Well, your tools wouldn't matter if I was dead, Liza," I replied,
trying (but failing) to hold back my frustration. "Which is what
would have happened if my magic hadn't stepped in."

I took a deep breath. "Look, I *am* sorry. But this once, can you
not harass me for making a mistake? I didn't enjoy taking that
life. And I feel bad enough about it as it is. So can you please just
. . . I don't know, *be there for me*?"

Liza had been helping me to develop and control my magical
abilities for several months. She was my teacher, my mentor, and
my guide, but I'd never fully seen her as a friend. She was always
so hard on me. And with good reason. She was trying to keep
me from turning evil, and that was a heavy responsibility. But as
the only person I knew with Pure Magic who might understand
what I was going through, sometimes I wished for a little more
empathy.

"Crisa." Liza's tone was softer. "Believe it or not, I am trying to
be there for you. I know I may not come across as compassionate,
but I really do care about your well-being. And not just because
your fate is tied to the realm, but because of you as a person.

"I have spent most of my life alone because of my Pure Magic
and the Author role that my sister saddled me with, so I don't
have great social skills. But I *am* very fond of you. I understand
your fear, I worry about your future, and I don't want you to
suffer. Don't mistake my nagging for lack of support or empathy.
I am only trying to help you avoid a terrible destiny."

Liza knew most of my secrets. And because of her visions of
the future, she probably knew more about me than I wanted her
to. But this was the first time I think I'd ever felt truly seen by her.

"I didn't know you felt that way," I said. "I didn't know we
were friends."

"Honestly, I think of you more like a daughter than a friend,"
Liza admitted. "I am protective of you because you are what I
imagine a child of mine would be like—magical, yes, but also
strong-willed, curious, and defiant. Which means maybe it is a
good thing, for the realm's sake, that I never had children."

"Um. Thanks?"

"Yes, well, now you know," Liza said abruptly, getting back to business. She really didn't have strong social skills. "We need to speak about more pressing matters. Did you say that your magic did not work in the Canyon of Geene?"

"Yeah, but I know the whole deal with Jacobee stone now. The only other weird thing was that when I tried to bring my wand to life in the form of a shield that didn't work either."

"No, I suspect not," Liza said. "Fairy Godmother wands are supposed to be conductors of magic, but since yours is already enchanted to specifically change into different weapons, I had a feeling that any other magical possession may be overridden."

"That's too bad."

"Not entirely," Liza countered. "It means that anyone else with magic cannot affect your wand either. Take that Morgause woman you mentioned. If your wand won't conduct other magic, then that means she cannot use her levitation powers on it either."

I perked up at that. At least there was one advantage.

"On a less positive note," Liza continued.

Oh, boy. I know that tone. That's Liza's I'm-about-to-give-you-bad-news-about-your-magic voice.

"I think it's time I was honest with you about something. Do you remember when I explained how when you have Magic Exhaustion you are not completely tapped out of magic? It is like any other form of exhaustion—your strength doesn't disappear, it is just extremely depleted. Therefore, it prevents you from doing anything of value except, in your case, getting your wand to change forms, which requires only the tiniest bit of magic."

"I remember."

"Well . . . that was not the absolute truth," Liza admitted. "Pure Magic is very powerful, Crisa, for some people more than others. I didn't want to bring this up until I saw how your powers developed. But based on recent events, I think you need to know about Magic Instinct."

Should I be taking notes? I feel like I should be taking notes.

"I want you to think of your magic like a virus in a symbiotic relationship with you, its host. The magic wants to corrupt you;

it wants to eventually overpower your will so it can exist at its full potential, in its pure self. By keeping a handle on it, you push back so that you and the magic can coexist. *But*, while your magic does want to overcome you, it needs you to survive. If you died, it would no longer have a host. And although magic can't be killed or destroyed—it can only change forms or change hands—when magic empties from a dead host to a new one there is no guarantee that the new host will bond with the power in the same way making it pure again. If that bond does not occur, which it hardly ever does, then the virus will die."

"Uh-huh," I said slowly. "Sooo you're saying my magic wants to protect me so it can corrupt me?"

"Precisely," Lisa responded. "Which is why when life *literally* hangs in the balance, a Pure Magic carrier can briefly overcome Magic Exhaustion. If the host is strong enough, the magic can come to his or her defense despite its state of depletion. Like how someone in mortal danger might still find the strength to run and fight even if they've been beaten to the very brink."

Like Bruce Willis in those Die Hard movies that Blue loves.

Suddenly a memory clicked into place. I remembered the day that Alex and Mauvrey led the commons rebellion attack on our castle in Midveil. I had exhausted my magic and shouldn't have been able to use my abilities. But when I was trapped in the burning castle and about to suffocate, I'd unleashed a small burst of power so I could escape.

In the aftermath, I'd wondered how that was possible. Now I knew: Magic Instinct.

"Liza, this would have been nice to know earlier," I said. "I'm constantly in peril. Being able to do this gives me a fallback if I'm ever without another means to save myself."

"Well, that's exactly why I didn't tell you about Magic Instinct." Liza sighed. "This is not another tool in your arsenal, Crisa. You don't control Magic Instinct, your Pure Magic does. The phenomenon only occurs when your Pure Magic detects that its host is at the doors of death, and it can happen whether you're magically exhausted or fully charged. Magic Instinct is what kicked in today when you faced the giant in the Canyon of Geene. I didn't want to overload you with information before, but Magic Instinct is also what helps you counteract the effects of the Poppies. Think about it. In any of the instances when you encountered Poppies, were you actively trying to channel your powers, or did they just come to your aid?"

"I—I didn't really think about it . . ." I cut myself off as a lump of sadness and fear stuck in my throat.

"Crisa, it's simple," Liza continued. "While Magic Instinct is designed to save you and keep you alive, it also corrupts you. It is the result of Pure Magic interceding on your behalf and filling the gap when your controlled magic falls short. However, if you ever face life-threatening trouble while you're suffering Magic Exhaustion, this instinct can be your salvation. Additionally, I believe you are getting strong enough now that you can call on it yourself. You don't have to wait for it to step in. If you actively choose to surrender control and let go to your emotions in moments of peril, you could potentially compel Magic Instinct to give you power when you are depleted in more situations."

"But isn't that *the opposite* of what you've been training me to do?" I argued.

"It is," Liza said. "Hence my warning to not actively pursue the use of Magic Instinct as a fallback option unless absolutely necessary."

I leaned against the headboard. I was less scared and sad now. I was actually a bit angry.

"Liza, I kind of wish you hadn't told me this. In the past you've given me instructions for things to completely avoid. This feels like you've given me the world's most delicious poisoned cookie. It's like, 'Oh, here's something that could save your life, but don't use it because it's super bad for you.' Why tell me now?"

"Because you deserve to know the whole truth about what your magic can do," Liza said. "Based on what I've foreseen, you may need this information soon. And while I don't want you to relinquish control to your Pure Magic, I want you to be dead even less. Knowing about this option may save you."

Liza shook her head and I couldn't tell if she was disappointed in me or herself. "You're growing very powerful, Crisa. You need to understand how your actions affect you and have a full grasp of what you're working with. You've always been a person driven to search for answers, despite the cost. Well, now you have them. And if you expect to grow into a strong, mature adult, you need to discover how to handle those realities for yourself. Your situation is tricky, but there comes a time when every girl needs to learn to control her own power."

All of a sudden my compact started vibrating again. "What's happening?" I asked.

"You're getting another call," Liza responded.

"Oh. I guess I should go then. It could be Peter or Dorothy."

"Very well. I will just leave you with one last instruction before I go."

"Let me guess. Try and stay out of trouble?" I said in jest, as that was what she usually told me.

"Not this time," Liza responded with a small smile. "I know trouble pursues you like a moth does a flame. I just want to say, take care of yourself, Crisa. I'm rooting for you."

With that, Liza's image vanished from the looking glass. The words "Accept New Call?" appeared in the center of the glowing mirror. Since the Mark Two was voice activated, I figured that was probably the way to respond.

"Um, call accepted?" I said.

The compact stopped vibrating and my brother's face filled the mirror. The moment I saw Alex, I involuntarily clutched the compact more tightly.

"You made it out of the citadel," he commented.

"You're a major jerk," I retorted. "See, I can state the obvious too."

"I didn't call to argue, Crisa. I just thought I would warn you that I passed the Boar's Mouth test. We're coming after Excalibur, which means you and your friends need to watch your backs. Arian doesn't need you alive as a spare anymore."

"That's not much of a warning, Alex. We've been forced to watch our backs since the first time Arian tried to kill us."

My hold on the compact grew tighter still; I wondered if the whole thing might shatter in my fist.

"I'm not talking about Arian," Alex said. "When you escaped the citadel, Rampart sent a legion of knights after you. And now he's spread word via Mark Twos to all off his main contacts in the realm, specifically the kingdoms that intersect the Passage Perelous, that you and your friends are headed to Avalon. Powerful families and common magic hunters alike are aware of you and where you're going, and they have the promise of your Pure Magic and a sizable reward from Rampart if they kill you and take it."

"Oh good," I said sarcastically. "And I thought getting Excalibur was going to be easy." I narrowed my eyes and sharpened my tone. "Alex, we talked about this. Save your warnings. I don't need them like I don't need you. But to make it even, I'll give you a warning of my own. You, Mauvrey, and Arian better watch *your* backs. Because my friends and I are walking away with that sword."

"You won't succeed," Alex said bluntly. "And when the time comes, I advise you to get out of the way. While I won't hesitate to take down any of your friends, I'd prefer to protect you from Arian if I can. He and Mauvrey don't need you alive anymore, Crisa . . ." His expression wavered. "But I still do."

Hearing the undeniable note of caring in Alex's voice caused my annoyance to boil over. Gray areas were insufferable and now they seemed to be everywhere—my Magic Instinct, the morality of taking a life, my relationship with Alex. While the former two on that list were likely going to plague me for a while, I would nip the latter in the bud right now.

"Alex, you're an antagonist. You don't need me alive. Why should you care about your little sister? My friends and I are not afraid of you or Arian or Mauvrey, so bring on the threat. Furthermore, stop calling me. Unlike you, who can't seem to pick a side, I've chosen mine. And no one is going to keep me from defending it."

"Crisa—"

"Good night!"

I snapped the Mark Two shut. Immediately, the compact started buzzing again. Filled with ire, I impulsively chucked the compact across the room. It sailed straight into the fire where it could burn—just like Alex would burn if he ever tried to hurt me or my friends again.

CHAPTER 12

Motivation

atalie Poole.

My dream zoomed in on the maple-haired girl as she leaned against the railing of a balcony overlooking a courtyard full of people. Some were carrying backpacks. Others sat at tables in the shade of a lovely pergola. A few chatted away by a fountain in the center of the courtyard, which encircled a lone statue of a man holding up a scroll. It was simple, but it had a powerful presence.

Opposite Natalie's balcony was another just as grand. There were several balconies protruding from the building overlooking the courtyard. The structure was modeled in the shape of a U. Immense iron lanterns with gold colored glass hung from majestic archways on the lowest level of each side. The regal setting reminded me of Lady Agnue's.

Over the years I'd dreamed about Natalie more than anyone else. She was a protagonist on Earth whom our antagonists were trying to destroy. They wanted to break her spirit because she had the potential to open the Eternity Gate, a legendary entrance that connected all the realms to a powerful land outside of time called Eternity. According to myth, when a world's dark magic (dark energy) outweighed its good magic (good energy), the Eternity Gate would open. If this happened, normal magic would shut down across every realm while Eternity's protectors examined the offending world. This included the magic of In and Out Spells (like the one around Alderon) and the magic of Fairy Godmothers.

That was why the antagonists were set on destroying Natalie. Acquiring Paige's memories to learn the location of Book's genies was only part of their plan. Natalie Poole and the Eternity Gate had always been the other main components.

Natalie's prophecy alluded that she would be primed to open the Eternity Gate by her twenty-first birthday. However, just like my friends and I intended to foil the antagonists' genie efforts, we fully intended to stop the Eternity Gate from opening and save Natalie Poole.

The Book to Earth time difference put us at a disadvantage. She was a child now, but that wouldn't last long. It would only be about eight months in Book before she turned twenty-one. Also working against us was that I didn't know exactly where she was on Earth or how to reach her. That was why I was trying to connect with her and warn her in an unconventional way. With a lot of training, carriers of Pure Magic could communicate through dreams with the people they often dreamed about. Liza did it with me periodically. Since I dreamed about Natalie so much, the idea was for me to achieve the same thing.

It was risky business trying to push myself to do this. Reaching someone through their dreams took a lot of energy even for experienced magic wielders like Liza. So I had to work to enhance the strength of my magic without allowing it to become stronger than me. But for now, reaching out in a dream was my best bet for warning Natalie of what was coming. I only hoped I would get powerful enough to do it before it was too late.

As I watched Natalie observe the courtyard below—a rare expression of contentment on her face—I knew putting myself at risk to save her was the right decision. Like so many sacrifices my friends and I had already made for the sake of protecting our realm and others, it was a price that needed to be paid. And I was the only one able to pay it.

Natalie appeared about twenty in this vision. It was the oldest I'd ever seen her. The vibrant strands of her maple hair were pulled back in a bun. A tattered backpack was draped over her shoulders.

"Saying one last goodbye?"

Natalie turned at the sound of the familiar voice. Ryan Jackson—the boy I knew was destined to be her One True Love—

came out on the balcony. He wore a navy t-shirt that complemented his blue-gray eyes.

"We don't leave for a week," Natalie replied as he stood beside her and looked down. "I'll probably eat my lunch up here at least three more times before we go."

"By 'eat your lunch' do you mean sketch the people down there while some random squirrel makes off with your salad?" Ryan retorted.

"Don't make fun," Natalie said, swatting at him playfully. "That squirrel was creepy. He looked like he could eat *me*. So if he wanted my Cobb salad, then . . ." Natalie stopped talking as something across the courtyard caught her attention.

"Nat, what's wrong?" Ryan asked, trying to see what she was looking at.

"That girl . . ." Natalie spoke like she was in a trance. *"I know that girl."*

My dream perspective followed Natalie's line of sight to the balcony on the other side of the courtyard. Standing at the railing was me. *Dream me.* And dream Daniel. They saw Natalie and Ryan just as the pair saw them. They stared at each other from across the distance and all the sounds of the busy courtyard faded away.

The scene shifted.

Rampart and Arian were in the Knights' Room of Camelot's citadel castle. Arian rapped his fingers on the Round Table in frustration. "You said you kept Ozma's crown in your study, Rampart."

"I said that as a test, Arian," Rampart replied. "I had a feeling you might try and take it before fulfilling your end of the bargain."

"Rampart, I am going to live up to my end of the bargain. Alex is going to retrieve Excalibur, I'll use it to access Paige's mind from Glinda's memory stone and find out where the genies are, and then you can do whatever you want with the blasted sword."

"That all sounds fine in theory, Arian," Rampart countered. "But as Ozma's crown is my only bargaining chip, you'll excuse me if I want to keep its location hidden."

The scene started to fade. However, as it did, my perspective shifted to the fireplace at the rear of the Knights' Room and zoomed in on the gold florets on the mantle. A bright flash of a thin gold crown in someone's hand suddenly consumed my vision. Then I was somewhere else.

I faced a great battle. The sky was bright and brilliant despite the absence of the sun. Streaks of pink, purple, and lime zigzagged over the starry heavens. They cast the entire world in a dizzying glow. This surely was the Vicennalia Aurora in full effect.

I was at the border of Alderon. The dome-like force field of the In and Out Spell, normally invisible, sparkled furiously. In addition, silvery cracks that looked like thick lightning strikes were corrupting the sphere, making it look like an egg about to hatch. Only unlike an egg, I knew that the beings trying to get out of this enchanted shell were bent on our realm's destruction.

Inside the crackling dome, an army of humans and monsters was ready to charge. At the front of the assembly was a small line-up of men and women whose forms glowed with black energy. The black energy flowed from their hands into the In and Out Spell as they tried to demolish the force field.

Somehow, I knew they were all carriers of Pure Magic. I could feel it. These were victims of the same disease I suffered from, except they had turned dark and been sent to Alderon to live out their days as malevolent witches or warlocks.

There were at least thirty of them. Time and imprisonment in this wasteland had made them older and more ragged, but they were still strong. More than strong, really—they radiated power. And one look into the intensity of their dark, glowing auras told me that they were not afraid to use it.

On the other side of the In and Out Spell, two dozen Fairy Godmothers fired their magic into the force field with equal fierceness. Their wands were pointed directly at the dome. Mighty blasts of scarlet-colored energy poured out of them, but it was nothing compared to the Pure Magic wielders on the other side.

Among the Godmothers I saw Lena Lenore.

The Fairy Godmother Supreme's normally polished attire was sullied and torn, and her beautiful dark hair was frazzled, as if a wild animal had attacked her. There was a ferocious but fearful glint in her hazel eyes as she sent her own magic to strengthen the In and Out Spell.

It occurred to me that I'd never seen the Godmother Supreme look nervous before. She was always so confident, so powerful, so intimidating. But the desperation in her expression here was as evident as the fact that the Godmothers were losing.

The In and Out Spell around Alderon was crumbling and the Godmothers didn't appear to have the numbers or the strength to hold it off much longer. I couldn't believe it. Book had experienced the Vicennalia Aurora many times before; I was told we were prepared for this. Every time the event occurred, Fairy Godmothers dedicated themselves to keeping an eye on Alderon's In and Out Spell. But clearly the majority of the Fairy Godmothers weren't here.

"They just took Daisy and Erin!" someone shouted.

Debbie Nightengale appeared from behind Lenore. My own Fairy Godmother looked even more disheveled than the Godmother Supreme. She had fresh scratches all over her arms, including a particularly large gash by her shoulder. Her red hair was a mess. And her dress—a light green gown with moving swooshes of color that matched the Vicennalia Aurora—was ripped in at least ten places.

"How many of us are left?" Lenore called back, sweat dripping from her brow due to the exertion.

"Seventeen, myself included," Debbie replied, shooting a bolt of red energy out of her wand at something behind the Godmothers, which was cut out of my perspective. "What do we do, Godmother Supreme?"

Lenore gazed at the force field and the army of villains behind it. "The Aurora has never had this kind of effect before. It really is making people with Pure Magic stronger and normal magic like ours weaker."

The more I studied Lenore's distraught face, the more I realized I preferred my all-powerful enemy in her state of superiority. Seeing her so worried made me feel extremely unsettled, and the news she just shared was beyond troubling. I'd already learned that normal magic was going to be weaker on the day of the Aurora. But I didn't know Pure Magic would be stronger. I'm not sure anybody was prepared for that. Lenore clearly wasn't.

"Godmother Supreme." Debbie's eyes pleaded with Lenore as she fired bolt after bolt of magic at an unseen enemy. "Please tell me you called for reinforcements before the Mark Twos went dead."

Suddenly, I perceived a terrible and familiar sound. Up 'til now, my dreaming consciousness had not heard it, as if a layer of the dream had been on mute. Now though, vicious, memorable screeches pierced the air. My viewpoint changed and I was finally able to see what Debbie and several other Godmothers were defending themselves against from behind. Flying monkeys.

Dozens of the winged, fanged monsters from Oz were flapping across Book's sky—releasing their blood-curdling cries, swooping down with claws outstretched to assail the remaining Godmothers, and bobbing and weaving past the bolts of magic being shot at them.

I watched Debbie fire in defense, but the creatures were too fast, their flight patterns too erratic. I saw one circling far above. He was coming in at an angle behind Debbie and Lenore, headed straight for them, but neither of the two Godmothers noticed. The flying monkey closed in—fifty feet, forty feet, thirty feet, twenty feet, ten feet, and then . . .

Visions began flashing through my head at rapid speed.

I saw creatures that were half human and half animal. Their bodies were of men dressed in sleek silver suits. Their fist-sized eyes were giant and black and set in furry, white faces.

Next came Kai, Daniel's girlfriend from Century City. She was in a forest, masterfully fending off magic hunters with her sword. I saw Daniel fighting beside her.

The images came faster. My mother's glass slipper shattering. Man-sized boot prints in the snow. Natalie running through a dark alley lined with dumpsters. A lavender-colored cat with giant green eyes and a creepy grin. An old woman I'd seen in my dreams before.

The scene expanded around the old woman. She was in the

middle of the woods. Seven magic hunters stood behind her. They all faced a grand cave with a mouth blocked by an enormous stone. The old woman was nervous. With that many magic hunters aiming their weapons at her, I could understand why. But what was strange was that she looked more worried about the stone in front of her.

I'd envisioned this before. With a flash my dream then changed to another familiar scene. Hills with blue colored grass rolled in the distance. A huge river surrounded by embankments of gray sand resided next to a great battle unfolding. Jason, SJ, and Blue were fighting at least thirty enemy knights in gleaming black, gold, and blood red armor. While Blue and Jason harnessed the power of their respective weapons to fend off the attack near the river, SJ was more inland. Focused on firing her portable potions, she didn't see a knight coming up behind her. He struck her in the back of the head with the pommel of his sword. She fell to the ground. He rushed in and raised his blade.

My perspective snapped to Blue. She was wearing a brown vest over a navy romper. Out of nowhere she was hit hard and thrust off her feet. She tumbled down the riverbank—the gray sand sticking to her hair and clothes like breadcrumbs on a chicken breast.

She tried to stand but another attacker slammed his shield against her head. Blue leapt up into a spinning kick to knock the knight away. But when she whirled around anew, a different knight came charging with a spear aimed directly at her chest. The blade reflected in her eyes. In that spilt-second I'm sure she thought she was done. But before the blade pierced her, Jason leapt in front of Blue and the spear went through him instead.

"*Jason!*" Blue screamed.

My friend fell to the ground. The knight who'd struck Jason yanked out his bloodied spear. He hinged to take another shot at Blue, but she launched herself at him before he got the chance. She tackled him to the ground and smashed his face with her fists over and over.

More attackers drew in, but she jumped up and annihilated

them all. Wielding the fallen knight's spear, she combined its force with her own—punching throats, flipping bodies, and slamming every enemy that came at her.

Suddenly the ground began to rumble. The panicked shouting of the other knights filled the air. A great, golden glow washed over their faces like an incoming tidal wave.

My focus returned to Blue, who took the opening to race back to Jason. She dropped to her knees in the gray sand. Jason did not move. His shirt was stained dark red around his stomach. Blue grabbed him by the shoulders and shook him, calling out his name. He did not respond. She touched her hands to the wound and blood soaked her skin.

The terrain continued to tremble. The river sloshed. The glow in the background grew brighter. Eventually the glow became so strong it washed out everything and then—

"Wake up, Sleeping Beauty."

My eyelids fluttered open, and I sat up. My friends were in my room. Jason was standing by the fireplace, poking the charred logs with a wrought iron rod. SJ had just thrown open the light pink curtains that matched my comforter. Daniel was going through my backpack. Blue stood by my bedside, smirking.

"Thanks, Blue. I love being woken by an insult," I replied with a yawn as I sat up. I rubbed my eyes. "What's wrong? Why are you guys all here?"

"Dorothy called Blue. She's been trying to get a hold of you all morning," Jason responded. "And I think I just figured out why she wasn't able to reach you." He dug the poker through the ashes of the fireplace and pulled out my charred compact mirror. "Geez, Crisa. This takes re-gifting to a new level."

I shook my head. "Sorry. Alex called last night. I got angry and overreacted."

"How unlike you," Daniel commented.

Fully awake now, I hopped off the bed but stumbled back when I saw what Blue was wearing. Before we'd parted ways last night, I'd given her back her clothes and utility belt of throwing knives, which had been stashed in my backpack. She now donned the latter, but her new outfit caused me great alarm.

"B-Blue," I stammered. "Where did you get those clothes?"

"Elaine has a daughter and a son about our age. The son, Galeschin, is away with Morgan's son Ywain helping the Gwenivere Brigade. The daughter, Elaine Jr., has been missing for a few years. Elaine Sr. said we could help ourselves to their clothes." Blue shrugged. "It feels kind of weird wearing a missing girl's outfits. But Jason left his clothes in the carriage last night, and the rest of us were almost murdered by pumpkins, evil scarecrows, and pirates in our old get-ups, so we agreed it was time for a change."

I noticed that all my friends were wearing new clothes. They'd kept parts of their old looks—Daniel still wore his leather jacket and Blue her brown boots for instance—but new pieces had been incorporated.

The outfits caused me great horror. Blue donned the navy romper I'd just seen her wearing in my dreams. A brown, halter-style vest that matched her boots, utility belt, and sheath lay over the top. SJ and Jason also wore the same clothes I'd envisioned them wearing in my dream. Which meant . . .

Oh no.

I thought I had time to make my magic strong enough to save Jason, but I didn't have any time at all. His death, that battle—it was all about to happen!

"Crisa, are you okay?" Blue asked. "You look pale."

"I'm fine," I said quickly. I crossed my arms self-consciously when I realized I was only wearing a nightgown. I grabbed a robe from a hook behind the door and plunged my arms through its soft sleeves. "What did Dorothy say?"

"She told us to call her back when you were awake," Daniel replied. He reached into his pocket and tossed me his Mark Two.

I flipped open the compact and spoke Dorothy's name. After a few rings she answered. The face of the familiar, gangly brunette filled the looking glass. "Crisa!" she exclaimed.

"Morning, Dorothy." I gestured for my friends to huddle around as I held up the compact. "What happened yesterday? Has Arthur really been captured?"

"I'm afraid so," Dorothy responded. "He successfully helped

all of the Lost Boys and Girls escape, but at the last second Arian got to Peter. Arian threatened to kill him if Arthur didn't surrender, so Arthur surrendered. But Arian didn't set Peter free. The antagonists are keeping him and Arthur somewhere in the forest. The fairies, Lost Boys and Girls, and I are trying to find them. I just thought I should tell you."

"Thanks for the update," I replied. Then I paused, thinking on the dreams that had passed through my head last night and the questions I'd been mulling over since I'd learned the antagonists were after Excalibur.

"Dorothy, random question, but did Ozma have some sort of crown on her when you were separated in Camelot?"

"Um, yeah," Dorothy replied, confused by the abrupt change of subject. "The Simia Crown. It's an old family heirloom that's part of a set. One crown is always worn by the ruler of Oz, and the other by her advisor so the power can be shared. The crowns were stolen many years ago. When Eva was still the Wicked Witch of the West she possessed them both. But once she was cured of Pure Magic Disease, she returned them to Ozma and Julian. Unfortunately, when Glinda turned dark, she stole Julian's crown, but Ozma was still wearing hers the last time I saw her. For as long as I've known her, she's never gone anywhere without it."

"Why are the crowns important?" I asked. "I had a vision of Rampart talking about Ozma's crown with Arian. I think that crown is the reason why Alex and Mauvrey were already going after Excalibur before they knew about Paige. Rampart has it, and is offering it to Arian in exchange for Excalibur."

"Crisa . . ." Dorothy looked frightened. "You *cannot* let that crown fall into the antagonists' hands."

"Why not? What is it?"

"The Simia Crowns are not ordinary crowns. They allow their wearers control over flying monkeys. One crown controls the females, the other the males. There are two crowns so that if one crown wearer tries to use the power for destruction, the other can challenge them."

Double oh no.

Everything made sense now. Arian wanted the Simia Crown

so he could orchestrate an attack on the Fairy Godmothers during the Vicennalia Aurora. That distraction would thin out their ranks and detract from their magical focus, allowing the antagonists in Book to break down Alderon's In and Out Spell. Rampart had acquired the crown when he'd captured Ozma. The thing that Rampart wanted most was Excalibur—hence the trade.

"Dorothy," I responded. "I'm going to need to call you back."

I caught my friends up on my conversation with Alex and everything I'd dreamed about (leaving out the part regarding Jason's death, which Jason had asked me to keep a secret).

"I thought the antagonists' plot only had two parts," Blue said. "Find the genies and harness their power for evil, and then destroy Natalie's spirit when she turns twenty-one so she'll open the Eternity Gate. Why are we only learning about their plan for the Vicennalia Aurora now?"

"The antagonists are not fools," SJ responded. "If they have been plotting to overthrow Book for as long as it seems, then it stands to reason that they have more than one plan. The reason for them opening the Eternity Gate is so that all normal, presently active magic is rendered useless—bringing down the In and Out Spell around Alderon and extinguishing the power of the Fairy Godmothers. As we deduced in Oz, should they find the genies, they would not release them until after that. For if the genies are still dormant during the Eternity Gate reset, then their magic will be preserved. The antagonists could then free them later on and use their power to take over the realm."

"But finding the genies and getting Natalie to open the Eternity Gate are not sure things," Daniel tagged in. "So like SJ said, they have contingencies. If there's an opportunity to break out of Alderon before then—"

"They're going to take it," I finished.

"It is an admirably detailed plan, really," SJ commented. "If Arian succeeds in acquiring the Simia Crown, flying monkeys could prevent the Godmothers from properly protecting the In and Out Spell when the Vicennalia Aurora hits. The spell could come down, and if that happens the antagonists could invade the realm, spread their forces across Book, and weaken it as an initial assault before the final blow from the genies and the Eternity Gate."

"I definitely think that's their plan," I said. "Which means we need to adjust for it. SJ and Blue, can you give Dorothy a call back and update her about finding Ozma and her slipper in Rampart's dungeon? I was so focused on the Simia Crown I forgot to tell her. She's going to flip when she finds out that Ozma is alive and Julian betrayed her."

I turned to the boys. "Can you guys talk to our hosts about the quickest route through the Passage Perelous? Now that Alex has been blessed by the Boar's Mouth, our competition for Excalibur just got kicked up a notch. We need to get to Avalon ASAP."

"What are you going to do?" Blue asked.

My lips tightened with displeasure. "I'm going to have a conversation with my least favorite Fairy Godmother. Assuming she's not still blocking my calls."

"Crisanta, the answer is *no*."

I stood on the outer wall of Gwenivere's castle. The sun was bright but hazy as it shone through the Poppy mist. Countless fireflies continued to flicker through it. Ormé had explained that they were drawn to Poppies—called to the flowers like bees to a hive. As such, they'd disregarded the memo about morning and their luminescent rear ends continued to glimmer.

The cold air of Camelot lapped against my face. I regretted not changing before coming outside. I'd mistaken the brightness for warmth and the robe I had over my nightgown was not getting the job done.

For the last five minutes I'd been trying to convince Lenore about the revelations my friends and I had just arrived at. Luckily, since the attack in Midveil she'd unblocked me as a caller on her Mark Two. Unluckily, she was still being difficult.

How unlike her.

Lenore and I had been at odds since the moment we met.

Even before she suspected I had Pure Magic she'd considered me a threat. The woman loved order and things she could control. To her, I was a defiant, anti-archetype flaw in her perfect world. Meanwhile, I considered her an intimidating combo of shrewd, strategic, and vicious, with narrow-minded views when it came to how to best protect our realm.

"Lenore, you have to believe me. The antagonists are going to unleash a flying monkey attack during the Vicennalia Aurora. I don't know where else you could possibly be planning on sending your Godmothers that night, but you need to gather them at Alderon's border. Otherwise the In and Out Spell is going to come down."

"You have been gone a while, Crisanta," Lenore responded. "You have no idea what's happened here."

"Then enlighten me," I responded.

"The assaults on your castle in Midveil and the other kingdoms were just the beginning," Lenore said. "Since you left, there have been commons rebellion attacks all across the realm. My Godmothers and I are stretched to our limits trying to keep the situation under control, but their forces are getting stronger. The only places that remain completely untouched are Clevaunt, Coventry, Ravelli, the protagonist schools, and—thank the skies—our beloved capital. If I move even a handful of Godmothers away from their assigned posts, a well-executed attack could cost an entire kingdom to fall."

I raised my eyebrows. "I didn't realize it was that bad."

The common characters of Book had tried to rebel in the past. In a way I didn't blame them. Our realm's division of power and importance wasn't fair.

People who were chosen by the Author were named protagonists and given every advantage. People who weren't chosen were labeled ordinary and not given the same regard. I believed each situation had its caveats. As a protagonist, my kind was forced into archetypes and supposed to live up to the specific life plans that the higher-ups set for us. As a common, you were left to your own devices and could pursue whatever path you desired. The problem with that was the realm higher-ups acted like you didn't matter. You had no say in how the realm was governed and couldn't count on the people in charge for the same type of help and opportunities given to main characters.

Still, my sympathy for the plight of the commons was not great enough to excuse what had happened. I believed in change and taking charge of your destiny, but not through murder or bloodshed. My growing conflict over the morality of taking villains' lives did not apply here. There was no excuse for hurting innocents.

The attacks on my castle and other kingdoms had crossed a line. Whatever compassion I once held for the commons fighting back had died that day, along with a lot of people. So while Lena Lenore and I were rarely on the same page, I felt for her here. The commons were becoming dangerous. And there were a lot more of them than there were protagonists and realm leaders.

And yet . . . I had to keep my eye on the big picture.

I recalled my time interrogating Anthony Graystone, a former member of the Midveil King's Guard who'd been a part of the commons attack on my castle.

"There is something big coming, something to do with the Vicennalia Aurora," he'd said.

My enemies must have been intending to unleash the flying monkeys the day of the Aurora this whole time, knowing that if the Godmothers were preoccupied with commons rebellion threats across the realm, their forces would be divided. Then the few Godmothers I'd foreseen assigned to the Alderon border would be assaulted by the flying beasts and rendered incapable of a proper defense.

It was a smart tactic. As SJ said, our enemies were not fools. They had multiple lines of strategy in place at once—Natalie and the Eternity Gate, Paige Tomkins and the location of the genies, the commons rebellion and the Vicennalia Aurora.

For months now, my friends and I thought we knew what the antagonists were up to. But all this time it seemed we'd only scratched the surface. Over the last few days the breadth of their schemes had come to light. And unlike the Eternity Gate plan, which would occur at the end of the year, the antagonists had other plans meant to come to fruition in a matter of days.

"Look, Lenore," I continued. "I know the situation is rough, but if the spell around Alderon falls then the destruction you're seeing will only be a hiccup compared to what happens next. I honestly think the commons rebellion is a distraction and we need to shift our focus elsewhere."

After my dream about the Vicennalia Aurora and the flying monkeys, I believed this wholeheartedly. I'd long suspected that the antagonists were using the commons to weaken our realm while they worked on their long-term plan. I still thought this was true, but now I realized it could also be simpler than that. Arian and the antagonists' might just be escalating the commons rebellion to distract us from their greater plot.

"A distraction?" an offended Lenore repeated. "Crisanta, you *saw* the threat that the commons rebellion poses firsthand. Your own castle was attacked and half destroyed with countless people killed in the process. Several other kingdoms experienced the same fate. Are you honestly telling me that this doesn't matter?"

"No, the rebellion matters to the commons, I'm sure," I responded. "But again, I think the antagonists are using it as misdirection to beat you."

"The nerve you have," Lenore huffed.

"It's not nerve; it's pragmatism," I asserted, clutching Daniel's Mark Two firmly in my hand. "I'm not saying the rebellion isn't a formidable threat, I'm just saying it shouldn't be our main priority. The antagonists don't care about the plight of the common person. They're not humanitarians; they're villains. Their main play is elsewhere. They're going to try and break down Alderon's In and Out Spell on the night of the Vicennalia Aurora. You *need* to concentrate all of your forces there."

"The numbers I've assigned to guard the spell on that day will suffice," Lenore said dismissively. "I will personally be there, and I'm sure we can handle a little magic instability."

I wanted to tell her that this Aurora was going to produce more than a little magic instability. Thanks to my vision, I now knew from Lenore herself that the Aurora was going to make Pure Magic stronger while it made normal magic weaker. However, I couldn't tell her that without revealing my dreams of the future. It was the same reason why I couldn't tell her that I knew with absolute certainty a flying monkey attack was going to happen.

As mentioned, Lenore had been trying to prove I had Pure Magic for a long time. The two signs of a person carrying Pure Magic were an inability to remove magic and dreams of the future. Thanks to an incident with a Stiltdegarth, Lenore knew my magic couldn't be removed. As a result, she regularly sought confirmation of the second bit of criteria. If she had proof that I dreamed of the future, she could send me to Alderon along with all other people who'd contracted the disease, aside from Liza.

Unless I wanted to doom myself, I was stuck. So all I could say was, "Lenore, I'm just trying to help."

Lenore scoffed. I was always amazed how her beautiful face could hold so much cruelty.

"It may have escaped your notice, Crisanta, but this realm existed just fine before you came along. We don't need you to save us or guide us. I have things perfectly under control."

"No you don't," I said flatly. "You're letting your pride and dislike of me get in the way of your judgment."

"And you, Crisanta Knight, are letting you self-endowed chosen-one syndrome get in the way of yours. Let's say I listened to you and moved all of my Godmother forces to the Alderon border, *despite* the fact that my sources say that the commons have a multi-kingdom attack planned for that evening. Who will defend the innocent against their onslaught?"

I paused then bitterly admitted the truth. "I don't know."

"Exactly," Lenore huffed. "And that, young lady, is precisely why I *will* send you to Alderon one day when I have proof of your Pure Magic. Despite what my sister thinks, I know your heart is destined for darkness. You have more inherent coldness in you than many Pure Magic carriers I've known in the past. It's obvious in the way you care so little about people."

"I care about people!" My voice rose an octave in surprise and offense.

"Really?" Lenore replied condescendingly. "Because you are asking me to abandon entire kingdoms without any kind of contingency. Did you even think about that before you called me and made your case?"

I was at a loss for words. That hardly ever happened.

"That's what I thought," Lenore responded. She shook her head. "Crisanta, thank you for the warning, but I caution you now like I always have to know your place. Whatever mission you and your friends are on, you're in it alone. I have too much responsibility to Book and its people to compromise my judgment for you."

With that, she hung up. I closed the Mark Two and stared into the mist. I hated that Lenore hadn't listened to me. I hated more that she'd made some good points. I knew my reasoning regarding Alderon was good, but I couldn't believe I hadn't considered what would happen to the innocents throughout the realm if they were left undefended against rebellion attacks that night. It hadn't even crossed my mind.

Was Lenore right? Was I inherently coldhearted?

As her words rung in my ears, I headed back to meet my friends in the dining room of the castle as we'd agreed to do before separating. SJ and Blue were already there. They were having breakfast with Ormé, Elaine, and Mindy. Jason and Daniel must've still been talking with Morgan and Gwenivere about the best way to get through the Passage Perelous.

When I entered, SJ and Blue raised their gazes to meet mine.

"What did she say?" SJ asked.

"We're on our own," I replied.

Blue shrugged nonchalantly. "What else is new?"

CHAPTER 13

Elaine the Younger

ver the next half hour many plans were formed.

I was going to lend my Hole Tracker to Ormé and a faction of the Gwenivere Brigade so they could get to Neverland, find Arthur and Peter, and free them from the antagonists. My friends and I were going to use our map of Camelot, which our hosts helped us improve, to get to Avalon. And Gwenivere and Morgan were going to move forward on their original plan with renewed vigor.

Before we even came along they'd been planning to siege the citadel on the night of the Vicennalia Aurora. With Rampart and his forces distracted by the festivities, it was the perfect time for an invasion. That was what Gwenivere's closed-door meeting last night had been about. Some of the queen's key allies across Camelot were having second thoughts about attacking Rampart's forces, fearing that they weren't ready. But with our arrival and word that Arthur was still alive, Gwenivere and Morgan were able to convince everyone to carry on with the plan.

And so, we decided on the following: My friends and I would retrieve Excalibur and rendezvous with Gwenivere's troops at the edge of the Forest of Mists at five o'clock on the day of the Vicennalia Aurora. We'd help our new allies take the citadel, restore Gwenivere to the throne, and free Ozma. After that, we would return Ozma to Oz and use the sword to liberate Paige's mind from Glinda's memory stone. And finally, we'd head back to Book to aid the Fairy Godmothers at Alderon's border and stop the antagonists from destroying our home realm before returning Excalibur to Arthur, its rightful owner.

Easy peasy.

JK. Not even close.

The newest information regarding the flying monkeys made things even trickier. My vision told me that one way or another, those flying monkeys were coming to our realm. There were a lot of ways this could happen. Alex could beat me to Excalibur, which would lead to Arian swapping the sword with Rampart for Ozma's Simia Crown. If I succeeded in claiming Excalibur, Arian could still get Rampart to give him Ozma's crown, probably by force. Or perhaps Arian would take Glinda's Simia Crown during our inevitable confrontation with the witch in Oz.

Whatever ended up happening on that front, we had to assume two things going forward. One, Arian would get a Simia Crown at some point, so we should try to do the same in order to at least counteract the flying monkey attack. Two, whether Lenore wanted to listen to me or not, she needed backup and we were going to give it to her.

That part of the mission, however, seemed a million miles away. Just like fulfilling my oath to the Boar's Mouth by getting the "lost king" to sit on Camelot's throne. There were so many instances of possible death between now and the climax of this story arc that I wondered if it would be best to push factors like this out of mind for the near future and concentrate on the first task at hand. Our immediate obstacle was traversing the Passage Perelous. According to our hostesses, it could take anything from hours to days to weeks to get through it and reach the Isle of Avalon. Some who ventured inside never returned at all.

Given that, I wasn't sure what the odds were that we could get to Avalon and back before sunset two days from now. When I raised this concern, Gwenivere laid it out quite plainly.

"If you are truly the Knight of the prophecy, you will return in time. If you are not, then you won't make it in time and all will be lost."

"Is there a third option?" Blue joked.

Gwenivere did not laugh. None of us did.

After our plans were set, Ormé and a troop of twelve girls from the Gwenivere Brigade geared up to leave straight away.

I strapped my Hole Tracker to Ormé's wrist as we stood on the edge of the castle's outer wall.

"Be careful with it," I said. "A really nice White Rabbit gave it to me and I owe him a rain check."

"Will do," Ormé replied with a smile.

The Gwenivere Brigade girls huddled together in three groups and Morgan began the process of creating a wind orb around them one unit at a time to transport them to the other side of the Poppy moat. When the Brigade was out of sight, Gwenivere and Morgan met with their attendants to further their plans. They had a lot of Mark Two calls to make.

While SJ, Blue, Jason, and Daniel got ready to depart, Elaine took me to her daughter's old room. It was a tad awkward. The woman had been present at breakfast and during all of our planning, but she was nowhere near as vocal as Morgan or Gwenivere. She seemed quite timid, and I really hadn't interacted with her beyond our first meeting. As we walked together to the room, I thanked her for healing Jason.

I also asked Elaine if there was any chance her healing magic could bring people back from the dead. Alas, she said it couldn't. It was a long shot, I know, but Jason's clock was ticking and I had no idea if my current magical chops were strong enough to save him.

I didn't want to overemphasize this insecurity, but I did want to warn him of the fate that was closing in (or suggest that he wear extra sturdy armor under his shirt as we proceeded). Unfortunately, I hadn't gotten the chance to talk to him alone this morning. I hoped an opportunity would present itself later. With SJ's SRBs allowing us to remain in the same clothes for long periods of time, the battle of Jason's death may not be in the immediate future. Still, I aimed to talk to him by the end of the day.

The room of Elaine the younger had dark rosewood floors with hues of rich red. Onyx paint covered the walls. Maroon curtains blocked out most of the natural light. The bed frame, desk, and armoire were made of iron.

"Are you sure this is okay?" I asked Elaine as I looked into the open closet.

"Take whatever you want," Elaine said sadly as she ran her finger along the iron frame of the bed. "My daughter has likely been dead for some time, and I've made peace with that."

I turned around, shocked that any parent could utter those words so calmly.

Elaine sighed heavily. "Ever since King Arthur was taken from us, this realm has been marked by death and despair. There have been many wars for the throne, many struggles even before Rampart came along." She sat on the edge of the bed. "Morgan and I were both queens once, you know. She was married to King Urion, and I to King Nentres of Garlot. But both our husbands were killed in the conflicts. And now look at us. We are confined to live in this island of a castle, separated from everyone and everything. Our children are brave; our sons continue to fight and serve Gwenivere's cause despite the risk. But years ago, a battalion of the Gwenivere Brigade, including my courageous Elaine, was attacked in the Passage Perelous. Only one Gwenivere Brigade girl made it back."

"You don't know for certain that your daughter was killed though," I said, trying to be optimistic.

"But I do," Elaine responded. "I know in a way that only a mother can. She is gone, like my husband and so many of my friends and relatives. And I accept that. I have to in order to keep breathing. I just wish . . ." She looked at me solemnly. "I just wish I could speak with her one last time."

Elaine exhaled and stood up. "Her clothes should fit you," she said quickly as she headed for the door. "Maybe not the pants, but definitely the tops."

She closed the door behind her with a soft click. I gazed again into the wardrobe of Elaine the younger. It still felt weird to go rifling through the girl's things. But Blue was right; a person could only fight monsters and bad guys in different realms for so long without feeling like a change of clothes was necessary.

Keeping on my black combat boots and sturdy leggings, I grabbed a simple black tank top from one of the hangers and a forest green leather jacket from another. Straightening out the top in the mirror, I caught the reflection of a picture on the far wall.

The oil painting was of Elaine's family. I assumed the young man in the center was her son Galeschin. He was short and had strawberry blond hair like Elaine. In this picture he was around Alex's age.

King Nentres—proud and strong with a black beard and intense eyes—had his hand on the shoulder of the girl next to him. I guessed she was Elaine the younger. She had black hair like her father with short, choppy bangs across her forehead. Dark kohl rimmed her eyes, which made her look edgy and defiant.

Entranced, I touched my hand to the painting for a moment. Then I headed for the door.

Before leaving the room, I realized I'd left my backpack by the bed. On an impulse, I held out my hand and concentrated. I commanded the backpack to briefly come to life and come to me. My hand flared with its familiar golden glow and the backpack rose and moved to rest by my feet. I released my control and frowned. Thoughts crowded my head in regards to Liza's revelations last night.

Magic Exhaustion was a formidable limitation. The fact that I had grown strong enough to potentially overcome it was pretty awesome. It meant I was getting more powerful. However, the new information Liza had shared was upsetting on two levels. First, while it was good to know that if my life was in peril I might be able to harness Magic Instinct through emotion and relinquishing control, I knew I wasn't supposed to do either. That was fundamentally a bad road to go down because it's what fed my Pure Magic Disease.

The other reason this whole thing irked me was that I was beginning to appreciate how much more powerful I could be if I *did* relinquish control and leaned on emotions. Between the incident with the giant and my immunity to Poppies, I had the potential to do a lot more than I was currently doing. And that was tempting in a toxic way.

As these thoughts whirled in my head as I stood on the threshold of Elaine's room, I vowed I would try my best to avoid actively harnessing Magic Instinct. Having more power would be nice, but it was not worth the risk of falling deeper into the clutches of my disease. And frankly, even if being corrupted weren't a risk, I liked being in control and I didn't want to surrender it. I'd fought too long and hard to be a girl who was firmly in charge of her own destiny and lived by her own rules. I was not about to forfeit that mastery of free will for the sake of power. No matter how strong it could be . . .

CHAPTER 14

The Big Shift

he mist from the Poppies dissipated with each step as the five of us trekked through the forest away from the castle. Fully restored to health, Jason led the way with our newly revamped Camelot map while I pulled up the rear with my newly adjusted view on power. In tune with my wish to avoid using Magic Instinct whenever possible, I had let myself get wind orbed over the Poppies like everyone else. Today was a new day, and I was going to be in control.

We made it through the morning without incident, eventually emerging from the forest into an extensive valley dotted with villages. In the distance, a cluster of bluish mountains crowned the valley. The center of that range was our destination; it was where the Passage Perelous began.

The journey to the mountains was long and tedious. Around midday, we stopped at a tavern in one of the villages to grab a bite to eat. Morgan and Gwenivere had generously given us more money for our quest, which I had put in my backpack for safekeeping. There wasn't much else inside the bag. Aside from the money, I had two granola bars, Daniel's Mark Two (which he said I could hang on to until I got a new one), and my dream journal. It was such a slim volume; I'd almost forgotten it was in there.

I'd started writing the text last December to keep track of my dreams, which might offer insights of the future that I didn't yet understand. Eventually I would need to add my most recent dreams to it, but who knew when I'd get a chance to do that.

Being on a multi-dimensional quest didn't exactly allow much time for journaling.

After we finished eating, we looked for the village stables. Morgan and Gwenivere hadn't just given us money so we could buy lunch. They knew that some of the villages in the valley had stables with horses for rent, which would speed up our journey.

While my friends haggled with the stable men to make a deal, I wandered around to the side of the stables and sat down, flipping through my dream journal and scanning the bullet points.

Girls in red dresses, dancing at a ball with Chance, giant teddy bears, cheese balls falling from a serving tray, Chance sword fighting with Daniel—

"Moo!"

I jumped in surprise. I'd been so lost in thought that I hadn't noticed a small brown cow that had wandered over. Her giant eyes stared at me.

"Come along, Milkshake," her owner said, tugging the rope loosely tied around the cow's neck. The cow mooed again and trotted after her owner.

I continued reading until my eyes landed on a bullet point halfway down.

Nyneve.

I snapped the book shut. So much had happened since I had woken up this morning that until now I hadn't put two and two together. Gwenivere had mentioned Nyneve in her workshop! She was the half magic hunter who Merlin had taken on as a potions apprentice—the one he'd fallen in love with and who Gwenivere believed had something to do with his disappearance.

I had dreamed about Nyneve last night, as well as many nights ago when I was back at school. On both occasions I also dreamed about Jason's death so, although my visions didn't normally show me things in chronological order, I wondered if experiencing them together twice was a sign that they would happen in close proximity time-wise. If Jason's fate was fast approaching, was Nyneve's also nearby?

Jason's fate . . .

I felt guilt well up inside me. Yes, I intended to talk to Jason regarding the closeness of his death as soon as I had a chance with him alone. However, since I hadn't yet, all morning I'd been making casual conversation with my friends like everything was normal despite knowing one of them was meant to die soon. I knew I had to keep up these appearances because the others didn't know about Jason's doom, but I was surprised how easily I'd been able to block out my concern for him on the trek. It felt wrong that I was able to do that, even if it was necessary.

Lenore's words echoed in my skull.

"I know your heart is destined for darkness. You have more inherent coldness in you than many Pure Magic carriers I've known in the past. It's obvious in the way you care so little about people."

"Hey! Are you looking for the bathroom too?"

I looked up and discovered Blue walking toward me. "Just reminding myself of some past dreams," I replied, holding up my journal.

"You sure that's all it is?" Blue asked, coming to stand in front of where I was sitting. "You've got your pensive-Crisa face on."

"I have a pensive-Crisa face?"

"Uh-huh. Lately, it's been one of your most frequent expressions. So, what's wrong?"

"Nothing, I just . . ." I bit my lip. "Blue, do you think I'm cold?"

My friend looked puzzled. The sunlight hit the back of her hair, making it look more golden than normal. "Where's this coming from?"

"Lenore. She said that I'm coldhearted because I care more about keeping the Alderon In and Out Spell up than protecting the people of the realm who are in danger because of the commons rebellion. It really bothered me that she said that. I guess I could just use a second opinion."

Blue sat down against the stable wall next to me. "Well, do you think SJ is coldhearted?"

"What does that have to do with anything?"

"Plenty. Crisa, you and I both know that SJ is one of the kindest, most compassionate people alive. But to people who don't know her like you and I do, she might not seem that way. She is very logical and calculating. And those kinds of qualities can make someone seem cold. Sometimes you're like SJ in that way. But just like it doesn't make her cold, it doesn't make you cold either. And anyway, you're only half like her," Blue said. "Your other half is a lot like me. While SJ runs on logic, I run on instinct. I'm all fists and fire, and you can be that way a lot of the time too. It just kind of varies depending on the situation. What doesn't change is your intention to do what you believe is right. And that, my friend, is what matters."

Blue slapped me on the leg affectionately then hopped up and began to walk away.

"Wait, you're just going to make a speech like that and slap out?" I commented.

"Crisa, I love you. And I'm here for you. But I came out here for other reasons. I have a small bladder and a big lemonade sitting in it. Nature calls."

The proprietor of the stables had seven horses. He allowed us to rent five with the caveat that he and his assistant ride us to our mountain destination. That way, they could rope up the steeds when we were done and steer them back home.

We agreed and saddled up.

As I was hoisting myself onto a caramel brown horse with white patches around his ankles, I saw SJ approach her steed gradually. The creature huffed and stamped his feet anxiously when he saw her coming.

"You okay?" I asked. "You know you can share a ride with me."

"No, no," SJ insisted, drawing closer to her horse. "You know I have been practicing. I can do this." She scrambled on top of the horse and grasped the reins tightly. The horse whinnied and bucked a bit.

"Whoa. Steady. Steady," she said.

After a moment, the horse calmed down and she grinned at me. "See. I told you."

I smiled back. I was proud of her. Despite SJ's strong connection with animals (like her mother Snow White), horses had always disliked her. Harnessing the will to face her fears on her own terms was hard, but it looked like she was making progress.

We galloped out of the village and continued our journey toward the mountains. We covered ground much faster on horseback. At a brisk canter, we reached the base of the mountains by two o'clock and followed the map up the winding path.

Eventually we came to a tunnel that carved through the mountain. On the other side was an enormous gorge. The only way to cross it was a thin rope bridge that stretched about a hundred meters and swung uneasily in the breeze.

"This is where we leave you," said the stables' proprietor as he dismounted. "The Shifting Forest is at the bottom of the mountain on the other side of this bridge."

"How much farther is the Passage Perelous entrance after that?" Blue asked.

"You misunderstand. The Shifting Forest is part of the Passage Perelous," the man replied. "It goes on for miles and connects many of Camelot's far-off kingdoms. But be warned, it is one of the trickiest, most dangerous landscapes you will ever encounter. The forest is built on tectonic plates that shift regularly. And the magic inside disrupts all kinds of technologies—from regular compasses to those Mark Two magic compact mirrors that just came out. It makes it very easy to get lost and disoriented, which in turn makes you an easier target for the monsters and villains that might be inside."

"I don't suppose there's a way to get to the Isle of Avalon without going through there?" Daniel asked Jason.

"Sadly no," Jason responded. "But don't worry, Morgan said we would be fine as long as we followed her instructions. Plenty of people maneuver through the Passage Perelous. You just have to know what you're doing and be able to defend yourself."

We dismounted and the men from the stables began steering our steeds back through the tunnel. The five of us started across the rope bridge, which teetered beneath our footsteps. I was not afraid of heights, but the unfathomably big drop below gave me pause. A mass of sharp, unforgiving rocks pointed up at us. Falling into it would be like plunging into the open mouth of a dragon. I kept expecting one of the wooden planks to snap under our weight. It would be classic us. Thankfully, we touched down on the other side without anything horrible happening.

"Wow, that has to be a record," Blue commented as she bent down to retie a loose bootlace.

"What?" SJ asked.

"We've gone nearly two-thirds of a day without being attacked. We should start taking bets about when it's going to happen. Goodness knows it can't be long now."

"Real optimist, aren't you?" Daniel commented.

I smirked as we continued on our way.

The journey descending the mountain was swift. It was a much more direct path than the winding one we'd taken to reach the bridge. While the majority of that travel was uneventful, there was one point that took my breath away.

Halfway down, we came upon a cliff's edge with an un-obstructed view of what was waiting for us below. As we looked out at a rather intimidating ocean of trees, a sudden subterranean grinding sound emanated from the forest. That's when we witnessed our first "shift." Chunks of trees moved like they were on tiles being pushed around a game board. A flock of birds flew into the sky, angrily squawking from the disturbance. My friends and I exchanged a look but didn't say anything. We continued forward.

When we reached the base of the mountain and were on the threshold of entering the grand forest, we saw a dirty wooden sign that rang a bell of familiarity in my head.

"Welcome to the Silva In Motu," I read out loud.

"It's Latin," Jason explained. "Many generations ago that was Camelot's native tongue. I studied the language a bit in preparation for this quest. Gwenivere confirmed that we might come across some signs in Latin in the Passage Perelous. 'Silva In Motu' loosely translates to 'Forest in Motion' or Shifting For-est.

"You learned *Latin* for this quest?" Blue exclaimed, impressed.

"Hold on," I said. I took off my backpack, pulled out my dream journal, and passed through the pages quickly in search of a description of a dream I'd had not so long ago. I knew I'd seen it earlier while flipping through the text.

"*Silva In Motu*," I read out loud, coming upon the page. "Tell the hunters to be waiting for her there. Then let's see how strong Crisanta Knight is when her precious friends aren't around to protect her."

I shut the book. "Arian said this in a dream I had back at school. He was talking about this forest. Between that and Alex's warning, I'm almost certain there will be magic hunters in there searching for us. They're going to try to kill me for my magic and they mean to do it by separating us." I groaned in frustration. "Every time I've been attacked by magic hunters, I've been alone. This is like really annoying deadly déjà vu. I've been lucky so far, but if history keeps repeating itself, I don't know how long my luck is going to hold out."

"History is not going to repeat itself," Blue said assertively. "Like you said, all those times you've been alone. Now you have us. Nothing is going to tear our group apart, not Arian or this stupid forest. You're not going to die here, Crisa."

Blue wore a face of confidence and I nodded in agreement and fashioned one as well. We forged on. There was no other option.

The tips Gwenivere and Morgan had given us to get through the Passage Perelous had a lot to do with plants and colors. No matter how the forest's tectonic plates shifted, moss always grew facing north, providing us with reliable navigation. If we came upon trees with a reddish tint, we were close to monster-dense areas. Mushroom circles meant we were near pixie or fairy habitats. And the leaves on the trees turned blue if a person had passed by recently.

Despite the perilous nature of the Passage Perelous, sometimes people did try to traverse it because it connected many kingdoms in Camelot. Cutting through it was much faster than going around, although your odds of dying were significantly higher. It was sort of a win-lose.

I was on my toes throughout the journey. On more than one occasion I instinctively reached for my wand when a deer or squirrel startled me.

These little surprises were nothing, however, in comparison to the jarring occurrences of the forest's actual shifting. Sections of land—trees, rock, and all—would periodically move like we'd seen from the mountain. It would begin with a rumble. The dirt beneath our feet would tremor like an earthquake. Then, all of a sudden, the ground would shift in different directions. We'd stagger until we caught our balance, then stand still and ride it out until the episode ended.

Jagged cracks in the earth showed some of the boundaries of the countless tectonic plates in the forest. If any number of these tectonic plates moved at once, each shift had the potential to dramatically rewrite our route. Accordingly, every time the forest experienced a shift (which could last up to a few minutes) we had to reevaluate our position and reset our course. We'd gone through three shifts thus far and while we were getting used to them, that didn't make them any more fun.

You know what else wasn't fun? The monsters we ran into.

By late afternoon we were exhausted. I definitely understood better why no one had claimed Excalibur in all the years Arthur had been gone. We'd been in this forest for an hour and had nearly been killed a half dozen times, despite having a detailed map and the helpful advice of Camelot royalty.

First, we ran into a tribe of ogres twice our height and five times our weight. Next came an onslaught of green spiders the size of watermelons. They spun webs that froze anything they latched onto, making a high-pitched hissing noise that echoed through the forest when they attacked. After that there were the mega toads—toads the size of small cottages that shot their long tongues at anything that moved. (We witnessed one latch onto the waist of a full-size Griffin that'd been taking a drink from a pond, and then swallow it whole.) After that, a swarm of possum bats arrived. Then, wrapping up the hour, a monster emerged from a pool of quicksand. That monster—you guessed it—was made of quicksand.

Avalon was still far away, and at this rate I didn't how we were going to get there in one piece. The five of us only lost more energy with every attack. We were getting tired, but we trudged on.

The forest groaned. Another shift was starting.

Great.

Once again, the pebbles around my feet quivered and bounced as the tectonic plates picked up speed and power. I noticed a section of forest moving closer to us. The trees were gray and they had blue leaves on the branches. A lot of them. People had been through here recently.

"Whoa!"

I whirled around at the sound of Blue's voice and saw that my friends and I were moving in different directions. Blue, SJ, and Jason were on one tectonic plate that was heading off to the left. Daniel stood on a plate that was being pulled deeper into the forest ahead. And my own shaking section was quickly shifting to the right.

I decided to try and jump over to Blue's tectonic plate. I was about to make the leap when out of the corner of my eye I saw something spiraling in my direction.

Instinctively I ducked. My instincts were good. The object was a net that had been meant for me. It hurled over my head and caught SJ's arm instead. I glanced over my shoulder and saw two men in grungy attire with rusty weapons standing beside a tree. What'd I'd been fearing had found us.

"Magic hunters!" I called to my friends. "Move!"

The hunters started shooting arrows through the trees. The shifting forest messed with their aim but also made their fire erratic and unpredictable.

Lapellius.

Shield.

I blocked as I ran and jumped onto the plate with Blue, SJ, and Jason. Blue was trying to free SJ from the net. Jason had activated the force field of his axe to protect them, but it wasn't large enough to offer full coverage. A violent tremor caused him to stumble forward and his magical force field extinguished for a moment. That was the opening the hunters needed. Another weighted net flew toward us, entangling Jason and pulling him to the ground.

Knife.

I bent down and tried to slice through his net, but then another tremor threw me back, slamming me into a tree.

"The one in the green jacket!" one of the hunters called. "She's the one with the magic. Kill *her!*"

I couldn't see where the shouting had come from. The directions were all spliced together as the shift turned us around. This also made it difficult to see how many hunters there were.

"Daniel, watch out!" Blue yelled.

I pivoted to where Blue was looking. Her warning kept Daniel from getting hit with a net. I saw another coming at me from that same direction and leapt aside to avoid it, but I was caught by the ankles and taken down.

As I clambered to my knees, I saw three hunters fighting Daniel. His plate was moving closer to ours again. As he valiantly fended off the attackers with his sword, I spotted another hunter in the trees with a net launcher. He'd been the one to trap me.

How many of these guys were there?

I cut through the net around my ankles and got to my feet. Blue had freed SJ and was moving on to help Jason while SJ began to unleash the fury of her portable potions. The guy in the tree was nailed with a giant blob of slime. He looked like a fly trapped in a web of mucus. Another three hunters were frozen solid with one of SJ's ice potions.

With Jason nearly free and SJ defending them, I rushed to help Daniel. I wasn't sure how much more he could take. Two additional hunters had just crossed onto his tectonic plate.

I bobbed and weaved, swatting arrows away with my shield. I rolled to the ground to evade another net and saw a hunter closing in, knife in hand. I ducked low and spun, hocking his leg out from under him. Once he'd fallen, I lunged back down and punched him in the face so hard he was knocked unconscious.

The victory was short-lived. Two sets of hands grabbed my arms from behind and threw me to the ground. My knife fell out of my grip. One of the hunters lunged at me and I kicked him in the chest. The other hunter was too close for a kick so when he rushed at me I let him come. I grabbed his wrist when his dagger was eight inches from my nose and yanked him toward me. His blade pierced the ground beside my head and I used his arm as a boost to launch myself up. My eyes darted about in search of my wand.

"Knight!"

I turned, but the warning came too late.

As the bronze arrow flew through the air, and my mind registered it would strike true, I felt like I was watching it in slow motion.

The arrow pierced me in the chest right where my heart was.

I staggered. I barely had time to look down and see the blood soaking my top before I collapsed.

I tried to keep my eyelids open, but I faltered as life drained out of me. All that was left was the haziness of the forest, fallen blue leaves, and the smell of disturbed earth—the last things, I imagined, I would have to remember this world by.

CHAPTER 15

Death (Or Something Like It)

expected death to be more permanent.

The last thing I expected after getting shot through the chest was to wake up again. But lo and behold, that's exactly what happened.

My return to life was slow. Shades of black and red pulsed through the inside of my closed eyelids. I heard whispery, warbled voices. Eventually, I started to make out the words.

"What's happening? She's not breathing. The magic should have been released from her by now. What's that glow?"

My eyelids snapped open. I was lying on the grass. My wand lay a couple yards away still in its knife form. Strength and vitality surged through me and a gust of air rushed into my lungs, causing me to sit up. I looked into the surprised faces of two dagger-wielding magic hunters standing over me. One held the arrow that had killed me. He'd pulled it from my body and its bloodied tip matched the arrow's dark crimson tail feathers.

I glanced down at my chest where I'd been hit. A bright burst of my magic was shooting out of the point of impact like a ray of light, sealing the wound. The veins in my arms were glowing too. The brightness shone out of the sleeves in my jacket, and I could feel the stinging. It was a similar sensation to when I made contact with Poppies.

The hunters were stunned, but when the beam of light subsided so did their shock. One of them pounced forward, his dagger aimed at my face. My reflexes did not delay—I caught his arm and heaved my body back, twisting and throwing him forward so he landed beside me.

Hunter Two charged in. While I pinned Hunter One to the ground, I kicked Hunter Two in the side of the knee, causing him to buckle. I released Hunter One's arm and forcefully hammered his bicep. He let go of his dagger. I grabbed it and stabbed him in the thigh, then sprang forward and slashed Hunter Two across the legs. Dropping the loaner dagger, I grabbed my own knife and ran. I ignored the cries of the hunters, the shaking of the shifting earth, and my own bewilderment at how I was still alive. I just ran.

I felt nauseous and disoriented. In the distance I heard shouts, but they kept changing direction and were getting farther away. Trees and stones blurred together and I found it impossible to tell whether this was due to my wavering perception or because the forest was shifting so fast that I was literally running in circles.

Where were my friends?

I considered calling out to them. But as Daniel's name formed on my lips, I thought better of it. The hunters were probably a lot closer than my friends were. Calling out would give away my position.

I darted through the changing setting, jumping from one tectonic plate to the other, but soon the shouts were gone. I couldn't hear my friends, or the hunters, or anything else except my own agonizing heartbeat. Pain pulsed through my body. My chest stung with every breath. However, that was nothing compared to the fear and desperation that ached through me. I didn't know how long I had been out, but in that interval of death I'd lost my friends.

The shifting forest came to a stop and I collapsed to my knees. I dropped my knife and slammed my fist into the dirt as I cried out in frustration.

No one responded. The forest was quiet and I was alone while Jason, Daniel, SJ, and Blue were out there somewhere, facing the wrath of the magic hunters Arian and Rampart had sent after me. Did my friends think I was dead? Were *they* dead?

The stinging in my veins felt like lemon juice in a wound.

Golden light continued to pour out of my sleeves although the burst of energy emanating from my chest had long ceased. I pulled down my tank top to inspect the spot where the arrow had pierced me. There was a scar across my skin, but it was sealed shut. That's when it hit me.

No, no, no!

At first, I was upset. I'd only promised myself this morning that I would avoid using Magic Instinct as a means to save myself. But my frustration dissipated when I appreciated the miracle of what had just occurred.

I'd come back to life! My magic, which I could use to give life to other things, had brought *me* back to life. I sat motionless on the ground as that fully sunk in.

Like Jason, I had theorized I might eventually get strong enough to use my powers to restore life to others. But I never thought I could . . . That my powers could . . .

I carefully touched the scar on my chest, but even the gentlest poke of my finger caused me to wince. Like a rock falling through the surface of a lake, a ripple of pain exuded from the wound and pulsed through me. When it subsided, I found my way to my feet. My chest still hurt bitterly, and now that the adrenaline was fading, I felt tired. *Very* tired.

Suddenly I had an idea. I slung off my backpack and dug around for Daniel's Mark Two. I flipped open the compact and tried to call SJ, then Blue, then Jason. Unfortunately, none of the calls went through. Each time I tried to activate the compact, the ringing was drowned out by harsh static.

I recalled the warning of the man from the stables who'd taken us up the mountain. He'd said that this forest disrupted magic tech, including Mark Twos. I guess I just wished he'd been wrong.

Defeated, I put the Mark Two in my bag and returned my wand to hairpin form before clipping it to the bra strap beneath my tank top. That's when I heard something rustling in the trees behind me. I whirled around but the sound stopped, and when I stalked through the trees in investigation, there was nothing to explain it.

I trudged on through the forest in search of my friends, but soon even this grew difficult. I may have been super charged when I'd first come back to life, but my exhaustion and pain were growing as time passed, causing me to feel heavy and stiff.

Things went from bad to worse a few minutes later. Distracted by the aching and dizziness, as well as the sound of rustling leaves that had started up again, I took a wrong step and fell through an animal trap. The hole was maybe eight feet deep. It had been covered by leaves and woven grass, which made it blend into the ground. I crashed to the bottom.

As if through a long tunnel, I looked up at the hole above me and saw a flash of silver and fur. My head felt woozy and I knew I was about to go unconscious. So I found myself praying to any higher power who might listen that this whole "bring myself back to life" thing did not have a time limit.

CHAPTER 16

Choker

lass, may I have your attention?"

The classroom of young adolescents looked up from their work. Among them was Natalie Poole. She sat at a desk near the front of the class. Ryan Jackson sat a few seats behind.

The students minded their teacher—a slender, caramel-skinned woman with curly hair and horn-rimmed glasses. The shadow of someone standing in the hallway cast its way across the floor.

"I would like to introduce a new student," the teacher said "She just moved to Los Angeles and will be starting class with us today."

A girl with long, platinum blonde hair, shining pink lip gloss, dark black eyes, and perfect porcelain skin entered the room. She smiled at the class and winked at Ryan Jackson when their eyes met. Then her gaze fell upon Natalie. She continued to smile, but the grin seemed different, somehow sinister.

The blonde girl appeared slightly older than the rest of the kids. Natalie moved uncomfortably in her seat as the teacher put her hands on the girl's shoulders.

"Everyone," she said. "Say hello to Tara Gold."

Natalie snapped the pencil in her hand. The image of Tara—Arian's right-hand woman who was charged with the campaign of destroying Natalie's life on Earth—faded to black.

I was now looking out at a spectacular view of snow-covered mountains. I leaned my hands against a low stone wall. The feeling of cold against my cheeks and the soft snowflakes that fell on my hands confirmed that I was not an observer in this scene, but a player.

In most of my dreams I was an omniscient presence who simply saw what was going on. Once in a while I had dreams where I was full-on present and talked to Liza in a void. This kind of dream was something in the middle. I was very much aware and a part of my surroundings, but it felt like I was not in control of anything I said or did. It was like I was on autopilot.

"I'm sorry I couldn't be more helpful."

My ears perked up at the recognizable voice. The last time I'd heard it in real life had been close to a year ago.

"Mark," I said, turning to see my old friend approaching from across a snowy courtyard.

Mark, prince of Dolohaunty, had been Jason's roommate and a friend of ours for a few years. But he hadn't returned to Lord Channing's last fall, so Daniel had become Jason's new roommate and joined our group as a result.

The staff at Lord Channing's said that Mark was taking a temporary leave of absence due to an illness, though later we discovered that the antagonists had also been targeting him just like they'd been targeting me, my friends, and any other protagonists they deemed a threat to their plans. We'd been extremely worried about him until Liza shared that he was okay, actually had been sick, and that we would reunite with him in the fall. I'd had a vision to confirm this, which helped, but sometimes I still wondered about what had happened to him.

Looking at the prince now, he seemed perfectly healthy and fit as ever. His dark skin stood out against the sharp white snow. The silvery dress regalia he wore, the glowing lights of the palace behind him, and the long-sleeved, sparkling purple gown I was wearing told me that we were at some kind of formal event.

"You've been enormously helpful," I found myself saying. "We'll figure out the rest as we go. There's still some time left."

"Not a lot of time when you're preparing for the end of the world," Mark responded.

"Then it's a good thing I'm not doing that," I said.

"What do you mean?"

"I'm not preparing for the world to end. I'm preparing to save it."

It was so strange to feel like I was reciting lines from a script I hadn't read. This vision was also more detailed and longer than other autopilot ones I'd experienced in the past. Maybe my visions were getting more powerful?

Mark leaned against the wall beside me. He tilted his chin up at the starry sky and closed his eyes for a moment. Tiny snowflakes fell on his face. He looked peaceful but also a bit sad. I didn't know why, but I felt my heart hurt with empathy.

"You're not just hiding from the crowd, are you?" Mark commented after a beat.

My eyes flicked to him. "What else could I be hiding from?"

Mark smiled sympathetically. "I know it's been a while since we've seen each other, Crisa, but I still remember how you like to run away."

"I do not." I frowned, genuinely insulted. "I never run from a fight if I can help it. I've faced every monster and antagonist this realm and others have thrown at me."

"I didn't mean from a fight," Mark said calmly. "I meant from people. You've always been like that—pushing people away, keeping friends at arm's length, never letting your guard down completely."

"I'm not like that anymore," I said flatly. "At least, I try not to be. Last year I had to deal with all that stuff you're talking about. It took a lot, but I overcame it. I've let a good number of people in since then—SJ, Blue, Jason, Girtha, Chance, Daniel . . ."

Mark nodded. "I guess old habits die hard with the last two."

"How do you mean?"

He raised his eyebrows and gave me an incredulous look. "Crisa."

My gaze darted away from him. The snowfall was picking up; a storm was coming. In that flurry of frozen fractals, the scene faded away.

Now I was in Rampart's castle, in the Knights' Room. Arian was glowering over a pair of nervous magic hunters—the ones who'd been standing over my undead body in the Shifting Forest.

"What do you mean she's alive?" Arian barked. "You just told me that you killed her."

"We did," one of the hunters said apprehensively. "She was dead . . . and then she wasn't. That life magic of hers is way more powerful than we thought."

Arian looked angry enough to kill someone himself. In the next instant, he did. Faster than I could look away, Arian drew his sword from its sheath and cut down one of the hunters. Blood and body fell to the otherwise glistening floor. The other hunter took a step back.

Geez, I wish someone had given my subconscious a warning. I did not need to see that.

"Let that be a lesson to you and the rest of your men about what happens to those who don't complete their orders," Arian said menacingly. "Now get out of my sight. The next time I hear from you, I better have news that Crisanta Knight is *actually* dead. Or Merlin has been captured."

The hunter bolted out of the room. Arian bent down and wiped his bloodied sword on the jacket of the dead hunter. Rampart, who'd been sitting in his chair at the head of the Round Table, shook his head and sighed. "I just had this floor cleaned, Arian. Next time you kill one of your henchmen, couldn't you do it in the courtyard?"

Arian scoffed, stowing his weapon as he stalked toward the king. "Watch yourself, Rampart," he said. "You may have this kingdom at your command, but don't forget whose orders you follow. Nadia and I helped put you on that throne and we can easily take you off. Which I'll take great pleasure in doing if you screw up again."

"First off, you didn't exactly help my grandmother and I take over Camelot out of charity," Rampart argued. "You did it so that when you made a play to take over your realm, you would have allies and armies to back you up. And second, *I* am providing *you* with the Simia Crown in exchange for Excalibur."

"And thanks to your ineptitude, that mission is in jeopardy too."

"Don't blame me for your little Knight dilemma," the king said defensively. "You instructed me to keep her here until you arrived. If you'd have just let me execute her on sight, then she wouldn't be on the loose right now."

"We had to make sure her brother was viable, you know that. Now that we're sure about Alex, her being alive is a major problem."

"Okay, so turn that problem into an opportunity," the king said. He got up from his throne and walked to the other side of the room. He gestured to a tapestry above the door. It was the gold and black one with a design of crossed swords in the middle.

"Have I ever told you about this tapestry?" he asked. "It's a symbolic depiction of the tale of Sir Balin, The Knight of Two Swords."

Arian rolled his eyes. "I don't have time for a history lesson, Rampart. In case you haven't noticed, my kind isn't so fond of old stories."

"Yes, I know you antagonists hate the old tales. But if you look close enough, you can find inspiration in them. Take this tale for example." He gestured at the tapestry. "Sir Balin won the magic sword that made him famous because of his goodness. Only a hero of the purest heart and truest courage could claim it, and of all the knights in Arthur's court, he was the only one able to. As the blade was enchanted to grant its owner great strength and skill in combat, he wielded it proudly for many years."

"And let me guess," Arian said. "He became some big, important hero in Camelot and—I don't know—got a castle named after him. Happily ever after."

"Not even close," Rampart responded. "What Balin didn't know was that while the blade's enchantment gave him great fortune, it would also lead to his destruction. Like Excalibur, his sword originated on Avalon. However, unlike Excalibur, which Arthur earned, a dark wizard stole this blade from the Isle. In revenge, the Lady of the Lake placed a curse on it. Whoever wields the sword is doomed to use it to kill the person they love most. In the end, Balin unknowingly killed his own brother with the sword, and later killed himself from the grief and guilt."

"So what?" Arian said. "You think we should try to use this sword to stop Crisanta Knight?"

Rampart shook his head. "We have no idea where the sword is. The blade couldn't be destroyed, so after Balin's death Merlin put a spell on it to make it difficult to find. A couple other knights have run into it over time. It's my understanding that Sir Lancelot took possession of the sword and killed his best friend Sir Gawain years ago. And Sir Galahad fell victim to the curse as well. However, after each owner of the sword fulfills the curse, it transports to some other place per Merlin's spell. Since the unpleasantness of Sir Galahad's fate, no one has seen it."

"Okay, then why are you bringing it up now?" Arian asked, frustrated.

"Because of the meaning behind the story," Rampart replied. "Balin's internal strength—that which gave him his power and made him so formidable—is the same quality that set him on his path to destruction. The sword that he was given because of his goodness was what caused his demise. Why not set up Crisanta Knight for the same fate?

"Her prophecy says that she's meant to either help or stop your takeover of the realm, but you've been acting like she's predetermined for just the latter. Prophecies are vague for a reason, Arian. People change. Their choices are not set in stone and neither are their futures. So instead of seeing this girl as a problem who must be eliminated, why not consider her power as untapped fuel for your cause? Why not turn her strength for heroics into a tool for devastation?"

Face pensive, Arian studied Rampart.

"Arian," the king said steadily. "Why not turn Crisanta Knight the *enemy* into Crisanta Knight, the *asset*?"

For a final time, my dream shifted. I entered a white void and found Liza sitting at a simple wooden table.

"You haven't tried to talk to me through my dreams in a

while," I commented as I walked over and sat down in the empty chair across from her.

There was a porcelain teapot and two teacups on the table. Liza poured. "I gave you the Mark Two so I wouldn't have to," she said. "Reaching you this way is much easier now that your magic is getting more powerful, but it's still extremely taxing. I will probably wake up feeling completely drained. However, your Mark Two isn't getting a signal, so I saw no other choice than to call on you like this."

"What's going on?" I asked. Liza gestured toward the teacup but I waved it away. "I don't like tea."

"Hey, it's your dream." Liza shrugged, taking a sip. She put the cup down then folded her hands on the table and looked at me solemnly and sternly. "I felt bad about how we left things and I wanted to talk about your Magic Instinct again. I've had too many visions of your future not to push the subject. I'm worried that if I don't, something terrible might happen to you."

"Something terrible already did," I said. "I died today, Liza. A magic hunter shot me in the chest, but Magic Instinct kicked in and brought me back to life." Liza's eyes widened, but she didn't seem too shocked. "Did you know it could do that?" I asked.

"Not for a fact," she replied. "However, I am not surprised given how powerful your magic is becoming."

"That makes one of us," I commented. "I honestly can't believe it. If I can do that, who knows what my limits are."

"I couldn't say," Liza responded. "I'm not sure how far this ability can stretch, or what its restrictions are. But perhaps more important for the moment—if you were dead, then *you* didn't activate that instance of Magic Instinct, Crisa. You didn't choose to let go, and that's what I am attempting to hammer home. It's why I called on you in this dream now. I know you don't want to let go of control when using your magic—I'd prefer it if you didn't too—but I'm afraid you need to accept that soon enough you will have to. I didn't want to push too hard during our last conversation, but to survive the trials ahead, you're going to need more power than full control currently allows."

"Liza, I really think that's a bad idea," I argued. "I agree with everything you've taught me about control before now. I don't want to relinquish that for the very reason that my magic *may be too powerful*. I mean, look at what it just did. I was dead and it brought me back. If I let it off the leash intentionally, who knows what it could do. What if I can't contain it?"

"I know, Crisa. I know. And again, I understand how this goes against so much of what I've tried to teach you. But the situation has changed. My visions have foreseen this as a necessity."

"But what if—"

"Crisa, you've never been ruled by the fear of what could be. I tend to be the cautious one in our dynamic. You are always pushing yourself."

"Playing with fire is different than diving head first into it, Liza."

The room began to shake. Liza's image faded as she took another sip from her teacup. More of her vanished with every second.

"You're waking up," Liza said. "And I have a feeling we won't speak again for a while. So I'll just say this. Magic runs deep in your blood, Crisa. It is a part of your very essence and your powers have a greater range than you realize or may even want. I can't promise you that you will be able to handle the challenge. But then, I never have and you've charged ahead anyway. You have never simply played with fire, my girl. You've lived in it. Now I am just asking you to be brave enough to walk in deeper."

Liza disappeared. The teacup she'd been holding fell and shattered.

When I opened my eyes, I was lying on a bed, definitely not in the animal trap I'd last been in. The bed had crimson silk sheets, pillows, and canopies. Every inch of the floor was covered in blue rose petals—the world's most fragrant and fragile carpet.

I sat up and looked down. My SRB and Alex's bracelet were gone, as was my wandpin. My feet were crammed into high heels instead of combat boots. And I was wearing a full-on, floor-length ball gown.

I leapt off the bed and looked myself over.

The dress was blood red, A-line, and sleeveless. The material was hard satin with pleats around the skirt. A dark silver belt with a hexagon pattern of chrome-colored crystals sat around my waist.

I was horrified. I didn't know how I'd come to be wearing this dress, but it didn't matter. Even if magical bunnies had wiggled their noses and caused my previous outfit to morph into this one through a flurry of rainbow sparkles, it was a violation.

You don't change a girl's clothes without her permission. That's just messed up.

I had no idea where I was. The walls of the room were built from giant gray stones and there were no windows. A single panel radiated pale blue light from the ceiling, and a dark wooden door resided on the far wall. I dashed over to it—my long dress dragging against the flower petals and leaving a trail of clean floor in my wake.

Surprisingly, the door was unlocked. When I stepped into the hall it was eerily quiet, but there were a few other girls wandering down the red-carpeted corridor in dresses just as long and scarlet as mine. I hurried over to a pair of them.

"Um, hi," I said.

"Hello," they said in unison.

One girl had lustrous black hair that hung down to her waist. Her red silk dress featured long sleeves and a low-cut neckline. The second girl was wearing a strapless red organza dress. Her chocolate brown hair was twisted up in a taut updo that showed off her high cheekbones.

I noticed that each of the girls wore an impressive choker made from rubies. Their necklaces were so tightly wrapped around their necks that it looked like the accessories were strangling them. I instinctively put my hand to my neck and realized I was also wearing a choker. I tried to pull it off, but it wouldn't budge. I couldn't find a cord to untie it either. The thing was inexplicably attached to me like a second skin.

"Where are we?" I asked. "Who are you people?"

The chocolate-haired girl looked nervous. "I'm Shiondre and this is Darcy," she said. "And please, you have to listen to us. I can see that you're new, and this might be overwhelming, but you have to behave yourself or else—"

A hypnotic, musical chime echoed through the corridor. It was so loud it caused the blue, shimmering tapestries that lined the hallway to shiver. At the same time, the blue panels of light that were spaced along the ceiling started to flash. They did so in a pattern that matched the chime's tune.

The girls in the vicinity seemed to tremble at the call of the ominous chime. As it continued, they began to walk down the hall, falling into single file. Shiondre grabbed me by the wrist and pulled me along as she and Darcy joined the line of girls.

I shook off Shiondre's grip and repeated my question with more urgency. *"Where are we?"*

"We are in Bluebeard Tower," she whispered. "And for your sake, I hope you're good at keeping a low profile."

I wanted to ask more questions—and mention that keeping a low profile was the opposite of what I was good at—but Shiondre and Darcy refused to look at me.

I walked behind them as other girls poured in from connecting corridors and merged with our procession. Each girl wore a unique red dress and the same ruby choker. The girls' eyes were filled with fear. It quivered where the light of life should've been. I had a very bad feeling about what was coming.

I ran through the synopsis of Bluebeard's story in my head.

After taking a wife, a monstrous, demonic man named Bluebeard went on a business trip. Before he left, he gave his wife keys to every room in his castle with only one instruction: don't open the chamber on the bottom floor. She could go anywhere and everywhere else, just not there. Of course, girl *had* to go and open that chamber. And when she did, she discovered the bloodied bodies of all the dude's previous wives. Bluebeard found out and was going to kill her like he had all the other girls, but in the end she was rescued and *he* was killed. End of story.

Or maybe not.

The line of girls entered a grand ballroom as the chiming continued. The room's floor was checkered tile. The walls were almost too tall to see the ceiling, but something up there made it worth a tilt back of the head to look. Sprouting from the ceiling was an enormous electric chandelier in the shape of an upside-down daffodil. The thing was easily three times the size of a carriage. A myriad of metal chains intertwined with clear-colored crystals draped from the fixture, glistening in the blue light that it emanated and connecting with the ceiling in big whooshes.

It was not the only impressive thing in the ballroom. While three of the walls were made of stone, the wall on the left was comprised entirely of giant windows in different shapes and sizes. A school of orange fish swam past one and I finally understood why I hadn't seen any other windows in the compound until now. We were underwater. At least I hoped that was water. The liquid beyond the windows was blood red. The color cast a menacing red shadow over us. It made the whole place feel like some kind of underworld where demons dwelt and the wicked spent eternity.

In front of the wall of windows was a regal cobalt throne positioned on top of a twelve-step, wraparound staircase. A dais stood on ground level next to the stairs. Sitting atop the dais was an open leather-bound book and a jar of ink with an aged quill sticking out of it.

The chiming stopped as the last of the girls hurried into the ballroom. We were lined up in single file across the floor, facing the iron doors that we'd come through.

I was about to say something to Shiondre when the sound of heavy footsteps diverted my attention. Two men marched into the ballroom. One was near thirty years old with a thin blond mustache and pointy chin. A mustard yellow cape hung from his shoulder pads, matching his puffy, pleated shirt. He seemed relatively normal, apart from his fancy outfit—especially compared with the other man.

This guy was over eight feet tall. He was burly in a strong-like-a-bear kind of way and had hands so big they looked like they could crush your skull like a walnut. He wore a glistening red ring on one hand while the other hand was gloved. The monster man's outfit was different shades of blue—from the tip of his shoes to his collar and cape—with plenty of platinum and gold trimmings that shined in the chandelier's electric light.

The most striking part of the creature was his face. It was half man, half wrinkled beast. His eyes were small, but they twinkled. And attached to his hard, intimidating jawline was a thick beard that was bushy and dark blue like the deepest waters of the ocean.

"Quite a collection, Daverose," said the man in the yellow cape as they approached.

"We've expanded our selection a bit since your last purchase, Lord Cramer," the blue-bearded man said. "We have fully restocked our redheads, and now offer thirteen ethnicities."

"Very good," Lord Cramer replied. "I'm thinking of a brunette this time, maybe something more exotic."

"May I recommend one of our younger models?" Daverose replied. "Perhaps this one."

Daverose walked up to Shiondre. I could see the bloodlust in his piercing blue irises. Shiondre gulped as he studied her. She looked down at the floor.

Daverose snapped his fingers and three creatures with bodies of men and faces of white tigers hurried into the room. I'd only just dreamed about such creatures. Their eyes were black and big as teacup saucers. They wore silver suits over black collared shirts and ties. Matching silk pocket squares sat in their jacket pockets. Each creature had one gloved hand and one hand that wore a ring made of the same red gemstone as Daverose's.

"Report," Daverose said to the tigermen.

"Yes, Master," one of them replied. He looked at Shiondre, opened a scroll, and cleared his throat. "Shiondre Louise Cunningham—age twenty-three, princess of Maramour, one hundred and nineteen pounds, five-foot-eight, no genetic defects, allergies, or unfixable quirks."

Lord Cramer moved closer to Shiondre and she stiffened in discomfort. My eyebrows narrowed and my protective instincts kicked in. However, before I could step between her and Lord Cramer, the man's eyes darted to me.

"Hello, who's this?" Lord Cramer pointed at me. He also had a ring on one hand and a glove on the other. He looked me up and down and smiled. It was all I could do not to punch him in the nose.

"Daverose, old boy, you've been holding out on me. Who is this lovely creature?"

"Alavaster," Daverose said to the scroll-wielding tigerman.

The tigerman took a step in my direction and glanced at his parchment nervously. "Um, sir, she is new. We still need to gather information on her. If Lord Cramer would like to select a different bride in the meantime . . ."

"No," Lord Cramer said. He continued to study me with a sick grin. "I understand if she needs time to be prepared. Put her on my backorder tab and message me when she's ready." He winked at me. "Yes. She'll do just fine."

He reached out his fingers as if to stroke my cheek, but I seized his hand and twisted it sideways.

"Try that again, and you'll lose that hand," I said, glaring at him.

Half the girls in the room gasped. All of them turned in my direction. Daverose pushed Cramer out of the way and towered over me.

"You have no idea where you are, do you?" he asked. "Or who I am?"

I didn't have time to respond. Daverose grabbed me by the neck with one of his massive mitts and tossed me clear across the ballroom. I slid over the smooth tile until I collided against the staircase leading up to the throne with a rough thud.

Ow.

"This is Bluebeard Tower," Daverose said as he marched toward me, his shadow elongating behind him thanks to the glow of the chandelier. "I am Lord Daverose Bluebeard. And you are my property."

I clamored to my feet and backed up against the dais next to the throne staircase. Glancing over my shoulder, I saw that the book was a kind of registry. On the left side of the pages were the names of men. Many of these names had a fancy title in front of them like Lord or Monsieur, but all had the last name "Bluebeard." On the right side of the pages, meanwhile, were the names of girls: Alladine, Ygraine, Bellangere, Ariane, and so on.

I snapped my attention back to the threat. Lord Cramer's

ordinary human body suddenly contorted. His limbs stretched and he grew to the same massive height as Daverose. His hands and head bulged as his eyes turned blue and menacing. His jaw and brow line stretched and warped. He looked like a lion, bear, and troll had donated their genetics to create a monster. For a finishing touch, his blond whiskers transformed into a ragged blue beard.

I swallowed the impulse to cower and stood up straight to address Daverose. "You're right," I said. "I don't know where I am, or who you are. But since I'm apparently not on your little scroll there, let me tell you who I am. I'm Crisanta Katherine Knight—Princess of Midveil, five-foot-six, a hundred and twenty-five pounds, no allergies, and most definitely *not your property*."

Daverose raised his eyebrows at me before glancing at Lord Cramer. "I'm afraid your backorder won't be ready for at least a month, Cramer. Even with regular disciplining, she'll probably take a while to rein in."

"Understandable," Cramer said. "We wouldn't want one of your brides leaving here with free will. People might start to talk."

Daverose snapped his fingers and the tigermen surrounded me. All three drew batons from within their jackets. The batons elongated to a foot in length and began to crackle with electricity.

"Tell me, Crisanta Katherine Knight," Daverose said. "Does obedience come easily to you?"

"Order me not to hurt you and find out," I countered.

Daverose grinned wickedly before turning to the line-up of ladies. "Get her settled, will you, girls? You know the drill. Fill her in on the rules, teach her the ropes, and show her around the castle. Anywhere and everywhere but my Little Cabinet. You all know what happens if you set foot in there. For now though, a small reminder of what happens if you disobey your master."

Daverose nodded to the tigermen. They lunged at me—their electric batons sizzling with the threat of shock. I side-stepped the first tigerman and ducked the strike of the second. I spun around, but the third creature hit me in the sternum with his baton. Electricity passed through my system with a curt, violent jerk.

It felt like part of my heart had gotten deep-fried. I staggered but managed to elbow the tigerman who'd shocked me. He fell back and I jumped out of the way to avoid the second tigerman as he swung at my chest. Alas, I backed up into the baton of the first creature. This time the electricity surged up the base of my spine. My knees buckled and I winced in pain. Before I could recover, the second and third tigermen were on either side of me. They jabbed their batons into my ribcage simultaneously, sending electricity through my body.

"Aaargh!"

One of the tigermen slammed his foot between my shoulder blades, flattening me to the ground. For a moment before I passed out, I thought I saw something. It was like a ripple over the environment. Everything in my vision—the walls, the chandelier, the floor—turned red and warbled, but no one else in the room seemed to notice . . .

CHAPTER 17

The Impossible Place

hance Darling was looking out the window of a tower. An elevated bed was in the middle of the room. Mauvrey lay upon it, sound asleep. Her hands were folded over her chest, which barely moved with breath. Her expression was soft and her skin was pale.

The prince walked over to the princess and studied her. The door across the room opened. A tall girl in her late twenties entered. She had wavy auburn hair that cascaded down her shoulders and framed her face. She wore a shimmery, long-sleeved olive dress, which was short in the front—showing off her pants and boots—but spilled out regally with a full bustle behind her. I didn't know who this girl was, but she had Chance's eyes and a similar bone structure, so I wondered if they were related.

"Should you really be spending your free time with an unconscious girl when you have a live one downstairs?" the girl asked.

"It's my turn to keep watch," Chance replied. "Blue will be up here in a few minutes to relieve me."

The auburn-haired girl moved over to stand beside Mauvrey and huffed. "I cannot believe this is the girl you were into for so many years."

"Mauvrey was an easy choice," Chance replied. "She was shallow and beautiful and didn't require me to be anything greater. When I was younger, I thought that was a good thing. Now I know better. The person you love should not make you want to settle for the easiest version of yourself. They should make you want to be the best you can be."

"I could not agree more," the girl said. "But be careful, little brother. My job as one of the heirs to our throne may be to protect this kingdom, but my job as your sister is to protect you. We are already making ourselves vulnerable by keeping Mauvrey here and hosting Crisanta Knight. I would hate to think you are also making yourself vulnerable for someone who might not feel the same way."

"Crisa has feelings for me, Daphne," Chance responded confidently. "I can see it. And I'm not giving up on her."

Again, I awoke in a rose petal covered bedroom. I took a moment to process. The dream of Chance and his sister disturbed me. The whole Mauvrey thing was weird, but I wasn't complaining; seeing my archenemy look like she was half-dead was actually rather satisfying. But the things that Chance had said made me feel uncomfortable in an unfamiliar way.

I shook it off and shoved the dream to the deep recesses of my brain. My most pressing objective was finding a way out of Bluebeard Tower. I got up and began my search of the mysterious compound, talking to different girls and exploring all the nooks and crannies like a hound on the hunt.

Unfortunately, I couldn't find a single way out. The only windows were the enormous ones in the ballroom, which would've led to a red, watery death if I so much as cracked one. I didn't know how deep we were underwater, and even if I could break those thick panels of glass, the water would probably rush in and drown me before I got out.

Oh, and aside from not having my wand, my magic wasn't working.

I'd expected my powers to be drained after that miraculous resurrection stunt in the Shifting Forest. But even when I was tapped out, I could still feel the presence of magic inside me. Now I felt nothing. It was like my powers were completely gone.

"There has to be a way out of this castle," I huffed as I entered the ballroom for the fourth time.

Shiondre and Darcy had been following me. They'd wanted to

make sure I was all right and had also been answering my many questions.

They told me about the water outside the Tower, which they were pretty sure was a lake. They explained that the massive chandelier in the ballroom was the only source of electricity for the entire compound—it single-handedly powered all of Bluebeard Tower's blue light panels. But most importantly, I learned that the chokers around our necks were designed to inhibit magic. Over the years Daverose's minions had abducted several enchantresses, so every girl kidnapped was fitted with a choker as a precautionary measure. The necklaces would stop girls from magically fighting back against Daverose, the tigermen, and their future husbands.

That's what we were doing here, you see. We were the matrimonial inventory for a malevolent race of monsters.

It turns out that Bluebeard was not just one man, one monster. Bluebeard was a *species*. To the outer world, his kind looked like regular men—often wealthy, handsome, high-society types. But Bluebeards were like wolves in sheep's clothing. They had a powerful bloodlust and a hobby of collecting new wives. In the olden days, this habit was much harder to maintain without drawing attention from the community. After all, a local lord who married every six months without giving an explanation for what happened to his previous wives was bound to raise a few suspicions.

As a result, the industrious Bluebeard known as Daverose had established a business that would remedy the situation. Setting up shop deep in the Passage Perelous where the Knights of the Round Table and other heroes couldn't find him, Daverose had made the buying and selling of wives a lucrative business for his kind to enjoy.

With the help of the demonic tigermen, Daverose abducted young women from the Shifting Forest and imprisoned them in Bluebeard Tower. Bluebeards from different realms made regular pilgrimages to this Tower. When they arrived, they looked over the selection of girls and paid Daverose a hefty sum for the ones they wanted. Soon after, the selected girls would vanish from the Tower.

My anxiety about the whole thing increased with each passing minute, especially knowing what was in store for me personally. Darcy and Shiondre explained that the tigermen conducted "disciplining" sessions every day. These were spontaneous torturing and brainwashing sessions administered to girls who fought back or got feisty. They were not scheduled for any specific time, so the girls were always on their toes. Daverose had specifically mentioned my "disciplining" when we'd faced off, so I knew I was on the tigermen's list and they could come for me at any moment.

"How often does Daverose bring a buyer here?" I asked as I glared into the depths of the red lake.

"There is no real consistency," Darcy responded. "There is a large crank on the third floor landing. One of the tigermen winds it and that sets off the chiming throughout the Tower, letting us know to report to the ballroom for assembly."

"And how many tigermen are there?" I asked.

"We don't know."

"Well, where are they now?"

"We don't know that either," Darcy replied. "The tigermen only appear when our master does. We have never seen them around the Tower except for when we are called for assembly."

"Okay, one, stop calling him our master," I said. "He's not our master and calling him that isn't helping. Two, they have to be around here somewhere. This building is *underwater*. It's not like they've got scuba gear in one of the armoires and can just swim to the surface."

"Scuba gear?"

"Forget it." I began to pace. My hand absentmindedly reached for my stomach. The last time I'd eaten had been in the village before we entered the Passage Perelous. I should've been starving by now. Yet I felt an uncharacteristic lack of hunger.

That's when a crazy notion hit me.

I closed my eyes and thought back to the moment before I passed out from the electrical shock of the baton. The way this room had flickered, it seemed like . . . like it wasn't real.

"Darcy," I said. "How long have you been here?"

"I am not sure," she said. "A while."

"What about you, Shiondre?" I asked. "How long have you been here?"

"A while."

Their responses made my crazy notion get all tingly as conversations I'd had with other girls throughout the day came back to me.

"And when was the last time either of you ate?" I asked.

"What?"

"You heard me," I replied. "You said you never see the tigermen or Daverose or any other outsiders except during the assemblies. I've been all over this Tower and haven't found a single staff member, let alone a kitchen. So that begs the question—where do you get your food from?"

"We've eaten," Shiondre insisted.

"Okay, then tell me when, where, *how?*"

Darcy pursed her lips and frowned. "We must have. I mean, we've been here—"

"A while, I know," I interrupted. "It's funny. I've asked a few other girls that same question and they all said the same thing, but no one can tell me any specifics."

"Crisa, what are you getting at?" Darcy asked.

"What I'm getting at is this place makes no sense. You all claim to have been here for a while, but there is no food anywhere. Aside from the one I woke up in, the bedrooms appear to have never been slept in. And there is not a speck of dirt on any of your dresses even though that's the only thing you ever wear."

"Crisa . . ." Shiondre tried to interject.

"And if we're underwater," I went on, "How are Daverose and his tigermen able to come and go? If they are not in the Tower, then they would have to leave somehow."

"Maybe there is a way out through the Little Cabinet?" Darcy suggested.

Shiondre elbowed Darcy and gave her a frightened look.

I frowned. "I heard Daverose mention that. What is it?"

Despite Shiondre's reluctance, Darcy answered. "The Little Cabinet is a test, Crisa," she said, lowering her voice to a whisper.

"For the most part, Daverose leaves us alone within these walls. The only thing we are forbidden to do is enter a room Daverose calls his Little Cabinet. He trusts us to obey this one rule and never go inside. Since that is the only place in the Tower that none of us have ever gone into, I have to imagine that Daverose's way out is through there."

My eyes nearly popped out of my head. "Why didn't you tell me this before? If there's even a possibility of a way out then why haven't any of you gone to investigate?"

"Because the Little Cabinet is a death sentence," Darcy responded.

"More so than waiting around here?"

"Yes," Shiondre interceded. "Crisa, please. You cannot go in there. You will die. You think you're the first girl who's wanted to escape through the Little Cabinet? There have been others, and all of them met the same end—a gruesome fate that Bluebeards have been bestowing upon disobedient brides for millennia." She shook her head and shuddered. "Any girl who passes through the Little Cabinet vanishes from the Tower. But soon after, Daverose assembles us in the ballroom, and . . ." She turned away with a sob.

"What?" I asked.

"He shows us their heads," Darcy finished for her friend.

I took a step back. "Wait, you mean like—"

"I mean like he and his tigermen gather us in the ballroom and he holds up the head of the girl who went through the Little Cabinet," Darcy said. "Shiondre has seen it happen twice. I've only seen it once. But believe me, it makes an impression. So that is why we don't go into the Little Cabinet. We're not stupid; we know there could be a way out through there. But we also know the brutal fate that awaits us if we try and take it."

I let the information sink in. It fit with the Bluebeard narrative—the whole "forbidden room filled with death" thing. Actually, now that I thought about it, I was pretty sure I remembered reading a couple of eclectic versions of the story in my Fairytale History class where the chamber that held the bloodied bodies was referred to as a Little Cabinet.

Goosebumps crawled up my skin. I'd been all fire and determination the moment Darcy had mentioned the Little Cabinet, but now I was hesitant. Even though I had miraculously come back to life once before, I wasn't sure how my life-restoring capabilities worked. Could what happened in the Shifting Forest occur again, or was it just a one-off? And did that ability only apply to certain forms of dying? I was clearly capable of resurrecting myself from an arrow through the chest, but was being beheaded an entirely different form of death that my powers couldn't protect me from?

Furthermore, what if the technicalities didn't even matter? This choker inhibited my magic. So if I faced off with Daverose again, I wouldn't be able to use my powers to save myself. Without that, or my wand, how good were my chances against such a barbaric monster? I would only have *myself* to rely on.

I exhaled deeply and centered.

That would have to be enough.

Time was running out on so many levels—I still had to find my friends, beat Alex and the antagonists to Excalibur, complete our quests before the Vicennalia Aurora, and save Jason from his imminent fate. I hadn't even had a chance to warn him this morning that his death was close at hand.

Daverose's threat was scary, but I would risk anything and everything for my friends and to stop my enemies. My head included. I turned back to Shiondre and Darcy.

"Are you guys going to show me where this cabinet is, or do I have to find it myself?"

Darcy and Shiondre walked me to a stairwell at the back of the Tower in silence.

There was a secret passage behind a tapestry. *Typical.* We climbed down it to the basement level of the compound. We arrived at a long, narrow stone corridor lit by two torches. At the end of the corridor was a single metal door.

"Best of luck, Crisa," Darcy said. "I hope . . . I hope we don't see you again."

"If I find a way out I will come back for you. I promise," I said.

Shiondre just nodded. "Goodbye, Crisa. Remember, we tried to warn you." Then she yanked on Darcy's arm and the two of them headed back the way we'd come. I marched toward my supposed doom, halting just before the door.

Deep breath.

In spite of the monsters that potentially awaited me on the other side of this door, I couldn't stay and cower when there were people and realms counting on me. Not now—not ever—would I forget that I had a responsibility to them first.

I reached for the iron handle and pulled. The unlocked door creaked outward and revealed blackness inside. Not blackness like a dark room, but like a void straight out of one of my nightmares.

My fingers stretched into the abyss. It felt cold and damp. I didn't know where this would lead me, but I was certain it was a way out of this place and that was good enough. I stepped into the darkness.

I gasped loudly as blood rushed to my head.

The moment I'd stepped into the void, it'd felt like I was falling. Then I suddenly sat up to the sound of small jewels clattering to the floor.

What? Where?

I continued to gasp for breath as my racing heart tried to calm down. At first, I could only make out a bright blue light overhead and the wash of dark crimson that seemed to consume everything. Then I closed my eyes, concentrated hard, and inhaled deeply. When I opened my eyes again, clarity had returned to my vision, but not my understanding of the situation.

I was in the ballroom of Bluebeard Tower, but it looked very different. While the window wall remained the same, the lower parts of the other walls had stone beds jutting out of them like shelves. Every girl from the Tower was asleep on top of a stone bed. It was bonkers. I was on the level closest to the floor. The next row of shelves was just a few inches above me when I was sitting up.

I swung my legs over the edge of my bed shelf and my boots dangled an inch from the floor.

My boots!

I was no longer in heels. I was wearing my familiar boots and leggings, though I still had the same red dress on over them. Also returned to their place were my SRB and Alex's wristband. I reached up to my bra strap and sighed with relief. My wandpin was there too. Which meant there was only one thing left to check.

I held up my hand and focused. A single golden spark flew from my fingers, but the attempt to produce anything more caused me great pain. I wasn't alarmed though; I knew that pain. It was Magic Exhaustion. Bringing myself back to life in the forest must've drained me pretty thoroughly. I barely had any power left.

Still, even though my magic was exhausted, knowing that it was there was a relief. Based on the Magic Exhaustion, and the vague ache I felt in my chest where I'd been shot, I concluded that it hadn't been long since I'd faced the magic hunters. Which meant it hadn't been long since I'd been separated from my friends.

I hopped off the stone slab to the checkered tile but almost slipped. My choker was lying on the ground with the rubies scattered everywhere. I touched my neck. Weird. Somehow the necklace had come off and shattered apart.

I hurried to the center of the ballroom. The epic electric chandelier was still there, seventy feet above me. The cobalt throne remained at the top of the twelve-step staircase with the dais at the base. However, aside from the bed shelves there was another key difference about the space. There was now a ladder in the room.

And I wasn't talking about the kind of ladder you'd use to paint a house or change a light bulb. This was an extensive stone ladder by the window wall that went from the ground to the ceiling. It reached up to an open doorway near the roof. I raced toward it but before starting to climb I took out my wand, transformed it into a knife, and cut the hem off my gown six inches above the knee. I tucked my wand back into place then began my ascent.

The steps of the ladder were huge, so it took quite a lot of effort. From the size, I surmised that this ladder was built solely with Bluebeards in mind.

I arrived at the doorway and found myself in a small landing area where an enclosed stairwell zigzagged upward at least eight stories. I raced to the top and found another door. This one was closed. When I burst through, the sunlight nearly blinded me. I was standing on a bridge that stretched over a massive, crimson lake. The water was gruesome in color but glassy in appearance. I walked out onto the bridge.

The doorway I'd come through was housed within a simple yellow stone building that looked like a small fort floating on the water. In the distance, rocky gorges soared into the sky, and from them red waterfalls poured into the lake. Although they were miles away, I could hear the thundering boom as the water broke the surface.

A deep grinding sound abruptly turned my attention the other way. On the opposite side of the bridge was a thick forest. I watched disgruntled birds flutter into the open as the trees moved.

The Shifting Forest . . .

I had escaped Bluebeard Tower! The possibility of reconnecting with my friends and recommencing with my mission was right over there! However, when I tried to move my feet in the direction of freedom, my body seized up. I couldn't leave. The other girls were still trapped inside. I'd promised Darcy and Shiondre that if I found a way out I would go back for them. I'd meant it. Moreover, Daverose had to be stopped. Not just in his efforts to control these girls, but permanently. I couldn't walk away from here without seeing to that.

Taking one more glimpse of the forest and a final breath of fresh air, I went back inside the stone fort and shut the door. Hurriedly I descended the enclosed stairwell and the stone ladder until I reached the ballroom floor. When I arrived, I carefully took stock of the environment again. I walked over to the nearest wall of sleeping girls. The first girl I approached was a blonde who I hadn't met yet. Her hair was in two braids and her red dress was one-shouldered. I felt her wrist for a pulse and found one.

"Hey, wake up," I said, snapping my fingers in front of her face and shaking her shoulders.

It didn't work. I gingerly put my index finger on her eyelid and pushed up. Beneath the lids, her eyes were glowing bright purple.

Yikes.

I gazed at the dozens of unconscious girls. They looked peaceful but comatose. And they all wore ruby chokers.

Wait. Not rubies.

I studied them closer. That's when I realized the tiny red gems on the girls' necks glowed meekly. These most certainly weren't rubies like I'd originally thought. Nothing about this place was what any of us originally thought.

The girls had been lied to. Bluebeard's chokers didn't prevent magic; they had magic in them! The chokers were clearly keeping the girls in some kind of shared enchanted sleep. Exiting through the Little Cabinet had broken my enchantment, blown my necklace to bits, and allowed me to exit the fantasy. Getting these necklaces off was therefore my best bet for rousing the girls from their magic slumber.

I tilted the blonde's head to the side. Unlike the chokers I'd seen in the enchanted sleep version of Bluebeard Tower, these had ties on the back. I simply had to undo the knot. I gazed around the room. There were a lot of girls in here. This could take forever. I stepped back and did a proper count.

Ten, twelve, eighteen, twenty-f—

A bone-chilling noise caused me to freeze.

The ballroom doors.

I pivoted sharply as they opened. Daverose and a half dozen tigermen stood in the doorway.

Crud.

The tigermen charged at me immediately. They were as agile as the cats their faces resembled. I yanked out my wandpin.

Lapellius.

Knife.

My weapon morphed, emitting a pale glow in the shadowiness of the room. I ducked under the first tigerman's swinging fist and jabbed him in the shoulder with my blade before pivoting around to duck the second creature's assault.

Shield.

The animal's claws scraped against the metal.

Spear.

I swung the staff out as the other tigermen reached me. I managed to slam it into two of them, but their catlike reflexes paired with human limbs made their movements unpredictable and faster than most of my previous opponents.

Shield.

Knife.

Spear.

Axe.

Yikes!

I was plucked from the fray. While I had been fighting the tigermen, Daverose had calmly approached. I could not stop him from grabbing me by my weapon-wielding arm and lifting me off the floor. He dangled me for a moment before roughly tossing me to the side like a sack of dirty laundry.

I hit the checkered floor. My wand, still in its axe form, slipped from my fingers. I rolled to a stop with the wind well knocked out of me. Despite being dazed, I jumped up and tried to make a break for my wand. The tigermen cut me off. Daverose sauntered toward me looking unruffled and almost amused.

I tried to summon my magic, but nothing but a few sparks arose. I still didn't have enough strength. Too late to think of another plan; Daverose loomed over me. He abruptly swatted me with the brute power of his backhand.

I was glad that he wasn't wearing the same big ring as before (weirdly, none of the tigermen were wearing their rings either) because that would have been like getting hit with brass knuckles. Nonetheless, I went sprawling over the tile again. My head spun.

"I had a feeling you were going to be the next one," he said.

I tried to get to my feet, but Daverose was already standing over me. His enormous gloved hand grasped my neck, lifted me a bit, then slammed me back against the cold floor. I tried to fight it, but I couldn't; my vision darkened. In the next instant, sight and sound slipped away and I blacked out. But not before Daverose's final words echoed in my ears.

"Take her to the Chamber."

CHAPTER 18

Blood & Water

didn't often have peaceful dreams. But at the moment I found myself staring up at a chilled gray sky that filled me with calm.

I was lying on the grass beneath a tree. I glanced over and saw Daniel beside me, his hands folded behind his head and his deep brown eyes focused on the branches above us. The branches were blackened—charred like they'd been burned—but small buds of green had sprouted here and there as the tree came back to life.

Without warning, words began coming out of my mouth. It was happening again. I was participating in my dream on autopilot like when I'd dreamed of Mark.

"Hey, Daniel," I said.

"Yeah."

"I can't imagine going through this without you."

There was a short pause then Daniel responded. "Good. Because I promise you'll never have to."

At that, I gently drifted awake and found myself in a setting that was the exact opposite of the tranquil dream I'd just been in. I was in a dungeon.

My wrists were cuffed and attached to chains dangling from the ceiling, keeping me in a standing position. The stone-walled square cell was dark, dank, and smelled like death and metal. To my right was a stairwell. It led up to a trapdoor in the ceiling that I could only barely make out. My chains allowed for very little sideways movement. I couldn't take more than a step in any direction.

I tried to focus my magic, but the moment my fingertips started to glow, pain reverberated through my arms like fire. I recognized this pain. It wasn't Magic Exhaustion; it was Stiltdegarth blood. The cuffs must've been forged with it. Even if I wasn't experiencing Magic Exhaustion, there would be no using my powers so long as I was constrained like this.

My worry escalated and I pulled harder on the chains, which were attached to a mighty hook bolted to the ceiling eighteen feet overhead. I could only see traces of the hook. Three feet below it, a maze of water pipes ran around the area. Most of them were on the left side of the room. They ended a little ways past the hook keeping my chains and me upright.

As I struggled, a fat droplet of water dripped from one of the pipes and ran down my face. I looked down as it trickled off my chin and fell to the floor. I nearly shriveled out of my skin when I discovered the dark stains on the ground around me.

Dried blood.

The room had limited luminescence. A dozen small lanterns encased within glass shells emitted pale blue light and rimmed the higher part of the walls. A dark shade of red also came from a small, thick-glassed window on the back wall near the ceiling that I could make out between the pipes. Still, I didn't need more lighting to be sure that these marks on the floor were blood. I could smell it.

The trapdoor at the top of the stairwell opened. I turned and saw hefty boots coming down the staircase. Daverose.

"I know what you're thinking," he said. "*How can I get out? How do I escape?* I assure you, it's a waste of time. There is no way out of the Chamber for you, at least not while you're alive."

"Actually, I was thinking of investing in some high-quality hand cream, what with the frequency people have been cuffing me lately," I said. "But escape is definitely up there on my list of priorities too. That, and tearing you a new one."

As Daverose came nearer, I spotted my wand. It was still in its axe form and glowed dimly from where it was attached to a holster on the side of my captor's belt.

Daverose loomed over me and smirked. "I must say, of all the girls who've ever gone into the Little Cabinet, you're one of my favorites. If circumstances were different, I'd probably keep you in my collection. Such a shame to kill so rare a bird."

Daverose moved to touch my face and I acted on impulse. I wrapped my fingers around my chains, boosted off the floor, and kicked my captor in the chest. Big as he was, the sudden shove jolted him back a couple of steps. I ricocheted off his body from the force. My good sense returned a moment later as I found my feet.

I shouldn't have done that.

Don't get me wrong, it felt great. But I hadn't thought the impulse through. I was restrained there with nowhere to go. My magic was inactive. Daverose had my wand. And he was twice my height, five times my weight, and in a very good position to crush me like a handful of cereal.

Luckily, Daverose didn't smash me to smithereens like he very well could have. Instead, he stepped forward and punched me so hard in the stomach I was surprised his fist didn't come out the other side.

I would have collapsed to the ground had the chains not been holding me upright. Wheezing and gasping, I thought I might pass out again, or throw-up. But I made it through and slowly my breathing calmed.

"One of my servants will be by shortly to prepare you," Daverose said nonchalantly as he headed back up the stairs. "I like you girls to be presentable when I kill you and, at the moment, you look more like a wild creature than a delicate maiden."

"Thanks," I coughed as I straightened myself out with a grunt. "I try."

Daverose shook his head in amusement. "On second thought, I think I'll enjoy killing you. My kin will certainly enjoy watching it. I have sent word to my nearest Bluebeard brethren. At sundown today, over a dozen of them will come to witness your demise. That's not long from now; you were asleep for a while." He grinned wickedly. "Enjoy your remaining time, Miss Knight. I hope the accommodations are suitable." The white of his grin and the malicious glint in his eyes sparkled in the shadows of the cell. He rose through the trapdoor and slammed it shut. I heard bolts slide into place on the other side as he locked it behind him.

Great. Now what? I talk a good game, but that doesn't change the fact that I'm chained here without any way out of these cuffs.

"This sucks," I sighed to myself.

"You don't know the half of it yet," someone replied.

I turned in surprise to see a girl floating through the back wall. She was around my age, tall and thin with wavy hair and a tattered gown. Most notably, though, she was see-through.

Her skin, clothes, eyes—all of her—was translucent white. The edges of her dress and hair flowed around her as if trapped in an invisible breeze. She levitated closer, causing me to realize that she didn't have feet. Her spirit form ended with the frayed hem of her dress.

"You're a ghost," I said, stating the obvious.

"Yes," she replied. "And I must say you're taking it rather well. Most people are much more frightened when my sisters and I appear. My name's Hannah."

"My name's Crisanta Knight," I responded. "And most people haven't faced Therewolves, Headless Horsemen, and Stiltdegarths. Trust me. I've seen way worse." I paused. "Wait. Did you say sisters?"

Fifteen other girl ghosts passed through the walls and floated around me with troubled expressions on their faces. They were all young and dressed in gowns like the first ghost—and like me. A lump formed in my throat and my stomach lurched. I looked down at the splatters of dried blood on the floor.

"You were all . . ."

They nodded.

"Here?"

They nodded again.

"I think I'm going to be sick."

"Not yet you're not," said a ghost with high cheekbones. "Daverose said you have until sundown. Which means you have twenty minutes to escape."

"Well, I'm open to suggestions. Have any of you ever found a way out of here?"

"Does it look like we found a way out of here?" replied the same ghost, raising an eyebrow.

"Oh, sorry. Stupid question."

The first ghost who'd entered, Hannah, crossed her arms and sighed. "We all ended up here when we escaped Daverose's dream state through the Little Cabinet. He put us in those same chains you're in and none of us were able to break free. Not even magic worked thanks to the Stiltdegarth blood in the handcuffs."

"You had magic?" I asked Hannah.

"I did," another spirit with choppy bangs replied, floating forward. I recognized her instantly.

"Elaine!" I gasped. "You're Morgan La Fay's niece."

The ghost raised her eyebrows. "How do you know that?"

"I met your aunt. And your mother."

"Oh." The ghost hung her head sadly. "How are they?"

"About as good as can be expected with you missing all this time and Rampart out there ruining the realm."

Elaine nodded. "I wish I could see them. Spirits can sometimes visit the living, but none of us can. Ghosts can't leave the place they were killed if there's still unfinished business. All of us are trapped in Bluebeard Tower so long as Daverose's dark magic and dark purposes remain active."

"Hold on," I said. "I'm still not entirely sure what is going on in this Tower. What kind of dark magic is Daverose using on all those girls? It's coming from the chokers, isn't it?"

"It is," a young ghost replied, gliding forward. She had bushy hair in a ponytail and there was a well-placed mole on her left cheek. "I'm Colleen. I got killed most recently, so it's my job to explain. First off, do you know what Avalonian glass is?"

I shook my head.

"It's a type of magical material that can only be found on the Isle of Avalon," Colleen explained.

"When properly forged, it can do all sorts of things," Elaine added. "Like absorb magic, contain and sustain it, or conduct and project it."

"I was getting to that, Elaine," Colleen said with a pout. She pivoted toward me again. "A long time ago, Daverose started his business when he purchased a dark magic boulder from a black market vendor in the Passage Perelous. Those who touch the rock are sent to a dream version of their present environment. He has the boulder in the Tower, siphons off its magic, and puts it into gems cut from Avalonian glass. Those are the gems in the choker necklaces, which are keeping every girl trapped in a dream state."

"The wretched part is that simply being aware of the enchantment could free them all," Hannah said. "That's the way the magic dream state works. Those who are aware of the illusion can take control of it—shift the environment and make alterations. It is why the dream version of Bluebeard Tower is different than the real thing. Daverose is aware of the illusion. So in the dream version of Bluebeard Tower he removed the ladder in the ballroom, the exit that leads to the surface of the lake, the bed shelves with the girls, and other rooms of consequence."

"He basically changed the environment to make us believe there is no way out, keeping us from suspecting what is really going on," I summarized.

"Exactly," a gangly ghost responded. "And again, the sad thing is that any of us could have altered the environment in the same way had we known it was a dream. But we didn't learn that until we were dead."

My mind connected more dots. "Those rings that Daverose and the tigermen wear. They have the same magic as the chokers, don't they? The Bluebeards and the tigermen put them on to enter the dream world at will."

Several of the ghosts nodded. I was catching on.

"They keep the rings in their pockets the rest of the time," Hannah said. "That's why they always wear a glove on one hand, for handling the rings. The moment their skin touches the magic in those Avalonian glass gems, they're sucked into the dream world."

"So how do they get out?" I asked. "I escaped when I went through the Little Cabinet. That's when my choker fell off. But once Daverose and the tigermen put on the rings, they're in there with the rest of us. Is there someone on the outside to take the rings off?"

"No, their exit is much easier than that," a wavy-haired ghost replied. She seemed to be about my age. "I'm Charlotte," she said. "And the Little Cabinet is everyone's way out. It's simple really. Every disease has a cure; every curse has a fix; and every form of dark magic has a loophole. In the case of this magic dream state, there's an exit portal. However, Daverose has manipulated the environment to mask it behind the door of the Little Cabinet so girls won't leave."

"But it's just a door," I protested.

"It's not just a door; it's fear manipulation," Charlotte responded. "Daverose calls that door the Little Cabinet because most of us are familiar with the old tales of Bluebeard. Since the Bluebeard species originated in Camelot, as kids we grow up with our parents telling us different scary stories about them, serving as warnings not to go off into the Shifting Forest alone. As a result, we associate the Little Cabinet with the death sentence that it carries in the stories, making us predisposed to be afraid of it. Between that and the reinforcement of showing off the heads of the girls who've disobeyed and gone through, Daverose is able to control us with fear. The majority of the girls he kidnaps are too scared to take the risk of opening the door because it takes a very special kind of defiant to choose almost certain death over servitude and obedience."

I stared at the ghosts. There were sixteen of them. Sixteen girls who, like me, had broken out of Daverose's illusion because they'd rather risk death than stay someone's prisoner. Sixteen girls who were strong and strong-willed and who didn't deserve to die here.

"When you all broke out of the dream world, you didn't make a run for it, did you?" I asked, although I was already certain of the answer. These girls were just like me. Their hearts had taken them down the same path. "The reason Daverose captured you was because you hung back and tried to figure out what was happening to free the other girls, right?"

The ghosts nodded again.

"I'm sorry," I said. "You didn't deserve this and I'm not leaving here without helping the other girls and helping you. If ending Daverose's wickedness is the only way to complete your unfinished business and free your spirits of this place, I'll get it done. For your sake as much as theirs."

"Those are nice sentiments," Charlotte said. "But I'm afraid you're missing the obvious."

"Which is?"

"You need to escape from this Chamber."

"Well, that goes without saying, doesn't it?"

"Currently it goes without doing either," Elaine commented. "I don't see you making any headway."

"Um, hello? I've been kind of busy listening to the backstory. I'm totally on it now." I pulled pointlessly at my restraints.

"Yeah, real impressive." Elaine rolled her eyes.

"Oh, hush," I said.

I glanced at the ghosts. They were staring at me expectantly, but also with a kind of worry that caused my anxiety to grow. I would never be able to think clearly with all those translucent faces watching me, reminding me of what lay in my near future if I didn't move fast.

"Look," I finally sighed. "This is hard enough without a ghostly peanut gallery. You guys want me to have a shot? For now, go into the halls and let me know if Daverose or one of the tigermen is coming. But one of you should come back in five minutes to check in on me, okay?"

"Okay," Hannah responded. "But, Crisanta . . . do you really think you can do it?"

The ghosts looked at me with sincerity and sadness.

"Yes," I said simply. "I haven't survived seven Wonderlands to die here. I'm getting out and so are you. Oh, and you can call me Crisa."

Some ghosts appeared hopeful; others seemed skeptical. Most of them respected my request for space and wished me luck before passing through the walls again. Only one ghost stayed behind. She was the most mature-looking specter and wore a long-sleeved, lace dress.

"You shouldn't give them hope with such talk," she said.

"You sound so sure I won't succeed," I commented.

"Because I'm all but certain you won't," she replied. "I was the first girl that Daverose killed. My spirit has been in this Tower longer than you can imagine. I've watched fifteen other girls attempt to break out of these chains just like I did. And I've watched fifteen girls die because in the end, without the key, those cuffs are locked onto you."

"There has to be a way."

"Perhaps there is, but I have no idea what it might be. I've seen everything. Several girls have tried picking the locks with hairpins or clips. Others like Charlotte used earrings or jewelry in their attempts at the same. Elaine employed a head-on assault to try and get the keys for the cuffs. When one of Daverose's tigermen came to ready her, Elaine attacked him. She managed to head-butt him, kick him in the groin, and bite off a chunk of his left ear before backup arrived. Colleen tried something similar, only she wrapped her legs around the tigerman that came at her and nearly strangled him to death. But, just like with Elaine, all the servant had to do was shout, and reinforcements came running."

"Okay, well that's a just a few methods I won't try then."

"You're not listening," the ghost protested. "Again, and again, even the most aggressive and imaginative solutions for getting out of these cuffs have failed. I even witnessed one girl with amazing core strength lift her feet up to where her hands were hanging and remove a knife she had hidden inside her boot. But she failed too."

"Not that I'm not loving the pep talk," I said irritably. "But what's your point?"

"My point is that the girls who escape Daverose's dream world are strong, bold, and relentless, but none have managed to succeed here. So I think it is wrong of them to expect anything different from you."

"You don't know me, um . . ."

"Laurel."

"Laurel," I repeated with a nod. "I don't think I'm stronger than any of the girls Daverose has killed, but I have one quality that others don't."

"And what's that?"

"Unapologetic crazy."

Laurel gave me a final pitying gaze and then disappeared in silence.

Good, I don't need her negativity.

I had no doubt that the girls before me had tried every plausible way to break out of these cuffs. I wasn't going to waste my precious time attempting the same. Intelligence and creativity were great, but what had kept me alive this long was my tendency to disregard the likely and court the risky. Implausible, long-shot plans were my specialty.

I glanced up at the hook my chains were hanging from. It wasn't small like the hook of a mountain climber's rigging. It was thick and looked to be constructed of iron. There was no way I could break it with my weight, no matter how much force I applied.

As I stared up, another droplet of water leaked from the pipes and hit my forehead. When it splashed down, so did an idea. There was a decent amount of space between some of the pipes, particularly the few above my head. What if I got up there and then . . .

I worked out a few calculations in my head, taking into account the approximate length of my chains and the width and height of the room.

Hmm. If my plan didn't work, it would get me killed before my scheduled execution with Daverose. If it did work, I would be free.

Definitely worth the risk.

I braced myself and crouched down as low as my restraints would allow. From that hinged position, I launched myself off the floor with the most powerful jump I could muster and wrapped my fingers around the chains. With a grunt and a heave, I pulled my body up. Slowly but steadily, I climbed the chains like they were ropes in a gymnasium, only this was way harder because of the slippery metal and the weight of the chains that increased as I went higher.

I was thankful that I'd spent so many years working out. Even so, my core burned with agony. By the time I made it up to the level of the pipes, my diaphragm was shaking like mad and my arms were one good quiver away from giving out. With a final jerk, I grabbed the nearest pipe with one hand, then the other. Hanging high above the ground, the pounds of chains weighing me down and begging me to let go, I harnessed my ferocity to pull myself up and swing my right leg over the pipe.

I made it.

I scooted myself onto one of the thicker adjacent pipes and lay down for a minute to catch my breath, resting like a bear in a tree.

That was hard.

Sadly, there wasn't time for more than that. I sat back up and continued with my plan. The iron hook holding up my chains was directly over my head. I inspected it and my assumption was confirmed; it would be impossible to break. No matter, that hadn't been my hope when I'd climbed up here. I had another play.

I stretched up and grasped the hook with both hands for support. Then I extended my legs, shoved one boot against a thick pipe for resistance and support, and proceeded to ram my other boot against the thinnest pipe within reach where it connected to another. I kicked it again and again and again until the pipes separated. Immediately red water started pouring out from both ends. It cascaded to the floor and began to fill the cell. After a few moments, I realized it wouldn't be enough. I needed more.

My eyes flicked to the small window on the back wall near the ceiling. It separated my prison from the dense waters beyond. Despite my heavy chains, I managed to crawl over the maze of pipes to reach it. When I was near enough, I braced myself before kicking determinedly against the thick glass. It took a lot—so many kicks, in fact, that I worried I might break a bone before I broke the glass—but finally a crack formed in the window. Four kicks later, and the weight of the water outside became too much for the damage to handle.

Shards of glass spewed inward along with a gushing, window-sized wave. The red water began filling up my cell much more quickly. As it continued, I crawled to the end of the maze of pipes, which stopped nine feet from the top of the staircase and the trapdoor.

I swung my legs over the last pipe, reeled in my chains so they were hanging off it too, then bided my time. It was an oddly peaceful pause as the room beneath me filled with water and I waited for one of the ghosts to return. When the water level reached my boots, Elaine came through the wall, right on cue.

"What in the—" she exclaimed, flailing her arms. "Was the sunset deadline not a quick enough execution? You're going to drown!"

"Not if you help me," I said calmly, kicking my feet lazily in the water as it rose to my ankles. "I need you and the other ghosts to cause a commotion. Get the attention of one of the tigermen and get him to come here quickly. But let me know when he's thirty seconds away."

"You're crazy."

"It's part of my charm. Now hurry. I know what I'm doing."

Elaine passed back through the wall. Seeing that the dangling slack of my chains was now fully submersed, I readied myself for the next step.

And here comes another great payoff for all that swimming practice I did in Midveil.

I took a huge breath, slid off the pipe, and plunged into the water. The chains weighed me down, but way less than before. I was able to swim toward the stairwell.

The length of the chains had kept me and any other girl from taking more than a step in any direction. Even if one of the girls had thought to climb the restraints, the distance from where the maze of pipes ended to the staircase was too far to jump, especially when combined with the weight of the chains and the obvious laws of gravity. So, I'd eliminated those issues. Once the water level was high enough, it allowed me to stretch the chains in a horizontal fashion, counteracting their weight and gravity just enough for me to bridge the distance between the pipes and the steps by swimming there.

I felt the pull of the restraints as I paddled, but the plan worked. Soon enough, my hands grasped the highest stair and I pulled myself up. My face broke through the surface and the trapdoor was only a few inches above me. The water level was barely four feet from the ceiling now. I quickly reeled in as much of my chains as I could. Doing so gave me about three feet worth of extra slack to make my next move. I crouched on the stairs and wiped the water from my face.

Elaine's upside-down face suddenly passed through the trapdoor—and my head. The rush of her ghostly form phasing through me felt like pure ice shooting across my brain.

"Ow, Elaine! Get out!" I cringed and brought my hands to my head.

"Sorry," she said, floating a few feet away. "I just came to tell you that you've got a tigerman incoming any second, so you'd better—"

Only then did Elaine seem to realize where I was and what I'd done. Her expression was priceless—a mix of shock, disbelief, excitement, and admiration.

"You used the water . . ."

"Yes."

"You're brilliant."

"Also yes. But trust me, you're not gonna want to see this next part. I'll meet you up top when I'm done."

Elaine gave me a solemn nod and disappeared through the ceiling.

I waited. My mind flashed back to Jason in the Mercy Pit. He had killed Gaheris to protect Blue and himself. He had done it because there was no other way.

I knew I had to keep this inbound tigerman from calling out for reinforcements when I jumped him. I also knew that he would not willingly give up the key to my cuffs. A fight was imminent. How it would end was less certain.

The water was almost up to my neck. I heard the sounds

of latches and bolts being undone. I swallowed all doubt and surrendered to my instincts. They were all I could rely on now. I had to trust them, and trust that when the time came my heart would steer me correctly.

The trapdoor swung open. A tigerman held it open with one hand while his other gripped a key ring.

"'Sup," I said.

He didn't have time to respond. I lunged out of the water, grabbed the tigerman by his belt, and pulled him forcefully into the Chamber. The trapdoor slammed shut behind him. He plunged into the water and I followed. I dove after the creature and ripped the key ring from his fist. Unfortunately, my triumph didn't last long. The surprise had worn off by then, and with it went my advantage.

The tigerman jettisoned toward me just as I was about to unlock my first cuff and rammed me into the wall. The keys fell from my hand and began to sink. I kicked the creature in the stomach, knocking him away.

I swam to the floor of the Chamber and snatched up the key ring. There was more than one key attached to it, but in a matter of seconds I found the right one, shoved it into the cuff on my left wrist, and unlocked it. The restraint fell away. One down, one to go.

No time for it now though. The tigerman had recovered and was swimming for the trapdoor. He was going to call for help. I put the key ring around my freed wrist like a bracelet and propelled myself off the floor with such speed that I shot through the water like a minnow.

The tigerman reached the top of the stairwell. His head burst through the surface and he began to push the trapdoor open. I emerged right behind him and gripped him by the collar. Taking a deep breath, I yanked him back into the water.

The two of us darted about the Chamber like fighting octopi. We kicked and thrashed and entangled with one another until we crashed against the pipes. The water level was only a foot short of the ceiling now. We were running out of air.

My lungs felt like they were about to burst. I grabbed one of the pipes and pulled myself up. I gasped, inhaling as much air as I could. No sooner had oxygen rushed into my lungs than a hand grasped my leg and dragged me back under.

I stomped the tigerman's face with my other foot. He let go. He started to reach out for my face, but I lifted my cuffed wrist and slammed the hard metal between his eyes. Then, before he knew what was happening, I wrapped the cuff's chain around his neck. He thrashed about, but I held on tight while my free hand wriggled the key into the lock of my right cuff. With a final twist, it came off. The moment it did, I pulled away. However, the tigerman managed to snatch my arm with one hand while his other attempted to untangle the chain from his neck.

My head felt like it was going to explode. I only had seconds before my lungs gave out. Instinctively I grabbed the open cuff dangling from the chain I'd wrapped around the tigerman's neck. With a swift jerk I attached the cuff to his wrist and snapped it shut. Locked. Then I flipped backward, kicking the tigerman and using him as a boost to shoot toward the stairs. My boots pounded against the steps and I pushed open the trapdoor to freedom.

Air hit my lungs like a painful punch and I fell to the carpeted hallway with an exhausted thud. The trapdoor slammed shut behind me.

My heart pounded as my SRB magically dried me off. I wanted to take a moment to rest, but instinct told me to stay alert. Only, that's when I completely realized that no one was coming after me. At least the tigerman wasn't. And I knew why. The key ring was still in my hand.

I stared at the keys, then at the trap door, processing what I'd done. My mind went blank. There were no words to express the stillness I felt.

Water was beginning to rise out of the trapdoor. With the window busted open, the red lake would continue to pour through until the rest of Bluebeard Tower was flooded. Little by little, this place would fill with water. And if I didn't move fast, the innocent girls trapped in here would eventually drown too, just like the tigerman I'd left down there.

"Crisa!"

I jumped up and dropped the key ring. Elaine, Charlotte, Laurel, Colleen, and two other ghosts zoomed over.

"You're alive!" Colleen said excitedly. "That was amazing! Did you really—"

"I'd rather not talk about it," I said, awkwardly kicking the key ring away. "What's the status on Daverose and the other Bluebeards?"

"Daverose and a dozen of his kin are upstairs in the parlor, taking their pre-slaughter drinks," Charlotte said. "Sunset is in less than ten minutes, which means that's how long you have before they head down here and realize you've escaped."

"Is the ballroom clear?"

Charlotte nodded.

"Good," I said. "Let's go get the girls. This horror ends today."

I pushed aside my feelings about what I'd done to the tigerman. Lead by the ghosts, I sprinted through Bluebeard Tower. I needed their help. They were right; the architecture of the real Tower was different than the dream version. I passed a few rooms and corridors that hadn't been in the dream state. For example, at one point I had to stealthily sneak past a grand room where tigermen were weaving red dresses on giant mechanical looms.

We made it to the ballroom and I darted for the stone bed shelf where I'd woken up. My broken choker was still on the floor. I tore a small piece of cloth from my dress and picked up one of the Avalonian glass gems. The electricity of the humongous chandelier overhead sparked liked the fire in my soul.

"I need someplace safe," I said to the ghosts. "A supply closet, a bedroom I can lock, anything."

"Out here," Charlotte said, waving toward the ballroom doors.

We hurried out and made a sharp left turn. Ten feet away was a small door. I threw it open and discovered what I'd asked for—a supply closet filled with mops, brooms, and cleaning supplies. I shut the door and the ghosts came through.

"Good luck," Elaine said.

"Be quick," Charlotte added.

"And, Crisa," Laurel said. "Bring them home safe. I was wrong to doubt you."

"No, you weren't," I replied. "You were being practical and realistic. I've just never had the luxury of being either." I gave her a small smile, sat down, put the glass gem on my lap, then touched it.

Snap.

I was suddenly in the dream version of Bluebeard Tower. The ghosts were gone. My head felt dizzy and my stomach was choppy like the sea, but I stood up and burst into the hall. I needed to gather all the girls and I could think of only one way to do it fast. I headed for the stairs, bolting past confused girls in red dresses. When I reached the third floor, I found a large crank like Darcy had described. I wound it forcefully a few times before letting go. The chime that summoned all the girls to the ballroom for assembly pulsed through the Tower and the pale blue panel lights began to flicker in accordance. I ran and made it back to the ballroom before the last chime rang out.

Ticking clock aside, I couldn't help but make an entrance. "Nice of you all to join me," I said as I strode in with my arms crossed.

"Crisa!" Darcy and Shiondre shouted in unison.

"How are you alive?" a girl with blonde pigtails asked in awe. "Shiondre told us you went through the Little Cabinet."

"Where is Daverose?" a girl with black bangs and thin eyebrows whispered fearfully.

"Is this a trick?" a brunette piped in.

I ignored their questions and strut across the ballroom. "Listen up!" I shouted. "This is a long, weird story with a ticking time bomb for an ending. So pay attention, because I'm only going to give you a short summary. This whole place isn't real." I gestured around the room. "You're trapped in a dream state because of the chokers that you're wearing. That's why I don't have one anymore. The exit to this dream world is a portal disguised as the Little Cabinet. When I went through it my necklace came off. That's how we can escape. Now come on, there are a lot of

Bluebeards on the other side and we need to get out before they stop us."

I waved for them to follow me, but none of them moved. "What are you waiting for?" I asked.

Some girls murmured worriedly.

"Hey," I said, marching closer to them. "Don't you want to save yourselves?"

There was silence for a second then a mousy redhead stepped forward. "That's not how this works. This isn't Oz, or Book, or the North Pole."

I whipped my head toward Darcy. "What's she talking about?"

"She means this is Camelot, Crisa. Our realm has a certain dynamic when it comes to danger. Only a knight can save us."

"Present and accounted for. Now I'm telling you, *we gotta move.*"

The girls still didn't budge. Their expressions were skeptical.

"You don't believe me, do you?" I said.

"Well, it's a bit farfetched," Shiondre replied. "You expect us to believe that this world that we can see and touch and feel is not real. We've all been in this Tower for a while and it appears to be pretty real as far as any of us can tell. How can we disregard what we know based solely on the word of someone we just met? You're asking us to trust you—a stranger—and go into the one place that our master has forbidden us to go. A place that all of our experiences have taught us to fear and stay away from."

"That's what Daverose is counting on," I argued desperately. "He's using your fear to blind you. The Little Cabinet in this Tower isn't a death sentence; it's a hidden way out. And *this is all a dream.*"

They still looked doubtful. I wanted to cry out in frustration. There was probably only a few minutes left before sunset. How was I going to prove to them that this place wasn't real?

My eyes fell upon the side of the ballroom where the ladder out of here resided in the real world. An idea popped into my head. The ghosts said that anyone who was aware of the illusion could manipulate the environment. I was aware of it now. Maybe I could use that to prove what I was saying.

Not entirely sure what I was doing, but sure of what I wanted to do, I held out my hand and concentrated like I did when I activated my magic. The girls must've thought I was crazy at first, but after a few seconds the room began to change. It was super trippy. The floor started to ripple; the walls contorted; the chandelier shifted in size; the windows inflated and deflated like balloons. I didn't know how to manipulate this world in terribly a controlled way, but boy did my actions give the girls a show.

After a few more seconds I stopped concentrating and the room snapped back to Daverose's version. The girls were shocked. Silence pulsed through the ballroom before Darcy stepped forward.

"Lead the way, Crisanta Knight."

I couldn't help but smile as I led the full assembly of girls out of the room and toward the Little Cabinet. As we approached, I realized that the passage there was very narrow and it would take a long time for all of us to escape, so I tried the dream manipulation again. This time I focused harder, hoping to produce a more controlled result.

I channeled all of my will and energy into the action I visualized. Sure enough, it worked. The tapestry that covered the secret passage to the Little Cabinet warbled and faded away as we drew near. Then the stairwell behind it shook and expanded in one big burst—transforming from a tiny staircase to a massive one.

Excellent.

We bolted to the bottom of the stairs and funneled into the tiny corridor. I manipulated the environment again, expanding the narrow pass. It was now twenty times its original width and instead of two torches lighting the way, there were at least two dozen. The door at the other end also quadrupled in size. We raced toward it.

I threw the door open by its iron handle and we faced the black void. The portal to freedom was now wide enough for at least half a dozen girls to leap through at a time.

"Don't touch your choker necklaces once you're free. The

magic is in the glass gems. Just make for the ladder and go all the way up; you'll see it." I stepped aside and waved the girls forward. "Go, go, go."

They filed past, bounding into the darkness and out of sight. When the last girl had gone, I jumped through myself.

Flash.

I was back in the supply closet. Elaine and Hannah were there waiting for me. I stood up and the glass gem in my lap clattered to the floor. When I exited the dream state my real body must've stopped touching the magic source. Since the chokers were attached tightly, they burst off violently. This time, my hand must've simply withdrawn from the glass gem.

"I got all the girls out," I told the waiting specters. "They should be in the ballroom. How much time do I have?"

"Practically none," Elaine responded. "The sun is setting now. The Bluebeards are on the way to the Chamber. You haven't got long before they discover you're gone."

I ran out of the supply closet and into the ballroom. The stone floor was scattered with broken chokers. The girls in red were climbing the ladder to the exit door by the ceiling seventy feet above. Their progress was slow because of their long, red gowns, but the first group of ladies was about to reach the exit and pretty much all of the girls had started climbing. The stone ladder was so massive it could support many people at once.

I turned around and realized that all the ghosts had materialized and were floating behind me in a half circle.

"You freed the girls!" Colleen exclaimed.

"Which means I'm fifty percent done," I said. "For your spirits to be free of this place, all of your unfinished business needs to be completed. I need to stop Daverose and his kind from doing this ever again."

"Crisa . . ." Charlotte said. "The Bluebeards and tigermen are inbound. You've done enough. You should get out of here while you have the chance. You can't save everyone, so just focus on the living, not the dead."

"No way," I said. I glanced up at the grand electric chandelier.

It crackled with conductivity as fiercely as my brain did. "Besides, I have an idea."

I raced over to the ladder and called up to the climbing girls. Several had already gone through the door and the last one on ground level had just started her ascent. "Hey! Keep going up no matter what. You girls on the lower rungs, hold on tight!"

"Why?" one girl near the middle shouted.

"Because there's going to be a flood. This place needs to go down."

I didn't wait for them to respond. I dashed to the dais by Daverose's throne staircase. The ghosts surrounded me. "Keep the girls climbing. I'll probably need you in a minute."

Laurel looked worried. "Crisa, what are you going to do?"

"This." I planted my hand on the dais. My magic had been resting for a while now; I felt sure I could muster one shot. It took a lot—everything I had left, as a matter of fact—but I forced the magic out of me. I commanded the dais to break a window. My power enveloped the hefty podium, lifted it off the ground, and sent it toward a lower window with maximum force.

Bam!

A large crack formed at the point of impact. The fissure began to spread menacingly until jagged streaks consumed a huge section of the glass. The dais knew its job was not done though, so it pummeled the window twice more.

Crash!

The glass shattered and a gargantuan red wave swept across the ballroom. It would have carried me away and slammed me against the back wall had I not veered for cover behind the wraparound staircase that led to Daverose's throne.

The water poured into the room and the girls on the ladder froze. "Keep going!" I yelled. They got over their shock and hastened their ascent.

I found my footing despite the fast-moving current that thudded against my legs. Since the ballroom doors were wide open, the water began pouring into the Tower at large, which meant the ballroom wouldn't flood until the rest of this floor was covered too. I felt certain the girls would have enough time to get out.

I tried to summon my magic again, just to see if I could, but it was no use. That really had been my last manageable burst. No matter how hard I focused, I could not muster a spark. I felt the depletion of Magic Exhaustion.

That's when I swallowed the bitter truth. Liza had said that soon enough I would have to call upon Magic Instinct. I knew this time was about to be upon me.

"I take it back." Elaine said by my side. "You're not brilliant. You're straight-up insane."

"Po-tay-to, po-tah-to," I said with a shrug. "Just make sure all the girls get out, no matter what happens."

"Why? What's going to happen?"

"We're going to have company."

I took my leave and began to skid down the splashy corridors of Bluebeard Tower. When I arrived in the east wing, the entire first floor was already submerged in one-and-a-half-feet of water and mounting.

I sped in the direction of the Chamber, as I knew that's where the Bluebeards had been headed for my planned execution. I desperately wanted my wand back, but my overall goal was to lead the monsters to the ballroom where I could see my plan through. I needed them all in one place in order to—

I shook my head. I didn't want to think about it right now.

I rounded the corner and spotted my whole assembly of enemies fifty meters away—Daverose, twelve extra Bluebeards, and plenty of tigermen. They'd already been hastening in the direction of the ballroom. In retrospect, the water had probably been a dead giveaway that something was awry. Level rising, I stood my ground as the dark red lake spilled into my boots.

"Catch me if you can, Beardos!" I shouted.

Boy did that do it. They took off after me with more bloodlust than a clan of vampires after a fast.

I spun on my heels and moved as fast as the water would allow. By the time I made it to the hallway that led to the ballroom, the water was past my waist and my enemies were less than twenty feet behind.

Eep!

I began to swim. Wading wasn't going to do it anymore.

When I reached the middle of the ballroom I paused and looked up to discover that only a dozen girls were left and they were on the highest third of the ladder. The ghosts were hurrying them along.

I whirled around as Daverose and the rest of the monsters burst in. They had transformed into their beastly other halves en route and had become a gathering of the most gruesome-looking creatures I'd ever seen. They also appeared ready to tear me apart.

Daverose's monstrous eyes nearly bugged out of his skull when he realized that his precious birds were fleeing the coop.

"Stop them!" he shouted. "Bring back the girls, dead or alive!"

"I don't think so," I said. I planted my feet firmly on the floor of the drowning ballroom, the rising red water up to my chest.

Daverose narrowed his eyes at me and removed a dagger from a sheath at his hip. When he brushed aside his cape to do so, I spotted my wand still in its axe form.

"You have something of mine," I said.

"Bring back the others, but kill her first," Daverose said, ignoring me and glancing at his brethren. "First one to sever her head gets fifty percent off all purchases for the rest of their lives."

Anger surged through me as I thought about what a despicable character Daverose was. Fear of being killed in eight different ways pounded my nerves. My desperation to save the girls, free the ghosts, and end this nightmare pulsed through me with the strength of a Category Nine earthquake.

Instead of pushing all that emotion away, I leaned into it.

As the Bluebeards charged, I let the emotion fill me like the water filled the room. Power boiled within. I could feel my body protest from Magic Exhaustion, but I forced my way past the hurt and did that which came least natural to me. For the first time, I completely let go.

A bright, painful glow erupted from my body and rippled through the water. It felt like a blow to the stomach. It ached worse than when Daverose had sucker-punched me in the Chamber. Then Magic Instinct took hold. What I did next was a reflex, like my body was already in motion before my brain decided on the intention.

I stomped my foot onto the checkered floor. The tiles rose up like a tidal wave and crashed into the onslaught of monsters heading toward me. The resulting splash of foes and loose tiles caused the room to shake, but I held steady.

I now understood the meaning of the saying "It hurt so good." For only in surrendering to the power inside me did I finally comprehend how hard I actively worked to keep it in check. I was like a prisoner who had been incarcerated for so long that I had gotten used to the restraints. Now with a taste of freedom, I realized what I'd been missing. Magic Instinct was intoxicating. That burst of emotion-driven, autopilot-generated power had felt incredible.

In spite of this, I shook my head and reined in the emotion and power again so I could take stock of the situation. All the girls were gone now, free and in the clear. The ghosts were floating near the ceiling. I whistled and they came whizzing over as I treaded water. "Help me distract them." I gestured to the fallen Bluebeards and tigermen. "Give 'em a head rush!" The ghosts understood what I was saying and began rushing in and out of our foes' heads mercilessly.

The monsters hollered with pain as my specter friends repeatedly inflicted the type of brain freeze Elaine had given me earlier. I saw Daverose across the room. He'd been taken down by the tidal wave but was getting up. I paddled to the steps of the throne and scaled them. Half were already submerged; the water level was easily up to six feet now.

At the top of the staircase I zeroed in on the glow coming off Daverose's side—my axe—before locking eyes with the monster himself. "Hey!" I yelled. "You and me, Gigantore. Let's go!"

Daverose came at me, accepting the challenge. With his

massive stature he could cut through the water much more easily than I could.

"Elaine, Charlotte, Colleen!" I shouted and pointed.

Just before Daverose reached me, Elaine plowed through his skull. Colleen and Charlotte followed. The Bluebeard roared in pain and I dove off the platform into the water and shot around his side. As my ghostly friends continued to assault him, I went for my axe hanging from his belt. Swiftly I grasped the handle.

Wand.

Lapellium.

The weapon morphed and shrunk down instantly, slipping out of the attachment to Daverose's belt. I quickly moved away and secured the wandpin to my bra strap.

Check that off the list.

I darted to the surface and back to the stairs of Daverose's throne. The ghosts were doing good work, but they were only stalling. The water level was not high enough yet. Some of the Bluebeards and tigermen were already swimming in my direction or toward the ladder to go after the girls.

I need more water.

Magic Instinct was my only option. It might cost me down the line, but I would worry about that later.

I unleashed.

Again I experienced a sucker-punch to my gut. Letting go to my magic and emotion was a double-edged sword. I had great power locked away inside, but it was painful for my physical body to sustain it while under the duress of Magic Exhaustion. And yet, releasing that level of power was so fundamentally satisfying. Best I could describe, it was difficult to endure but felt effortless to surrender to.

Fueled by the emotions overtaking me, a golden glow radiated off my skin like flames; even my eyes seemed to burn with it. I was not in control of my actions, but my Magic Instinct seemed to know what I needed in order to protect myself. My body jolted in reflex and I shot out my hand. A condensed ball of energy pulsed forth like a comet. The light blasted across the room into the grand doors of the ballroom. The exit slammed shut, obeying the wishes of my Magic Instinct. The force of the water pummeled against the doors, but they refused to budge. The water level began to rise much more drastically as a result.

I kept letting the fear, anger, and desperation overwhelm me. My subconscious deep inside remained anxious about this choice, but as I filled with strength, there was no denying the truth I'd feared discovering: letting emotion run wild was a way easier means for channeling power than forcing focus.

The energy throbbed inside me. My magic could not have felt more painful and delicious. Though my body was feverish from exertion, my glow only brightened. It liked being unleashed.

Several Bluebeards had almost reached me at that point. I moved on autopilot and gripped the back of Daverose's throne, Magic Instinct still raging through me. In a swift jerk, the throne followed the instinct—ripping itself from the platform and smashing through another section of window.

Water blasted through. I dove off the other side of the throne steps to avoid the wave. The nearby Bluebeards did not escape the rush. When it burst through, it swept them away.

I swam as hard as I could to make it to the ladder on the side of the room. By the time I did, the ballroom was half full.

I clutched the ladder and hoisted myself up, barely moving fast enough to outclimb the rising water. The monsters bobbed around, swimming for the surface. Many were caught in the swell I'd released; some had gotten pushed against the back wall. I didn't know where the ghosts had gone. Maybe they couldn't sustain their forms in this level of rushing water. I hoped they were okay.

I reached the final step and ascended to the doorway of escape. I spun around and gulped. My silver SRB sparks flickered like the nervousness inside me. Everything had been leading up to this moment.

Daverose and several of his kin were seconds from reaching the ladder. Soon they would come after me and the girls. They would continue to come after any maiden in Camelot unless someone stopped them.

My heart throbbed with uncertainty, but there was no time left to stall. I'd hatched this plan and needed to shut out the second-guessing and see it through. I swallowed down my reluctance and sense of mercy. I could not give either a place here if this evil was to be stopped and the girls and I were to survive.

My eyes darted to the chandelier.

I'd figured out how to destroy the Bluebeards when I'd first returned to the ballroom after escaping the Chamber. It was a natural solution inspired by our escape from the citadel, and it was the only way to protect myself from all these monsters that wanted to kill me. I had faith my Magic Instinct would feel the same way and respond accordingly if I gave it the chance. So I did.

For a final time in this chapter, I let myself fall into the intoxicating toxicity of Magic Instinct. It was more painful this time; I was pushing myself way past the limit. But I grit my teeth and did what had to be done. I let go and trusted my magic would finish the job.

Channeled by Instinct, all my residual power consumed the immense electric chandelier. The bright blue thing cringed in my golden aura, coming to life. Then the draping garlands that connected it to the ceiling hinged back like spider legs. In a magnificent thrust, the whole fixture ripped itself from the roof, pushed off the ceiling, and dove toward the water—its torn-out circuits spraying sparks like mad.

I bolted through the door but glanced back over my shoulder just in time to see the chandelier and its dozens of electrical wires plunge into the flood. Electricity surged through the water like lightning. I turned away and slammed the exit door behind me, trying to drown out the sound of the agonizing final screams of the Bluebeards.

CHAPTER 19

First Contact

he sky was streaked with orange and navy as the sun set in the distance.

I stood on the bridge outside the fort that led to Bluebeard Tower. The water level of the lake was slightly lower—a side effect of the massive amount needed to fill the compound. As a result, the wooden bridge no longer sat on the surface of the lake, but several inches above it. Droplets ran off its wooden edges in an almost peaceful manner.

Now that the adrenaline was starting to fade, I took a knee on the bridge. While Liza had been right about me being powerful enough to use Magic Instinct even while in a state of Magic Exhaustion, she hadn't mentioned how much it would hurt. I was ninety-nine percent sure that if someone killed me at that moment, my magic would not bring me back. My bones and blood ached terribly.

Alas, I could not rest. Now that this mission was done, I had to reunite with my friends and return to my actual mission of finding Excalibur. I was about to cross the bridge and head to the forest when a myriad of white lights jettisoned out of the water like shooting stars. They swiftly came down and levitated in front of me, transforming into human shapes.

The ghosts!

My transparent friends from the Tower had made it! Each ghost smiled widely while the sunset spilled colors through their white forms and caused them to shimmer.

I crossed my arms and grinned back at them. "Still think I'm crazy?"

"Yes," Elaine replied. "But you're right; it is part of your charm."

"I still cannot believe it," Charlotte said. "What you did back there was amazing."

"It was a lot of things," I responded steadily, looking away as I thought about the dozens of dead monsters I'd left in my wake. "But I don't know if amazing is one of them." I shook off the darkness plaguing me for the sake of the group. "At any rate, I'm glad you're all okay. And thank you for the help. I couldn't have done it without you."

Laurel laughed lightly.

"What's so funny?" I asked.

"Crisanta, *you* just saved *us*. We should be the ones thanking you. Though I have no idea what kind of a gesture would be big enough to even begin to convey what we owe you."

"You don't owe me anything. I'm only sorry I couldn't have done more to help. I may have set you free, but you guys are all still . . ."

I hesitated, not wanting to say the word.

Laurel smiled at me warmly. "Death is not always the end, Crisanta Knight," she said. "There is more to existence beyond what the living understand. Now that we are free from Bluebeard Tower, our spirits are preparing for the journey and choices that come next."

I nodded, trying to pretend like I understood what she was talking about. I got the whole "death is not always the end" thing. I'd literally experienced that this afternoon when I'd come back to life. But as for everything else, well, maybe it was a ghost thing.

"In lieu of a thank you card or a fruit basket," Elaine said, "we have decided to offer you something else. Hold still, all right?"

The ghosts joined hands in a circle around me, spinning quickly until their forms blurred into a white aura of energy that whirled over me like a cyclone. I felt my skin turn cold and a tingle go up my spine. Then the ghosts ceased spinning. The dark silver belt around my waist was glowing, but the effect only lasted another second before fading back to normal.

"Ghosts can put energy into objects," Charlotte explained. "That's how fortune tellers sometimes communicate with the dead through talismans. We each put a little of our energy into that belt of yours. Now *it* is a talisman. If you ever need help, hold the belt in front of a flame and call on us. It will only work once, but our spirits will respond and we'll come find you."

Awesome! Ghostly backup could definitely come in handy someday.

"Thanks," I said, touched by their gift to me. "So where are you off to now?"

"We are going to seek out our living family members and friends," Colleen responded. "They deserve to know what happened to us."

I pivoted toward Elaine. "You're going to visit your mother I take it?"

"Definitely," she said. "Until we meet again, Crisa. Good luck."

"You too—all of you. And Elaine, tell your mom I said hi."

With that, the ghosts took off. Their forms glimmered brighter for a second and then each of them zoomed toward the sky and disappeared into the dusk. Once they were out of sight, I turned my attention back to the bridge. The group of my freed, former co-captives was waiting for me on the other side—their long red gowns dragging in the pebbly marsh that rimmed the lake. I sucked in my pain and exhaustion and slowly made my way to their waiting throng.

When I reached them, I was consumed in a swarm of hugs and cheers. The hugs hurt, but the cheers felt good. I walked with the girls to the edge of the forest as they gabbed and gushed and each tried to thank me individually. It was flattering. They made me feel like a hero. For a moment I forgot that in order for me to earn their praise I'd had to kill so many others.

The thought of it sickened me with moral conflict.

As I made my best efforts to swallow the guilt, I glanced up from a tight hug bestowed upon me by a girl with blonde bangs and thought I saw something in the distance. I moved my way through the group so I could see better.

There was a tall figure emerging from the forest—a familiar-looking person with dark brown hair and a posture I recognized.

I continued walking toward the figure until he looked up and saw me. He stopped, just like my heart did for an instant when I realized who it was.

For a second we stared at each other across the expanse—both of us trying to be sure we weren't seeing a mirage. And then . . .

"Knight!"

I don't think I'd ever been so happy to hear someone say my last name.

"Daniel!"

A jolt of exhilaration and relief propelled me to run to him. I forgot all my pains and aches. I was so happy that when I reached him I leapt into his embrace and wrapped my arms around his shoulders. He threw his arms around me and lifted me off the ground, spinning me for a second.

"I was so worried!" I exclaimed when he put me down.

"*You* were worried? Knight, I saw you get shot. I thought you were dead!"

I shrugged, smiling at him. "Well, you know me. I'm not that easy to get rid of."

He looked me up and down and noticed the new red dress I had on over my leggings. "I see you had a costume change," he said.

"I did."

He leaned in closer. "What's wrong with your eyes?"

"What do you mean?"

"They're kind of dull and gray. Actually . . ." He took a step back and studied me properly. "All of you seems pretty drained. What happened to you?"

"In a word, Bluebeards," I replied. "But I'll live. What happened to you?" I asked as I looked him over, noticing the thin scratches on the side of his neck. Without thinking, I reached my hand to his face and turned his chin to get a better look. "Are those *cat* scratches?"

"I had a run in with a not-so-friendly Puss in Boots," Daniel said, swiping my hand away. "Let's just say my dislike of cats is now irrevocable."

"Crisa?"

I turned around to find Darcy and some of the other girls standing near us. "Who's this?" she asked, staring at Daniel with intrigue.

"This is Daniel," I said. "He's a good friend of mine. Daniel, these are, uh, some new friends."

Daniel lifted his hand in a wave and smiled. "Hi there."

A flutter of giggles went through the group. Some girls waved, others said hello, a few just smiled and nodded. Their response irritated me slightly—like the mermaids' reactions to the boys in Neverland—but I let it go. Daniel was handsome. Girls getting all girlie around him was part of the deal.

"Ladies, give us a minute, will you?" I said.

The girls went back to chatting lakeside. When they'd gone, I returned my attention to Daniel. "Are the others with you?"

His expression darkened and he shook his head. "No. I got separated from them in the Shifting Forest during the attack. I've just been heading north trying to find them and . . . maybe you too."

"I thought you thought I was dead."

"Yeah." He shrugged. "But I hoped you weren't."

Nightfall was imminent, and considering the Shifting Forest would be even more confusing after dark, our group decided to make camp for the night. The lakeside was flat and we could see clearly in all directions. No monsters or magic hunters could sneak up on us.

We didn't have any food and the grass we lay down on was far from cozy, but nobody complained. Roughing it for one night sure beat an eternity of being prisoner to a human-trafficking monster.

Even though it was a warm evening, we built a campfire. After being captive for so long, the girls were happy to sit in the open around its glow. Daniel and I volunteered to collect more wood but were careful to keep the luminescence of our camp within sight in case the forest shifted again.

My pain had diminished, but I felt utterly exhausted. Daniel and I had too much to catch up on for me to go to sleep yet though. I told him about coming back to life after the hunters shot me, being imprisoned in Bluebeard Tower, and the development of my Magic Instinct. I told him everything except about the dreams I'd had. My visions about Chance, Mark, and him and me lying beneath that tree felt too personal, and I didn't feel comfortable sharing them. Plus, they didn't really seem important or relevant.

When I'd completed my recap, Daniel told me about the shenanigans he'd gotten into during our time apart. They involved a giant iguana, a duel with a local warlord who'd kidnapped some duchess, and a surprisingly vile encounter with Puss in Boots. The outcome of his adventures? The iguana was extinguished, the duchess was saved, and Daniel's distrust of cats was cemented in stone.

"So, do you think that thing with your powers bringing you back to life was just a one-off, or will it work every time someone kills you?" Daniel asked as I split a branch with my axe.

"Honestly, I don't know," I replied. "I didn't exactly mean for it to happen, and I have no way of testing it unless, you know, I get killed again."

"Let's call that a Plan B," he said. "Still, it would be pretty awesome if you could learn to control it. You'd be unstoppable."

"I don't know if I want to be *unstoppable*," I said with a sigh. "I'm not sure anybody should be. Power like that is too corruptible. It's the whole reason Pure Magic is dangerous, *and* the whole reason I'm supposed to keep a tight rein over it. What I did today with Magic Instinct in Bluebeard Tower was necessary for my survival, and the survival of others, but I don't want to unleash like that again if I can help it. You don't know how horrible *and* wonderful it felt to give in to such power. It was sensational in a destructive way that I can't fully describe." I shook my head, feeling conflicted. "I have to contain it. If I start thinking of myself as invincible—if I let it go to my head—then who's to say I won't wake up tomorrow with a wicked heart?"

"I don't know," Daniel admitted. "But I think you're being too hard on yourself. I know that every person with Pure Magic—apart from Liza and apparently Merlin—has changed. But you've been working really hard with Liza. You've got your powers under control and I don't think a few episodes of Magic Instinct are going to change that. You're honestly the last person who I would ever worry about turning dark. That's why Arthur knighted you in the first place, right? You're like the poster child for the moral compass."

"I wouldn't bet on that . . ." I said uneasily. "Not after what I did to the Bluebeards and the tigermen today." The air abruptly felt colder and darker. The mere mention of the merciless actions I'd taken this afternoon filled me with unease.

Like Daniel said, the whole reason Arthur had knighted me—given me The Pentecostal Oath and thus the gift of being able to claim Excalibur—had been because he thought I was honorable. But I had just taken so many lives. They may have been monsters, but did that really make a difference?

Was killing the Bluebeards and tigermen acceptable because they'd killed so many innocents themselves?

Could a person truly be good when they did things that seemed so outwardly terrible?

"You know, I passed my second Valiancy Test today," Daniel said suddenly.

I turned toward him, surprised. "You mean—"

"I killed two magic hunters," he said bluntly. "It was during the attack in the Shifting Forest. I didn't mean for it to happen," he continued. "But it happened."

I stared at Daniel, the one person who always told me the truth even when I didn't want to hear it. His eyes looked hard, but then, they almost always did.

"Do you regret it?" I asked.

A beat passed between us. He exhaled deeply. "I don't believe in regret, Knight. It's a waste of energy. What I believe in is learning from my mistakes so that I'll be better prepared next time."

He sat down on a large tree root with the bundle of firewood we'd been collecting at his feet. I sat beside him, returning my axe to wand form. Its glow made my hand look ghostly, like the dead girls from Bluebeard Tower.

"So, do you?" I asked. "View it as a mistake, I mean?"

"Honestly, no," he responded. "Those guys were trying to kill us. Killing them was not an easy thing to do, but I know it was the right thing to do."

"But even if it was the right thing to do? Was it *wrong* to do it?" I pressed.

Daniel cocked his head. "Are you asking me that question, or yourself?"

"I don't know." I kicked at the pile of branches at our feet and gazed into the shadowy forest.

"Well, let me ask you this," Daniel replied. "Do *you* regret what you did to the Bluebeards and the tigermen?"

I thought on the question. When things were about to go down in Bluebeard Tower, I remembered telling myself that when the time came, I would trust my instincts. I would trust my heart to weigh the options and make the right call.

It was true that killing others—in general—was bad. But at the end of the day, I had acted defensively and protectively. I wondered if maybe that was the difference. I hadn't sought out Daverose and his kind to end them. And while I'd harnessed darker emotions to evoke Magic Instinct, I'd been motivated by good intentions rather than revenge or hate. I had made the choice to take down the Bluebeards because it was the only way to save myself, the other girls, and the ghosts, while ensuring that future generations of innocents didn't suffer the same ordeal.

I leaned back and glanced up at the starry sky through the canopy of trees.

"I regret that it was necessary," I thought aloud. "But I don't regret doing it. They'd already murdered so many people. And if I hadn't stopped them, they would've continued. I made a decision. The morally superior might look down on me for that, but I stand by it. Whether that makes me a good person or a bad person, I'm not sure."

"I couldn't tell you," Daniel said with great care. "I'm not an ethics professor. But it sounds to me like your heart was in the right place. That's gotta count for something. Whether you're able to justify your actions with your own sense of morality though is on you alone. I'm not your conscience, Knight."

"Aren't you?" I asked, half joking—but half serious.

We sat there in silence for a minute. Eventually Daniel picked up the pile of firewood and bundled it under one arm. He extended his free hand to me and helped me off the ground.

We started back toward the glow of the campfires. Just before we stepped into the lakeside clearing, Daniel spoke again.

"For what it's worth, I think you're a good person. I know you're worried about your magic, and what you can do. But if I had to trust anybody with that kind of power, I'd trust you in a heartbeat."

I looked up at him and found myself feeling grateful, not just for what he'd said, but for him too. "Thank you, Daniel. I mean it."

"Any time, Knight." He paused for a second then regarded me sincerely. "And I mean that too."

I stood on the edge of a jagged cliff overlooking a gorge that seemed to go on forever.

The sky was honeydew green. Hazy sandstorms swept across a distant horizon while black and gold sparks of magic carried on swirling winds.

Tall rock formations stuck out from the misty depths of the gorge. The decaying remains of buildings protruded from them like blemishes. These intriguing buildings had nothing on the ones hanging from the sky. Like stalactites in a cave, severed castle towers, parapets, and turrets hung upside down from absolutely nothing. They floated across the entrancing sky like clouds.

The snap of a twig caused me to turn around. Mauvrey was standing behind me. Her golden-blonde hair was swept back in a long ponytail. She wore jeans, heeled boots, and a camel-colored leather jacket over a plain white t-shirt. Her fingerless metallic gloves encased her hands. There was an odd black vein pattern going up along the right side of her neck that was creepy like a viral crossword puzzle.

Despite this strange affliction, the expression on her face was even more unusual. It wasn't filled with its usual condescension or superiority; rather, she looked at me with genuine concern.

Just past her, two other people were approaching—Natalie and Daniel. Natalie was the same early twenties age that I'd dreamed about recently. The wind swept her maple hair across her shoulders. It was redder in this light, as were her eyes. She'd been crying.

I was speechless at the sight of them all together. A person I cared for, a person I hated, and a person who I was supposed to save, all standing side by side in this unexpected place.

"You're going to want to hide."

I spun at the sound of the male voice. When I did, the fascinating dreamscape of the gorge and honeydew sky vanished along with Daniel, Natalie, and Mauvrey.

Now I was in a white void with an old man standing before me.

I recognized him. He was the only person besides Liza who'd ever contacted me through my dreams. The mysterious man was about sixty with a long white beard and a silver-and-dark-blue robe. He wore a utility belt with a variety of leather pouches around his waist and carried a staff with a ridged point like a mining drill in his right hand.

I didn't know who he was, but he'd directed me to begin our search for Paige Tomkins in Neverland, which was how we'd ended up meeting Arthur and Peter.

"When you find the magic hunters, you're going to want to hide," he said. "I can take care of myself."

"What?" I stammered.

Then the man brusquely vanished.

"Hey!" I shouted.

No response. He was gone, but I heard someone else.

"Would you like some more tea?"

I whirled around. Natalie was sitting in the void. But unlike the version of her I'd just seen, this Natalie was no more than nine years old.

While my side of the void was white and vacant, hers featured a field of flowers paired with a pink and purple sky. She was sitting at a round table with a lace tablecloth. The little girl wore a glittery lavender dress and a plastic tiara. Around her sat a raggedy stuffed bear, a furry bright blue monster toy, and a plush peach rabbit with a bow around his neck and a missing ear.

Natalie poured tea into white teacups. Butterflies flitted around her, their wings sprinkling golden glitter.

As I drew nearer, I noticed the white clouds overhead were twisting into the most brilliant shapes—dragons, castles, pirate ships, and Pegasi. Looking closer, I also discovered the flowers in the field were like living drawings—renderings made by a child that had sprung up from the pages of a coloring book. All the scenery was that way. The trees and bushes and even the swirls of the sky were a living work of art.

I was a few feet from Natalie when I collided with an invisible force field. I placed my hand against it, sending out a glistening ripple that appeared to go on infinitely in both directions. I had no way of knowing where or if it ended, but the force field prevented me from getting any closer to Natalie.

"There now, Vincent," she said as she poured tea for the peach rabbit. "See, all you needed was a little tea to get your inspiration back. Soon you'll be good as new and we can paint some more."

I pressed my hands onto the force field, causing it to warble. Natalie was so near, but she might as well have been a million miles away.

I gazed at her sympathetically. She was so young and happy. It hurt me to know that so much darkness was coming for her. She didn't deserve enemies like Arian or that blonde witch Tara who would eventually come for her. Natalie was an innocent in all of this, an accidental pawn in the schemes of others. And the only thing that could help her was my intervention.

Closing my eyes, I pressed my forehead against the force field.

"Don't worry, Natalie. I will protect you. No matter what, I'll find a way to save you. I promise."

"Who said that?"

My eyes snapped open. Young Natalie was now on her feet, looking around curiously.

"Is someone there?" she said to the sky. "You said you'd save me. Save me from what?"

I tilted my head. "Natalie?"

Natalie perked up. She stepped closer to the invisible wall between us but didn't appear to notice its presence, or mine.

"Where are you?" she asked.

Excitement filled my chest.

"I'm here!" I shouted.

Alas, Natalie couldn't see me. Whatever dreamscape she was in only allowed my voice to seep through. I pressed both hands against the force field and bent down. Natalie's face was inches from mine, but she had no idea. She gazed into the distance behind me.

"Natalie," I said. "Can you hear me?"

"Um, a little," Natalie said nervously. I noticed that the flowers and swirls of the sky in the background had turned gray. The clouds thickened and began to cluster together. The butterflies paused like they'd been frozen in time.

I understood what was happening. When Liza first tried to contact me through my dreams our connection wasn't very strong, so communication was difficult. I couldn't see Liza in the beginning; I could only hear her. And even so, we only had seconds to talk before her voice faded out. I had to choose my words carefully and quickly.

"Natalie, listen. There's a girl named Tara. You have to watch out for her. She's bad."

"Hello?" Natalie began looking up at the sky again. "I . . . I can't hear you. You said something about a Tara? What's a Tara?"

"Tara's a girl," I said louder.

"What? I can't—"

"Natalie, beware of Tara." I banged my fist against the force field, causing the energy to violently ripple. "Beware Tara Gold!"

Natalie's side of the world went dark. Then everything went dark.

The sounds of crickets filled my ears. I opened my eyes and saw the glowing embers of a campfire and several girls in red who were keeping watch around it. I rolled to my side and sat up.

"Daniel," I said, shaking my sleeping friend's arm.

He grunted and shrugged me off. I shook him harder. "Daniel," I repeated.

He grunted again, but this time he opened his eyes. Seeing the urgency in my face, he sat up. "What's wrong?"

"I did it," I said. "I reached Natalie in her dreams. She couldn't see me, but my voice got through. It was like when Liza first contacted me in my dreams. My dreamscape collided with hers."

"Wait, hold on," Daniel said, trying to fully wake up. "What are you saying?"

"Daniel, it finally happened; what Liza has been training me for. I contacted Natalie through her dreams and . . . *she heard me.*"

CHAPTER 20

Well, This Is Awkward

n the morning we journeyed alongside our herd of red-gowned girls for a few hours until an area of the Shifting Forest opened up to reveal a small kingdom. Having explained that Daniel and I were on a mission, my new friends and I parted ways. The girls intended to make their own treks home but needed to rest and regroup first. They thanked me profusely and wished us luck on our quest ahead.

So onward we went, trying to find Avalon and our friends along the way. I truly despised the Shifting Forest, but at least I had Daniel to navigate it with me. Although we'd traveled without incident all morning, every time the earth moved and the terrain began to change, I felt the hairs on my arms rise. I couldn't shake the feeling that any second a magic hunter was going to pop out of the bushes and kill me. Again.

Ongoing run-ins with the homicidal had been a part of my life for a while now, but I felt a lot less equipped to handle them at the moment. Magic Instinct had taken me far beyond the recommended cease-and-desist point with my powers. Today I was feeling the repercussions. Usually, when my magic was temporarily wiped out, I was tired. Now I felt a simmering soreness underneath my skin that was a deeper level of draining. I had woken up feeling like a piñata at the tail end of a kid's birthday party. I'm sure I looked it too.

Despite this, the most worrisome thing was, even with the exhaustion, I sensed power bubbling inside me. I could always feel my magic when I had Magic Exhaustion, even if I couldn't channel it. But this time was different. In the past when my magic was rebooting, it felt like there was a steel wall that I couldn't cross until the full rest period was done. Today it felt like that wall was penetrable, as if I could tap into whatever magic was on the other side before I was fully recharged.

This was bad. My spirit hummed with temptation, trying to convince me I had plenty of power, but logically I doubted if I had the physical strength to sustain it. If I pushed myself too far, I'd reach Magic Burn Out and get obliterated to the point of no return.

And yet, the magic still itched within me. The irrepressible sensation of power I had experienced yesterday hovered around my shoulders like a phantom.

I mentioned my Magical Exhaustion to Daniel as we walked, but I didn't want him to know the full extent of my pain and tiredness. We couldn't slow our pace. I could keep up just fine when I was properly motivated, and boy did I have plenty of motivation. The Vicennalia Aurora and our one chance to free Paige's memories from Glinda's memory stone would come after sunset *tomorrow*. Arian, Mauvrey, and Alex were racing toward Avalon to claim Excalibur and meet the same deadline. And on top of everything, I had to get to Jason before he was killed.

Based on the clothes my friends had been wearing, I knew his time was coming. Maybe it was going to happen in a few days, maybe in a few minutes. All I knew for sure was that I had to do everything in my power to beat the clock and reach him before it happened.

Not that I was sure how much help I would be even if we did find him in time. With this serious case of Magic Exhaustion, the extent of my powers was pretty vague. And if I *could* channel my powers in this tired state, would I even know how to save Jason? I'd brought myself back to life by accident. I'd killed that giant in the same way. I'd never actively tried to manipulate an already-living being's life energy. The terrible thought occurred to me: what if I couldn't? What if I was only that powerful when I relinquished control of my magic and let it take over?

"Knight, watch out!" Daniel curtly held up his arm, causing me to stop in my tracks. I'd been so lost in thought that I hadn't seen the covered pit in the ground. Daniel had prevented me from falling into another animal trap.

"Thanks," I said.

"You're welcome. Just focus, okay?"

I nodded and followed after him.

"I really hope that the magic hunters won't bother SJ, Blue, and Jason without me around," I asked, stepping around a mushroom circle in the dirt.

"Maybe in the past that would've been a thing," he responded. "But there are literally rewards for our kill or capture."

As if to prove a point, we passed another tree plastered with Wanted posters. We'd come across them throughout the day. The faces of my friends and I were all over the deeper part of forest. The flier I saw now was for Blue. I raised my eyebrows as I took in the contents. Just like the newspaper we'd read in the citadel, Blue's Wanted Ad was slightly different than ours. Printed beneath her name was the message: *If unable to detain, kill with extreme prejudice. Threat to QB mortality. See authorities for details.*

I still didn't understand what that meant.

Suddenly the earth began to move. Daniel and I stopped walking as the tectonic plates of the forest shifted around us. I stayed vigilant as I watched the ground change.

Daniel and I had been working with very little to go on as we navigated the forest. Jason had our customized Camelot map and we didn't have Mark Twos to communicate with our friends. I had left mine in my backpack, which I'd lost during the Bluebeard Tower episode. Everything else inside was gone now too. I lamented the loss of my dream journal in particular; there were months of catalogued visions in there.

Without our customized map or Mark Twos—which might not have worked anyway because of the Shifting Forest—we were left with three tools to navigate to the Isle of Avalon. The first was Gwenivere and Morgan's advice regarding the Passage Perelous. The second was Daniel's memory. He had been with Jason yesterday morning when our allies edited the Camelot map. And the third was our new map.

We'd acquired a simple map from a bookseller in the kingdom where we'd parted ways with the girls from Bluebeard Tower. It was lucky that Daniel had some money hidden in his left shoe, as my money had been in my backpack. When I asked him about it, Daniel said he always kept a bit of money in his shoe, a habit he'd developed when he was young and spent a good deal of time in the streets.

"After my parents died, I had to protect the little I had," he told me. "And I wasn't that big or strong. Other street kids would always gang up on me. I could outrun or outsmart them most of the time, but a backup plan was always good in case they caught and robbed me."

Like it always did, this precious sliver of honesty that Daniel shared caught me off guard and moved me. Unlike earlier in our friendship, now we were comfortable enough with each other that he didn't make a big deal about it and neither did I.

The shifting of the forest finally stopped. Our section of the ground had moved and we came upon a small cliff. Leading up to it was a cluster of boulders surrounded by trees. The leaves of the trees were blue, signifying that someone had passed through recently. Hearing voices, I pulled Daniel by the jacket and we crouched behind the boulders, trying to survey the scene below.

Oh, crud.

"Open the cave, Nyneve," said one of the seven magic hunters standing in a half circle around an old woman. The magic hunter wore a burnt-orange scarf and a light brown leather jacket. The men behind him were dressed in similar grungy earth tones, and all of them had weapons. I counted four daggers, one sword, and two bows.

My mind flashed to the old man in my dreams. "When you find the magic hunters, you're going to want to hide. I can take care of myself," he had said.

I didn't need to know to hide. But the second half of that statement implied that the old man was nearby. That piqued my interest.

One of the archers stepped forward and pointed his bow. "Now," he barked.

Hm. I wonder if I'll ever get used to seeing the images in my head blossom into reality.

While I'd long adjusted to having magic at my fingertips, being able to see glimpses of the future and then witnessing them turn into the present was always unsettling. It made me feel both larger than life and completely powerless.

Daniel and I watched the old woman—Nyneve. Like I remembered from my dreams, she was shaking with nerves. She stood in front of a cave with an opening that was blocked by a large, smooth stone.

Nyneve was probably in her late eighties or early nineties. She had white wavy hair and a pasty complexion. Her blue eyes regarded the cave with more fear than she showed for her captors.

"I am warning you one last time," she said, pivoting to the hunters. "Moving this stone will bring you nothing but destruction. He is too powerful. You are no match."

The hunters dismissed her warning. "Open it," barked a magic hunter wielding a sword. "We'll see who is outmatched."

Nyneve turned back to the cave and stared at the boulder blocking its entrance.

I leaned in to Daniel. "I dreamed about this," I whispered.

"And?" he whispered back.

"And nothing. I don't know what's behind the stone. I do know her though. Gwenivere told me that Nyneve was Merlin's half-magic-hunter girlfriend. She was also his potions apprentice before he went missing."

"Then I have a pretty solid guess what's in the cave."

"You do?"

He raised his eyebrows and gave me a patronizing look. "You really never do the reading assignments at school, do you?"

I was about to retort when Nyneve raised her hands and placed them on the boulder. She took several deep breaths, closed her eyes, and concentrated. After a few seconds, the stone started to emit a pale green glow and the cave began to tremble.

I was nervous about what was going to happen next, although Daniel seemed calm. I guess he knew something I didn't.

The cave shook harder as the glow increased, and the boulder began to move. It rolled to the side like an egg on a counter until the entire cave mouth was unblocked.

From our vantage point, I couldn't see directly inside. The moment the stone came to a rest, Nyneve took several steps back. Instinctively, I drew my wandpin.

The hunters began to move forward, pushing Nyneve along with them. They made for the cave's entrance and disappeared inside. Daniel and I held our positions. There was silence for about thirty seconds before the first scream. The cave shook again. More shouts followed. It sounded like the hunters were under attack. Daniel and I looked at each other. We weren't on the hunters' side, so we certainly weren't about to rush in to help them face an unknown enemy.

Suddenly, one of the magic hunters flew out of the cave with a surge of bright blue smoke. He collided against a tree. A second hunter sailed out after him and rammed into a boulder. The other hunters appeared next, driven from the cave as they fought defensively with their weapons.

I still couldn't see what was attacking the hunters. Frankly, I wasn't sure they could either. There was definitely something taking shots at them. Every few seconds, I saw one of the hunter's bodies jolt like he'd been punched. Their limbs and clothes were slashed, as if invisible blades had assaulted them. And once in a while, a blue blast of smoke would appear and blast them away. Whatever this unseen enemy was, it was tearing into the hunters with unbelievable ease.

After a minute, all of the hunters lay unmoving on the grass. That's when their attacker finally shimmered into existence. A golden flash appeared in the center of the battleground. Standing there when it vanished was a man about sixty years old with long white hair and a beard that hung to his waist over a silver-and-dark-blue robe.

The man from my vision!

He dusted off his robe and adjusted the utility belt around his waist. The belt had leather pouches hanging from it; he closed one on his left hip by snapping its latch. In his right hand was a fascinating staff. The pointy end had spiraling ridges like a mining drill. The mysterious man wiped the drill blade against the grass to get some of the blood off, then spun the staff and tapped the blunt end against the ground twice. This caused the drill blade to retract, converting the staff into a regular walking stick.

The man turned around and spotted Nyneve at the threshold of the cave. She'd been watching the battle unfold from a safe distance. As the man walked over to her, the terror in her eyes was unmistakable.

"Nyneve," the man said.

"Merlin," she responded.

Merlin!

I shot a look of amazement at Daniel, but he didn't seem surprised in the slightest.

Nyneve clenched her fists and sighed. "If you're going to kill me, just do it."

Merlin reached into one of his leather pouches and withdrew a pinch of a purple substance that looked like powder or sand. He threw it at the ground by Nyneve's feet.

"Ignus," he said.

A cloud of purple smoke enveloped Nyneve for a moment. When it dissipated, she was no longer a feeble old woman in her eighties. Now she was about forty. Her wiry, white hair had turned brown and lush. Her posture was straight and the brightness in her eyes had been restored.

She held up her hands and gasped. "I don't understand," she said to Merlin. "I trapped you in that cave for years. Aren't you angry?"

"Anger is a waste of time, Nyneve," Merlin said. "I have much bigger fish to fry. I simply want to look at your true face when I kill you."

The fear returned to Nyneve's eyes.

"Spiralis," Merlin said. In an instant, the drill blade at the end of his staff reappeared. Before Nyneve could take a step back, he drove the blade straight through her. She dropped to the ground, dead. He casually wiped the drill blade on the grass again then thudded his staff twice to rescind it.

My mouth hung open in shock, but instinct kicked in as I saw one of the hunters moving in my peripheral vision. While Merlin was distracted with Nyneve, the hunter had regained consciousness and drawn an arrow from his quiver. He raised his bow.

"Look out!" I shouted.

Lapellius.

My wand transformed and I leapt out from behind the boulder. The arrow shot through the air, but thankfully my warning had caused Merlin to step aside, avoiding a shot to the spine and only getting a glancing blow to the shoulder.

Merlin stumbled forward, dropping his staff. A second hunter jumped to his feet. These guys weren't as dead as I thought. Dagger in hand, he bolted for Merlin. This time I had a proper chance to intercept.

I morphed my wand as I darted between Merlin and the hunter.

Spear.

I slammed the staff into the magic hunter's forearm and pushed him back. With a side kick to his ribcage and a thwack to his shoulder from my staff, he went down. I kicked him in the head again for good measure before realizing that the hunter with the bow had reloaded.

Shield.

The arrow ricocheted off the curved metal front of my shield.

Knife.

I chucked my blade and it spiraled through the air, lodging directly into the hunter's thigh. Blue would've been proud.

By then Daniel had jumped into action too. As the hunter painfully pulled out my blade, my friend rushed in and roughly struck the pommel of his sword into the side of the hunter's head, knocking him out.

Daniel picked up my knife, wiped it on the grass, and brought it back to me. "I'm getting sick of these guys," he said, restoring his sword to its sheath with a huff.

"I'd imagine so," Merlin said.

Daniel and I turned around. Merlin had retrieved his staff. It looked like the arrow had done nothing more than nick him; only the tiniest bit of blood stained his robe and he seemed unconcerned by it. "Crisanta Knight. Daniel Daniels. Nice to finally meet you." He nodded at each of us like he was paying respects.

I was pretty stunned meeting the famous Merlin. Most people talked about him like he was dead. But then I was Miss Resurrection, so maybe I shouldn't have been so susprised to see him waltz out of a cave. I was more astounded by the fact that Merlin had been the guy talking to me in my dreams. I understood that he had Pure Magic, but he'd made a choice to contact me specifically. Between that and the fact that he'd left the Questor Beast book for me to find in Gwenivere's castle, I wondered how much of my future he had seen.

I opened my mouth to voice some of this, but Merlin held up his hand. "All in good time, Crisanta Knight," he responded. "But before we get into that . . ." Merlin glanced over my shoulder.

The hunter I'd kicked in the head was starting to get up. Daniel made to go toward him, but Merlin stepped forward first. He drew some white sand from another pouch. As he did, I noticed the metallic bracelet on his wrist. Part of it extended along his hand with bulging end points that met in the middle of his palm.

"Ignus."

When Merlin said the word, the bulging end points struck against each other, producing a tiny spark that ignited the sand in his hand. The grains began to sparkle before he threw them on the hunter's face. On impact, the now-sparkling sand created a white wisp of smoke that swiftly popped like a bubble. When it vanished, the hunter collapsed back to the ground. I thought he was dead until he snored as Merlin closed the pouch the sand had come from.

"What was that?" I asked.

"Potion sand," Merlin replied. "Condensed magic particles of my own design. But that's not important right now. First and foremost, you probably want to know why I keep reaching out to you in your dreams."

"Um, okay," I said, taken aback by the way he treated me with such familiarity.

"I've had visions of your future for some time, Crisanta," Merlin said, pivoting on his heel and heading back toward the cave. He beckoned for us to follow. "Fascinating stuff. I feel like I know you and your friends quite well. You really are something. Come. This is a show-and-tell type of situation."

Merlin stepped over Nyneve's body like it was a pothole.

I scrunched up my face, put off by the action.

What was with this guy? In the last few minutes he'd defeated a bunch of magic hunters while he was invisible, murdered his ex-girlfriend, and now he was talking to us like we were long-lost colleagues whom he couldn't wait to catch up with. For someone who was supposed to be a respected wizard, he didn't act as prim and formal as Julian, the current Wizard of Oz. And for someone who was supposed to be a powerful wielder of Pure Magic, he sure didn't give off the wise, all-knowing mentor vibe that Liza did. My first impression of the guy was that he was peculiar and shifty.

The infamous wizard hurried ahead of us into the cave. I restored my weapon to its wandpin state and pursued him. Daniel and I moved around Nyneve's body and stepped into the cave. The entry sloped down substantially and the dirt was slippery; I had to watch my footing.

"So, is this who you thought was in here?" I whispered to Daniel.

"It's in *Le Morte d'Arthur*, the famous book about Camelot's history," Daniel replied. "I remember something about Merlin being trapped in a cave that could only be opened by the same person who sealed it. Jason and I had to read the book for our Chivalry class. I'm actually surprised you didn't know. Blue said you guys were reading it for your Damsels in Distress course."

I narrowed my eyes. "It's a fourteen hundred-page book, Daniel. And I've been kinda busy trying to save the realm, not turn evil, and avoid being killed. I haven't had a lot of spare time for reading lately."

The ground leveled out and we passed through a stone

archway. I went under with no problem (like I imagined Merlin did since he was about five-foot-six like me). Daniel had to crouch a bit. When we came out the other side we found ourselves in a huge cavern lit with a bluish hue. The ceiling was very high and the floor was dotted with indigo rocks. A small, silvery pond at the back of the cavern rippled from the fountain protruding from its center.

The bluish hue came from clumps of luminescent moss growing on the ceiling and around the cavern walls. They lit up everything with perfect clarity, including the words and drawings on the walls. When I saw them, I shivered. It felt wondrous and spooky, like when we went to Liza's home and saw how she kept track of her visions with paintings and diagrams.

Merlin had used fragments of the indigo rock like chalk to write and draw all over the cavern. I saw my name, Daniel's name, and the names of many of my friends on the walls. I also saw phrases including "captured by Rampart," "killed by magic hunters," "Simia Crown," and "Pure Magic" written near my name. I followed those phrases along the wall, pursuing their trail in a trance.

"Lady of the Lake, Century City, Potions Professor, Chance Darling, Dreamland, M.R.I., Big Bear. . ." I read out loud.

There were phrase trails for Daniel and my other friends too. Between our trails were fairly impressive sketches. I saw an illustration of Jason standing in a wooden boat crossing a lake. A drawing of five weirdly shaped hummingbirds flying over my head. A rendering of Chance Darling and Daniel arguing.

I stopped when I came upon a sketch of me facing off with Mauvrey. I'd seen the image in a dream. I was holding her by the throat, strangling her. The expression on my face was so ruthless it caught my breath.

"Like I said . . ."

I turned to face Merlin.

"I know you."

My lips tightened into a frown. I'd always felt uncomfortable with how much of my future Liza knew. It made me feel inferior— like she was a god and I was her subject. After we met and got to know each other, that discomfort had lessened slightly because we were no longer just dreams to one another; we were real. She typically didn't lord her power of foresight over me, and as our relationship had grown I didn't feel so violated when she did reference my future. With all the work she'd put into training me, she'd earned that familiarity, and my trust.

Merlin, however, had not. We had no relationship, but he was clearly privy to the turns of my fate before I was and didn't seem to have any qualms about showing it off.

Another thing that bothered me was that while I knew Liza's motivations for helping me, working with me, and interfering in my life, I didn't know Merlin's. Why had he been communicating with me through my dreams? Why had he left that book for me at Gwenivere's castle? His motives were not evident and that was disconcerting.

Furthermore, Liza never mistook seeing my future as a write-off for not needing to understand me in the present. I think that, above all other reasoning, was why Merlin's last statement perturbed me so much. Merlin didn't *know* me. Knowing someone and knowing their future were two very different things. I didn't appreciate him acting like they weren't.

"There's not much to do in this cave except sleep and meditate," Merlin said, not paying any mind to the annoyed expression on my face. "The result is a lot of visions. I came to learn a lot about you and your friends' significance while I was stuck here."

"How long has it been since Nyneve trapped you in the cave?" Daniel asked.

"Based on the way Nyneve looked, I would say about ten years," Merlin said.

"How does Nyneve's age let you know you've been here for ten years?" I asked. "And if that's really the right amount of time, how the heck did you survive that long?"

"The potion sand in my third pouch is for rapid aging," Merlin said, gesturing to his utility belt. "It makes people age five years for every one year that passes."

"Why have a potion that does that?"

Merlin shrugged. "I don't like to kill my enemies if I can help it. I prefer to punish them. I'm vindictive like that. So I always carry some kind of suffering-based potion. One shot activates it; a second will reverse the effects like you saw with Nyneve a few minutes ago. That's how I know the approximate amount of time I've been here. Nyneve was forty when she trapped me, but I managed to hit her with some potion sand before she sealed me in.

"As to your second question, this cave is enchanted. Time moves very slowly inside. For me, it's only felt like a couple of months have passed. And I've had the Fountain of Youth to keep me alive." Merlin gestured to the fountain in the middle of the pond like it was no big deal.

"The water contains nutritional powers that provide your body with everything it needs to sustain itself. It can't heal the sick or the wounded, but it can prolong a healthy life indefinitely if you keep drinking. This cave used to be the home of the Holy Grail for that reason . . . But that's another story."

Merlin huffed in amusement as if he was remembering something funny. "Anyway, being trapped in here hasn't been so bad. I've just hated that I haven't been able to protect the realm and the people I care about for so long. I've had many visions about Camelot's fate under Rampart and Morgause's rule, as well as what has befallen Arthur. It is regrettable. Now that I am free I can help proactively. We must depart for my compound immediately. I have to make preparations for what's coming and there are some things that you need."

Merlin slapped Daniel on the back. "Let's go, tall guy."

Daniel was surprised by the sudden, familiar gesture, but he followed the wizard out. They ducked under the arch we'd entered through. I hesitated before going after them, taking one last gander at Merlin's work on the walls.

"I don't suppose we can take some of that water from the Fountain of Youth with us?" I heard Daniel ask as they ascended toward the mouth of the cave.

"Nice try, kid," Merlin responded. "But the magic waters only work if you drink them in the cave while it's sealed shut. You can only reap their benefits if you're stuck in here like I was. It's a bragawash clause, but all magic comes with a cost."

I stared up at the sketch on the wall of me throttling Mauvrey. "Don't I know it," I muttered.

CHAPTER 21

Forget-Me-Nots

erlin seemed to know all the moves the Shifting Forest was going to make before it made them.

The wizard twisted through trees and glens and natural undergrowth tunnels with the utmost confidence even as the ground was moving. He explained that the forest's tectonic plates shifted in certain patterns, which had to do with the time of day. He'd memorized these patterns long ago.

During the journey, Merlin told us more about the potion sands he kept in his leather pouches. Like SJ and her portable potions, the wizard had invented a way to crystalize his magical brews into a more travel-friendly form. While SJ had figured out how to condense hers into marble-sized projectiles, Merlin had reduced his potions to grains of sand. All it took was a spark to ignite them and release the enchantment contained inside. The metal bracelet he wore was designed to produce the necessary spark when he—or whoever wore it—spoke the command, "Ignus."

Merlin was legendary for his magic and his influence over Camelot as Arthur's right hand. The potion sands that Merlin carried with him explained his wide range of powerful abilities, which had helped foster the mythology of him being the "greatest wizard of all time." The only power that was not a result of his inventiveness was the gift that resulted from his Pure Magic—invisibility.

Like me with my powers of life, or Liza with her powers of

teleportation, Merlin's Pure Magic had bestowed him with one incredibly powerful ability. Not only could he make himself invisible, he could project that power onto other beings and objects as well.

Nyneve had been right; those magic hunters had been no match.

After walking for half an hour, we reached a stone wall that encircled a massive property. Vines covered much of the wall and mushrooms sprouted at the base. At the top of the wall were long, sharp spikes like the points of Twenty-Three Skidd lacrosse swords.

Merlin led us along the barrier until we reached a silver gate decorated with crystals. I imagined they must've been stunning once, but like the gate itself, they were now dull and weathered.

The gate did not have a handle or a keyhole. Instead, there was a large, translucent disc with a round opal at the center. I stared at it curiously. It looked like an eyeball. Then the thing blinked and I jumped away.

"Many years ago, I put an enchantment over this property," Merlin explained. "If the walls and the spikes don't deter trespassers, this little guy stops them in their tracks."

Merlin held his palm up to the eye. It blinked before a wave of blue energy rippled across the wall.

"How does it work?" Daniel asked, eyeing the eye suspiciously.

"The eye scans anything alive within one foot of the wall all across the compound. If it does not see me, then it will release a warning. If that warning is not heeded, then the trespassers face an electrifying consequence." Merlin looked up at a dove in a nearby tree. "Here, I'll show you. Both of you step back a few feet."

"Wait, what are you gonna—"

"Crisanta. I'm working." Merlin held up a finger for silence then shooed Daniel and me behind him.

It took all of my strength not to let my irritation show. I hadn't gotten shushed like that since I was at school. My impression of Merlin was not improving.

Merlin removed one of the pouches from his utility belt and

shook it upside down on the grass several inches from the gate. A few small particles spilled out.

"More potion sand?" I asked.

"No," he replied. "This is trail mix. I ran out a while ago, but I thought I might have some crumbs left." He whistled lightly to get the attention of the dove. Curious, it flew over. When the bird landed on the ground to eat, Merlin retreated and joined us.

At the center of the gate, the shimmering eye blinked again. Its opal cornea shifted in the direction of the dove. After a moment, a wave of blue energy passed over the wall like it had before, only this time right after it finished a loud chime sounded and a wave of red energy followed. Then a warning was issued. It was loud but calm.

"Please step away from the wall. You are trespassing on the property of the almighty, and incomparably handsome, Merlin. You have five seconds to move away."

A bad feeling started to creep up my throat. "Merlin, it's not going to—"

"Shh." Merlin smacked my arm with the back of his hand. "I like this part."

The dove continued to peck at the crumbs.

"Four," the voice counted. "Three, two, one."

As I'd feared, something horrifying happened on "one." The wall crackled with white-hot magical electricity. Then a single pulse shot out of the bricks closest to the bird. The delicate dove never knew what hit him. He was dead instantly.

"You killed him!" I dashed forward and came to my knees in front of the ill-fated bird. There was a small black scorch mark on his otherwise pure white coat, right above his heart.

"Relax," Merlin said as he held his palm up to the gate's eye anew. Blue light flashed over everything as he shrugged. "It was just a bird. Nothing to get yourself into a twist about. It's not like it was a person."

"Have there been people, though?" Daniel asked sternly. "Killed by this gate, I mean?"

"Nah," Merlin shrugged. "I had this enchantment in place for years before I got trapped. It only kills the occasional woodland creature. It's never hurt a person. People are smart enough to move away once they hear the warning."

Merlin snapped his fingers in front of the eyeball. The gate vanished.

"Now, onward," Merlin said. "If you two hope to complete your long-term mission, you'll need some of the magical items I have inside."

"Keep them," I said, glaring at the wizard. "I don't want anything from you."

My irritation at Merlin had blossomed into mild anger. He couldn't just go around killing things. I was still on the moral fence about taking life where bad guys were concerned, but I knew that taking life to prove a point was a hard wrong. I figured everyone knew that.

"I thought you were supposed to be a good guy," I said to Merlin.

"I *am* a good guy," Merlin replied. "I just focus on the big picture to accomplish the most good. I never do anything without a reason."

My glare persisted, but Merlin took in my sour expression with ease. "Not a fan of my methods, Crisanta Knight?"

"Hardly," I huffed.

"That's fair," Merlin replied. "I've been told I'm an acquired taste. Like croquet or sushi."

"Sushi?"

"It's like raw fish, only fancier. When you go to Earth, I recommend a place called Sugarfish—I've foreseen tiny portions, but excellent quality."

My annoyance with the wizard melted into confusion. I raised my eyebrows and looked to Daniel for help. "Okay. Now I'm lost."

Merlin shook his head. "No, no. That's not supposed to happen until Book Seven."

I turned back to him. "What?"

"Never mind. I'm getting ahead of myself. Been in that cave a bit too long, you know." Merlin knocked on his head, which made a disturbingly hollow sound.

I blinked hard and long. Merlin threw me for a loop. One

minute he was cold and calculating. The next he was babbling like a quirky hobo living behind a dumpster.

"You're not making any sense," Daniel said.

"Or am I making all the sense in the world, but it is a world you're unfamiliar with?" Merlin countered. I opened my mouth to speak, but Merlin held a finger to my lips, shushing me preemptively. I had to fight all my instincts not to break that finger.

He pulled away and crouched down to my level. "Crisanta Knight, I'll admit that being in that cave alone with nothing to do but get lost in my visions has made me a tad more unstable than usual. But make no mistake: I am not a fool. And no action I take is without purpose or meaning. The help I'm offering will be vital to your destiny. As a matter of fact, this dove was killed just for you."

Merlin's irises flared with the stern intensity of someone strong, powerful, and more brilliant than anyone I'd ever known.

"You're a smart girl, Crisanta," he said. "And I know there's been a theory burning in the back of your mind about the extent of your powers. You want to know whether you can actively use them to restore life to others like you accidentally used them on yourself. More specifically, you want to know if you can use them to bring back a friend."

Daniel glanced at me. "Knight? What is he talking about?"

I chose my words carefully. Jason had sworn me to secrecy over his fate, but I had to give Daniel something.

"It's precautionary," I replied. "It'd be a good back-up plan to have if something awful were to happen to one of us. The problem is, I don't know if I'm strong enough without Magic Instinct to intentionally harness that kind of power."

"Which is why I have provided you with this dead creature," Merlin said, gesturing to the dove. "I can tell by the grayness in your eyes that you're in the midst of a grueling spell of Magic Exhaustion. But I had a vision about your time in Bluebeard Tower. You're powerful, and given the right motivations, you can harness your magic before it's done rebooting."

"But that's only with Magic Instinct," I argued.

"You can do it without Magic Instinct," Merlin insisted. "I've done it. And I have a feeling you have the potential to be even more powerful than I am."

"But I—"

"Crisanta, you have to try. This is a safe space to experiment. If you can't restore life to this tiny creature in this controlled environment then you'll have no hope when a friend's life is on the line."

Silence hung for a few moments as I thought it over.

I sighed. "I wouldn't even know how to start."

"I don't believe that," Merlin stated. "Harness your emotions the way you did before but combine them with your will. Magic Instinct is a defensive tactic. You lose control because you are in immediate peril and the power protects you like a reflex. I'm telling you that you can be that powerful without letting go or being in direct danger. Use your emotions like an offensive tactic. Gather all that focus you've been training with, but don't block out everything you're feeling like you're some kind of level-minded machine. Allow the emotions to build inside and then give them purpose."

I looked at the dove and bit my lip. Then I picked up the creature and cupped it in my palms.

"Strong emotions run inside you, Crisanta," Merlin coached softly. "You bury them a lot of the time because they lend your Pure Magic power. But the other side of that coin is that they give *you* power. I understand it is dangerous, as letting emotion fuel your magic could enhance your odds of turning dark. But feeling things deeply is genuinely your only shot at becoming more powerful. And in the long term, becoming more powerful is your only shot at saving the ones you love."

I was still weak from Magic Exhaustion, so this was a bad idea. I didn't exactly trust Merlin, so this was a bad idea. My magic training with Liza had always been about trying to avoid combining emotion with magic, so this was a bad idea. And I hated how intoxicating that emotion-fueled rush of power felt in Bluebeard Tower, so this was an *exceptionally* bad idea. Yet I closed my eyes and let the feelings flow.

Merlin may have been a lot of unlikeable things, but he was right about this. If I couldn't garner the power to bring a bird back to life, I had no hope of restoring life to Jason. And doing that was more important than protecting myself against my power-hungry Pure Magic. Protecting the people I cared for was more important than protecting myself, period. I was willing to put myself at greater risk of turning dark if it meant I'd have the power to truly make a difference and save my friends.

Since I didn't have a strong emotional connection to this dove—past my general desire to save it—I had to dig deep for an emotional charge. I thought about my desperation to enhance my magic to use it on Jason, my fear that I wouldn't be able to, and my love for my good friend that was causing me to do this. Those feelings mixed with my will as I concentrated on what I wanted to happen. I imagined the small dove's heart beating, his eyes bursting open, his wings flapping into the sky.

I felt magic searing through me. Waves of pain radiated through my body. It was much worse than anything I'd felt all day. My system was not strong enough in this recuperative state to sustain much, but I forced myself to continue. My eyes burned beneath the lids, causing me to open them.

"Knight, your eyes," Daniel said in shock. "They're . . . glowing."

I was too deep in the trance to respond. Daniel seemed miles away. I focused harder, letting the emotion I normally contained swell so much that it hurt. Then I breathed out a single word, a command full of my absolute will.

"Live," I whispered.

A golden aura flowed down my arms until it culminated in my hands, which pulsed like two petite suns. Then, all at once, the energy was sucked into the body of the dove. The creature's charred plumage shone beneath a small beam of light that burst from its chest. Then the plumage changed to white and the bird's tiny black eyes peered up at me. In the next instant, he flipped over in my hands and flew off.

I grinned ecstatically, but only for a moment. A second later my glow shut off like an extinguished candelabra and my stamina went with it. I collapsed to the grass. I heard Daniel say my name, but again it felt like he was far away.

Even dressed in armor and dripping with sweat from a Twenty-Three Skidd match, Chance Darling still looked perfect.

He dismounted his Pegasus and handed the reins to a waiting attendant while tucking his silver helmet with forest green plumage under his arm. As he made his way into the tunnel that led to the arena's locker rooms, Girtha caught up with him. She too was dressed in armor, and her massive right hand clung to a helmet with the same color plumage as Chance's. They were on the same Lord Channing's team, after all.

"Darling," Girtha said as she approached. "What's the work schedule look like tomorrow? You got enough people on overtime? Spring break is almost over, which means Crisa will be back soon and we've still got a lot of construction to do on the upper levels."

"I know," Chance responded. "But we'll be fine. Between your volunteers from Lady Agnue's, the workers I hired, and the solid team of guys from Lord Channing's assisting in the endeavor, we should be able to get the job done."

"Cool." Girtha nodded. "By the way, I've been meaning to ask you something. I get how being the grandson of King Midas lets you turn stuff to gold and afford the workers, but how did you get so many volunteers to help out? Some heroes might be tempted by the gold, but the princes from Lord Channing's don't need the money. And good guys or not, staying at school and volunteering their spring break to do this . . . Well, it just doesn't add up."

"Their assistance cost me a lot," Chance admitted. "Plenty of guys were willing to pitch in for free because they were already staying at school for the break, but many weren't. I had to exchange a lot of favors to get the support I needed. I've been doing homework for younger students whose classes I've already taken. In my spare time I'm giving private training sessions to guys on the fencing, archery, and swim teams so they can make first string next term. And I've traded away my prized horses back home. Just to name a few things anyway."

"Dang, man," Girtha said in awe. "You must really like her to go through all that. Does she know you feel this way?"

"I don't think so. But I don't blame her," Chance replied. "With my history, Crisanta has every reason to doubt me. And if I'm honest, even now I'm not sure if I am worthy of her forgiveness or good graces."

"Aw, cheer up, Princey," Girtha said, throwing her massive arm around Chance's shoulders and crushing him a bit. "I used to think you were a total tool, but now you've got my full respect. Crisa may not be quick to trust, but she's got a good heart and she believes that people can change. And you, my friend, have changed."

The scene shifted to a wintery forest. A multi-story wooden cabin came into view. Sleek silvery railings and metallic ducts ran along the outside and through the compound like tunnels in a hamster cage. Smoke poured out of the cabin's stone chimney. Several guards in black turtlenecks, pants, and parkas paced around the area. They were each holding dark, long-nosed things, which looked like weapons I'd seen in the *Die Hard* movies we'd watched on Earth.

Machine guns, I believe they were called.

Snow clung to the roof of the large cabin and the pine trees that surrounded it—falling here and there when a bird or squirrel rustled its integrity.

Suddenly a loud shriek pierced the air. The birds took flight in panic. Even the guards looked a bit disconcerted. Their reaction to the noise had nothing on mine though. I knew with utmost certainty that the scream in the dream was my own.

I woke from the nightmare and found myself lying on a dusty suede couch. It was maroon and smelled like old cheese. The room I was in had a glass ceiling that was covered in vines and cobwebs. It seemed I was in some sort of greenhouse.

I sat up and saw that behind the couch the greenhouse was so overgrown with trees and plants that I had no way of telling how big it was. However, the area immediately in front of the couch was modeled like a small den.

Bookshelves with vines growing through holes in the wood

stood against the back wall. Every shelf was loaded with withered, damp-looking books and miscellaneous knickknacks. The floor was all grass and weeds, forming a thick, organic shag carpet. Flowers I didn't recognize grew from clumps of moss that covered the coffee table across from the couch. There were vines along the couch too, which had somehow wrapped around my left leg and arm. I had to yank really hard to get them to release their grip before I could stand up.

That's when the pain came like a wave. It felt like a Giant of Geene was sitting on me. Every breath felt labored. Every cell ached. And my throat hurt the way it did whenever I had consumed too many cough drops—sour, but kind of icy.

I grabbed the edge of the couch to keep from stumbling.

"Daniel? Merlin?" I called out.

Two seconds later, Daniel and our wizard host emerged from the greenery.

"Glad you're awake," Daniel said.

He was carrying a lumpy burlap sack. Merlin had a sack of his own. I was about to inquire as to their purpose when I noticed Daniel was staring at me. Not in a you've-got-chocolate-on-your-face kind of way, but in a I'm-really-worried-about-you kind of way.

"You shouldn't have used your magic, Knight," he said anxiously. "Even if you were trying to test its capabilities, you were already drained from your Bluebeard chapter. It wasn't safe to try anything so soon."

"Merlin wanted me to test it and I'm glad I did," I admitted. "Now I know that I *can* use my powers to save others."

"Only if you live long enough to get the chance," Daniel countered. He set his sack on the coffee table and several red potatoes spilled out. There was a dirty, broken mirror that hung in a rusty frame on the wall adjacent. Daniel went over to it, selected a shard, and brought it over to me. "Powers of life or not, you keep pushing yourself and that same magic that saved you is gonna burn out and destroy you."

He held up the mirror fragment, forcing me to look at myself. My face was so white it would have given ghosts a reality check.

My normally forest green eyes were a creepy silver color. Not only that, my pupils lacked all brightness. They looked dead. Sort of like how I felt inside.

"All right, I see your point," I said. "I'll take it down a notch with the magic."

"Try ten notches," Daniel replied. "I'm all for you improving your powers, but doing it while you're in a state of Magic Exhaustion is too dangerous. Luckily, Merlin says he can fix up a potion to restore some of your strength."

Daniel gestured at Merlin. The wizard had his arm elbow-deep inside a potted plant and seemed to be ignoring us.

"Um, Merlin?" Daniel said.

"Hang on, I've almost got it," Merlin mumbled. "Here we go!"

He gleefully pulled out a silver coin the size of a sand dollar from the pot, then moved across the den and placed it in a circular indentation on the bottom level of a bookshelf. The slot accepted the coin like a vending machine. In response, the bookshelf shifted aside and revealed a dark shaft. Inside was a thin metal pole like you'd find at a fire station, leading to who knows where.

"The potion shouldn't take me more than an hour to prepare," Merlin said as he rolled up the sleeves of his robe. "You kids can make yourselves a snack while I work. First though, I want to give you those magical items I mentioned."

Merlin grabbed his sack of ingredients and the sack Daniel had put on the table, swinging them both over his shoulder. Then he slid down the metal pole with one hand.

"Wahoo!" he shouted as he disappeared from sight.

"Are we supposed to follow him?" I asked.

"I guess," Daniel said. "You wanna go first?"

"Um, why don't you lead?"

Daniel shrugged, put the mirror shard on the table, and approached the shadowy shaft. He leapt off the ground and slid down the pole. I scurried to the edge and peered down after him, but by then he was lost in blackness. When I heard a thud indicating he'd found the floor somewhere below, I took it as my cue to go.

The pole was four feet away from the edge, so jumping was

a necessity. I summoned all my strength to bridge the distance, bounded into the shaft, and grabbed onto the cold metal pole with my hands while my legs wrapped around it.

My hair and dress whistled through the updraft of the shaft. Things grew darker and darker until I could not even see an inch from my nose. Then abruptly I dropped into an amazing place that was like nothing I'd ever seen.

I landed on the grassy floor of a cavern, which was a cross between an elaborate potions lab and a mystical, underground garden. Merlin was off to the side explaining something to Daniel and pointing at the silvery stone walls, which displayed everything it would take to keep SJ occupied for a hundred years.

And I thought Julian's potions lab back in Oz was impressive.

Beakers, test tubes, and other lab equipment cluttered the solid gold countertops. Many containers on display were glass, but plenty of others were reinforced with gemstones. Some were even *made* of gemstones.

Liquids streamed steadily from fountains that stuck out along the right wall. The spouts were stone renderings of animal faces—deer, fish, ravens, squirrels. The liquids they emitted were all different. While a thin purple stream pouring from one spout smelled like grape juice, another next to it ejected a much thicker substance that looked a lot like blood. Each of these liquids poured into a gold basin also sticking out of the wall about a foot beneath each fountain.

I opened one of the cabinets beneath a countertop and discovered it was stocked with a myriad of jarred ingredients—golden eggshells, a lone monkey foot floating inside greenish oil, a pink yogurty substance labeled "Flower Child Phlegm," blue radishes, moldy pie, and countless other weird things.

On the opposite wall were more countertops and cabinets. There were also several sinks, cauldrons of various sizes, and large piles of scrap metal. On one of the countertops I spotted a big glass jar full of bolts and screws.

Instead of fountains, the wall on the left featured grand glass dispensers. Each of these vessels contained different colored sand—Merlin's various potion sands I presumed. It was all terribly impressive.

And yet, as mesmerizing as the potions laboratory was, the rest of the room was even more awe-inspiring. It was beautiful and bewildering all at the same time. Above us, where the roof of the cavern should have been, a night sky swirled with deep shades of navy and onyx and twinkled with stars. Meanwhile, a gorgeous acre of flower bushes grew over the ground. They featured only one type of flower—blossoms with tiny blue petals and bright yellow centers. These flowers gave off such a radiant glow that the entire area was lit up by their mystical aura.

"It's amazing," I commented as I stepped into a pathway between one of the rows of flower bushes.

"Forget-Me-Nots," Merlin said looking around the room, which I guess he hadn't seen in a long time. "A very useful plant. It has many magical properties and can create a powerful potion."

Merlin picked up a small device from one of his countertops. It looked like a compass, and he began wading through the bushes with it. The compass made beeping noises that changed in pitch as he delved through the garden. After about a minute of hastily combing the rows, the compass chimed loudly and Merlin dove into one of the dense flower bushes. He eventually popped back up, his sleeves dirty and his beard full of leaves and twigs. Between his fingers he clutched a single flower that was the same shape and size as the others but was all yellow.

He returned to Daniel and me and held it up for us to study more closely. "One in every three thousand Forget-Me-Nots has a special bit of magic that can let you see people's memories," he explained. "It needs to be brewed carefully with a reverse Sleeping Capsule Spell by a master potionist, but the end result is quite extraordinary. That is one of the magical gifts I'd like to give you, Crisanta Knight," he said, looking at me seriously. "In warfare, there is no greater power than understanding your enemy. So, given how many enemies you have, I am offering you this flower—and a second one as soon as I find it—so that in the future you can be better prepared to face the people who threaten you."

"Um, thank you," I said.

I was grateful, as this truly was a special gift, but Merlin's shifting personality was keeping me more off balance than the Shifting Forest. I was still pretty sure I didn't like him, but here he was giving me magical gifts and preparing to brew a potion to restore my strength. What the frack was this guy's deal? All I could say for certain was that he was a puzzle.

"I'm not done," Merlin replied. He pulled out a box from beneath one of the cabinets. Inside the box was an assortment of necklaces with tiny glass test tubes hanging from the cords like paper clip-sized pendants. He popped the Forget-Me-Not into one and sealed it with a purple stopper. Then he placed it on the counter and took out a second cord necklace, which he uncorked. He went to a dispenser on the wall that contained a mauve potion sand. There wasn't much left. He held the tube beneath the dispenser and pressed a button that caused the last of it to pour into the tube.

"The Forget-Me-Nots are for you to use a while from now, Crisanta," Merlin said. "That test tube necklace is made of unbreakable glass, so they will be safe. As for you, my boy . . ."

Merlin closed the second test tube with a blue cork and offered the necklace to Daniel. "This one is not unbreakable because, by nature, you're going to want to break it. This is the last of my Ally Aid potion. In the very near future you will need help to survive. When that time comes, break this tube and the person you need most will appear by your side."

Daniel took the cord and hung it around his neck. "Thanks," he said appreciatively.

"Now then," Merlin continued, "You two go relax while I hunt down another flower and prep the potion that will restore Crisanta's strength. She's barely a sniff away from Magic Burn Out. Oh, but one more thing first. I want you to meet someone."

Merlin punched a green button attached to an intercom on the wall and shouted, "Expecto Bizzario!"

"Is that some kind of incantation?" I asked.

"That was no incantation," Merlin replied. "I was calling my dog."

A metal hatch suddenly opened in the wall. Out leapt a dog the size of a Labrador, made of bronze and copper. When its red eyes saw Merlin, it barked happily and pounced on the old wizard, knocking him over. Merlin did not seem to mind.

"I missed you too, boy. Here, here." Merlin went over to the big glass jar containing screws and bolts. He opened it and threw a handful of bolts at the creature, who crunched them down gladly. When it finished eating, the mechanical Labrador jumped into Merlin's arms.

Surprisingly, Merlin was able to hold him up. "Expecto Bizzario, meet Crisanta and Daniel. Crisanta and Daniel, meet Expecto Bizzario," Merlin grabbed one of the creature's paws and waved at us with it. "I used to have normal hounds, but they were regrettably fragile things. They accidentally consume one chemical or lick even slight remains of loose potion sand and they would keel over faster than a ten-year-old at a Bat Mitzvah. So a while back, I built Expecto Bizzario. He's indestructible, a great guard dog, and not limited by mortality. Good thing too, because I'm pretty sure going ten years without being fed would've been a problem for normal dogs."

Merlin put Expecto Bizzario back on the floor. The dog trotted over to us wagging its tail, which made a slight grinding sound. Daniel and I patted him on the head while Merlin went over to a dispenser with teal potion sand. He poured a handful into his palm and trotted back to us. Expecto Bizzario returned to his master's side.

"I imagine most of the food in my kitchen has expired, but please help yourselves to whatever you find. Just don't touch the licorice. It's poison. And I think the cookie jar has some flesh-eating crickets inside. They're probably dead now, but don't open it just in case."

"All right," I said. "But how do we get to—"

"Short Range Teleporting potion," Merlin said, shaking

his closed fist. "See you two in a bit." He tossed the sand in our direction while his bracelet sparked at his command word, "Ignus."

A teal cloud erupted at our feet. When it dissipated, Daniel and I were in a cobweb-covered kitchen. I coughed as the last of the smoke vanished.

"Well, I don't know about you, but I'm thoroughly weirded out," I commented.

"Weirded out enough to not go looking through this guy's cabinets for something to eat?" Daniel asked.

I raised my eyebrows. "What is this, your first day?"

CHAPTER 22

The Window

fter a thorough search of Merlin's untidy kitchen, Daniel and I discovered a cabinet full of packages labeled "Insta-Supper."

The average package was the size of a postcard and the weight of a hacky sack. There was a picture of a food item on the front of each one. After tearing them open, we only found pieces of foam inside. However, after some experimentation we realized that by adding water (and taking cover when a small, green combustion occurred), the food on the label magically appeared in place of the foam. We feasted on roast beef, freshly baked bread, and potatoes au gratin. All of which made me very happy.

After we had eaten, I was too anxious to relax like Merlin had suggested, so I decided to explore the famous wizard's home instead. Daniel came along for a while, but when we discovered a living room with some comfy-looking silver couches, he tapped out.

"If Merlin's going to be busy for a bit, I think I'm going to see if I can get some rest," he said, removing the dusty quilt that had been covering one of the couches to reveal a moderately clean area underneath. "With our luck, it might be our only chance before someone tries to kill us again. You should probably do the same."

"I think I'll pass," I said. "I've spent more time unconscious in the last twenty-four hours than any person ever should."

He frowned in disapproval. "Knight—"

"Daniel, I may be in pain, I may be tired, and I may appreciate your concern, but you have to let me be. You know how I am. I need time to . . ." I gestured at my head with both hands. "Mentally sort stuff out."

Daniel let me go without further protest. I continued exploring, wandering through countless dusty, darkened rooms. I paused when I came to a music room of sorts. A lonely gold harp resided at one end, leaning against the wall like the torn off wing of an angel. There was also a gray grand piano in the corner by a window with drawn curtains. A few rays of light escaped through the blinds and shone on the keys. I wondered if Merlin played. Shelves on the wall with folders and bound books containing sheet music certainly suggested so.

Between the shelves hanging on the walls were various framed maps and paintings. I paused when I came across a small frame perched on a shelf that featured someone I knew.

It was Arthur, just a much younger version. In this picture he was around Alex's age. Merlin was also in the photo, and he looked so young I didn't recognize him at first. I picked up the frame and blew dust off the glass. When I did, I noticed that the picture was unusual, almost holographic. It reminded me of the screens that the projection orbs lit up. Arthur and Merlin's image moved slightly when I moved the picture, causing me to wonder if there was some kind of magic involved.

I studied the image. Although Arthur and Merlin were both in formal attire, as if about to attend an important ceremony, Merlin had one arm around the king's neck and was using the other to give Arthur's blond head a noogie. They were both in mid-laugh when the picture had been captured. It warmed me inside to see them like that. I put the picture down and added it as a piece to the growing puzzle that was our new ally downstairs.

Eventually I ended up at the front doors of Merlin's compound. I pushed them open and daylight streamed into the cold stone foyer. I stepped outside.

The stretch of grass between the main doors and the enchanted wall that guarded Merlin's home was overgrown—way more so than the grass in his magically sustained greenhouse and Forget-

Me-Not cavern. It billowed around my shoes in thick waves that were knotted together like the fur of a wild dog.

I walked down the cobblestone path that led to the gate. At one point when I thought I was stepping on some dried leaves, I leapt back in terror when I realized I was crushing the charred, severed wing of a long-deceased pigeon.

"Ew, ew, ew." I shuddered as I scraped my boot against the cobblestone, trying to shake off the feeling of grossness.

That's when I noticed clusters of bone hidden in the grass close to the wall that I hadn't seen when we'd entered. Tiny skeletal remains of birds and the occasional squirrel were scattered about like a graveyard. I imagined these were other animals that'd been fried by Merlin's guard wall. It seemed even if they made it over they were punished for getting too close to the barrier.

My gaze fell upon an area of the grass where a dead red-chested hummingbird lay. It had not been there long. Its body was still whole; it must've died fairly recently.

Once Merlin brought me whatever strength-booster he was brewing, I decided I would try to bring it back to life. For the first time since I'd foreseen Jason's demise, I had a plausible way to save him and I wanted to get in as much practice as possible. If I was going to be of any use to my friend, I had to get good at this.

"It won't work."

I jumped. Merlin appeared behind me, looking completely changed. His beard was now short and sleek, like something a wealthy businessman would sport. His hair was neatly trimmed and his wild eyebrows had been shaped. He'd changed out of his dirty robe and now wore a freshly pressed maroon one with gold piping. He'd transformed from looking like a crazy old man to a distinguished elderly gentleman—like someone who might be a professor at Lord Channing's or an ambassador to one of my realm's kingdoms.

Merlin pointed at the hummingbird I'd been staring at. "You can't save it."

I rolled my eyes. "I know, I know—I'm too weak right now. But after you give me whatever it is you've concocted to fix me up, I should be able to, right?"

"I'm afraid not. Even once your strength is restored, that bird is beyond saving."

"What do you mean? The bird is dead. I bring things back to life. If I harness my emotional power like I did before, why can't I save him?"

"When creatures die, their souls hang on to their physical bodies for precisely three minutes," Merlin explained. "Whether they go by natural causes, or unnatural ones like murder, poison, or dark magic, they only have three minutes to be saved. After this window closes, no amount of magic can help them. Not even yours. Think about that poisoned Snow White corset that your classmate Mauvrey tried to kill you with last semester."

I opened my mouth to ask how he knew about that, but he waved me off.

"I've had a lot of visions of your future, Crisanta," he said dismissively.

Oh. Right. He knows all about me.

Ugh. That still didn't sit well. How much of my life had this guy seen in his head? And how long had he been having visions about me? Despite being from different realms and him being trapped in a cave for a decade, he seemed to know the answer to every question I was going to ask. He didn't even appear to be curious about my backstory at all. Perhaps he already knew enough?

"Like you," Merlin continued, "Snow White only survived the poisoned corset because it was removed in time. If it was left on for much longer, both of you would've been beyond rescue. Do you understand, Crisanta?"

I understood the example. A while back SJ had explained about the poisoned corset the evil queen had used on her mother. But the rest of it . . .

I blinked at the man. Merlin sighed.

"Even you, with all your power, would have been a goner if that corset was left on long enough because your window would've closed," Merlin said. "The bottom line, Crisanta, is that you can't save everyone."

My heart was struck by the news. My plans to save Jason were flawed. After he was killed I only had three minutes to get to him. But in my dream, he, Blue, and SJ had been on their own. What if I didn't reach them in time?

"I don't know if you make it," Merlin said abruptly.

I met his gaze.

"I've seen a lot of your future, Crisanta, but I've only seen fragments. It's why I wasn't surprised when you and Daniel showed up at the cave I was trapped in. It's why I am giving you these specific magical objects. And it is why I instructed Arthur to be pushed out onto the Lake of Avalon should he ever find himself mortally wounded. It's always been tradition that Pendragon kings restore Excalibur to the Lady of the Lake when they aren't long for this world. But in Arthur's case, it was more than that. Ordinarily, kings can just summon the Lady of the Lake wherever they are to return the sword. Arthur didn't know that; I lied to him so he would end up in that boat on the lake. I knew a Wonderland portal would open and take him to Neverland where he would be preserved, thus buying time for your storyline to catch up with his.

"With your powers, I believe that you can save him. I haven't had any visions to confirm that this comes to pass, but I've known that you were coming for many years, so you have always been my plan where Arthur is concerned."

"That's why you came to me in my dreams these last few months," I thought aloud. "You wanted my friends and I to go to Neverland—not just because we'd get the clue that would lead us to Oz to find Paige Tomkins. You wanted me to meet Arthur."

Merlin nodded. "It was destiny that you would find him. I just wanted to help you along. Now the next time you reconnect with Arthur, you can use your magic to counteract his mortal wound. Hopefully."

The truth sunk in. I was both impressed and a touch scared. The idea that Merlin had taken steps so many years in advance to influence the futures he'd envisioned was astounding. At the same time, the fact that he was *that* calculating and *that* good at manipulation was enough to make anybody uneasy. Particularly the girl he seemed to be doing so many calculations and manipulations around.

"You knew that I had this power all along," I said slowly. "Not just the magic to give life to the inanimate, but the ability to infuse life into the dying. You knew that I'd learn how to use my abilities to resurrect the dead."

"I didn't know how long it would take you, nor how many years would pass between Arthur's supposed death and your arrival, but my visions told me that you would have this power, and that you would come. Which is why, since I first uttered the Great Lights Prophecy, I have been making preparations, waiting for the day when the right Knight would appear to go after Excalibur and restore it to the rightful king."

The right *Knight* . . .

Merlin wasn't playing games here. Me saving Arthur was just one of his plans in motion. He must've foreseen Alex and me coming for Excalibur, and who knew what else.

"So you know about Alex, Arian, and Mauvrey?" I asked.

He nodded.

"But you're not sure it's me either, are you?" I said. "Like Arian and Rampart, you don't know if I'm the 'right Knight' meant to claim Excalibur. It could be my brother. He meets the same qualifications as I do. Which means he could be the one destined to decide the fate of this realm. I might not be the hero you need me to be . . . Just like I might not be the hero Jason needs me to be."

Merlin put his hand on my shoulder. I cringed a bit. He wasn't being cruel to me in any way; he'd actually been generous, kind, and helpful. However, he was also curt, ambiguous, and patronizing. Best I could describe, he made me feel like I was a lab rat in a maze and he was the clever scientist. He knew about the twists and turns I'd taken, the obstacles that lay ahead, and he was set on watching me run for his own purposes including saving Arthur, claiming Excalibur, and probably other things too.

The shaky fact was that I didn't know what all his motives

were. Now that our fates had finally collided, I had a feeling that my role in his vision for the future was only just beginning.

"No. You might not be the right Knight," Merlin agreed. "Frankly, from what I've seen, you might very well doom us all."

I glowered. "Thanks for the encouragement."

"Crisanta, you don't need the encouragement of others," he said firmly, squeezing my shoulder. "Such words are fleeting. Whether you succeed or fail, the main faith to keep going has to come from you. Otherwise, when push comes to shove, you will stumble and fall."

A half hour later, Merlin escorted Daniel and me out of his home with Expecto Bizzario trailing us. The metallic dog was biting at Daniel's pant leg as we walked, slowing him down. I would have laughed, but I was concentrating on not hurling all over the path as I swallowed the last of my unappetizing medicine.

Yuck. Magic granola bars are not delicious.

Merlin had brewed me a power-restoring potion in the form of two chewy, stale-tasting snack bars. I was forced to eat one before leaving and ordered to consume the other in the evening as a chaser.

The wizard swore that by morning my magic and I would be restored to full strength. However, the caveat was that I could not use any magic at all until then. Should I disobey the instruction, Merlin warned that even if I could overcome the pain of Magic Exhaustion, there would be no coming back. If the dismal state of my strength didn't annihilate me on the spot via Magic Burn Out, his granola bars would. Their ingredients needed time to work. If I didn't give them long enough, they would have the opposite effect and turn into poison, corroding my small intestine like an out-of-control acid monster.

No wonder Merlin has never submitted the invention for mass production. Something tells me that any kind of public health and safety board wouldn't approve a snack bar that could disintegrate your insides.

I couldn't wait to continue on our way to Avalon. While this stop had provided me with magic-restoring snack bars, taught me about my resurrection abilities, nourished us with actual food, and more, I was anxious to get going.

I was kind of relieved that Merlin had opted not to come with us. His presence continued to make me feel uncomfortable. Even so, I did hope he would rendezvous with us later for the good of the group.

Daniel and I had told the wizard about our plans to reconnect with his old pals Gwenivere, Morgan, and their allies for the siege on the citadel right before the Vicennalia Aurora. Our hope was that Merlin could meet up with us then. We'd definitely benefit from having a powerful wizard on our side as we took on the citadel of Camelot.

He was excited about the invasion invitation but vague about accepting. Although the idea of dethroning Rampart pleased him, and he was adamant that his whole purpose in life was to help Arthur and the Pendragon royal family, he said he would only join us if "other forces" did not get to him first. He explained that his visions indicated certain antagonists needed him to serve a purpose on the day of the Vicennalia Aurora—that's why they'd hired the magic hunters to capture Nyneve and force her to open the cave. He'd also foreseen that he would not be able to elude them forever, so he couldn't commit to reconnecting with us for the siege.

This news was worrying, but Merlin insisted we had enough to concern ourselves with. He could take care of himself and would face and outwit fate on his own terms like he'd done a hundred times before. Having done the same multiple times, I understood where he was coming from. Though I still wished he'd let us help. While I may not have trusted the guy completely, he was a fellow Pure Magic wielder and was important to Arthur and this realm, so I felt bad about leaving him to fend for himself.

Alas, Merlin would have none of our assistance. He maintained that we focus on the priorities he deemed *our business*.

"Crisanta," he said as we walked across the front lawn. "You've seen visions of the Vicennalia Aurora. You know how much more powerful Pure Magic is going to be when the event hits. But this magic fluctuation will not be a sudden change; it will be gradual. The closer the event draws, the more power will surge throughout all the realms. It's been happening for days now, building up. Even the wormholes that create portals from one realm to the next have been appearing more frequently."

"I noticed that when we arrived in Camelot," I responded.

"The intervals between wormholes will only keep getting shorter until the Vicennalia Aurora arrives at 7:30 p.m. tomorrow evening," Merlin continued. "By then they'll be coming every few minutes, maybe seconds. This build up will affect all Pure Magic carriers in the same way. As early as the morning, you should start to feel potent magic in the air. Waves of increased magic energy will also roll across the atmosphere during the day, affecting you in short, mighty bursts. Your power will grow more and more until it climaxes during the Aurora. In other words, once you're healed, with each hour that passes tomorrow you will become stronger, just like anyone else with Pure Magic, including me, Glinda, and all the Pure Magic-wielding witches and warlocks in Alderon."

"While people with normal magic like the Fairy Godmothers become weaker," I said.

"Exactly," Merlin confirmed. "While those with Pure Magic will grow increasingly formidable as the Aurora approaches, those with normal magic will experience the opposite effect. Some people who have normal magic may still pack a punch, depending on their individual strength. For example, I know Morgan La Fay and Morgause are extremely strong; even if it hurts them, they'll still be formidable. But for the most part anyone and anything powered by normal magic will be handicapped."

"Yeah," I sighed. "I've foreseen it. The antagonists in our realm are going to use that as a means to break down the magical barrier imprisoning them. Their Pure Magic carriers and other ploys will be too much for the limited number of Fairy Godmothers assigned to stop them."

"Have you told the Godmothers?" Merlin asked.

"I tried to warn our Fairy Godmother Supreme about it, but she wouldn't listen."

"Even after you alerted her of what you'd foreseen?"

"Well, I didn't tell her about my vision exactly," I admitted. "I just gave her a general warning."

"Why wouldn't you tell her?"

"Because if Knight admits that she has Pure Magic, then the Godmother Supreme will toss her into Alderon," Daniel explained, shaking Expecto Bizzario from his pants leg again. "Pure Magic isn't looked upon favorably where we're from."

"In all honesty, it's not looked upon favorably anywhere," Merlin said, "given the rate of how it turns people evil. But considering what's at stake, I would think Crisanta would have sought the path that's right, not the path that's easy."

My eyes narrowed as his words struck a chord.

Is he suggesting what I think he's suggesting?

A cluster of red-chested hummingbirds flew by. Merlin used it as an excuse to change the subject before I could retort. He was really good at cutting me off when I was trying to think through his cryptic talk.

"Hummingbirds are one of Camelot's most prolific species you know. Anyhow, as promised . . ."

My head whirled from the sharp subject changes as he presented me with a cord necklace with two tiny yellows flowers in the tube. "Remember, in order to bring out the memory magic of the Forget-Me-Nots, they need to be brewed with a reverse Sleeping Capsule Spell, so you'll need a skilled potionist to develop them properly. I take it finding one won't be an issue?"

"Not even a little," I said. "One day you'll have to meet our friend SJ. You two would have loads to talk about on the potions front."

I slung Merlin's cord necklace around my neck and tucked it inside my collar. Then I shoved my sword into the sheath Merlin had lent me and secured the strap around my shoulder. Since I couldn't use any magic *at all* until tomorrow, I'd transformed my wand into a sword before consuming the first granola bar. My wand could operate even during periods of Magic Exhaustion; it just needed the absolute tiniest spark of my power to work. But Merlin warned that even this could trigger the granola bar's poisonous erosion, so it was in my best interest not to risk it. As a result, my trusty weapon was now as stuck as I was.

I would have felt a lot more comfortable carrying around a spear, as I was way more skilled with the wand in that form. However, lugging around a five-foot-long staff wasn't exactly practical. And given how many quick escapes we'd had to make in recent days, I needed something simple and portable.

"A couple more things," Merlin added. "When you decide to use the Forget-Me-Nots and brew them into the memory potion, you'll need a single hair from the head of the person whose memories you want to see."

"All right," I said, bending down to pat Expecto Bizzario. "Anything else?"

"Two words of advice," Merlin replied steadily. "Choose wisely."

The sternness in his eyes stopped me cold. Then Merlin pivoted toward Daniel and gave him a look that was even harsher. It was a combination of warning and worry—like the wizard wasn't sure whether he wanted to protect Daniel or blast him to dust.

"She's not what you think," he said.

Daniel shot me an uneasy swift look.

Before either of us had the chance to respond, Merlin took a fistful of teal potion sand from his utility belt and threw it at the ground by our feet, surprising us.

"Ignus!"

A moment later, Daniel and I appeared in the Shifting Forest. The wall encircling Merlin's property was about forty feet behind us and Merlin was on the other side of the gate.

"Bye now! See you eventually!" he called.

Another teal cloud exploded around the wizard and Expecto Bizzario. In an instant they were gone and Daniel and I were left in the quiet forest.

"I don't know whether that guy is crazy or brilliant," my friend said.

"Trust me," I said, shaking my head. "The two aren't mutually exclusive."

CHAPTER 23

The Reinforcement

 efore we left, Merlin had given Daniel a new map of the Shifting Forest. It was the size of a placemat, but it had magical properties. The map changed with the movements of the forest. So, thanks to a nifty "You Are Here" icon that was linked to the map, we were able to navigate a hundred times faster.

Ugh. I hated that I couldn't hate Merlin. He was irritating and a mystery, but he was just so darn helpful.

The Isle of Avalon was clearly marked on the parchment. With each step we drew closer to it, and hopefully finding our friends. Continuing to head toward our mutual goal was our best bet to reconnect with them. And thanks to this map, our odds of reaching them before Jason's death, and reaching Avalon before our enemies, was *way* more likely. Not even the couple of monster attacks we had along the way deterred my spirit. With our swords and teamwork, Daniel and I bested whatever was thrown at us.

We traveled earnestly for the rest of the day, stopping only once to rest. Even then, we barely paused for a few minutes. As soon as we heard rustling in the trees, we booked it. There were too many things out there that wanted to kill us or capture us or eat us if we slowed down. Now that the Vicennalia Aurora was barely more than a day away, I was beginning to feel the pressure of the climax. Jason's death, Excalibur, and my next confrontation with Alex were drawing close.

I was distracted by this thought when Daniel lifted up his hand and stopped.

"Do you hear that?" he asked.

I paused and listened, looking at the elongating shadows of the trees. Night was nearing. We probably didn't have long before it got dark.

"Voices," I said quietly, making out the vague murmur of several people talking. "Maybe thirty feet away."

"Let's move," Daniel whispered.

We accelerated our pace through a cluster of trees but halted again when we heard more voices. These were much closer— probably fifteen feet away. Thinking fast, Daniel and I skidded down a steep slope and ducked inside the hollow trunk of a tree.

It was a tight fit and we were crammed together pretty closely. The voices grew nearer and I tucked my knees against my chest as we waited them out.

A few minutes later, all was silent again and we crawled out of the tree. I was astounded at how much darker the sky had turned in just that interval. A shade of shivering blue soaked the land. We'd have to stop and make camp soon, but not yet. Every ounce of daylight mattered when you were up against the clock.

"We're supposed to go north, which is that way," Daniel said, pointing. "But maybe we should hold off. Whoever was up there could still be in the area. It'd be safer to go east for a bit and then arc around."

"No way," I replied, unwilling to sacrifice any amount of time. "We stay the course. Straight north; no delays."

"Knight, I'm just as adamant about finding the others and Excalibur as you are, but we need to think smart. An extra half hour playing it safe isn't going to kill us."

True. But it could kill Jason.

"Daniel," I said calmly. "Our friends are in trouble more than you know. I had a vision a while back about Jason, but he made me promise not to tell anyone. I'm keeping that promise, but you have to know that when I say we can't afford to waste any time, I mean it. That vision is going to come true very soon and I need to be there when it does. Otherwise . . ." I shook my head. "Otherwise nothing. We just have to get there as quickly as possible, okay?"

I expected Daniel to protest, but much to my surprise he nodded.

"Okay," he said. "I'm with you."

He reached up and picked a small twig out of my hair. Then he adjusted the sheath of his sword and began to climb back up the inclined earth. I followed. We had to stop halfway as the forest shifted. The vibrations were strong, but thankfully short. We continued our ascent not half a minute later.

When we reached even ground, Daniel checked the map to reorient our path before pushing on in the growing dark. Everything was bathed in the shadows of twilight. As a result, my partner and I failed to immediately notice the color of the leaves.

Daniel was walking slightly ahead of me. I stepped over a root and ducked under the low-hanging branches of a willow tree, pushing one away to clear my path. When I did, I looked up and paused.

Are those leaves blue?

In this light everything looked that shade. I paused and really studied the leaves.

They were definitely blue, which meant someone had been through here recently.

"Daniel—"

From the depths of the forest, I saw a coil of brown spiraling toward me. I sidestepped in the nick of time. The net ensnared the helpless tree to my left. I threw myself to the ground as a second net came hurtling after it. When I glanced up I saw what I'd been afraid of.

Dang it! Again?

A surge of magic hunters sprinted out of the trees. I leapt up instantly. Daniel raced toward me, but a volley of arrows forced him to dive left while I went right. There were at least twelve hunters and they were spread out.

Why did these guys always have to travel in packs?

I drew my sword and met the blade of an incoming attacker. I kicked him in the chest, pushing the hunter back as I whirled around to block the strike of another.

While Daniel fought the four men closest to him, I rammed the neck of a magic hunter with the hilt of my sword, sliced some guy's forearm, and ducked a blow to the head. With a roundhouse kick I launched another hunter against a tree then bounded aside and narrowly avoided being shish-kabobbed by a sword.

Daniel and I were managing to hold our own despite being greatly outnumbered. However, several magic hunters had elected to stay out of the fray and launch nets in our direction whenever they saw an opening. I felt one after another whizz by as I fought. The nets were connected to their firing mechanisms via long ropes. Whenever a net missed, the hunters flipped some sort of switch on their guns and the nets detached as new ones loaded into the barrels.

I was mid strike when the edge of a net caught hold of my sword and pulled it out of my grip. A long blade swung toward my face. I rolled to the side. Just as I was about to reclaim my weapon, another net fell on top of me. Instead of the net being released, it tightened around me and started reeling me in toward the hunter who'd scored the hit.

"Daniel!" I shouted.

He tried to come after me, but now that I was out of commission, all the other hunters turned their attention to finishing him off.

They formed a circle around him. Daniel was one of the greatest sword fighters I'd ever known, but even he couldn't fend off so many attackers alone. Realizing the same, he did the only thing he could. He ripped the cord Merlin had given him from his neck, threw it to the ground, and slammed his foot on it.

Crud. I didn't see that coming. I thought the payoff for that gift would come much later in the story.

A huge cloud of mauve smoke erupted and the hunters instinctively withdrew. My hunter temporarily stopped reeling me in. I twisted a bit to get a better visual on what was happening. When the smoke cleared, a girl with wavy black hair, olive skin, and intense dark eyes appeared. I almost had a stroke from the shock. Daniel was even more stunned.

Kai.

Daniel's girlfriend took in the situation in half a heartbeat.

She had a sword in a sheath swinging from her shoulder and she pulled out the blade as a magic hunter charged. Instinct kicked in and she gracefully side-stepped him, ramming her elbow into his face, pounding her pommel onto his hand, and slamming her boot down onto his foot as he passed.

Daniel evaded the blade of a different magic hunter, popped up next to Kai, and the two were back to back.

Kai was clearly surprised but all she said was "Hey, Daniel." She didn't ask any questions or demand any explanations. She merely kept fighting as if she were engineered solely for that purpose.

In that moment, I could understand why Daniel liked her so much. Years of being a bladesmith's apprentice had made her skilled and strong. As outnumbered as the two of them were, they now posed a serious challenge to the hunters.

It made me feel embarrassed for having been taken out of the game so easily. I was better than that. However, I didn't have much time to dwell on my shame as the hunter with the net gun had started to reel me in again, dragging me across the forest floor.

Eep!

Seconds later I arrived at the hunter's feet. He drew a large, deadly sharp axe from his sheath. With no weapon and no wand, my brain squeezed out the only non-magic idea I had left.

Fake it 'til you make it.

"You might want to duck," I said, pointing behind the hunter.

There was nothing there, but the hunter didn't know that. When he pivoted around, I used all my force to plow a kick into his front leg. His fall forward made him pass close enough to me that I could reach my hand through a hole in the net, grab him by the jacket, and throw him hard against the dirt to my left.

He and his net gun crashed to the ground. I spotted a knife at his side and clambered forward to try and reach it. Unfortunately, the hunter recovered too quickly. He launched himself toward me and tackled me flat against the grass again. Quick as a whip, he snatched his dagger and rotated his arm back. My eyes widened in panic. Then, from out of nowhere, a boot went into the small of the hunter's back and he flew forward. I rolled to the side to keep from being hit by his body and blade.

Kai stepped in front of me triumphantly. With classic Crisa style she kicked the hunter in the ribcage, then the head to knock him out. She lunged down and sliced through the front of my net with her sword.

"Hey, Crisa," she said, giving me a wink before shoving her sword into its sheath and grabbing the net gun the hunter had dropped. With a small frown, she studied the mechanism momentarily. Then she flipped a switch, which released the rope attached to my net and reloaded the barrel. Kai took aim and fired. A net spiraled out and trapped a hunter charging us. The gun had a lot of kickback, but she'd braced herself well and absorbed the shock.

I climbed out of my net as she flipped the release switch and loaded another shot. It looked like the gun had two rounds left. Kai used the first on a pair of hunters sparring with Daniel. The net ensnared them both, but this time the mechanism's kickback slammed her shoulder hard. She winced but shook off the pain and prepared to fire again.

She aimed her last shot low at two more hunters. The net entangled their feet, causing them to trip. Daniel darted over to us as I kicked the last of my net off my ankle. He had picked up my sword along the way and tossed it to me without breaking stride. I caught it and shoved it in my sheath. Kai dropped the empty net gun and the three of us broke into a run. This was our only chance to escape. Several hunters were still on their feet and the entrapped hunters were already breaking free.

We bolted through the forest for thirty seconds before reaching the edge of a cliff. The crumbling, jagged ridge dropped off into a gorge below. Four separate rivers rushed over the ledge, creating waterfalls that spilled into silvery water churning eighty feet beneath us.

Kai wheeled on Daniel. "Do you remember when we were twelve and I taught you how to swim?"

The first four magic hunters burst out of the forest twenty feet away. Four more were right behind them.

Daniel shot a puzzled look at his girlfriend. "Taught me how to swim? Kai, you pushed me off a—"

Before Daniel could finish his sentence, Kai shoved me from behind. It was hard to say whether I was more surprised, terrified, or enraged by the move. But figuring out my exact emotional state hardly seemed important as I plummeted to the water below. In those kinds of situations, screaming tends to take priority over pretty much everything else.

CHAPTER 24

I Make a New Friend

t's difficult to start a friendship with someone when they push you off a cliff.

I'd only met Kai once before—when Daniel had brought us to her house in Century City. She and I hadn't become instant besties or anything, but she'd seemed like a cool person and I'd liked her just fine. Now though, was a different story. As I dragged myself out of the river, I was not happy with her.

After the visceral drop to the icy waters, I was roughly dragged under the current and had come very close to smashing into some partially submerged rocks. It had not been fun. Thankfully, the current had leveled off downstream and I was able to wade to the riverbank. Silver sparks from SJ's SRB whirred around me.

I looked around. Beyond the gorge swallowing us, the twilight sky had turned cloudy. The day was over and night was setting in.

Exactly one day left until the Vicennalia Aurora.

I continued to cough up water as Kai and Daniel paddled out of the river behind me. Kai started wringing out the water from her hair but stopped when she saw me.

"Why aren't you wet?" she asked. She turned and saw that Daniel was suddenly dry too. A few fading silver sparks danced around his clothes. "Why aren't *either* of you wet?"

"This is an SRB," he said, holding up his wrist. "It's a bracelet that's been laced with a potion to keep us clean and dry no matter what kind of mess we get into."

"Where'd you get that?"

"SJ made them," Daniel said. "Here, give it a try."

Daniel removed his brown rope bracelet and placed it around Kai's wrist. Then he kissed the top of her head. A slew of sparks skimmed across Kai's body as he pulled away. A blink of an eye later, she was dry.

"Wow. Okay, so that's one good explanation. Now I need about a dozen others," Kai said as she handed the bracelet back to Daniel. "Where are we? What am I doing here? And, Daniel, what kind of greeting was that?"

Daniel grinned. "Sorry."

The two of them exchanged a brief kiss. It was short, but it irritated me.

"How about we start with a question for you," I replied, crossing my arms. "What were you thinking pushing me off a cliff like that?"

"I was thinking about saving our lives," Kai countered, crossing her arms as well. "It's not like we had any other option."

"You could have at least warned me."

"There was no time. You might have argued. Besides, the drop wasn't so bad and we can all swim."

"You *assumed* I could swim," I countered. "What if you'd been wrong?"

Kai shrugged. "Yeah, you're right. I knew Dani could swim, but with you I did kind of assume. Sorry. Everything still worked out though, didn't it? So no harm, no foul."

"That's not exactly how I would phrase it," I replied. My gaze narrowed and drifted to Daniel. "Of all the people you could've summoned to help us—Jason, SJ, Blue, Peter Pan, Eva in Oz, heck, I would've even taken the Headless Horseman—you used Merlin's potion to bring *her* here?"

"What's that supposed to mean?" Kai asked defensively.

"Nothing," Daniel intervened, putting his hand on her shoulder. He glanced at me and I saw remorse in his eyes. "Knight, I didn't choose to bring Kai here. I smashed the vial on the ground like Merlin said and the person that we needed most showed up. You saw Kai; she saved us both. If it weren't for her sword skills," he gave her a small, affectionate smile, "and quick thinking, we would have been toast."

Kai smiled back at him and the two bumped shoulders.

"Yeah, I know." I sighed, feeling frustrated. "But what are we supposed to do now? We've still got a mission to complete and since the Gwenivere Brigade has my Hole Tracker, we have no way of finding a portal to send her home."

"Home?" Kai repeated. "Forget it. Ever since the lot of you came by my house and told me about your mission to find Paige Tomkins, I've regretted not going with you. It sounded then like you could use some help, and now I'm sure of it."

"Reason with her, please," I pleaded to Daniel. "She's not safe here."

Kai raised her eyebrows. "*I'm* not safe here? I just took out half a dozen magic hunters while you were trapped in a net. If anyone's not safe here, it's you."

For a split second I wondered if punching Daniel's girlfriend would violate my promise to protect her. Deciding that it would, I let the matter drop. It was cold and getting darker and we needed to make camp.

"I'm going to get some wood to make a fire," I said, drawing my sword from its sheath.

Daniel stepped toward me. "Knight, you shouldn't—"

"Relax," I said, waving him off. "I'm not going far. Just fill her in on the story. A lot has changed since we saw her last. If she's going to stay, she needs to know exactly what she's getting into."

When I got back with the firewood, it was too little too late.

During the extra time I'd taken to cool off, Kai had chopped firewood, done some fishing, and cooked us dinner while Daniel caught her up on our tale. Unlike the second granola bar from Merlin that I had to choke down, Kai's grilled fish with wild herbs was delicious. I didn't compliment the chef though. I accepted that she was stuck with us, but I was still mad at her for pushing me off a cliff. Daniel clearly noticed my irritation.

After dinner, Kai decided to take a short stroll along the river to process everything we'd told her; she promised not to wander out of sight. I sat on a log by the fire staring at the flickering flames. Daniel sat next to me. We sat in silence for a minute.

"You're mad at me," he said eventually.

"No, I'm not," I responded without looking up. "I'm just frustrated. You know why Kai shouldn't be here."

"You think I wanted this?" Daniel replied earnestly. "All I want is to keep her safe. Now she's stuck in the thick of it with us. You said it yourself; we have no way of finding any portals right now. Even if we found one, I doubt I could make her go."

"She's that stubborn?"

"No more than you."

"Then it's a lost cause."

I sighed. While I was upset with Kai's actions, I was more upset with myself. I felt so guilty. If I hadn't been caught in that net, Daniel wouldn't have used Merlin's gift. What were we supposed to do now? I attracted danger and death like flowers attracted bees. My promise to help keep Kai safe was in jeopardy and I hated that. Daniel had been there through the thickest of perils with me and I sincerely wanted to return the favor. After everything he'd given me, I owed him that. I wanted to give him that. However my story would end, I wanted to make sure his ending was a happy one. He deserved to be with the girl he loved. Hence my promise to help make that happen.

But now with Kai a hundred feet away, deep in the bowels of Camelot, I wondered if I had been kidding myself when I promised Daniel in Neverland that I would help protect her. I couldn't even protect my friends from the treacherous path I'd set us on. How was I supposed to guard the fate of a girl that prophecy literally predicted I had the power to bring down?

"I'm sorry, Daniel," I said, the words escaping my lips before I even realized I was saying them. "I promised I'd help keep Kai safe and all I've done is brought her closer to danger. If it wasn't for those stupid magic hunters, she wouldn't be here."

Daniel shook his head. "Knight, I know you feel bad, but this isn't your fault. Neither of us could've known Merlin's potion would summon her."

"Maybe not," I said. "But that doesn't mean that all of *this*," I gestured to the general area around us, "isn't my fault. I know you and the others are committed to being there for me. But be honest, did you really know what you were signing up for when we became friends? Magic hunters, antagonists, monsters—someone is always trying to kill us. And every sundown is just another tick of the clock closer to the next impossible quest we're embarking on."

I sighed deeply. "Maybe you *were* right all that time ago when we were trapped in the Therewolf camp. Maybe I did ruin your life. *All* of your lives." I shook my head bitterly. "I was in this from the moment my prologue prophecy appeared, or probably years before that when my godmother gifted me with magic in the first place. But you guys didn't have to be. I just keep entangling you in it further. Now look at us. Look at you. You're in constant mortal danger and the person you love most is now in it too. Of course I feel bad. It *is* all my fault."

Daniel stared at me for a moment. A frog or something croaked in the distance. Then he abruptly pushed me off the log.

I toppled backward and landed on my butt in the dirt. Confused, I looked up at him. "Daniel, what the heck was that for?"

He shrugged. "You needed to be knocked off your high horse. Knocking you off this log seemed like the next best thing."

I blinked in surprise.

"Knight, you need to understand something. You may be an important part of all this, but don't kid yourself into thinking you're solely responsible for everything that's happened. None of us—not me, SJ, Jason, or Blue—were dragged into this situation. We chose to be here. Not for you, but for us. Because defending our home, stopping the antagonists, and protecting those we care about matters *to all of us*. So stop talking about yourself like you're some kind of virus that's wreaking havoc on those around you. The five of us have been infected by the same fate since the start. We're all responsible because we're all in this thing together."

Daniel helped me back onto the log, keeping hold of my hand after I sat down.

"And as far as Kai goes . . ." he went on. "I'll admit I was hesitant at first when you offered to help me protect her. But now I'm grateful that you did. She's strong and skilled and beyond brave, but Camelot's nothing if not unpredictable. So if she is going to be traveling with us, honestly it would make me feel a lot better knowing there is someone else actively looking out for her too. That is . . . if you're still up for it."

"Um, yeah." I cleared my throat awkwardly. "Sure thing."

"Knight, I'm serious," he said, narrowing his gaze. "I know the two of you didn't exactly hit it off, but I need to know whether or not I can count on you."

I placed my hand on top of his and we locked eyes. "Daniel, I told you. I keep my promises. Whatever it takes, I will do *everything* in my power to keep Kai safe. You have my word." Then I cracked a smile. "Just promise me that from now on, I hold onto the magical objects we're gifted with. For someone who was poor as a kid, you're a bit of a quick spender."

Daniel laughed. I did too. For a moment it looked like he was going to say something else, but our time alone together came to an end. Kai was heading back toward the campsite. Daniel moved to join her. I didn't realize until he stood up that we'd been holding hands this whole time. The warmth had felt nice and I hadn't noticed it until it was gone.

As I slept, my brain struggled.

The more magic I used, the stronger my visions were. However, Merlin's granola bars must've warped my ability to see the future because I only had one clear complete dream.

The scene took place in a forest. It was night, but the setting was not dark. Fluorescent teal caterpillars the size of foxes wiggled across the dirt and up tree trunks. Luminescent pink foliage hung from the branches. The contrast of colors against the black sky was startling.

Blue, Jason, Chance, and Girtha were standing in a small

clearing within the enchanting setting. Chance and Jason were hanging back a little as Blue and Girtha argued.

"If you're wrong, then we won't save her and we'll *all* end up dead," Girtha protested.

Girtha's massive size would have intimidated most girls. But Blue stood her ground and talked to Girtha like this large younger sister of the *Hansel & Gretel* twins was an unimposing elf.

"Girtha, I've been friends with her way longer than you have. You may be a main character back home, but in this storyline, you're a supporting character at best. So stop acting like you have as much of a say here as the rest of us."

It was hard to tell whether the comment made Girtha angry or sad; both emotions flashed across her face. Jason took a risk and stepped forward.

"Blue," he said gently, putting his hand on her shoulder. "Maybe you should take it easy."

She glowered. "Why?"

"Because you need to get over yourself," Chance responded. Having found his voice, he stepped unapologetically into the conflict as well. "I get it, Blue. Girtha and I both do. You're protective of her because you've been closer longer and you've had stakes in the game since the beginning. But just because we weren't an integral part of this story when it started doesn't mean we can't influence the outcome. And it doesn't mean we don't want to."

Blue's fists were clenched, but she took a deep breath and steadied herself. She looked at each of the people around her, gears turning in her head like they did when she mapped out the terrain in a battle before charging in. My friend was fueled by instinct, and she could be hotheaded and impulsive. But she also had the intelligence and experience to fully assess a situation before she made the decision to jump in. She was fire, but fire that moved with purpose and understanding.

"I know what happened is my fault," Girtha said softer, trying to extend an olive branch. "But I—"

"No," Blue said suddenly.

Girtha blinked.

"It's not your fault. It's mine and the lot of you have been too nice to say it." Blue swallowed hard and a veil of guilt fell over her face. "I'm the reason Crisa's not with us anymore."

The dream blurred and disappeared. My mind tumbled through tons of disorienting, bright flashes. I only managed to make out a few images amongst them.

First, a high tower with a bronze turret. The background was a red sky with moving swirls of black. A horrible wailing pierced the air as shadowy blobs swarmed the tower, encircling it like a storm.

Then a mahogany house in a forest. Gold braziers held flames that crackled brightly. Daniel stood in front of the house and reached for the handles on the grand double doors.

Lastly, a woman. She was tall with bronzed skin and dark, curly hair, and her eyes were icy blue. She was somewhere in her late twenties and looked familiar.

The woman ran as a group of men chased her. The background was fuzzy, but for a split second I saw Arian. The attackers caught up with her and tackled her to the ground. The woman attempted to scream, but a hand was clasped over her mouth.

I sat up and put my hand to my head. Trying to dream while under the influence of Merlin's granola bars had given me a headache. And a backache. I must've been tossing and turning a ton. I was glad I had Daniel's jacket wrapped around me. Since I was only wearing my red sleeveless dress over my leggings, and he and Kai both had outfits with long sleeves, he'd offered me his jacket to keep warm for the night. He'd done the same thing last night when we camped out by the lake.

I looked over and saw Daniel asleep on the ground a slight way over. Kai, however, was leaning against the log facing the fire pit. She had volunteered to take the first watch while Daniel and I tried to get some rest.

I got up quietly and went to sit beside her.

"Hey," I said.

"Hey," she whispered back.

I looked up at the stars—glistening sparks of light that worked together to form the most beautiful constellations. The clouds had rolled out of sight, and the sky and moon had an uninhibited view of our world.

"Nice night," I offered, trying to make conversation.

"I'm sure you'd find it a whole lot nicer if I weren't around," Kai commented. "You've made it pretty clear that you don't want me here."

For the sake of Daniel, I took a deep breath, thought about what needed to be done, and met her gaze. "It's not that I don't want you here, Kai," I responded. "Really. I was just upset before. But I'm over it now, and I owe you an apology for losing my temper. You saved us and I'm grateful. Sorry for not saying it sooner."

The way Kai looked at me reminded me of how I used to look at Daniel—like I appreciated what he was saying but also wondered whether or not I could trust it.

"It's okay," she replied hesitantly. She tucked a strand of hair behind her ear. "While we're on the subject . . . I probably owe you a couple of apologies too. The first is for going off on you earlier. It wasn't right, and I knew it. But I get really ticked off when people think I can't fend for myself. It's sort of a sore spot."

"Yeah," I huffed in amusement. "Believe me, I practically wrote the book on the subject."

"Okay, good," she replied. "You get it. So that only leaves my second apology. One I should've opened with. I really *am* sorry for pushing you off that cliff, Crisa."

"Don't be," I said flatly. "In all honesty, if the situation were reversed, I probably would have done the same thing."

Kai nodded. "Daniel did say you and I are a lot alike."

I tilted my head. "Did he now? What else did our brooding hero tell you about me?"

"A bunch of stuff," Kai replied nonchalantly. "Not just today, but during the semester when we write to each other from school."

Daniel talks to Kai about me?

Do I know how I feel about that?

"One point he's driven home is that we would probably be really good friends if we didn't let our pride get in the way," Kai continued.

"That's a pretty tall order." I smiled a bit. "My pride is a force to be reckoned with."

Kai grinned back. "Not as much as mine. People talk about it far and wide."

"Oh yeah." My smile grew mischievous. "Well, mine's led good men to their graves."

"Mine's taken down whole cities," she countered wickedly.

I spread out my arms in a dramatic gesture and threw my head back. "Mine's conquered realms."

We burst into quiet, companionable laughter, which we tried to muffle so as not to wake Daniel. After a moment, Kai looked at me with a serious expression. "I like you, Crisa," she said. "Maybe Dani was right. Why don't you and I try being friends?"

"All right," I said. Then I bit my lip and thought quickly. "But I have one condition."

"Uh-oh."

"Relax, it's nothing terrible. I just want you to promise that so long as you're with us, you don't take any crazy, unnecessary risks. You let Daniel and I take the lead and don't protest when we try to protect you."

"I thought you said it was nothing terrible?" Kai huffed. "You know, I'm not sure what Dani told you, but I *can* take care of myself."

"I know you can," I assured her. "You made those armed magic hunters look like toddlers playing with sticks. But that's not the point. My condition has nothing to do with your ability. The fact is that Daniel and I have been dealing with this stuff a lot longer, so it'd probably be for the best if you hung back a bit."

"Crisa. I told you how much I hate it when people think I can't fend for myself. I don't like depending on others for the same reason. I don't want to give them any ideas about me being helpless."

My eyes traced over Daniel, whose sleeping frame hadn't moved since our conversation began. "You know, Daniel taught me something a long time ago," I said. "He showed me that asking for help doesn't make you helpless. Relying on other people doesn't mean you're weak; it means you trust someone else as much as you trust yourself. You trust Daniel don't you Kai?"

"Of course I do."

"Okay," I responded. "Then swallow that infamous pride of yours and agree to the condition. I get that it might seem like an annoying and maybe even insulting request, but that's not my intention. I'm making it in good faith and I want you to accept it in the same fashion."

Kai stared at the ground with her brow furrowed. For a moment, I worried she would reject my proposal. She eventually looked up and stuck out her hand.

"All right, Crisa. I'll abide by your condition. Just don't push it. And don't tell Daniel I agreed to this either. I don't want him going all hero-saves-the-damsel on me."

"Deal," I said, shaking her hand. "I won't tell him. Though I doubt that'll keep Daniel from trying to be your hero. He's still him after all."

"You're probably right," Kai admitted. "The guy believes in me and my strength more than anyone, but he's got a real deep protective instinct."

"I noticed," I said, leaning back against the log and turning my face up to the stars again. "Most guys at Lord Channing's have a hero complex that they develop at school, but his always seemed pretty instinctive. Has he always been like that?"

"Yeah. Even before he got picked to go to Lord Channing's, he was a natural hero. Loyal, determined, never hesitating to jump in to defend others—I've always felt like he can't help but try to protect people, like he's drawn to it or something."

"I wonder if it's because of how he lost his family . . ." I pondered out loud, thinking of the secret Daniel had shared with me in Neverland, that he was an orphan who'd lost his parents and kid sister when he was younger.

Kai didn't respond. When the silence persisted, I turned to discover a genuinely shocked expression on her face.

"He told you about that?" she asked slowly. "About his parents and younger sister . . . and the fire?"

I nodded. She continued staring at me in surprise, which started to make me feel uncomfortable. "What's that look for?" I asked.

"Nothing, it's just . . . I don't think he's ever told anyone before. I only know because my father and I were there the night it happened. You guys must be pretty close for him to open up like that."

I noticed her eyes dart to the jacket I was wearing. I was about to respond when Daniel shifted in his sleep. Although his eyes remained closed, Kai and I stopped talking.

After a minute, I cleared my throat and stretched my arms. "Honestly, I'm not going to be able to sleep right now, Kai. My head still hurts from the last attempt. Why don't you get some rest while I take watch? I'll wake you in a few hours so we can switch."

"All right. Suit yourself." Kai shrugged, abandoning the conversation.

She got up from our shared log and sauntered over to where Daniel slept. She lay down beside him and rested her head against his arm as she shut her eyes. I picked up the nearest stick and stoked the fire, watching it burn.

CHAPTER 25

Wave One

In my dream, I was standing in a classroom. A date was written in the top left corner of the chalkboard: *November 10, 2020.*

The floor was beige tile and the walls were brick. The wall on the left had tall, thin windows spaced along it. Arian's blonde crony Tara leaned against it with a book bag draped over her shoulder. Her dark eyes were fixed on Natalie, who stood in the center of the room.

"What exactly is your problem with me?" Natalie asked Tara.

"I have no problem with you," Tara replied evenly.

Natalie threw her head back and scoffed. Her maple hair brushed against the shoulders of her navy zip-up sweatshirt. "Drop the pretense, Tara. You have been tormenting me for years. And I get the whole high school mean girl 'you can't sit with us' thing, but high school bullying is supposed to end *in* high school. You chose the same college as me. We have the same major even though you have as much interest in art history as a cat has in swimming lessons. And I *know* it was you who sent the virus to my computer that deleted my term paper last night."

Tara shrugged. "Prove it."

"You think I won't?"

"I think you can't," Tara replied. She uncrossed her arms and slowly walked toward Natalie, drumming her fingers along the desks.

"Let's say you're right," Tara continued. "Let's say, theoretically, that I have been out to get you since the day I enrolled in your school. Let's say, theoretically, that my very purpose for being here is to make your life miserable. And let's say, also theoretically of course, that everything I do is intended to destroy your world until it eventually shatters. Why should I be afraid that you'll fight back now? You and I have been bound together for years, Natalie, and you've never challenged me before."

Natalie clenched her fists but held Tara's gaze. "For a long time, I didn't believe I deserved to be happy, and I didn't let love or light into my life because I thought it would be taken away from me like so many things I've cared about before. But I'm not the confused teenager I was when we first met. I'm stronger than you think, Tara. The girl I am *is* worth fighting for, and I'm not going to live in your shadow anymore."

Tara smirked as she sauntered over to the door. "I always thought you were strong, Natalie. That is why you *had* to live in my shadow. It is your destiny as much as it is mine. But don't worry." Tara's face reflected in a panel of glass above the door handle. "Our time together is almost up."

"What's that supposed to mean?" Natalie asked.

Tara glanced over her shoulder. "You'll see. Say hi to Crisa for me. I'm sure she'll be here soon." She opened the door and a blinding light burst through.

I saw flashes of Chance Darling, a thin gold tiara dangling from someone's fingers, and flying monkeys. Then there were short visions of Blue's eyes glowing bright green as fog swirled around her, SJ in Merlin's potion lab, and then SJ brewing something in Julian's potions lab in the Emerald City. Finally, there was Kai and Daniel. They were dancing at a ball at Lady Agnue's. Kai wore a shimmering gold gown and Daniel's smile lit up his face as he looked at her. That was the last thing I saw before the flashes faded and I was left standing in the void.

"Having a good rest, Crisanta?"

I turned at the sound of Merlin's voice. He was sitting on a pale blue wooden swing. The chains holding it up were covered in vines and disappeared into the void. The swing was the same one we had at my home in Midveil.

I felt a tad violated seeing Merlin using it. I wondered about the control he and Liza had in my dreams when they communicated with me. Last I'd spoken in the void with Liza she'd been drinking tea at a nice table set up. Then Merlin was using this swing. Were they able to shuffle through pieces of my subconscious and generate what they wanted? Or was my mind generating these things for them.

"It's your dream," Liza had commented when I'd passed on the tea.

"What are you doing here, Merlin?" I asked, walking toward him. "We just saw each other in real life. What's wrong? Did something happen?"

"Relax, Crisanta. Nothing's wrong; I just wanted to give you a warning. We talked about the Vicennalia Aurora increasing your Pure Magic's power, but as you go on to use that to your advantage, I wanted to emphasize that you need to be careful."

Really? He's bothering me in my dreams to give another warning. Between him and Liza it's like having magic mentor whiplash. One moment they're telling me about all this great power I have and all the big, important things I'm supposed to do with it; the next they're cautioning me about the dangers of using it.

"Being careful isn't my priority right now, Merlin," I said, a bit annoyed. "Fortune may not favor the reckless, but time does. And that is what I'm working against. You know that. I am on a deadline to save Jason, find Excalibur, and reach Paige Tomkins' memories. I'm nervous enough about what's coming without more things shaking my nerve."

"I understand that," Merlin replied. "And I helped you develop your powers for that reason. But after you left, it occurred to me that you're no good to me, or anyone, if you're dead. I should have sent you off with more than just granola bars and Forget-Me-Nots. You need this warning as much as anything else."

Merlin gestured for me to sit on the swing next to him, but I remained standing with my arms crossed.

"I know what you are up against, Crisanta," he said. "But do not get cocky with what you have learned. Just because your magic can resurrect people doesn't mean you should use that ability every chance you get. More importantly, just because that power saved you once doesn't mean it is something to be relied upon. All

magic—even Pure Magic—has limits. Remember what I told you
about the three-minute window you have to save other people's
lives? Your ability to restore life to yourself is also conditional. If
you have already used a lot of power, then your Magic Instinct
might not be strong enough to compensate. Try to harness it
without proper fuel in the tank and if your natural death doesn't
kill you, Magic Burn Out will."

"Are you sure you're not underestimating me, Merlin?" I said.
"I've done a lot, *despite* my episodes of Magic Exhaustion. Maybe
Magic Burn Out isn't as much of a threat to me."

Merlin waved his hand dismissively. A tiny red balloon
appeared in his palm. Again, I wondered if that was a result of his
mind's power or mine.

"Think of your body as this balloon," he said. "The helium inside is your magic."

The balloon began to inflate. "As that power grows, you
become something grander. But let it fill you up too much, let it
stretch past what your body is physically capable of, and . . ."

The balloon—which had stretched to the size of a hatbox—
exploded. Tattered pieces zipped around before crumpling to the
ground.

"That is how Magic Burn Out works," Merlin explained. "This
will always be true, no matter how powerful you become or how
powerful you feel. At the end of the day, there is only so much you
can do. *That* is what I am warning you to be careful about. When
you wake in the morning, it will be the day of the Vicennalia
Aurora and you will face one peril after the next. But I advise you
to hold back on using your abilities whenever possible in spite
of the energy waves created by the Aurora that will tempt your
magic otherwise. Trust me. You need to conserve your energy for
when it counts. If you use too much of your magic right away, you
may not have the strength to bring yourself or others back later.
Understand?"

I did understand. Daniel had suggested that my power might
make me invincible. It was scary to know for a fact that this wasn't
true.

And yet, I was actually more grateful for the knowledge than

I was fearful of it. No one was invincible. Everyone had limits and we needed them. I was appreciative to have this anchor of reality because frankly, if I was only going to keep getting more powerful, I needed something to rein me in and prevent me from letting my Pure Magic consume me with its tempting power. Perhaps the threat of mortality would do just that.

"Thanks for the advice, Merlin," I said, meaning it. "I'll only use my magic when necessary."

"Wise choice," Merlin said. "You avoiding Magic Burn Out isn't just for your own good, but everyone else's too. Take care, Crisanta. I hope to reconnect with you and your allies soon."

The wizard faded away. I was left in the void alone but felt myself waking up shortly thereafter. The time to face the inevitable had come.

When I opened my eyes morning had barely broken but Daniel and Kai were already up. The world was slightly chilly and coated in light gray. I took a deep breath. The Vicennalia Aurora would come to pass tonight, right after sunset. We only had one day to find Excalibur, aid Gwenivere and Morgan with overthrowing Rampart, return to Oz to free Paige's mind from Glinda's memory stone, save the scarecrow Fairy Godmother like I'd promised, and then help the Godmothers protect Book from Alderon's antagonists and the imminent flying monkey attack.

It was going to be a long day.

Barely 5:30 in the morning, we splashed some water on our faces, I gave Daniel back his jacket, and we got moving.

Merlin's map showed that the Isle of Avalon wasn't far. Diving into the gorge last night had actually worked out as a shortcut. I was grateful for this, and the fact that we still had the map. Daniel had shoved it in his jacket before he made the jump into the gorge, and luckily the document was made of magic paper that couldn't get ruined.

We walked briskly with renewed spirits, me in particular. Merlin said that his granola bars would have me feeling normal by morning, and he was right. I felt no pain and no exhaustion. A rosy glow had returned to my skin and my irises were back to their usual shade of green. I could also sense that my magic was fully replenished, but more than that, it was like every cell in my body hummed with electricity. I felt more alive than I had in a long time.

As I breathed in the cool morning air, I knew it was more than the granola bars making me feel this way. Merlin had explained that the shift in magic energy during the Vicennalia Aurora would affect me and other Pure Magic carriers throughout the day. I was already starting to be aware of it. I could sense the magic in the atmosphere as surely as I felt the breeze against my skin. There was power in the air—a power only I, and others like me, could detect.

I was stronger. My magic was stronger. If this was how I felt now, I wondered what would happen when one of those magic waves rolled through the atmosphere later.

Power fizzled in my fingertips as I walked, but I resisted the urge to test it. After Merlin's warning in my dream, I was hesitant to waste an ounce. I didn't even want to change my wand back yet. It was still in its sword form in the sheath bouncing across my shoulder.

Daniel, Kai, and I kept to the riverbank as we traveled. As daybreak approached, gold began to color the sky. The waters of the river turned navy while the sand revealed its true color—gray. It'd been too dark to notice the odd color of the sand when we'd washed up on the bank last night. Now it and everything else was coming into focus.

I stopped suddenly as a feeling of familiarity prickled the back of my brain.

"What it is?" Kai asked.

"This sand . . ." I thought aloud.

My mind flipped through a thousand memories. I had so many dreams, and the last few days had been so jam-packed with odd things and new information, that sometimes it took a second to be alerted by small details. I placed this memory, though.

Oh no.

The sound of a waterfall had been getting louder for some time. Sure enough, I could see the ground dropping off in the distance. The river was spilling off the edge of another cliff. You could slightly make out rolling hills beyond that, only they weren't green or brown.

I pointed at them. "What color are those hills?" I asked, though I already knew the answer.

Kai and Daniel followed my gesture. Kai squinted and tilted her head, a bit surprised. "They look kind of blue," she replied.

Daniel checked the map. "Those are the Blue Hills of Terrenore," he said. "I read about them back at school. It's an unclaimed area of land that intersects the properties of some of Camelot's oldest and most feared knights—the Gold Knights, the Black Knights, and the dreadful Red Knights."

"Good guys?" Kai asked hopefully.

"Not typically," Daniel said. "They descend from old and powerful families that command private armies. Sometimes they side with the king of Camelot; other times they just do whatever is in their best interest. The Blue Hills of Terrenore are their mutual ground because this land is equidistant to all their castles."

Black, gold, and red knights.

A navy river with gray sand.

Blue hills.

"Oh no," I said, out loud this time.

"What's wrong?" Daniel asked.

I didn't answer. I sprinted toward the edge of the cliff with Kai and Daniel following closely behind. My heart felt like there was a cord wrapped around it—tightening and pulling me forward.

When I reached the brink, I gazed down at the drop. It was at least a three-hundred-foot plunge—much higher than the jump we'd taken yesterday to escape the magic hunters. The river dove off into a massive waterfall that pummeled the jagged rocks of the cliffside before dumping into a much fatter river at the bottom.

My eyes followed the river to a spot about a half mile away. It was everything I expected and everything I feared. I could see a battle unfolding. The glint of the rising sun made the knights' uniforms glisten, even from this distance. There were no fewer

than thirty of them, and my friends were caught in the throng. I
knew it was them. Small eruptions of fire and lightning detonated
in the battle zone. That was signature SJ.

My dream of Jason's death was about to unfold.

"We have to get down there," I panted. "It's Blue, Jason, and
SJ. They need our help, *right now.*"

Daniel and Kai spotted the battle raging below.

"We'll never make it in time," Kai said, worry in her voice.

"Shut up," I snapped. "We have to." I paced by the edge in a
panic, trying to think. The only way down was to go around and
find a path through the Shifting Forest. But we could run at light
speed and still not make it before the battle was over.

I looked straight below at the waterfall pummeling against the
river.

Come on. Think. Think.

Suddenly a sensory charge passed through my system. It was
the first wave of magic energy from the oncoming Aurora.

What else could make me feel like this?

A jolt of energy set the hairs on my body erect. I sensed magic
in every part of me. It was like an intoxicating gas only I could
breathe in. And as I did, I felt like I could do anything. It was
caffeine directly to the bloodstream and adrenaline straight to the
core.

I didn't know how long this feeling would last, but I had to
take advantage of it.

Get to Jason. Get to Jason.

Enchanting the earth to form a platform didn't seem like a
good idea. It worked in Neverland, but that cliffside was basically
pure stone. At the Canyon of Geene, my section of earth had fallen
apart. And anyway, we didn't just need a way down; we needed a
giant assault in order to wash away the threat.

Wash away the threat . . .

An idea popped into my head as I stared at the throbbing
river, and then—

"Jason!"

The frightened sound of Blue screaming our friend's name
echoed across the valley.

"Knight!" Daniel grabbed my arm. "You said you had a vision about Jason. What did you see? What's going on down there?"

My face fell in fear. "Jason's dead, Daniel." Then my features hardened. "But not for long. Follow me."

I sprinted back along the river away from the cliff's ledge so the current wouldn't be so intense. Then I marched into the river. Daniel and Kai pursued me. I could only go about eight feet in; anything deeper and the pull of the current would surely sweep us off our feet. The water rose past my knees. Planting my boots firmly into the murky bottom, this was where I decided to make my stand.

"What are you going to do?" Kai asked.

"Something new," I replied.

I plunged my hands into the water and concentrated. I let the magic wave in the air rush through my blood as powerfully as the water coursing around my legs. Both were strong and visceral. The power felt both cleansing and corrupting.

I focused harder than I ever had, my mind visualizing what I wanted the water to do. Energy poured from my hands into the river, flooding it with so much golden light it looked like the sun was washing downstream. Then the water started to rise.

"I hope you guys can hold your breath for a while," I said, glancing over my shoulder at Daniel and Kai.

In a sudden burst, walls of water came up around us and began to take shape, resisting the pull of the current and responding to my will instead. The three of us were submerged in a sphere of water, which became the center of the creation I was building. Additional surges of water spun in tight, condensed cyclones and attached to our sphere like limbs, floating us off ground level. Soon we were twenty feet above the river in the belly of the enormous, man-shaped water monster I had brought to life.

I willed my water creature forward. Daniel and Kai were floating right behind me in the center sphere. We reached the edge of the cliff.

Okay. Here we go.

I focused my control then mentally commanded my creation to jump.

WHOA!

We plummeted three hundred feet down the waterfall. My fists tightened as I fought gravity and all the other relevant laws of physics to retain the monster's form. Sprays of water came off it like sweat, but its overall shape held steady at my will.

Keeping my eyes open in the water was difficult, but that was the least of my worries. We needed to stick the landing. When we were about to reach the river below, I directed my water creature to land in a crouched position on a single knee. It did, and with one of its watery fists slamming into the river. The collision caused a tidal wave to career downstream. Daniel, Kai, and I felt virtually nothing. The water we floated in cushioned all impact. We bobbed a bit in the sphere, but it was no different than being in a hot tub and feeling the swell when someone bigger jumped in.

It'd been close to twenty seconds since I'd consumed us in water and I knew we couldn't go much longer without breathing. Plus, retaining this level of power was taxing even with the help of the magic energy in the air, so I mustered all the strength I had on my next command.

Run.

The water creature picked itself up from its crouched position and began to bolt downriver toward the conflict. Each watery footstep sent a carriage-sized splash up the banks. The creature's limbs sloshed. My friends and I bobbed around from the continuous force of each heavy stride as we rapidly closed in on our destination.

Soon I saw the nearby flash of SJ's lightning potions; we couldn't have been more than sixty meters away. Unfortunately, that was as far as I could take us—my lungs were about to burst. Daniel and Kai were likely in the same state. I ordered the creature to let us slip out its back leg in the form of a mini waterslide. Our bodies rushed out in a wave and landed in the river.

SPLASH!

Air poured into my lungs. However, I didn't let the shock of the oxygen or the drop into the water diminish my focus. I kept all my energy fixated on my creation. I rose in the river and maintained magic control of the water monster as it continued to race forward.

The battle was now in clear view. This was my chance to eliminate the enemy threat and create my opening to save Jason.

My grand monster continued downriver—golden energy surging through its liquid skin and casting the battle ahead in a golden wave of light. Its massive footsteps caused the ground to tremble. I couldn't see the knights' expressions from here, but I suspected they were pretty surprised.

I heard yelling. The knights were bracing themselves. I braced myself too, but for another reason. Just as my water creature was thirty feet from the fight, I ordered it out of the river. Then I broke the creature apart. With a final push of magic, I transformed the monster into a colossal wave. I knew Blue and Jason were by the bank and I spotted SJ off to the left, so I aimed the wave directly at the center congregation of knights.

It was the stuff of sailors' nightmares. The wave careened toward the army and swept two thirds of it away. The knights I'd hit were splattered all over the blue grass like bug carcasses. SJ saw her opening and began firing on the rest; she knew what my energy signature looked like and was ready to jump into action.

I took a second to get my bearings, but that's all I could afford. Jason's window for being saved was going to shut.

"Come on!" I yelled to Daniel and Kai, racing toward Jason and Blue.

Normally I felt drained after using large amounts of magic and needed time to recover. But I didn't feel that way now. The wave of magic in the atmosphere was so strong, it nourished whatever my body had lost.

I moved so fast that the world blurred. Water, SRB sparks, and my own residual glimmers of golden energy trailed off me. As I closed in, I could see that SJ needed a hand to take out the remaining knights.

"Help SJ!" I called to Daniel and Kai. "I've got Jason!"

Daniel and Kai veered off to assist our princess friend while I zeroed in on the riverbank where Jason lay unmoving. Blue was kneeling over him, tears streaming down her face and Jason's blood all over her hands.

I didn't know for certain how much time had passed since Jason had been stabbed, but I sensed his window was moments from closing.

"Blue! Move!" I yelled.

She looked up. I skidded to my knees in the sand beside them. Seeing Jason dead in reality was much worse than seeing him dead in my dreams. I could smell the blood coming from the wound that stained his shirt. I could hear Blue convulsing in sobs. I could feel the ice cold of his skin as I touched his face.

"He's gone," she said in a whisper.

"No," I said willfully. "Today is not the day for him to die."

I'd only ever tried this on a bird. But I felt so sure it was possible that it was like I'd done it a hundred times. My body moved with a kind of magic muscle memory.

"Blue, let go," I ordered, gesturing for her to release Jason's hand.

She hesitated.

"Move!" I said. "We don't have much time!"

She let go and scooched away a couple of inches. I took Jason's hand in mine and placed my right palm on his stomach where the wound was. He didn't move. There was no breath or heartbeat inside his body, yet I could still feel life within him. It was hard to explain, but somehow I could sense his energy. It was fading by the second, but I knew it was there.

Life.

I didn't just concentrate on the word or my ability; I fixed all of myself—my heart, mind, body, and soul—on the spirit behind the word. I closed my eyes and let the emotion flow and intertwine with my focus. I thought of precious memories I shared with Jason. The night we met at our first school ball. The afternoon he taught me how to whistle. That time we broke into Lady Agnue's old dungeon beneath the kitchens. The day he came to visit me in the infirmary and smuggled in chocolate chip cookies.

Life.

The command reverberated in my skull. I felt a tug at my

heart that forced me to open my eyes. When I did, I saw immense golden light flowing out of me into Jason.

Life.

I thought of every laugh and smile and struggle Jason and I had shared. I thought of every moment with him I could remember and concentrated on the elements that made him *him*—his selflessness, his bravery, his goofiness, his warmth, his protectiveness, his heroism.

My light glowed brighter, but I began to feel weaker. I could sense that the Aurora's wave of magic energy had finished rolling through the atmosphere. No extra power boost was going to help me now. I had to do this on my own. With one final push, I gave Jason everything I had.

"Life!" I ordered out loud.

An enormous rush of energy zapped out of my hands like an electric shock. It was so powerful it knocked me back.

The energy discharged straight into Jason and my body stopped producing magic altogether. My glow ceased like I had ejected all of it in one burst.

I blinked. There was nothing but stillness for a second then, all of a sudden, the glow came back—not out of me, but out of Jason. Golden energy shot from his wound like a geyser. The veins in his arms glowed too, like mine did after I'd resurrected myself. When the burst from his chest dissipated, Jason's golden veins began to fade to normal.

I clambered to my knees and leaned over him, waiting in silence. Blue was beside me. I realized SJ, Daniel, and Kai were standing behind me too. Having wrapped up their battle, they were witnesses to the miracle that happened next.

Jason coughed. Then he opened his eyes. They were bright blue with rims of gold around the irises. He looked up at me and managed a small, pained smile.

"What took you so long?"

CHAPTER 26

Blood on Her Hands

n the immediate aftermath of Jason's resurrection, my friends drilled me with questions while he rested. Personally, I could have used a short rest too. The magic wave had made me feel exceptionally powerful but raising that water creature and bringing Jason back to life had taken a lot out of me. And yet, I knew I was still quite strong.

I was definitely a bit tired, but yesterday I'd passed out after bringing a bird back to life. Today, I'd created a super-sized water monster to do my bidding, resurrected one of my best friends, and I was still standing. That was definitely progress. As long as I had a little time to recharge and no one tried to kill me in the next couple of hours, I would be fine.

"So, let me get this straight," Blue said. "Not only can you pop back up when someone smacks you dead like a human version of whack-a-mole, now you can bring other people back to life too?"

"Yup," I said. "That's the short version. I'll explain more, but can we walk and talk? Half those knights might be encased in SJ's ice or goo, and the others may have retreated, but we're still out in the open and need to keep heading toward Avalon."

"I can't believe this!" Blue groaned.

I was surprised by her frustration. "Why are you mad? This is a good thing."

"Agreed," Jason said. "Being dead is not my favorite state."

"I'm not mad, I just wish you could have given us some indication that you had this power," Blue replied. "Do you have any idea what the last couple of days have been like for us, Crisa?

We weren't sure if you were dead or captured or what. We've just been heading toward Avalon hoping to the heavens that we would find you and Daniel along the way."

I softened. I had been worried about SJ, Blue, and Jason, but I hadn't thought about how they must've felt since our separation. They did watch me get shot after all.

"I'm sorry," I said. "Let's just be grateful that we're all together now."

"And that we got a bonus character," Jason added, starting to get up. Blue and Daniel lunged in quickly to help him. He smiled appreciatively then extended his hand to Kai. "Nice to have you on board."

"Thanks," she responded, shaking his hand. "I'm glad you're okay, Jason."

"We all are," Daniel seconded, patting Jason's shoulder.

SJ cleared her throat. "This is an emotional time for all, and there are still many questions that need answering, but I think Crisa is right. We should walk and talk. Jason, are you well enough to travel?"

"Yeah, I'm okay," he said. "Crisa may be new at resurrection, but she does fine work. Honestly, I feel great. Like I just had a good night's sleep."

As unbelievable as it seemed, it looked to be true. Except for the thinnest of scars, his wound had healed perfectly, like mine had after I'd been shot. Unlike me, however, Jason's post-resurrection state was free of all the pain and disorientation mine had been filled with. I garnered my reaction was probably a result of the intense strength it took to exert the feat, not the actual feat itself. As proven by both Jason and that bird yesterday, when my magic energy successfully infused into a dead creature during its three-minute window, it revitalized them in every sense of the word. I didn't get that benefit because I wasn't just *being* resurrected, I was *doing* the resurrecting.

Gazing at Jason's renewed state, I'd have been lying if I said I didn't feel proud, and overjoyed, and surprised, and incredibly relieved. Jason was alive and it was because of me. The vision that had been troubling us both for so long didn't matter anymore. We couldn't talk about this in front of the others, but we exchanged a knowing smile. Jason was going to be okay and I had been able to use my magic to achieve a game-changing result.

Everything would be different now.

My friends and I dove back into the nearby Shifting Forest with Merlin's magical map navigating us onward. While we maneuvered through dense trees and thicket, Daniel and I caught the others up on what we'd experienced since our group had been separated, including our encounter with Merlin and how Kai had come to join our gang. Daniel did a quick recap of his solo ventures, and then I shared mine. I described the discovery of my new resurrection abilities after I'd been shot; then I had to tell everyone about my escapades at Bluebeard Tower.

"So I sent the chandelier into the water and that was it," I finished reluctantly.

"That is awful." SJ shuddered.

"No, that's brilliant," Blue countered.

"I'm pretty sure it's both," I responded. "Anyway, it was a tough call but I made it. The ghosts needed to be freed and I couldn't let any more girls get taken. If I left without ensuring that, it would go against everything I stand for, right?"

"That depends," SJ said. "Is murdering your enemies one of the things you stand for now? Because you seem to be headed down that path."

"SJ, don't phrase it like that," Jason defended. "They were monsters, not people."

"And we're back to this debate again," I huffed. "Look, I'm only going to say this once. I've been through a lot these last few days—we all have—but I still don't completely know how I feel about the morality of taking life. I know you all have different opinions, and your opposing points are valid, but can you stop passing judgment on me until I can decide for myself? This is big. This is character-defining big. And the fact is . . . it makes me feel small by comparison. So can we drop it? Please?"

My friends nodded. They could tell how much this topic was

getting to me. I'd killed a giant and a bunch of Bluebeard monsters and tigermen since we'd arrived in Camelot, but my real enemies were still out there. Sooner or later I would have to face Arian, Mauvrey, Rampart, and even Alex, and if given the opportunity, I wasn't sure if I had it in me to end them. As I closed the lid on this anxiety for now, I decided that there was only one thing I was sure of. Like in Bluebeard Tower, when the time came, I would have to trust my instincts.

They were all I had in the end, and what I'd had since the beginning. I just needed to listen to them and hope that they, and my heart, were always based in what was right. As Daniel had told me in the woods the other night—that had to count for something. While my friends' voices clashed on the killing issue, this piece of wisdom called out to me. Which meant that at the very least, as I built my own perspective on morality, I would start with it as my guiding light.

Eager to change the subject, I showed off my cool new ghost talisman belt before imploring SJ, Jason, and Blue to tell us about their last couple of days.

The summary: after losing sight of Daniel and me, they'd used our original homemade Camelot map to continue on their way to Avalon. Their journey had included run-ins with a few ogres, a small, unfriendly dragon (not like my pet dragon Lucky back home), and some monsters called Samaracks—half scorpion, half meerkats that were eight feet tall on their hind legs and had massive pincers and fangs.

Hm. Not sorry I missed that.

"Word of Rampart's bounty on all our heads has reached every part of Camelot," Jason said. "We saw Wanted posters on trees in the Shifting Forest and in the villages we passed. But as we got closer to the Blue Hills of Terrenore, we noticed there were mainly Wanted posters for Blue. The knights who attacked us were fully focused on getting to her."

I raised an eyebrow. "Why?"

"Don't sound so surprised," Blue huffed.

"Sorry, I didn't mean it like that. I just mean why were they more interested in you than SJ or Jason?"

"You remember the Questor Beast—the monster that poisoned Dorothy and attacked her and Ozma near Avalon?" Blue asked.

Do I ever. I'll be lucky if I ever get the haunting pictures and passages from that book I read at Gwenivere's castle out of my head.

"Yeah," I replied.

"Well, like Dorothy said, the creature has all kinds of malicious powers, like producing its own fog to sneak up on victims, spitting acid, and tracking the scent of fear and adrenaline in its prey. What we didn't know was that it is supposedly nearly impossible to terminate. Unless you destroy the Questor Beast in a really specific way, every time you kill the thing it respawns somewhere else."

Courtesy of Gwenivere's book, I actually did know this.

"Blue, what's all that got to do with you?" Daniel asked.

"Everything," she responded with a heavy sigh. "It's my fate. My prophecy says that I am either going to be killed by the Questor Beast or be the one who finally destroys it."

"What? Since when?" I asked.

"Since forever. Or at least since I got my prologue prophecy last semester. I know I never told any of you exactly what it said," Blue met Jason's eyes for an instant, "but there's a part about the Questor Beast. I knew I would eventually have to face it. However, it wasn't until recently that I really understood what that meant. I couldn't find any information about the creature in our regular schoolbooks, but when we started reading *Le Morte d'Arthur* in Damsels in Distress class, I learned that the Questor Beast was from Camelot. I managed to get a bit more information from the texts in the restricted section of our school library. Unfortunately, even that wasn't enough to prepare me. After talking to Dorothy and some of the village locals in the last couple of days, I understand the truth now. And it's an awful lot to swallow."

"But why would Arian and Rampart care about you destroying the Questor Beast?" I asked.

"And why would anyone want to stop you?" Daniel added. "Wouldn't it be good for the people who live here if you take down a crazy monster?"

"Because it's not that simple," Blue said. She stopped walking and stared at the ground. She'd kept this part of her prophecy private for a long time and I could tell she was uncomfortable revealing the truth.

The hum of the forest whirred around us—finches chirping, breeze rustling the leaves, a lone crow cawing atop a nearby tree. We'd been hiking for about half an hour and I knew we were getting close to Avalon, but Blue's burden was worth the pause. I knew perfectly well what it was like to be choked by fate and strangled by prophecy. It was humbling, troubling, and infuriating. And sometimes a girl just needed to take a beat before she found the strength to voice her vulnerabilities.

Eventually, Blue sighed again. "Did you guys ever read a version of *Snow White* where the reason the evil queen wanted the huntsman to cut out Snow's heart was because the queen needed to consume it in order to remain beautiful forever?"

SJ raised an eyebrow. "Really? That is the example you are going with?"

"SJ, I am trying to make a point here," Blue said.

"Go on." SJ shrugged.

"My relationship with the Questor Beast is kind of like that," Blue explained. "According to my prophecy, if I destroy it, I will absorb its powers. But if *it* kills *me*, then it will become completely immortal and nothing and no one will ever be able to strike it down again. That's why so many people in Camelot—the knights who live nearby, especially—are after me. They want to kill me before the Questor Beast has a chance to. That way, I can't seal the prophecy and leave them with a horrible monster for eternity. Rampart and Arian, on the other hand, probably just don't want me to succeed in absorbing the creature's powers."

"Your Wanted poster said that you should be killed if you can't be detained, and that you are a threat to QB mortality," Daniel thought aloud. "So QB stands for Questor Beast." He gave Blue a sympathetic look. "Did you know?"

"I suspected."

"I have a question." Kai raised her hand. "I've caught up on most of the backstory now, but how did this Arian guy and King

Rampart even learn about your prophecy, Blue? Aren't those private?"

"Last semester we discovered that one of the Scribes who guarded protagonist books was working for Arian," Blue responded. "She told him when protagonists with important prophecies came along so he could eliminate them before they became a threat. I received my prophecy before the Fairy Godmother Supreme caught the Scribe and tossed her into Alderon. I figure that Arian has seen my prophecy just like he's seen Crisa's and probably Jason's and Daniel's too. He must've told Rampart about it when he learned we were on our way to Camelot."

"I'm sorry, Blue," Kai replied. "That's a rough hand to be dealt."

"I'm sure you'll overcome it though," Daniel said.

"Most people don't think so," Blue replied. "Hence why tons of them want me dead. Given what the monster is capable of, none of them believe I can actually take the thing down and they feel it'd be safer to bet against me.

"Well, they're wrong," Jason said, supportively putting his hand on Blue's shoulder. "You *can* beat it. And Rampart and Arian know it too. They wouldn't have let everybody know about you if they weren't afraid that you were going to win and absorb all that power."

"Exactly," Daniel agreed. "So let's focus on you winning, not losing. You said the creature has to be destroyed in a specific way right? Do you know how?"

"I do," Blue responded. "It has to be stabbed through the heart. The books I've read disagree on where the creature's heart is located, but the villagers we talked to about it believe that it is in one of its five heads."

"It's the center head. Beneath the chin," I stated.

They all turned to me.

"I read it in a book."

"Why didn't you say anything about it until now?" Blue asked.

"I didn't know the Questor Beast was so important to you until now; I thought it was just another monster. I was in the library at Gwenivere's castle when I came across a book with information about it. Merlin left it for me to find; there was an inscription from him to me on the inside."

"Geez," Daniel said. "How much of your future has that guy seen?"

"I've wondered the same thing myself," I replied. "It's creepy."

"How do you think we feel knowing that you can see our futures?" SJ commented.

Huh. I hadn't thought about it like that.

"So, did the book tell you anything else?" Blue asked, bringing the conversation back to focus.

"Well, there was this thing about death bl—"

I froze.

DING! A light bulb went on in my head.

The book I'd read in Gwenivere's castle said that the Questor Beast could only be destroyed if it was "stabbed through the heart by someone with the death blood of their one true love on their hands."

I stared at Blue. After Jason's ordeal, both she and I had wound up with his blood on our hands. We'd rinsed them in the river afterward, and SJ's SRBs had taken care of the rest. But despite that, I could still feel the blood on my skin. Psychologically, it was a hard thing to wash away.

My eyes darted to Jason. He had been dead. Not dying. *Dead.* The blood we'd gotten on our hands was therefore *death blood.* Which meant if Blue was successful in destroying the Questor Beast, Jason was her one true love!

Snap! I knew that Blue had been crushing on Jason for a while, but I didn't know her feelings ran so deep. Honestly, based on conversations we'd had, I wasn't sure she knew either.

"Crisa?" SJ said. "What were you going to say?"

Crud. What should I do here?

Revealing the death blood factor would let everyone know what'd I just realized—that if Blue was successful in the challenge fate had planned, it meant Jason was the *one and only* for her. I couldn't go blurting something like that out.

This was very personal, dynamic-changing information. Blue had sworn me to secrecy about her feelings for Jason because she was not ready to make them public. Moreover, Jason had died this morning, Blue had a mutant monster to face, and we all still had a million life-or death objectives to handle before the day's end. Now was not the time to interject such a revelation. Honesty was not the best policy when it could distract people before they engaged in a bunch of nearly impossible, perilous tasks.

"Uh, just that its death blood would smell a lot," I responded. "The book didn't say anything else of importance though. Only that the monster lives somewhere in the Passage Perelous."

"Actually, it lives near Avalon," Jason said. "That's why the colored knights were so intent on killing Blue. We're super close to Avalon now." He nodded to the map in Daniel's hand. "How far do we have left?"

"There's about another mile to go," Daniel replied, checking the map. "I guess we should proceed with extra caution if the Questor Beast lives around here. After all, didn't Dorothy say that when she and Ozma left Avalon it wasn't long before they were consumed by the fog that the Questor Beast produces?"

"You mean fog like that?" SJ said, pointing.

We turned and followed her finger. A thick cloud of fog was blanketing the trees. We barely had time to process it. The billows came in so fast that within five seconds anything that was more than fifteen feet away turned into a silhouette.

Suddenly, a roar echoed through the forest. Branches shook and pebbles trembled. I would have tipped my hat to the Questor Beast if I wasn't freaking out. Between the roar, the quake, and the fog, that thing knew how to make an entrance.

CHAPTER 27

For the Kill

Being so close to Avalon and finding Excalibur, it felt like a cruel joke that fate had thrown Camelot's most notorious monster in our path. Though not as cruel as the monster itself.

Daniel in the lead, we immediately made a break to the left, hoping that if we moved quickly and quietly we could maneuver through the forest without the creature spotting us. That was a naïve hope; the creature could track its prey by smelling fear and adrenaline, and we had plenty of both.

To my right I saw a flash of gold, which disappeared into the fog. The sound of hissing resonated through the forest. The fog grew thicker. A gust of cold wind whipped against me as something else whizzed behind us.

Daniel and SJ were the furthest out, Kai and Jason were in the center of the group, and Blue and I picked up the rear. She had her right hand poised by her throwing knives and her left hand firmly around her hunting knife. Her classic blue cloak blew behind her. I drew my wand ready to fight.

Shield.

I could feel the creature out there stalking us. The direction the hissing came from kept changing. As it grew louder, so did the pounding of my heart.

Blue's expression was determined, but I saw a hint of doubt. She didn't know if she could beat the Questor Beast. I didn't know if she could beat it either. But I had faith in her the same way she and the others always seemed to have faith in me. It was imperative that we clung to that; otherwise, we would have no chance.

SNAP!

A branch broke somewhere nearby. The hissing stopped.

"Look out!" Jason shouted.

A long tail with a spiked mace at the end swung out of the fog. Blue and I dove to the ground to avoid being decapitated. The tail recoiled into the fog.

The six of us formed a circle with our backs to each other, our eyes on the trees. It seemed like every noise in the forest had stopped. In this disorienting fog it felt like time itself had stopped.

CRACK!

A second later, a giant tree trailing dirt and roots came flying in our direction. We all leapt out of the way as it slammed into the middle of our clearing. A bird shot out of its leaves and flew into the sky.

That's when the Questor Beast appeared. It lunged out of the fog and I had my first clear view of the full creature. Like in the renderings in the book at Gwenivere's castle, it had five leopard heads with mouths full of fangs, fifteen-foot-long snake-like necks, and a gold-spotted body with legs the size of tree trunks.

Four of the Questor Beast's heads turned on Daniel and SJ while one aimed at Kai. She bounded out of range but had to roll to the side to evade the poisoned teeth that the beast fired at her. The teeth pierced the ground and caused the grass to wilt instantly. I watched the creature's fangs regrow with ease.

SJ managed to fire off one of her portable potions, but the lightning bolt barely caused the Questor Beast to flinch. As she reached into her potions sack to reload, the monster slammed one of its feet into the ground and the forest shook. SJ fell to the dirt and the fifth head charged at her. Blue flung four throwing knives at the creature. Two of them pierced the neck of the encroaching head. The monster wailed, which bought Kai enough time to swoop in and help SJ up. However, the Questor Beast abruptly pivoted and swung its mace tail toward us.

"Duck!" I yelled.

Most of us did, but Kai was struck. The side of the Questor

Beast's tail hit her like a battering ram and she disappeared into the fog.

"Kai!" Daniel shouted.

He moved to go after her, but the Questor Beast's first and second heads swiveled toward him and Jason. My friends dodged and began attacking the creature—Daniel with his sword and Jason with his axe. The two moved with such speed and precision that any other monster would have been dead in seconds. This one, regrettably, was agile, intelligent, and had a lot of attack options.

SJ tried to distract the beast's fourth and fifth heads with more potions. Unfortunately, the creature was learning. Before her potions could hit their mark, one of the Questor Beast's heads would spit a blob of crimson acid. The acid would encase the potion midair and cause it to drop to the ground like a dud cannonball.

I stayed with Blue, trying to draw the creature's center head forward so she might have an opening to take it down. Blue chucked one throwing knife after another, but the creature was too fast. Many of the blades missed their targets.

There was no time to clear my mind and focus on my magic. Not that I could see anything with enough clarity to project my magic into anyway. The only weapon I could actively utilize was my indestructible shield. I held it up as an assault of poisoned teeth rained down.

Blue launched another pair of throwing knives, but the center head bobbed and weaved. When I saw it draw back, I leapt forward, grabbed Blue's wrist, and yanked her behind my shield as a blob of acid was ejected in our direction. Glancing over my shield, I saw Jason activate the force field of his axe to protect himself and Daniel from the same kind of onslaught.

We continued to fight, but our efforts were pitiful. It was like the creature was toying with us. No one could get in a good shot. Worse? The teamwork we usually thrived on was foiled by the waves of blinding fog.

Suddenly SJ screamed. When I looked for her, I only saw the follow through of the monster's tail. She must have been knocked into the forest like Kai had. My heart raced with fear and a desire to go after her, but I couldn't. None of us could; we had to fend off the monster's attacks on us.

Now that there were only four of us left, the creature changed tactics and began to charge specifically at Blue. I wondered if it somehow knew that it would live forever if it killed her. The hunger in its bright-green reptilian eyes was enough to convince me it had a clue.

We were chased further into the forest as one head after another lashed furiously in our direction. The boys disappeared somewhere behind us. The dense fog caused us to lose visual on the Questor Beast too, but I could feel the earth shake from its nearby footsteps.

I could barely see three feet in front of me at that point so I had to rely on my sense of hearing. And right then, I heard the very specific sound of spit building up in the creature's throat. Blue and I skidded behind the nearest tree and not a moment too soon. Out of the haze, a blast of acid sailed right past us. Blue grabbed a low-bearing branch and swung herself into the tree. I transformed my shield back to a wand and followed her up.

The ground stopped shaking. Heartbeats racing, we waited in our perch, wondering where the predator was. Then the Questor Beast's tail wrapped around our tree trunk like a whip, ripped it from the earth, and hurled it across the forest. Blue and I hung on for dear life as we flew through the air.

We let go just before the tree hit the dirt and tumbled roughly onto the grass as a loud hiss reverberated through the area. It was like all five Questor Beast heads were in perfect harmony. I jumped to my feet as I made out an inbound shadow.

Shield.

I drew into a fighting stance, but then realized the shadow belonged to Jason. He was surprised when he bumped into me. We were both surprised when Blue tackled us a second later.

A blob of acid hit the tree behind us. The bark instantly smoked, sizzled, and began to disintegrate. Blue threw another series of knives into the fog before angrily turning to us. She grabbed Jason by the collar.

"Get out of here," she snapped. "I already lost you once today. Isn't that enough?"

A pair of glowing green eyes emerged from the fog, followed by four more sets. Slowly, the beast came into view as it stalked forward. Blue pushed Jason away before bracing her boots against the dirt.

"Crisa," she said steadily. "When I give the word, toss me your spear."

"Blue—"

"I know what I'm doing," she snapped. "Both of you, stand down. It needs to see me and *only* me right now, so take cover."

Her expression was so stern that neither of us questioned her. Jason and I ducked behind the nearest tree as the monster appeared in its full glory. It stretched out its necks and loomed over Blue. All five heads bore their fangs and simultaneously lunged at her. She dove forward and rolled closer to the creature. Several heads plowed into the dirt. Blue came out of the roll and rose to her feet. Darting around the right side of the beast, she speedily fired off eight throwing knives in a row. Her enchanted utility belt could barely replenish them fast enough to keep up with her.

Blue's aim was astounding. She managed to hit five of the creature's eyes—completely blinding the fourth head and partially blinding the first, second, and fifth. Lime green blood dripped from the Questor Beast as it wailed.

"Crisa! Now!" Blue yelled.

I hurried out from behind the tree, transformed my wand into a spear, and threw it at her. She caught the staff midair and made her move.

The first head dove at her with its mouth open, raring to take a bite. She raised my spear and thrust it upward, puncturing the creature's mouth like a skewer through a piece of meat as it bit down. With all her strength, she twisted the staff so fast that she broke the monster's neck. The snap was cringe-worthy loud and the rest of the Questor Beast reared in agony.

Blue yanked out the spear, spun around, and stuck the blade into the ground. The first head lay limply on the grass. In one fluid motion, Blue removed her cloak and flung it at the second head as it charged. She jumped to the side like a bullfighter, drew her hunting knife, and stabbed the partially blinded creature in the top of the head. It dropped dead as well.

My friend shoved her knife into its sheath then leapt back as the center head fired a glob of acid, just missing her. She ripped my spear from the ground and flung it at the Questor's Beast's chest. It was a direct hit and the monster staggered.

The fourth and fifth heads joined the center in defensively spewing acid. Blue backflipped out of the way and evaded their fire. She landed in a crouched position on the grass. The eyes of the center head locked with hers.

"Come on!" she shouted, drawing her hunting knife.

The center head hissed. Blue ran straight at it. At the last second, she slid directly underneath the head with her knife extended, trying to pierce the monster's heart. Unfortunately, the Questor Beast maneuvered to avoid her strike. The center head withdrew while the other two twisted around.

That was our cue. Despite Blue's wishes, Jason and I raced forward. He threw his axe at the fourth head, decapitating it swiftly with a forceful chop. I rushed to retrieve my spear, which was still stuck in the creature's body. Instead of ripping it out, I commanded it to morph into a wand. Once the weapon changed shape, it fell into the palm of my hand. Then I looked up.

Uh-oh.

I flung myself to the side to dodge incoming acid, rolling to a stop in the dirt. As I came to my feet, Blue zagged around the creature's assaults while Jason darted to retrieve his axe without getting killed. Seeing them dash around, I was reminded of our favorite team sport—Twenty-Three Skidd. It gave me an idea for how I could give Blue a clean shot at the center head's chin so she could end this. We only needed to take out the other remaining head first.

Blue and Jason were already ahead of me (no pun intended). That head was currently attacking Jason while the center one lashed out at Blue. I knew that despite their erratic movements, my two friends were operating under the same instinct. Somehow, they always seemed to be able to read each other's minds in battle. This time they were distracting the monster by splitting the focus of its heads.

Slowly but surely, my friends moved closer to one another until they were back-to-back. Then, in one precise moment, the fifth head fired a blob of acid at Jason while the center head lunged for Blue. My friends dove out of the way. The acid of the fifth head hit the center head, burning the creature's face. It snarled and hissed violently in pain.

That was our opening.

Lacrosse sword.

My weapon morphed into the traditional Twenty-Three Skidd weapon—a long staff with a big blade at one end and a large, netted basket on the other.

I rushed in, extended the basket, and snatched the center head by the lower half of its mouth—chin and teeth caught in the netting. Without breaking stride, I slid to the ground with all my body weight, bringing the Questor Beast's neck down low and twisting it sideways. Jason sped in to help me. We used all our strength to keep the monster's head down and expose its chin.

"Blue! Now!" I shouted, struggling to hold the creature in place.

Blue had been courting the attention of the fifth head while this had been going on. When she saw us, she tried to make a beeline for the center head, but the fifth head cut her off with another acid attack.

The center head thrashed harder. Jason and I used every ounce of our combined strength to prevent it from getting loose, but my grip was slipping.

"Blue, c'mon!" he yelled.

She shot me a panicked look. The fifth head charged at her and she flung a single throwing knife. Thank Book her aim was true. She took out the head's remaining eye, fully blinding it.

As the creature howled in distress, she bolted toward us, drawing her hunting knife. The weapon was silver, sharp, and tinged with green blood. Just as I felt my grip on the lacrosse sword slipping, she raised the blade high over us then plunged it down. I shut my eyes and turned my face away at the last second.

A horrible hissing sound sizzled in my eardrums. The struggling head stilled.

I opened my eyes to see the center head lying lifelessly in the tangle of my lacrosse sword basket. The Questor Beast's entire body collapsed to the ground with a mighty, final thud.

The monster was dead. More than that . . . it was destroyed.

Wand.

My weapon morphed back to its familiar form and Jason and I stood up slowly. Blue triumphantly yanked out her hunting knife from the beast's chin. She'd done it. She'd stabbed it through the heart. I exhaled deeply. It was over. Or was it?

Suddenly, the Questor Beast started to glow lime green. I jumped back.

Every trace of fog in the forest rushed in and was absorbed into the monster's body. In a matter of moments we could see the sky again. The sun shone and the birds chirped, but the creature still glowed. That entrancing aura slowly rose out of the Questor Beast like steam off a hot bowl of rice, forming a large ball of energy above our heads. It beamed brighter for a second, then zipped around like a comet before going straight into Blue.

Her body convulsed from the rush of power and she glowed momentarily with a green aura of her own. When Blue looked up at us, her eyes had become the same intense lime green shade as the Questor Beast's. Thankfully, after blinking a few times they returned to their normal blue color. The energy outlining her body disappeared just after.

"What the heck was that?" Blue asked.

"You completed a part of your prophecy," Jason responded. "You destroyed the Questor Beast, so that was you absorbing its powers like the prophecy said."

"Well, all right then." Blue cracked her neck and stored her hunting knife. "Celebratory nachos are on me when we get home. Now, shall we go find the others?"

"Wait, hold on," I said earnestly. "Blue, you absorbed the

Questor Beast's powers. We don't know what that's going to do to you. Don't you want to take a minute and take stock of yourself?"

"Did I grow four extra heads?" Blue asked.

"No."

"Then for now, I don't care. Let's get out of here. I am so over monsters."

CHAPTER 28

Hands Off

ow that the fog had lifted it didn't take long to re-connect with SJ and Kai, who had been thwacked by the beast, but were mostly unharmed.

Daniel was the hardest to find. At some point during the battle he'd been slammed into a tree, which had temporarily knocked him out. He was only starting to regain consciousness when we located him. Thank goodness he wasn't injured; although he was pretty ticked off about having been taken out of the fight.

"Who's the Sleeping Beauty now?" I joked. He glared at me. I didn't blame him. It wasn't particularly funny. But I had to say something to mask how worried I'd been. When we first spotted him lying on the ground, it felt like I had been shot in the chest all over again.

After regaling the others with the story of Blue's heroism against the Questor Beast, we consulted Merlin's map and continued to Avalon. The attack hadn't taken us far off course and luckily there had been no shifts in the forest during that time. We were closing in on our target, and that was so delicious we couldn't help but move faster with every minute.

The only thoughts that deterred my focus from our oncoming destination were related to Blue. Since she'd successfully killed the Questor Beast, I knew without a doubt that Jason was her one true love. I itched with desire to tell her, and tell him, however I knew in good conscience that I couldn't do either. To start with, there was the main reason I'd concluded with earlier about not wanting to distract them. Past that, after letting the revelation sink in, I decided not to tell them for a much more important reason.

Blue and Jason had to figure out who they were to one another for themselves. I'd made the choice a long time ago to never read my full prophecy because I didn't want that unnatural knowledge of fate influencing my decisions. I'd be a total hypocrite if I took that right away from my friends. So, finitely my mind was made up. I couldn't and wouldn't tell them.

Aside from the true love business, as we made our way to Avalon my thoughts also kept coming back to Blue because I was worried about her.

Absorbing the Questor Beast's powers was clearly having some unsavory side effects. As we journeyed, Blue periodically shivered and perspired. Her hands were pale and shaking. And her eyes kept flashing between that glowing, reptilian green and their normal blue. Although, whenever any of us asked if she was all right or needed help, her glare was so sour it caused us to withdraw and leave her be.

"There it is!" Kai suddenly exclaimed.

My head whipped forward.

Kai was gesturing excitedly through the trees to her right.

I dashed forward, thrust aside a branch, and saw it for myself—a crystal blue lake with ripples of turquoise. In the middle of the lake was an island of thick forests and purple mountains, the whole entity ringed by mist.

Avalon.

My friends and I pushed through the last of the trees and beheld it together. We were standing at the top of a steep, grassy slope that led down to the lake. We marveled at the view of Avalon for a moment before we spotted three knights on the bank below. They wore full armor and manned six horses that were tied to a few gnarled trees growing out of the white sand rimming the water. I instantly recognized the navy cape that one of the knights wore, and the boar-shaped brooch that came with it.

Rampart's knights from the citadel.

The knights noticed us, but before I could even reach for my wandpin, SJ drew a silver portable potion, sped down the embankment, and fired. Two knights were instantly encased in ice. The third knight ran across the sand but was swiftly taken out with a jade portable potion. It smashed into his helmet and a blob of slimy goo consumed him from head to toe.

Blue, Jason, Kai, Daniel, and I bolted down the hill to join SJ.

A bit of the green goo slid off the knight and trickled over the sand into the lake. The instant it did, the tranquil, crystal waters turned dark and murky. The center of the lake started to bubble and steam and radiate a silvery glow.

Now what?

From within the churning water, a ghostly figure began to rise. It was a woman. A spirit woman. Unlike the ghosts from Bluebeard Tower, her face and flowing robes were an icy, pale blue. Her hair and eyes were such a dark shade of black, ravens would've been jealous. I could feel those eyes burning into me.

She had to be the Lady of the Lake, the guardian of Avalon. This specter carried a lot of weight on our fate. We had to show her respect, do what she told us, and hope to the heavens that she and her lake spirits deemed us worthy enough to claim Excalibur.

Without warning she zoomed toward the bank. We took several steps back in awe and fear. I felt the urge to raise my weapon, but I restrained. Pointing a blade at her would not make a good first impression. The Lady of the Lake stopped five feet above the water just off the bank and hovered there. The force she'd churned up crashed against the sand in a rough wave. A silvery glow and a small cloud of mist hung around her. Meanwhile, her hair and robes flowed like a constant wind was blowing. I guess that was a ghost thing.

"No outside enchantments or magic permitted across the waters of Avalon," she bellowed. Her voice was deep and unsettling. It didn't sound like only one person talking. It echoed like eight different women speaking at the same time. Each syllable sent a chill up my spine.

The Lady of the Lake shot a piercing gaze at SJ. "That includes potions."

SJ hurriedly reattached the slingshot to her belt without saying a word. Daniel then stepped before the Lady of the Lake.

Her hard gaze and emotionless frown fell upon him but he did not waver.

"We've come for Excalibur," he said. He shot me a glance over his shoulder and waved me over subtly. I approached until I stood beside him.

"This is Crisanta Knight," Daniel continued. "She's been blessed by the Boar's Mouth and has sworn The Pentecostal Oath to the king of Camelot. If you give us passage across the lake, she can claim the sword as the prophecy says."

The Lady of the Lake turned her eyes onto me. I gulped.

"One has already come forward asserting the same mission," said the Lady of the Lake. "Your brother, Alexander Knight, is on the Isle of Avalon right now, searching for Excalibur."

I felt my muscles tense. After seeing Rampart's knights, I'd kind of assumed that this was the case. There were three of them and six horses, meaning that the rest of the party was elsewhere. Alex had beaten us here. We couldn't waste any more time on this bank.

"I can find Excalibur first," I said firmly.

The Lady of the Lake stared at me. After a pause, she nodded. "I will grant you passage. But for every person who crosses the lake, one person must stay behind as collateral. Should members of the search party fall victim to any of the traps on the isle, the souls of those waiting here will be my payment. Decide now who will go and who will stay."

I turned to my friends.

"Alex, Mauvrey, and Arian," said Blue.

"What?"

"They brought six horses and three of Rampart's knights stayed behind," Blue clarified. "I'd put money on the fact that Alex, Mauvrey, and Arian are the ones on the isle looking for Excalibur."

She was probably right, which meant the three of us who went after them would have to be ready for a brutal fight.

"I will stay," SJ said decidedly. "Should any monsters or magic hunters come out the woods, my potions will hold them back most effectively."

"I'll stay too," Kai said. "Based on what Daniel has told me, this isn't just business. It's personal. You guys should face them. I'm only a guest in this storyline."

Jason turned to Blue. "In that case, I think that Daniel, Crisa, and I should go. Blue, you should stay here with the SJ and Kai."

"What? No way!" Blue exclaimed, her eyes flashing Questor Beast green. "You died a few hours ago."

"Yeah, but I've fully recovered," he said. "You haven't looked right since killing the Questor Beast and absorbing its powers."

Blue could glower at us all she wanted, but Jason spoke the truth. She was still shivering sporadically, sweat beaded her brow, and her hands, which were normally so steady, were trembling. Blue looked seriously fragile and drained.

"Jason's right," I said. "We don't know how the Questor Beast's powers have affected you, Blue. Until we do, I think it would be safer if you stayed and Jason came with us."

Blue shot me a poisonous expression but nodded. "Fine."

I readdressed the Lady of the Lake. "We have our three,"

"Very well," she responded, slowly raising her hands. The water near the bank gurgled and a pair of graceful wooden boats rose from its depths and slid toward the sand

"Be warned," the Lady of the Lake continued, her eyes directly on me. "I am aware of every form of magic that enters the realm of Camelot. I do not care how powerful the approach of the Vicennalia Aurora is making you, child. As I said, any magic that did not originate from Avalon is not allowed beyond this point. You are not even permitted to transform that wand of yours once you step off this bank. Should you use even a spark of power, I will strike you dead. Do you understand?"

I nodded. I didn't question how the Lady of the Lake knew these things about me, but I was bummed that she did. I had hoped that my magic would give us a much-needed edge over Alex and company. Now our victory was less certain.

I'd grown to respect Arian's tremendous skill as a sword fighter. He'd nearly killed me quite a few times. I'd been humbled by Mauvrey's aptitude with her metallic gloves. She'd beaten me before and I would never forget it. And then there was Alex. He was my brother. He'd taught me to fight when I was growing up. He knew my moves and my instincts better than anyone. How could I go up against him?

"Do not be afraid," SJ said, reading my thoughts. She touched my shoulder and gave me a reassuring smile. "You can do this."

I put my hand over hers and smiled back. "Thanks," I said. "I wish you guys were coming with us."

"That would be too easy," Blue said. "The universe likes testing us."

She gave Jason an impassioned look. "Please don't die again, okay? And don't have too much fun battling the bad guys without me."

"I wouldn't dream of it," he said. "Just get some rest. You've already destroyed an immortal monster today. I think you're set for action in this act of the story."

I exchanged hugs with all of my friends except for Kai. She gave Jason and me an encouraging nod then kissed Daniel goodbye. A twitch of awkwardness passed through me and I darted my eyes away from their embrace.

"Take care of yourself," Kai said to Daniel. "I'm not going to be able to magically poof up next to you if you get in trouble and need someone this time."

"If he needs someone, we'll be there," I replied adamantly.

"That's right. We've got each other covered," Jason agreed.

I pivoted to address all three girls. "We'll be back soon to put an end to this story arc together. I promise."

I transformed my wandpin into a spear and Daniel passed Kai our Merlin map. SJ suggested that our SRBs would probably count as outside enchantments, so we took them off and gave them to her for safekeeping. Lastly, Jason removed his Mark Two—which he still had—from his pants pocket and handed it over to SJ as well.

That done, we were about to turn away when Blue abruptly embraced Jason again, quick and hard. She clearly surprised him; though it didn't surprise me. It made me smile. Seeing this display of affection between Blue and Jason warmed my heart— unlike what I'd seen between Daniel and Kai.

I walked across the sand with the boys. "We're ready," I said to the Lady of the Lake, who'd been patiently waiting for us to say our goodbyes.

"Only two per boat," she declared, gesturing to the vessels.

I climbed into the one on the left. Daniel followed me, so Jason hopped into the second boat. I looked around inside for the paddles, but the boat was empty. Before I could ask how we were supposed to row, the vessels began to skate across the water on their own. Pretty soon, SJ, Blue, and Kai were nothing but tiny figures on the bank.

It was smooth sailing for a minute, but the joy ride didn't last. The boats soon began to pick up speed. Then about halfway across the lake, Jason's boat veered right while ours went left.

I panicked, clutching the side of the boat. "Jason!" I called. But the boats moved too fast and the mist around the isle was growing thicker. I could no longer see his boat or the bank where we'd left our friends. The atmosphere had changed unexpectedly and even the sky had abruptly clouded over.

"What's happening?" I asked Daniel.

"I don't know," he said. "But we're slowing down."

He was right. Our boat had curtly changed speed and was now barely moving along. Something was about to happen. I could feel it. The mist was dense and icy cold. My skin felt clammy and I found it hard to breathe.

Daniel and I stood up in the boat—trying to make out the isle, or something, anything. That's when we saw it. Up ahead we spotted a slender, graceful arm stretching out of the lake like it was reaching for the sky.

An arm? Really?

My memory sparked.

I remembered this. I'd dreamed about this moment before. But what happened next? I racked my brain. There was the mist and the arm and then . . . then we were underwater and Daniel was in trouble!

"Daniel—"

"Knight, look," he said, cutting me off.

More arms were rising out of the water. They slowly extended from the lake like reeds. Each arm penetrated the surface up to the bicep then remained perfectly still. I wish they would've waved or given us the thumbs up or something. The way they reached up and froze like that was creepy.

Our boat passed through the watery field of arms. I moved closer to Daniel protectively. Alas, while my instincts were good, my understanding of the danger was not. In the next moment, we were attacked.

An arm shot out of the water by the side of our boat and extended past the bicep, but it was not connected to a shoulder— just more arm. The thing was like a giant noodle, and it snatched Daniel by the jacket and yanked him overboard.

"Daniel!" I lunged to my knees at the edge of the rocking boat, but he was gone. He'd been dragged under. The other arms that had risen out of the lake curtly disappeared below the surface too.

Crud.

Crud! Crud! Crud!

I dropped my spear in the boat, took a deep breath, and dove into the water.

I was surprised at how well I could see under the lake. It was like I'd entered a different world. The surroundings were beautiful but odd. Everything swirled with silver and blue strokes like I was trapped in an oil painting.

I spotted Daniel twenty feet down. Countless hands were dragging him below, each of them attached to a long, pale noodle arm that stretched so far into the depths I could not see where it came from. Other unfathomably long arms swayed in the water like disturbing sea kelp.

My own arms cut through the water sharply as I swam after my friend. I was a good swimmer, but as I went deeper and deeper, the creepy arms grabbed at my ankles, legs, and wrists. I dodged them for a while, but eventually a hand firmly wrapped around my forearm. Half a dozen more hands saw their opening and zoomed in to clutch my other limbs. Instead of dragging me down like Daniel though, they held me firmly in the water. I would have shouted angrily had I not been holding my breath. I watched a thrashing Daniel get pulled farther and farther into the darkness until he vanished completely.

Suddenly, the Lady of the Lake materialized before me. Her glow lit up the water like moonlight in a bleak December sky. She waved her hand and a silver bubble formed around my head. The bubble made my face dry and I could breathe.

"Your friend will not run out of air either," the Lady of the Lake said. "I have enchanted him as I have enchanted you. While his bubble has put him to sleep, yours will allow you to breathe and speak underwater."

"Can I *yell* underwater?" I asked with a scowl, trying to pull away from the hands that restrained me. "What's going on? Your weird lake arms took my friend. That wasn't part of the deal."

"It is for his own good, child," the Lady of the Lake responded in her deep, resonating voice. "The spirits of my lake foresaw some of your friend's immediate future on the isle. His fate will change in a very unfortunate way if he journeys there. Proceed with your other friend alone. The two of you can try to claim Excalibur and I will preserve this hero within my lake until you return."

I glanced into the depths where Daniel had been taken. "But I need him," I said. "Without him we won't stand a chance."

The Lady of the Lake studied me with a poker face that would've made a seasoned gambler wet himself. "The choice is yours," she said. "You are the one trying to fulfill the Great Lights Prophecy. However, I warn you that taking this hero to Avalon will result in a great challenge for him that no one should wish on a friend."

I thought hard on the proposition.

"But he's not going to die on the isle or anything, right?" I asked. "He won't get killed or badly hurt if he comes with us?"

"Not today. But my spirits can only see into the immediate future. As I said, setting foot on Avalon will only bring an unfavorable twist to his fate."

I considered this critically. I didn't want to saddle Daniel with anything bad, but I also knew that Jason and I would probably get killed if he didn't come with us. Without my magic, the two of us against Alex, Mauvrey, and Arian yielded very low odds.

This wasn't a fight we could afford to lose. If we didn't claim Excalibur, then Arian would trade the sword to Rampart for the Simia Crown and recover Paige's mind from Glinda's memory stone. And if that happened, then he'd learn where Book's genies were hidden and the antagonists would have all the power they'd ever need to take over the realm.

Daniel was too important to leave behind. I could feel guilty about this later. For now, I had faith he'd be able to handle whatever challenge the isle threw at him. I would help him get through it and protect him from whatever unfavorable twist of fate came next. We'd faced many obstacles together and always overcame them as a team. This would be no different.

"I need him," I said decidedly.

"Very well," said the Lady of the Lake, nodding solemnly. The giant noodle arms released me and shrank back into the depths. "I will break your breathing enchantments and you can try to save your friend before he drowns."

"Wait! I thought you were trying to help Daniel by keeping him from going to Avalon. Now you might let him drown? Taking away our ability to breathe makes no sense."

"Child, this is the Isle of Avalon. Valor, worth, sacrifice, heroism—these are words that matter here. Sense, fairness, consistency—those are words that do not. Everything is a test, and if you'd like to pass this one, I suggest you start swimming."

The Lady of the Lake snapped her ghostly fingers and the silver bubble around my head began to disintegrate. I took a deep breath before it popped.

"Better hurry," she whispered as she faded away.

Panic surged through me and I swam with everything I had. The water got darker and darker, colder and colder. My strokes were long and intense; my kicking was powerful and desperate. All that lit my way were tiny glowing fish like aquatic fireflies. Then I saw the arms.

The colony of arms grew from the squishy, glowing green floor of the lake. They swayed in the water like anemones. I found Daniel floating in a dense bed of them. The arms were not holding onto him any longer, but he wasn't moving and his eyes were closed.

I swam to him and pulled one of his arms over my shoulder. Then I grabbed him around the waist with one hand and boosted off a chunk of smooth underwater rock to propel us to the surface. I stroked through the water with my free hand while my feet kicked so hard that mermaids would've been impressed, Stella included.

The water changed from black to navy to crystal blue. The surface grew closer and closer until we burst through. I gasped for air, but Daniel was still unconscious. I looked around. Our boat was long gone, but the isle shore was barely fifteen feet from where we'd surfaced. Trying my best to keep Daniel's head above water, I paddled toward it.

When I felt sand under my boots, I grabbed Daniel under the arms and dragged him the rest of the way. Although he was heavy, I managed to heave him onto shore before collapsing on the white sand beside him. I turned Daniel's head sideways like I'd learned in First Aid class at school to allow any water in his mouth to fall out. Then I put my fingers to his neck. I couldn't find a pulse.

I placed my head to his chest and listened closely for a heartbeat. It was barely there, but it was there, which meant I could revive him. I carefully straightened his head and started chest compressions. I pumped hard and fast thirty times, but he was still unconscious. I was about to continue to the next phase of CPR—mouth-to-mouth resuscitation—when I hesitated.

If there was ever a time to use magic . . .

Daniel's face was white and still. My own chest tightened. I wanted nothing more than for him to open his brown eyes and look up at me. Water from my wet hair dripped onto him.

I'm sorry, I thought.

I closed my eyes, tilted his chin back with one hand, and plugged his nose with the other, and moved closer. Then something warm rushed against my skin. I opened my eyes and saw a silvery glow blow past us like a gust of enchanted wind. The

Lady of the Lake was hovering a few yards away. She smiled at me cryptically. Then Daniel coughed. I took my hands away and backed up as he sat up, hacking water.

He put his hand to his head and groaned. "Ugh, what happened?"

"Daniel!" I threw my arms around him and hugged him tightly, quick and hard like Blue's goodbye to Jason on the bank of the lake. My embrace surprised Daniel as much as hers had surprised Jason. I pulled away a second later, a little embarrassed.

"You, um, almost drowned," I said.

He glanced at me, warmth in his expression. "I guess the reason that sentence has the 'almost' in it is because of you?"

"The Lady of the Lake helped a bit," I said. I glanced up, but she had disappeared back into her depths. She did leave a parting gift, though. My spear, which I'd left in the boat, was now stuck in the sand a few feet away.

Water dripped down my face. Without our SRBs, Daniel and I would need to dry naturally. I brushed a strand of hair behind my ear and looked into the distance. I still wasn't able to see the other side of the lake where we'd left our friends. The ring of mist protecting the isle blocked the rest of the world from view.

Daniel got to his feet. I stayed on my knees for a beat and stared up at him. I couldn't believe how close I'd come to losing him. He gazed at the mist, but I continued looking at him—his eyes, his nose, his lips . . .

A weird tingle passed through me. It wasn't fear or awkwardness—it was a bit like electricity. I couldn't believe how close I'd come to . . . I mean, if the Lady of the Lake hadn't shown up and revived him, I would have continued with the CPR and had to . . .

Daniel tilted his chin down toward me. "What's wrong?"

"Nothing," I said, standing swiftly. "Um, are you okay to keep going?"

"Well, it's not like we can go back after that," Daniel jested. He started walking across the sand, heading inland.

The cold mist caressed my cheeks. "No. I suppose we can't," I muttered. I yanked my spear from the sand and hurried after him.

CHAPTER 29

Watch Your Glass

he Isle of Avalon was much larger than it'd seemed from the mainland. Lavender-colored mountain ridges began about fifty feet from the water and spiraled around the island like the spikes on the back of a dragon, reaching mighty heights.

The mysterious landscape concealed the heart of the isle from where we stood on the beach. We had no idea what could be hiding within the mountains. As we walked down the beach though, we spotted another boat coming ashore. It was Jason's.

The three of us were glad to be reunited, but our attitudes soured when we spotted something else on the beach a short distance away. Two other boats were resting on the bank—Alex and company's, no doubt. Our greatest enemies were already ahead of us on the hunt for Excalibur.

I chose to look on the bright side. If they hadn't returned to their boats, that meant they hadn't found it yet.

As we forged ahead, I detected a strong presence of magic in the air. I'd felt it since the morning, but now that we were getting closer to midday, the Aurora's energy was becoming more potent. I wished I could use my powers here—Arian, Alex, and Mauvrey would have no chance.

My eyes were wide and alert as the three of us trekked across Avalon in search of Excalibur. We knew for certain that it was on the isle but had no idea where. The legend (and instructions) that had been guiding us ended here.

While we scoured the terrain, I also looked for anything that resembled a pond or a spring. This isle was where the Four Waters of Paradise could be found—the waters with the power to cure my Pure Magic Disease. It was the only substance with the power to give me a clean slate and today, the day of the Vicennalia Aurora, was my only chance to use them. *If* I decided to use them.

Honestly, I still didn't know what I would do if I found the waters. I'd saved Jason already, so I didn't need to worry about that. But our conversation back in Gwenivere's castle haunted my conscience. Did I really *want* to cure my Pure Magic Disease? If you'd asked me a couple of days ago, I would have said yes. But now I didn't know.

If it weren't for my magic's growing power, I would have died when those magic hunters shot me, I would've been killed in Bluebeard Tower, and I wouldn't have been able to resurrect Jason. In the last couple of days, I was beginning to value my growing power on a new level and feel its strength in a more exhilarating way. But was that power and potential worth the risk of losing control, corrupting myself, and turning dark? Was it wiser to keep my Pure Magic so I could use it to make a difference, or should I wash myself of this affliction while I had the chance?

I dreaded having to make such a permanent decision.

None of us knew much about Avalon, but we knew that the isle was dangerous and full of treacherous obstacles. After twenty minutes, we came upon our first. It happened when we were passing beneath an arch of lavender rock that was encrusted with hundreds of barnacles. I placed my hand on the thick arch for balance as I stepped through. When I did, the previously unobtrusive barnacles started to flash red—slowly at first but speeding up rapidly. Then they starting making a high-pitched beeping noise.

My friends and I were familiar enough with danger—and the movie *Die Hard*—to recognize charges when we saw them. We dashed down the rocky path before the barnacles blew like explosives and the entire arch came crumbling to the ground. The boom and clatter echoed around the canyon. If Alex, Mauvrey, and Arian didn't know we were here before, they certainly knew now.

Our next obstacle occurred in the form of quicksand. The boys stepped in it and within three seconds they were consumed up to their knees. Luckily, I had been a few steps behind them at the time. I braced one boot against a rock as I extended the staff of my spear and pulled them out.

After that came the attack of the blue spider crabs, which, I hope you don't mind, I'd rather not relive through retelling. Let's just say they were furry, the size of bulldogs, and more than enough reason for me to never eat seafood again.

When that assault was over, I had to thoroughly wipe crab gut from the blade of my spear and scrape crustacean carnage from my boots. And just when I'd finished drying off from the lake too.

What a lousy time to not be wearing an SRB.

"Whoa, is that a wormhole?" Jason exclaimed from ahead.

I glanced up and saw a glowing red circle of energy floating in the air a half dozen yards away. It was a wormhole. A counterclockwise wormhole that would lead to Neverland. The wormhole flashed at us tauntingly and made me think of Peter and Arthur. I hoped the Gwenivere Brigade had gotten to them by now. I hoped they were all safe and that we would see each other again soon.

The wormhole suddenly shrunk and disappeared, closing the tear between worlds. When it did, our eyes nearly bugged out when we saw what had been hiding behind the portal. It was a sword shoved into a stone.

Holy bananas, is that . . .

We raced forward.

Sticking out of a smooth boulder right in front of us was a beautiful sword. About half of the weapon was stuck in the rock. The hilt was dark gray leather and the guard was silver. The blade itself gleamed with an onyx glint. I was over the moon until I tilted my head sideways and saw two words engraved in tiny letters on the flat of the blade.

"Gladius Cordis," I read.

"That's Latin," Jason responded. "I think it roughly translates to Sword of the Heart."

"Exactly how much Latin did you learn when you were prepping to come on this quest?" I asked.

"He switched his language elective to it," Daniel responded.

Jason shrugged. "I'd already learned mountain troll and gnome last year. And I like to be prepared."

I gazed back at the sword. "Well, I guess this isn't it."

"Then what's it doing here?" Daniel asked.

"I don't know. Maybe it's a test or a trap," I replied. "Like when we went to the Cave of Mysteries and there were all those other enchanted knickknacks trying to distract us from what we were after. I think we should stay away from it."

I moved past the strange blade and so did the boys. However, it seemed the sword was not so keen on being forgotten. Fifteen minutes later we passed through a tunnel and when we exited the other side, there it was again, stuck in another stone ahead of us.

"Did we go in a circle?" I asked, glancing around at our surroundings.

"No, I don't think so. Nothing looks the same," Jason replied.

"Except for the sword," I remarked. I kept my eyes on it as we moved away.

Another ten minutes went by. Then at the top of a gravelly slope, I stopped in my tracks.

"There it is again," Daniel said.

Gladius Cordis was shoved in a rock on a ledge to the right. I was about to comment on the sword when the air beside us began to shimmer. I backed up against Jason and Daniel. A new wormhole opened up. This one was orange, which meant it went clockwise in the Wonderland sequence.

"Another one?" Jason commented.

"Merlin said that because of the magic instability during the Vicennalia Aurora, wormholes would appear more frequently as the day goes on," I said.

"But we saw the other one barely twenty minutes ago," Jason replied.

I dipped my fingers into the swirling orange magic of the dazzling portal. "By tonight they're supposed to appear every few minutes, maybe seconds. We might not have seen any wormholes until now, but the Aurora must be affecting the Isle of Avalon faster because it has a higher concentration of magic. After all, it is home to Excalibur, the Four Waters of Paradise, the Lady of the Lake, and who knows what else."

Daniel reached over and gently pulled my hand out of the portal. "Don't want you to fall in," he said.

The three of us eased away from the mystic wormhole and continued. A few minutes later, the path we turned onto became fascinating. It was flanked by immense shards of red and blue glass. They stuck out of the sand hazardously like someone had shattered a giant stained-glass window and forgotten to clean up the pieces.

"What is this?" Jason said in awe.

"It must be Avalonian glass," I replied. "I learned about it when I was trapped in Bluebeard Tower. Mauvrey also mentioned it once too. Depending on how it's forged, it can serve a lot of purposes related to magic, like absorbing or containing it."

Extra purposes aside, the immense shards were super sharp, so we were careful as we made our way down the path. No one wanted to slip, fall, and accidentally slice off a limb.

The route was completely walled in by the glass. Between every few shards, however, there were these weird, door-sized walls of dark gray energy. They kind of reminded me of portals, but they gave off a seriously eerie vibe. I did not know where they led, and I did not care to deviate from our mission to find out.

We wandered through the glass-laden trail with our reflections following us in the shards for a few minutes until Daniel started to sink again. It was more quicksand. He yanked his foot out before he was past the point of no return. On closer inspection, the quicksand was slightly darker than the regular sand on the path, but not by much. We were *really* going to have to watch ourselves.

As the boys continued, I paused for a moment to inspect a particularly thick piece of blue Avalonian glass. Something about its sheen and radiance tickled a memory, but I couldn't place it. I put my hand against its smooth surface and gazed at the entrancing substance, my reflection watching me vigilantly.

I drew away from the shard and admired the pathway as a whole. My friends were a bit ahead now, about to turn a corner. I'd catch up with them in a moment. The sun reflected off the glass, casting beams of unintentionally sharp light on the ground. That's when I noticed one of the energy walls shimmering. It was three feet to my left. The disturbance only lasted for a second, like a hiccup in the grayness.

What in the—

Two shimmering wires abruptly shot out of the gray and wrapped themselves around my wrist. An electric shock came a split second later and zapped me so hard that I dropped my spear. The wires pulled me forward.

"Daniel!" I managed to yell.

I was yanked through the energy wall, which was, in fact, some kind of portal. A second later Arian's hand was around my neck, choking me.

"Did you really think I'd forgotten about you?" he asked.

I couldn't answer; his hand was crushing my throat. My eyes darted around. We were in some sort of cave. I'd seen no signs of caves on the isle a moment ago. I figured that the energy wall was a portal to an obscure pocket dimension—a hidden fold of space on the isle.

Why not? We'd encountered weirder.

The wires around my wrist recoiled and Arian threw me to the ground. I tried to pick myself up, but Mauvrey pushed her purple ankle boot against my chest and pinned me down.

Arian stood a few feet away. The cave around him had a low ceiling full of sleeping bats. Just like in Merlin's cave, indigo boulders and luminescent moss clumps were everywhere. Meanwhile, embedded in the stone wall of the cave behind me was a kind of window that looked out onto the Avalonian glass pathway where I'd come from.

This must've been the energy wall I'd been pulled through. There were two additional windows further down that were apparently energy walls connected to this cave too. I saw Jason and Daniel run past them. They didn't see me. They hadn't seen which energy wall I'd gotten yanked through.

Argh.

I cringed at the weight of Mauvrey's heel digging into my chest.

"Each energy wall leads to a different pocket dimension hidden on the isle," she explained, watching my eyes and confirming my theory. "On this side they all lead back to the same place. Daniel and Jason will never find you unless they guess the right one. Not that you will be alive even if they do."

Mauvrey raised a hand. She aimed the dual wires of her glove at my throat and fired, but this time I grabbed them out of the air before they reached me and yanked back with all my strength. Mauvrey was thrown forward and landed face-first on the ground. It was a small win, but Arian was standing above me with his sword drawn before I got any farther. My eyes widened in fear. His arm hinged back, but he faltered when a familiar voice came through the shadows.

"It's not here," my brother said as he emerged from the depths of the cavern. "Let's keep—"

Alex froze when he saw me. I used the interruption to my advantage.

I boosted off my hands and rear foot and kicked Arian's sword away—spinning to my feet and kicking Arian in the chest. The moment my boot jolted him back, I whirled around and dove through the energy wall. My boots skidded against the sand and I scooped up my spear just as Arian came through after me.

I lifted my weapon and blocked his strike. He spun around my side but I pursued him and countered his next move. My right foot rammed his knee inward, pushing him down. Mauvrey darted through the energy wall next. She was close enough that I was able to spin my staff and thrust the blunt end into her chest—knocking her back into the pocket dimension. I swiftly reversed the staff and jabbed Arian.

That's when Jason and Daniel emerged from their own energy wall. They must've been looking for me inside a different pocket dimension. Daniel immediately began to clash swords with

Arian. Mauvrey emerged with Alex by her side and Jason rushed to engage them. Jason swept low with his axe, but my brother jumped over the strike. He brought down the bottom of his sword to hit Jason in the lower back. I intervened and kicked Alex in the ribs.

Mauvrey fired both her metallic gloves. Wires shot out—one set at me, another at Daniel. I dodged, but Daniel didn't see them coming. As they connected with his arm, Mauvrey crossed her pointer and middle fingers and electricity surged through the wires, shocking Daniel. He dropped his sword but didn't go down. Arian took a shot at him, which Daniel managed to evade. However, when he tried to reach for his sword, Arian kicked it away.

I ran to help. Arian swung at my chest, but I side-stepped and elbowed him in the head. Arian faltered for a second but took a page from my playbook and kicked me in the stomach. I thudded roughly against a shard of Avalonian glass, cracking it.

Mauvrey reeled in her wires, which were still attached to Daniel. He jerked forward. Arian kicked him in the spine and my friend slammed into the sand. The wires returned to Mauvrey and she and Arian stood over Daniel. Mauvrey clapped her hands together and her gloves sizzled with electricity. Knowing what came next, I charged forward and plowed into Arian, using the full force of my body to ram him off his feet and straight into Mauvrey's electrified hands. The gloves were pushed against Mauvrey's chest and shocked both my enemies simultaneously. The two of them fell to the sand. Having been electrified by the gloves before, I knew they would need a beat to recoup.

I helped Daniel up and turned to collect his sword, but it wasn't where it had fallen. Narrowing my eyes, I spotted the hilt disappearing into the ground. It had been swallowed by the quicksand!

"Oomph!"

I whirled around. Alex had coldcocked Jason in the face with a hard punch. Good thing my friend knew how to take a hit. He recovered, blocked Alex's sword with his axe, then swung at Alex's sternum.

My heart stopped for a moment. Alex jumped back and I exhaled.

Ugh. I hate that I still care for him.

I realized I should be helping Jason, not gawking. That's when I noticed the sand behind my brother was slightly darker in color.

More quicksand.

The boys exchanged blows, but Jason was on the offensive and driving Alex back. I took advantage of this, skidding to the ground at his feet and sweeping his leg out from under him. My brother fell backward and landed in the quicksand. He immediately began to sink. I stood over him triumphantly and watched him struggle.

"Are you just going to leave me here?" he asked.

"Let your new friends help you." I pointed my spear at Arian and Mauvrey, who were slowly getting up.

I raced to join Jason and Daniel. "Come on. They were searching inside the pocket dimensions through the energy walls. Excalibur must be in one of them. Let's move."

We leapt through the nearest energy wall and into another cave. It was a lot like the one I'd just been in, but much smaller. We were able to search the entire thing in less than fifteen seconds.

"Next one!" Jason said, waving us back to the cave wall that faced the Avalonian glass pathway. Looking through the energy walls, we saw that Arian and Mauvrey were trying to wrench Alex free of the quicksand.

"Hold on," I put my hand in front of Jason. "They may not be able to see us, but they know which energy wall we went through." I pointed at three other energy walls along the side of the cave that connected back to the Avalonian glass pathway. "We should jump out of a different opening at the same time they jump through our original one. That way we can better evade them."

"Fine, but since multiple energy walls lead to the same caves, how will we know which ones we've already checked?" Jason asked.

"Here," Daniel responded. He picked up a piece of indigo rock. "This looks like the same stuff Merlin used to draw with." He bent down and slashed an X against the ground; sure enough, it worked like blue chalk.

I looked up to see that Mauvrey and Arian were nearly done pulling Alex free.

"Should we split up to cover more ground?" Jason asked.

"No," I replied. "Let's stick together if we can help it. Now let's jump."

Just as our enemies rushed through our original energy wall, we exited through one farther down then immediately darted across the Avalonian glass pathway into a different pocket dimension.

"I guess it's a race now," Daniel said as we started to search the new cave.

"It's going to be complete chance who finds Excalibur first," Jason said.

"This whole quest has been complete chance," I replied. "At least in this case we know it's going to end one of two ways."

We finished a sweep of the new cavern and found nothing. Before we left, we paused for a moment as we watched Alex and company exit one energy wall then run twelve feet down the Avalonian glass pathway to leap through another.

They no longer appeared to be chasing us. It seemed that after their initial pursuit, Alex, Arian, and Mauvrey had come to the same conclusion we did. Fighting it out was not the most important thing right now; the race was. Finding Excalibur was the number one priority for everyone. This entire storyline had come down to this head-to-head match.

Daniel marked a quick X on the floor, and the boys and I moved on to check other four pocket dimensions while keeping an eye out for our enemies. The sixth cave we checked was the largest by far. The ground was flat at the entrance, but immediately dropped into a steep descent. We took the slope in a run. Gravel scraped beneath my boots as I bolted down. Daniel was in the lead by about ten feet. Jason and I followed, all of us going dangerously fast. It was unfortunate, because all of a sudden, a bright orange light erupted in Daniel's wake and Jason and I were moving too rapidly to stop or swerve. We fell headfirst through the clockwise portal and into the realm that lay beyond.

No, no, no!

CHAPTER 30

Cloud Nine

fter plummeting for a few seconds, Jason and I dropped onto a fluffy, light pink cloud that smelled like rosewater. Instead of falling through it, we ricocheted into the air. The cloud looked fluffy, but it was actually springy like a trampoline. We bounced several more times before we were able to find our feet. Thankfully Jason's axe had been in its sheath at the time of our fall and I'd retained my grip on my spear.

I took in the mystifying surroundings. There were clouds everywhere. Some were light pink like the big one we'd landed on. Some were golden. Others were white with silver linings. And that wasn't me being optimistic. Glowing silver outlines literally encased some clouds, and silver lines cut across them like zippers.

All the clouds floated through a sky swirling with baby blue, royal purple, and fuchsia. Tiny sprays of stars stood out against the darker parts of the sky. Gleaming silver ravens darted across overhead and it looked like it was raining glitter. I held out my hand and itty-bitty gold flecks touched my skin before popping like bubbles.

"Cloud Nine," Jason thought aloud. "That's the realm that comes next in a clockwise rotation of the Wonderland sequence. Orange portals from Camelot lead to Cloud Nine."

I nodded, remembering the path now. "Then Oz, then Limbo, then the Portalscape." I looked around to find the portal we'd come from.

"There it is," Jason said, pointing at a hefty pink cloud thirty feet above us. The portal we'd entered through floated over it.

On this side the portal was red, as it led back to Camelot, which was a counterclockwise move in the Wonderland sequence.

The portal flashed for a second and then Daniel's head poked out.

"We're down here!" I shouted.

Daniel leaned forward like he was about to jump through.

"No, keep looking for the sword!" I shouted. "We have to get to it before Alex. The two of us will find a way back to the portal."

"You said we shouldn't risk splitting up."

"I said we shouldn't split up if we could help it. We can't now. You need to keep looking for Excalibur. We'll catch up."

"What if the portal closes before you—"

"Daniel, don't argue with me. Just go!" Since his sword had been lost to the quicksand, I realized that he needed a weapon in case he ran into our enemies. I glanced at the staff in my hand.

"Here!" I stepped to the edge of my cloud, drew back my arm, and hurled my spear upward like throwing a javelin. Daniel caught it with great dexterity.

"Thanks!" he called down. "Hurry up!" He ducked back through the portal and disappeared from sight.

"Okay, now what?" Jason asked.

I pressed my boot firmly into the cloud. I felt it wanting to push me back up. It really was like a big, poofy trampoline.

And if all these clouds are like trampolines . . .

"You remember the bunker we slept in when we stayed with the Lost Boys and Girls in Neverland?" I asked.

A mischievous grin spread across my friend's face. He knew what I was referring to—the delightful trampoline floor of the kids' bunker. "Last one to the portal has to clip Rampart's toe nails," he challenged.

I grinned and the two of us bounded off the cloud. I flew through the sky for a dozen feet before my boots landed on the pink cloud I'd been aiming for. I went sailing to another cloud after that, bouncing higher and higher from one level of the sky to the next as I worked my way up to the counterclockwise portal. Jason followed his own cloud trajectory. Showing off, he did a midair flip. He was ahead of me now, and by my calculations, only two clouds away from the portal. Make that one.

Jason sprung off a pink cloud, aiming for a white, silver-lined one. I expected him to bounce off it and soar up to our destination, but much to my surprise, he disappeared into the white cloud. It was like it'd swallowed him. The silver-lined cloud turned golden.

"Jason!"

My heart pounded with panic. I hopped over to the golden cloud as fast as possible, When I landed, I realized this one felt more like a cushioned mattress than a trampoline.

I got on my hands and knees and studied the cloud. It was slightly translucent. Inside I could see the hazy silhouette of a person. I tried to pull at the cloud or dig into it with my nails, but it was thick and impenetrable.

A silver raven suddenly landed on the edge of the cloud. Its eyes were like diamonds, and its feathers, feet, and beak were an enchanting shade of silver. Around its neck was a lavender cord necklace with a blinking yellow pendant that had the word *InfoRaven.* The pendant kept flashing like a button so I gingerly reached out and touched it. When I did, the automated voice of a woman came out.

"Welcome to Cloud Nine. What is your question?"

"Um. My friend fell into this cloud. How do I get him out?"

The InfoRaven tilted its head and the voice projected once more. "Cloud Nine is a place where people can escape to the world of their dreams—a fantasy where they are in their happiest place. White, silver-lined clouds are available cocoons. Golden clouds are cocoons in use. To exit the cocoon, the slumberer must will it to happen. If an outsider wishes to wake them, the outsider may enter the slumberer's Cloud Nine fantasy and try to convince them to leave."

"All right, let me in," I said.

The InfoRaven blinked. "Hold please."

Ugh. I didn't have time for this! The portal back to Camelot could close any second.

A silvery glow enveloped my entire body and in a flash I was standing in a forest. Jason's dream. It was probably the most picturesque, tranquil forest I'd ever been in. The trees were infinitely tall with lush green leaves. The sun was shining and the weather felt like it was in the perfect low seventies with a light breeze. Birds lent a soft background song to the environment. A deer cantered by in the distance. A family of rabbits scampered across my feet into a nearby hole.

I had no trouble believing this was Jason's happiest place. It was easygoing, woodsy, and full of warmth—just like him.

I heard familiar laughter and followed the sound through the forest to a gorgeous field of dandelions and sunflowers. I smelled pine, freshly watered grass, and . . . bacon (which was weird, but I wasn't complaining).

To the far right I saw a village of elaborate tree houses. On the left was a large lake the color of a blue jay's brightest feathers, with wild Pegasi drinking at the edge. Directly ahead was some type of small arena. There was cheering coming from inside, so I followed the joyful, enthused sounds.

The arena had an open roof and was lined with rows of bleachers filled with people applauding. At the center was an elevated combat floor. Jason and Blue were there, battling it out against a dozen black-armored knights.

Of course Jason's happiest place includes some type of combat. He's a hero and loves to fight. And he fights at his best with Blue.

I got closer to the elevated combat floor until I was standing right next to the floor at eye level.

My friends fought in perfect synchronicity like I'd seen them do a hundred times. Whenever one of them stabbed an opponent, that knight disappeared in a puff of smoke. One by one, my friends eliminated their rivals until there was only a single enemy left. The pair simultaneously struck the remaining knight, who evaporated in a final puff. The crowd went wild and jumped to their feet in celebration.

Blue stored her hunting knife as Jason raised his axe to the cheers of the crowd. I smiled. Then Jason put his arm around Blue and kissed her. Like *full on kissed her.*

I stumbled back from the shock and knocked over a vendor

who was selling turkey legs. The vendor crashed into several more people and the disturbance caused Jason to look over. When he saw me, his face paled like an anemic ghost.

"Crisa!"

Abruptly the combat floor, the arena, the crowds, and even Blue vanished. They were like a mirage that had never been there. Only Jason stood on the field in front of me.

I struggled to find the proper words. I knew Jason was Blue's one true love. I knew Blue had developed feelings for him. But I didn't know that he was already into her. Furthermore, I hadn't been prepared to see that level of an affectionate display right then and there. I felt super awkward to have witnessed such a private moment. My reaction had been a combination of *egads, that was fast, and whoa, too close and personal.*

"I didn't see anything," I felt the need to say, even though it was clearly a lie.

Jason blinked and glanced around. His look of embarrassment changed to confusion. "Is this a dream?"

"Sort of," I explained. "We're in Cloud Nine, remember? You fell into a cloud with a silver lining. This is supposed to be a fantasy of your happiest place."

"Oh," Jason said.

"The portal back to Camelot could close any second," I said quickly, changing the subject. "We need to get out of here. I think all you have to do is will yourself to wake up. So, um, if you could just—"

"Crisa," Jason said.

"Yeah?"

"About what you saw . . ."

"Jason, you don't have to explain, I just—"

"I like Blue," he said bluntly. "You saw what you saw and I'm not going to pretend that you didn't. I have feelings for her. I'm not ready to tell her. And now you know. Just promise me you won't say anything and we're good."

But you . . .

But she . . .

Argh!!!

"Fine, I promise," I said with a grunt. "Now get us out of here, will you?"

Jason nodded and closed his eyes. We were both enveloped in a silvery glow and a second later we were back in Cloud Nine. We stood on one of the pink clouds. Thank goodness the portal back to Camelot still flashed red in the distance. But it was shrinking.

"The portal's closing!" I said. "Come on! Stay on the pink clouds!"

Jason and I bounced from one pink fluffy formation to the next until we arrived at the portal. We dove through one at a time as it shrunk to the size of a carriage wheel. An instant later we fell on the stone floor of the cavern we'd last been in.

Daniel had left a blue X on the ground nearby. The marking strategy meant that we could at least see where he'd been in our absence. The question was, where was he now?

Looking through one of the energy walls, we saw Mauvrey and Arian race along the Avalonian glass pathway and leap into another pocket dimension. However, half a second later, Mauvrey went sailing out again like she'd been powerfully kicked.

"Daniel!" I gasped.

We bolted out of our cave, rushed past a still-recovering Mauvrey, and sped through the same energy wall she and Arian had just used. When Jason and I entered the pocket dimension, I saw several things that demanded my attention at once.

Arian was fighting Daniel, who somehow had a sword again. My spear lay on the floor. And Alex was on the right side of the cavern, approaching a glistening onyx stone that held the most beautiful sword I'd ever seen.

Excalibur!

This was the sword we'd been looking for. I felt it in my bones like fundamental instinct.

Alex reached out for the blade. Without thinking, I scooped up my spear and threw it at him with all the force I had. It plunged through my brother's thigh and he cried out in pain and fell to the ground.

I sprinted forward. Arian tried to stop me, but it was too

late. I reached the sword, gripped the hilt, and with one mighty, unstoppable move, yanked Excalibur from the stone.

Everything in the universe rippled.

Excalibur emitted a brilliant, ghostly blue glow like the Lady of Lake but a hundred times brighter. I shielded my eyes. A wave of magical energy spun through the air and I sensed power surge through my body. When I lowered my arm a sparkling, rainbow-colored aura rippled through the environment.

Everything felt calm and I admired the sword in my hand, which still glowed a mild ghostly blue. Excalibur's hilt was dark gold. The pommel and guard were carved with an intricate design. The blade, meanwhile, was long, sleek steel. Strange letters began to appear on the flat of the blade.

ƎX⊃ᴙ⅃IᙠYᗡ

⅂ƎɥᗡᗡᴙGᴑɥ

The letters shimmered ominously in the blue glow. I turned the sword sideways and the letters morphed. Like a mirage, they changed in correlation with how the light hit them. If I held the sword at just the right angle, the letters altered enough to spell something I could understand:

EXCALIBUR

PENDRAGON

I held the blade tightly, transfixed by its beauty. Everything about it was unique. More importantly, for the meantime it was *mine*. I'd done what we'd set out to do and claimed Excalibur. I'd lived up to Arthur's expectations, Merlin's hopes, and my own desires. I'd beat Alex and the antagonists, stopping them from claiming the sword for Rampart, and now . . . Now, here I stood with the most powerful weapon in all the realms in my hand and the future gleaming ahead.

I did it! I can't believe I actually did it!

It wasn't until that moment that I noticed the scene had grown quiet. I looked up and discovered that Arian and Daniel had ceased fighting and were standing perfectly still. Jason, Alex, and Mauvrey (who'd just come through the energy wall) were also frozen in place. They all twinkled slightly, like someone had coated them in glitter glue. Arian stood a few feet away. I walked up to him and poked him in the side of the head.

Nothing.

A bright flash appeared, and the Lady of the Lake floated before me. Although there was a smile on her lips, her eyes were black as ever. The combination made her look even more sinister.

"You are the Knight of the prophecy," she spoke in her creepy voice. "You have claimed Excalibur. The price of this is making a poor choice. One day I will appear to you again, Crisanta Knight, when you make the wrong choice at a crucial point in your journey. Until then, wield the blade with pride and power, and deliver it to the rightful king of Camelot as you have sworn to do."

The sword in my hand suddenly felt heavier. I'd known all along about the price I would have to pay for claiming Excalibur. But being reminded of it sucked the glorious feeling of victory from this moment.

"What happened to my friends?" I asked, gesturing at Daniel and Jason.

"I have frozen them along with your enemies."

"I can see that," I replied. "I mean, can I have them back now?"

"Yes, you may have them back," the Lady of the Lake replied. "They are worthy heroes so I will even reward you by transporting the three of you back across the lake."

"No boats?" I asked.

"No boats."

"And my enemies?"

"They can return to the mainland the old-fashioned way."

That was good news. It meant that A) we wouldn't have to

worry about the noodle arms, and B) we'd leave Alex, Arian, and Mauvrey in our dust as we made off with Excalibur.

I'd had my fill of Avalon and was eager to reunite with my friends across the lake. However, I knew there was one more thing I needed to do before we left. It was now or never.

"Before you send us back . . ." I took a deep breath. "Can you take me to the Four Waters of Paradise?"

The Lady of the Lake said nothing. Instead, she simply spread her hands apart. She and I were immediately wrapped in ribbons of white energy. An instant later, we were in a different area of the isle.

Wow. With her behavior swinging from helpful to hurtful, part of me didn't think she would be so hospitable. Was I actually about to find the waters?

We were high up on Avalon's mountains. I stood near a ledge and could spot the sand embankment of the lake hundreds of feet below. The Lady of the Lake was hovering above a small crater close by. Within the crater was some sand, dried pieces of vegetation, and a few small fish skeletons. But there was no water.

"The spring you seek dried up long ago," the Lady of the Lake stated.

I felt a tangle of emotions—sadness, disappointment, regret, and maybe a touch of relief. It was all very overwhelming and a bit somber.

"So that's it then," I said bluntly. "If there is no more water here, then I can't be cured of Pure Magic Disease."

"Can't is a strong word, Crisanta Knight," the Lady of the Lake replied. "You did not find the Four Waters of Paradise here, but that does not mean you will not find them elsewhere."

"What do you mean?"

The Lady of the Lake spread her hands again and we were consumed in her white ribbons of energy. Then we were back in the cavern with my frozen friends and enemies. Excalibur was still in my hand.

"The time for questions is over," said the Lady of the Lake. "Are you ready to leave the isle?"

"Give me a minute, will you? I just need to collect myself."

The Lady of the Lake nodded and vanished, leaving me alone. I turned Excalibur over in my hand as I thought about the Four Waters of Paradise.

It was true I didn't know what I would've done with them if I'd found them. But I liked having the option of curing myself out there. I knew some of my friends were going to be disappointed that this was no longer on the table—especially SJ, who seemed to be the most worried about me turning dark. However, the universe had spoken and unlike other times when fate could be challenged, there wasn't anything to be done here. I guess we would all have to deal with this reality. Eva in Oz would also have to accept it. I had promised her that I would bring more of the waters back to Oz to cure her sister Glinda. So much for that.

Sigh.

It was time to move on. I had to accept that finding the waters was no longer on my list of things to do and I couldn't dwell on it. I had bigger fish to fry.

I looked around the room at the frozen faces of my friends and foes. I saw that Alex was wearing a Hole Tracker so I went over to him, unfastened it, and attached it to my own wrist. Ormé had mine, so I could use this one.

Then I looked at my brother's leg. My spear stuck out of it at a hard angle. I was surprised how unapologetic I felt about it. Staring at his wound, I felt absolutely nothing.

However, as I studied his pained, still face that's when I realized something. Alex, Arian, and Mauvrey were all frozen. They couldn't move; they couldn't fight; they couldn't defend them-selves. All three stood before me like vulnerable statues and I had a deadly sharp sword in my hand . . .

The opportunity hummed at the back of my mind like a song. I approached Arian and stood inches from him. I looked into his vicious black eyes. I remembered the first time he'd gotten the jump on me in Century City and held a sword to my throat. Steadily, I raised Excalibur and brought it to his neck.

Blue was right. Villains didn't stay down. As long as they were allowed to exist they'd keep trying to destroy you. Arian would never stop. He was evil, and so was Mauvrey, and so was Alex. I could permanently stop any one, or all of them right here. Maybe I had a responsibility to. Maybe I'd wanted that for a long time.

It would be so easy.

My hand did not shake. I held the blade steadily. I thought I was going to go through with it. *I was so sure.* But then, at the last second my instincts pulled me back.

No.

I took a step away. I was surprised how fast my conscience had jumped into my throat. I swallowed hard and knew the truth.

I couldn't do this. My heart was in the wrong place. Killing in self-defense was one thing, but this didn't feel right. Murdering three people in cold blood was not an honorable course of action. I told myself I would trust my instincts where taking life was concerned, and right now they were telling me that this was not who I wanted to be.

I gazed at Arian and nodded decidedly. "Fight you another day."

With a deep exhale, I walked away. I honestly didn't know if this was the best decision, but it was what my heart deemed necessary, so I listened. I went over to Alex and yanked my spear from his leg.

"I'm ready," I called out.

The Lady of the Lake reappeared.

"Take us back," I said. "We're good to go."

"As you wish."

The Lady of the Lake spread her hands, and Daniel, Jason, and I were consumed in her light. I closed my eyes and let her magic wash over me—cleansing and purifying my unease. Maybe someday I would feel differently about what I'd decided here today. But for now, I knew I'd stayed true to my own morality. What that morality might become in the future was changeable, as I was changeable. However, I couldn't worry about that. I had to live my truth in the here and now. That's what I'd done. That was all I could do to hold my head high.

As the magic enveloped us, I looked at Excalibur in my right hand, the spear in my left, and at the cavern vanishing before my eyes.

I wondered when I would next see Alex, Arian, and Mauvrey. I wondered if I could control the magic growing and burning inside of me—keep its thirst in check the way I'd just kept my darker half in check. And I wondered what the Lady of the Lake meant about me finding the Four Waters of Paradise elsewhere . . .

I'd get the answers to all three questions eventually. As the scene melted away, I knew there were more important matters about to unfold. I had a realm to restore, a Fairy Godmother to save, an evil witch to defeat, and a kingdom of antagonists to stop. And I had to do them all before day's end.

Things were about to get real.

End of Book Five

About the Author

Geanna Culbertson is the award-winning author of *The Crisanta Knight Series*. Since Book One's release in May 2016, the series has won many awards, including a Mom's Choice Award for best family friendly media, a Living Now Choice Award for "best lifestyle and world changing books" in adventure fiction, a Benjamin Franklin Award for best books in Teen Fiction, and many more!

The Crisanta Knight Series is a proud sponsor of *Girls on the Run, Los Angeles* (GOTRLA). Driven by a heroine who is strong, smart, and bold, *The Crisanta Knight Series* is happy to be a continuous presence in the GOTRLA community, as both envision "a world where every girl knows and activates her limitless potential."

The series has been featured in *Girls' Life Magazine* as recommended reading for preteen and teen girls. Culbertson is also a regular speaker at schools for an array of age groups (from elementary schools to major universities).

Culbertson is a proud alumna of the University of Southern California where she earned her B.A. in Public Relations and triple minor degrees in Marketing, Cinematic Arts, and Critical Approaches to Leadership. She is a part of only 1.3% of her graduating class to earn the double distinction of *Renaissance Scholar* and *Discovery Scholar.* Her Discovery Scholar thesis "Beauty & the Badass: Origins of the Hero-Princess Archetype" earned her acclaim in the School of Cinematic Arts, and helped fuel her female protagonist focused writing passions.

In addition to authoring *The Crisanta Knight Series* (set to be eight books with the final release in spring 2021), Culbertson is a full-time manager at a leading industry digital marketing firm, representing over 30 clients across the world. When Culbertson is not working or writing, she can likely be found performing volunteer work at her local karate studio where she teaches martial arts (she is a black belt), going on adventures with her mother and best friend, and indulging her love of delicious food across the land.